DOWN AMONG THE DEAD MEN

ROBERT GREGORY BROWNE

PAN BOOKS

First published 2010 by Macmillan

This edition published 2010 by Pan Books
an imprint of Pan Macmillan, a division of Macmillan Publishers Limited
Pan Macmillan, 20 New Wharf Road, London N1 9RR
Basingstoke and Oxford
Associated companies throughout the world
www.panmacmillan.com

ISBN 978-0-330-50892-6

1 3 5 7 9 8 6 4 2

A CIP catalogue record for this book is available from
the British Library.

Typeset by Ellipsis Books Limited, Glasgow
Printed in the UK by CPI Mackays, Chatham ME5 8TD

Visit **www.panmacmillan.com** to read more about all our books
and to buy them. You will also find features, author interviews and
news of any author events, and you can sign up for e-newsletters
so that you're always first to hear about our new releases.

For Lani and Matthew

In memory of Ignacio 'Nick' Garcia
Rest in peace, old friend

PATIENT'S JOURNAL

Day 56?
11.36 p.m.

I don't remember the shooting, but I'll never forget the pain.

I feel it, sometimes, as I lie here in my bed, looking back at that night.

The night that changed my life.

In a distant corner of my damaged brain I see myself lying face-down on rutted pavement, my chest on fire, the faint sound of accordion music playing on some distant radio.

I don't know where I am. I'm not sure why I'm here. But there's something wet beneath me, and I don't know if it's blood or simply a puddle of water I've landed in after the impact.

I'm guessing blood.

Lots of it.

Then there's my head. Something wrong there, too. A damp spot. A pressure. As if someone is stepping on my exposed brain with a spiked heel. Leaning into it for maximum force.

That's the pain I'll never forget.

A pain that sends me drifting.

Then, the darkness comes – an internal darkness, where everything is loose and floating towards some black, nebulous nowhere.

A distant scream echoes. A high shrill keen followed by the tattoo of approaching footsteps that quickly fade into the ether as the darkness finally overcomes me.

And my last thought as I drift away is that I might never wake up again.

Sometimes I wish I hadn't.

Most times, in fact.

ONE

CASA DE LA MUERTE

VARGAS

1

They found the bodies in the desert, about twenty miles south-west of Tolentino.

Two Texas dirt bikers, father and son, had come down from El Paso to ride the dunes and discovered a dead woman lying in the scrub, her throat slit, her body half-drained of blood.

It didn't stop there.

Vargas had to give the two men credit for calling the local *policía* rather than packing up their bikes and hightailing it back across the border. Most Americans thought of this part of Mexico as some lawless, dirt-water hellhole full of corrupt *huta* who would toss you into jail at the slightest provocation. And taking ownership of a house full of corpses was always risky business for anyone, let alone a couple of *gabachos*.

But it seemed that the two had been genuinely concerned about doing the right thing, and Vargas admired that. Their willingness to walk him through the crime scene didn't hurt either.

The father, Jim Ainsworth, was a lean, sunbaked cowboy who reminded him of that guy from the 'Lord of the Rings' movies. Viggo something. They met on

5

a Friday afternoon at the Cafe Tacuba, a hole-in-the-wall place just off the 45, where they shared a booth near a window that hadn't been washed in a decade, if ever.

The accordion-laced songs of Julietta Venegas played quietly on a jukebox in the corner, an ancient, mule-faced waitress swaying to the beat as she dragged a damp rag across a tabletop.

They were just finishing their meal when Ainsworth said, 'You still haven't told me which one of the shit catchers you work for.'

Vargas raised his eyebrows. 'Shit catchers?'

'Newspapers. That's about all I use 'em for. Line my rabbit cages.'

There was a bit of a twinkle in Ainsworth's eyes and Vargas wasn't sure if this was a pointed jab or a just a piss-poor joke.

'No paper,' he said.

Ainsworth frowned. 'I thought you were a reporter?'

'Used to be. Now I'm freelance. I write books.'

That was stretching it a bit. Truth be told, this was Vargas's first stab at writing long form and he wasn't completely sure he had it in him. After fifteen years of turning in concise, thousand-word stories to the *Los Angeles Tribune* – and the *San Jose Reader* before that – the idea of pumping out four or five hundred pages of who, what, where, when and why seemed like a slow, uphill trudge. This book would either make him or break him.

Ainsworth nodded as he scraped the last of his beans

off his plate. Vargas had sprung for the meal, mentally counting every peso as he'd scanned the menu, wondering how much more spending he could get away with before his advance money was gone.

'I've never had much use for books, either,' Ainsworth said. 'My wife, God bless her, used to go through about every half-baked paperback she could get her hands on, but I never saw much point to it.'

Vargas said nothing. He wasn't interested in getting into a debate with this guy about the merits of literature.

'I've gotta admit,' Ainsworth went on, 'I didn't mind her reading the spicy ones.' He flashed a conspiratorial grin. 'She was a helluva woman.'

'I'm sure she was,' Vargas said, smiling politely. Then he nodded to Ainsworth's empty plate. 'You want anything else?'

Ainsworth leaned back and sighed, rubbing his stomach. 'I think that'll about do her.'

Vargas gestured to the plate next to Ainsworth's. Tacos and beans and Mexican rice that had barely been touched. The seat behind it was vacant.

'What about your son?'

'He's never been much of an eater,' Ainsworth said. 'He ever gets his ass back from the *baño*, I think we're good to go.'

2

They drove out to the desert in Ainsworth's F150, a couple of dusty red dirt bikes chained to its bed. Ainsworth had taken one look at Vargas's rusted, ten-year-old Corolla and offered to drive.

'It's these goddamn long legs,' he said. 'I need all the room I can get. Besides, I don't really want to leave these bikes out here.'

Vargas didn't mind. He figured he'd save on gas, and Ainsworth had said the truck was air conditioned, a luxury the Corolla hadn't been blessed with. It was late October, but the south-west was in the middle of a massive heat wave, and by the time Vargas had reached the cafe this afternoon, he'd been drenched in sweat.

He rode up front with Ainsworth, while the son, Junior, sat in the extended cab behind them. Junior was a lean, twentyish version of his old man, but there was something seriously off about the guy. He spent a lot of time staring at nothing and spoke about as much as he ate. The few words he *had* said had been accompanied by a loopy, half-there smile as if he were hooked up to an invisible morphine drip.

Ainsworth, on the other hand, seemed to enjoy talking.

'Me and Junior get down this way just about every couple of weeks. Nice to get out of Paso, you know? Just load up the bikes, hop in the truck and drive.'

'Why Chihuahua?' Vargas asked. 'There's plenty of desert up in Texas.'

Ainsworth shrugged. 'Something about this place, I don't know, everything's slower down here. Everybody pretty much minding his own business. Never in a hurry to get in your way.' He paused. 'Besides, you can't beat the price of that sweet Mexican *chocho*. Right, Junior?'

'*Chupamelo, mamacita,*' Junior said.

The words, which roughly translated to 'Suck it, baby', surprised Vargas. Junior seemed too simple minded and innocent for such a vulgarity, let alone in Spanish.

Ainsworth, however, chuckled, glancing at his son in his rear-view mirror.

'Your mother was still alive, she'd wash that mouth out with industrial strength Ajax.' He looked at Vargas. 'You'll have to pardon my boy's manners.'

'I've heard worse,' Vargas told him.

'And I've probably said it. I gotta admit I haven't been the best influence on the kid. Took him to his first whorehouse when he was fifteen. You shoulda seen how big his eyes got when he saw all them cute little bare-assed *chiquitas* lined up just for him. I swear to Christ it took him longer to make up his mind than it did to do the deed.'

'Slow draw, quick trigger,' Junior said. 'That's what Big Papa told me.'

Ainsworth summoned up a deep, lusty laugh this time.

'That I did, son. That I did.'

Twenty miles down the highway, they took the turn-off past a battered, bullet-riddled road sign that read DUNAS DEL HOMBRE MUERTO. Dead Man's Dunes. Vargas thought this was both ironic and appropriate, considering what the Ainsworths had found here.

A narrow dirt road took them to an abandoned Pemex gas station that looked as if it hadn't seen business since the early sixties. The windows had been boarded up decades ago, the plywood now grey and dilapidated, covered with layers of crude spray-painted graffiti written in both Spanish and English. '*Puta*' and '*Joto*' and 'Fuck' were featured prominently.

Ainsworth pulled onto the asphalt next to the pumps and killed the truck's engine.

'This is it.'

He gestured beyond the station to a wide expanse of beige, dusty earth, dotted with dunes and yellowing desert scrub. Nothing unusual. You could find miles of the stuff from here to Texas.

What set this particular piece of land apart was the house that sat in the distance. The one that had been featured on the local news and in the Chihuahua newspapers just two months ago, a crumbling adobe box with broken and missing windows and only half a roof.

Despite the heat, Vargas felt a faint chill. And a small tug of excitement.

'Take me through it,' he said to Ainsworth. 'Step by step.'

'That should be easy enough. Right, Junior?'

But Junior wasn't listening. He was staring at the house, his dopey smile gone. He looked as if someone had just ripped out his soul.

'I wanna go home,' he said.

'Come on, now, son, we talked about this.'

'I don't care,' Junior said. 'I wanna go. Now. I don't like this place. I don't like it at all.'

Ainsworth showed Vargas a tight smile. 'Boy hasn't been right in the head since the crash. Caved in half his skull. Almost joined his mama in the morgue.' He returned his gaze to Junior. 'I told you, son, I'm not gonna let you pussy out on me. We made this man a promise and by God—'

'It's not that big of a deal,' Vargas said. 'He can wait for us here if he wants.'

Ainsworth turned sharply. 'Did I ask you to butt in?'

'I'm just saying, if he doesn't feel comfortable . . .'

'If God had put us on this planet to feel comfortable, Poncho, we woulda all been born with Lazy Boys stuck to our hindquarters.'

Vargas stiffened.

'The name is Ignacio,' he said. 'I told you that. Most people call me Nick.'

'Fine, Nick. But we're doing you a favour here, so I'd appreciate it if you didn't try to get between me and my own goddamn son. He may be a half-wit, but he's twenty-two years old and it's about time he grew some motherfuckin' balls.' He eyed his rear-view mirror. 'You hear me, Junior?'

Junior didn't answer, lost somewhere inside his own head.

'You *hear* me?'

'I wanna go home,' Junior said. 'What if they're still in there?'

'Who?'

'Them people. The dead ones.'

'Now why would you think that?'

'I seen 'em. Laying there all shot up. They kept looking at me with them dead fish eyes.'

Vargas expected another flash of anger, and was surprised when Ainsworth softened, a genuine warmth in his voice.

'Listen to me, son. You're mixed up, is all. I promise you, they're not around any more.'

'How do you know?'

'The Mex police came and tidied the place up, remember? We were here when they came.'

Junior thought about this a long moment, looking thoroughly confused, then the sun slowly rose somewhere inside his brain, shining light across the memory.

He nodded. 'They asked us questions.'

'That's right,' Ainsworth said.

'And I didn't say nothin' wrong.'

'Right again. You made your papa proud.'

'And they put all them people in big black bags, threw 'em in the back of a truck.'

'Every single one of 'em. And we're here to show Mr Vargas what we found and where we found it. He's gonna write you up in a book, make you famous. What do you think about that?'

Junior's smile returned.

'Like Elvis the Pelvis?'

'Just like Elvis,' Ainsworth said.

3

The house was farther away than it looked.

They drove along what had once been an access road, but was now little more than chunks of broken earth, making passage by truck difficult and uncomfortable. Vargas had to hold onto the support bar to keep from getting knocked around inside the cab.

Ainsworth had offered to pull the bikes down, give Vargas a ride, but Vargas had declined. The one time in his life he'd taken a ride on the back of a dirt bike had scared the everloving crap out of him. Not an experience he was interested in reliving, especially with this guy at the wheel.

About halfway there, Ainsworth brought the truck to a stop and gestured with a nod towards a nearby dune, fronted by a patch of scrub.

'I came up over that rise and nearly put my rear tyre in her face. Almost took a header in the process.'

'She the only one you found out here?'

Ainsworth nodded.

'Sonsabitches must've used a razor sharp garrotte. Practically took her head off. Then they shot her a couple times for good measure. Local police figured she'd managed to run for it and got caught.'

'Oh? They tell you this?'

Ainsworth huffed a dry chuckle.

'Hell, no. They wouldn't give us the time of day. For a while there, I thought they were gonna cuff us both and send us off to no man's land. But that didn't seem to keep them from jabbering on in front of us. And I may have forgotten to mention to 'em that we both speak Spanish.' He grinned. 'Figured the more we looked like touristas, the better off we'd be.'

'*Mi padre es un bastardo elegante,*' Junior said.

Ainsworth smiled. 'You're right about that, boy. I'm what you might call a wolf in hick's clothing.'

They both got a good laugh out of that one as Vargas stared at the patch of earth where the body had lain. After several weeks, whatever blood there'd been had been absorbed by the dirt and brush and blown away by the wind and was no longer visible. But Vargas had worked a few crime scenes in his time, and it wasn't hard to imagine what the dead woman had looked like.

But then it wasn't imagination he should be relying on, was it? That would only get him in trouble again.

'What was she wearing?' he asked. 'Was she in her nun's habit?'

Another dry chuckle. 'You see any convents around here? She looked like a typical border bunny. Jeans and a T-shirt. First glance, that's what the *policía* thought they were. A buncha wetbacks, headed for El Paso.'

Vargas bristled. 'Are those the terms they used?'

Ainsworth studied him a moment.

'Look, Nick, you seem like a nice enough guy, but you start gettin' all holier than thou on me, you're not gonna get much of a story.'

Point taken. Vargas had heard his share of unrepentant bigotry over the course of his life, especially growing up around the fields of southern California, where the term 'berry picker' was not an endearment. His father had worked those fields for hours so long, at wages so low it would make you weep. But he'd never complained, despite the animosity he'd encountered on a regular basis. Much of it from the very families who bought those berries at prices his cheap labour made possible.

But this trip to Chihuahua wasn't about old wounds. When it came to work, Vargas had always tried to keep his emotions in check. No reason that should change now.

He gestured to the house.

'Show me where you found the rest of the bodies.'

BETH

4

'I don't know about you,' Jen said, holding the black cocktail dress against her chest and admiring herself in the mirror, 'but I plan on getting laid tonight.'

Beth knew she shouldn't be shocked by this pronouncement. Jen was painfully matter of fact about such things. About *most* things, if you wanted the God's honest truth.

But Beth was shocked nonetheless, and could only guess that this was because she'd been playing surrogate mom to the girl for nearly half their lives and felt some knee-jerk moral obligation to express disapproval.

'Do we really have to talk about this?'

'Little sissy's got a crush,' Jen said, blissfully ignoring the question as she laid the dress across her bunk. 'Did you see that boy's derrière?'

'Boy? I don't remember any boys.'

'They're all boys. You, of all people, should know that. Just look at Peter.'

This was another area of conversation that Beth would just as soon avoid. She was still smarting from the divorce and felt no need to go down that ruinous path. She was here to have fun. Maybe not as much fun as Jen was planning, but enough to help her forget what a mess her life had become.

The cruise to the Mexican Riviera had been Jen's idea. After her best friend Debbie had dropped out at the last minute, Jen had offered the vacant slot to Beth, and Beth had jumped at the chance to get away for a long weekend. She just hoped she wouldn't have to spend their entire vacation keeping tally of Jen's conquests.

The aforementioned boy was Julio, a bartender they'd met up on the pool deck, where they'd gone to get some sun before dinner. He wasn't tall, but he was definitely dark and handsome, and yes, Beth *had* noticed how nicely his derrière had filled out his tight white shorts, and she could fully appreciate Jen's enthusiasm.

'From what I can tell,' she said. 'Julio's no boy. Has hair on his chin and everything.'

Jen grinned. 'It's the everything that I'm interested in.'

'Doesn't the cruise line have some rule against the help fraternizing with guests?'

'Calm down, girl, you're not in court. We're on vacation here, remember? There *are* no rules.'

'You sleep with him, you could get him fired.'

Jen's grin widened. 'Trust me, I'm worth the risk.'

'Oh, brother.' Beth rolled her eyes.

'Why are you always such a prude?'

'I'm not a prude, it's just—'

'I know, I know, only when it comes to me.' Heaving a sigh, Jen pulled off her T-shirt, then reached back and untied her bikini top. 'I don't know if you've noticed, sis, but I'm all growed up now. You don't have to protect me any more. If anything, I'm the one who should be doing the protecting.' She paused. 'Speaking of which, how's your head?'

'Pounding, thanks to you.'

'Hey, I can't help it if you've got a stick up your butt about anything remotely provocative. If you were smart, you'd find a Julio all your own.'

'Not likely.'

Jen flung the top aside and Beth instinctively averted her gaze. She'd seen her sister naked plenty of times over the years, but suddenly felt as if she were invading Jen's privacy.

Maybe it was the boob job, which Jen didn't hesitate to flaunt at every possible opportunity. Or maybe it was the close confines of this budget traveller's stateroom they'd been stuck in. They didn't even have a window – or porthole, to be nautically correct – and the light in here was weak and depressing. They were practically on top of each other, and seeing Jen's newly acquired attributes waving hello from less than two feet away did not exactly warm and comfort Beth.

'I'm no doctor,' Jen said, slipping off her suit bottom now, 'but a couple of hours with the right guy and I'll bet those headaches of yours will clear up real quick.'

'That's your solution to everything, isn't it?'

Jen shrugged. 'More or less.'

'Just do me a favour and take your shower,' Beth said. 'They're seating us in less than fifteen minutes.'

5

Dining on a cruise ship is an elaborate affair.

Long, intricately set tables crowded with your ship-mates, some of whom are dressed to the nines. Two or more waiters. A five-course, gourmet meal that has the potential to be mediocre, but is actually quite good considering the amount of food being pumped out of the ship's kitchen.

Beth ordered an escargot appetizer, a Caesar salad, seafood chowder, medallions of beef, a plate of cheeses and a scoop of green tea ice cream. A definite case of eyes bigger than stomach.

They'd been surrounded by food from the moment they'd first stepped foot onto the ship that afternoon, but Beth had passed on the burgers and greasy fries and pizza slices and soft-serve ice cream offered upstairs on the pool deck. And by the time dinner came around, she was famished.

Jen, on the other hand, had opted for a liquid diet and was drunk before the meal was half over. Ordering only an appetizer and a small salad, she washed it all down with a couple of colourful rum drinks that came in tall glasses carrying the cruise line's logo. Add that to the three Dos Equis good old Julio had served her by the pool, and it wasn't long before she was a candidate for the Long Beach drunk tank.

Of course, they were quite a distance from port at that point, so Beth figured it didn't much matter. Still, she tried more than once to get Jen to slow down, but Jen wouldn't have it.

'Loosen up, Pollyanna, I'm just getting started.'

The problem was that her sister was wildly unpredictable when she got drunk. Or just plain wild. Once the liquid started flowing, you never knew which Jen would surface, and while all were quite beautiful, few of them were pretty.

By the time dessert was served, she was well into an unapologetic flirt session with the newlywed husband sitting next to her. Much to the chagrin of his sadly mousy wife.

Maybe flirt was too mild of a word. This was an all-out, full-frontal assault.

'Let's go dancing. You wanna go dancing?'

'I–I don't really dance,' the man said, shooting his wife an awkward glance.

'Oh? You look like a dancer to me.' She reached over and squeezed his bicep. 'There's a lot of muscle under that fancy jacket.'

The man coloured slightly, then shrugged. 'I work out.'

'Ugh,' Jen said, then put her lips to her straw and took a noisy final slurp of her second drink. 'I can't stand working out. The sight of all those treadmills up in the gym gives me hives. If I'm gonna get sweaty it had better be worth my while, if you know what I mean.'

Her speech was slurred, but she managed that patented Jen fuck-me smile, and Beth wondered what had happened to her newfound lust for Julio.

'When I need to shed a few pounds,' Jen continued, 'I just call the man with the magic wand.'

The newlywed's face went beet red then, and Jen laughed and shook her head.

'Not *that* kind of wand, dummy. My surgeon.'

'Surgeon?'

'You know. Liposuction?' She waved an imaginary lipo wand in the air, then turned in her chair, facing him, and leaned back slightly. It was a tricky manoeuvre for someone so drunk, but she managed to avoid falling on the floor. 'Take a guess.'

'About what?'

She cupped her breasts through the black fabric of her cocktail dress. It was obvious she wasn't wearing a bra. Not that she needed one.

'How much you think these babies cost me?'

Beth pushed her ice cream aside. 'All right, Jennifer, that's enough.'

Jen shot her a look, 'Polly want a cracker?' then turned again to the newlywed. 'Well? How much?'

Despite his scowling wife, the man stared openly at Jen's offering and Beth knew there'd be storm clouds in the honeymoon suite tonight.

'I dunno. A couple grand?'

Jen laughed. 'A couple grand? Where does your wife get her work done? JC Penny's?'

22

Her voice – almost a screech now – rose above the din of the dining room. Not only were most of the people at the table gaping at her (forks held in suspended animation above their creme brulees and flourless chocolate cakes) but a few from the adjoining tables were staring as well.

'Jen, please, you're drunk. Let's go back to the cabin.'

Ignoring Beth, Jen turned to the elderly couple directly across from her, and smiled at the silver-haired husband.

'Tell me the truth now. Do these look like they're only worth a measly two grand?'

And with this, she unceremoniously yanked down the top of her dress, exposing herself to their small corner of the world.

6

She threw up halfway back to the stateroom. They were on the stairs leading up to Deck 7, when she gripped the rail.

'Are we swaying? Why are we swaying?'

Beth steadied her. 'We're on a ship, remember?'

'Uhhhh. I don't feel so good. How many drinks did I have?'

'Before or during dinner?'

'It's the rum. I swear to God, I should know better. Rum always knocks me on my ass.'

'I don't think your ass is the problem.'

'Huh?'

'Never mind,' Beth said. 'Let's just get you into bed.'

They'd had plans to hit the casino after dinner, then maybe the dance club on the uppermost deck, but thanks to Jen's overindulgence and sudden need to express herself, it now looked as if Beth would be curling up with a paperback book.

'What happened back there?' Jen said. 'Am I dreaming, or did I flash my boobs again?'

Again?

Beth wasn't aware of any previous boob flashing – unless you counted the teenie-weenie bikinis Jen favoured – but then Jen had long been an exhibitionist. If she were drunk enough and some guy pointed a video camera in her direction, she'd surely be the first one to say, 'Why the hell not?'

In fact, she probably wouldn't even have to be drunk.

'Let's put it this way,' Beth said. 'I'm pretty sure you and your two new friends are the talk of the ship right now. And I can almost guarantee we'll be getting a phone call from the purser tomorrow morning.'

Jen slumped against the wall. 'I am *such* an idiot. Why do I always do this?'

'Let's save the pity party for later, okay?'

'I promised myself I wouldn't drink so much, and what's the first thing I do?'

'It's a little tough to say no when you're surrounded by the stuff.'

Jen shook her head. 'I am so fucking predictable. And I've ruined your vacation. I ruin everything for everybody.'

'Quit being dramatic,' Beth said, then tried a smile. 'If they don't throw us off the ship tomorrow, you've still got three days to make it up to—'

Jen clutched her stomach.

'Uhhhh. Tell it to stop. Make it freaking … ohhhh, shit.'

Then it came. Jen's appetizer, dinner salad, three beers and two Bahama Mamas, all over the standard-issue cruise-ship blue and green carpet—

—and Beth's brand-new Kenneth Cole sandals.

Her smile abruptly disappeared.

'Oh ... My ... Fucking ... Lord ...' she said, and nearly threw up herself.

VARGAS

7

He never thought he could be so easily creeped out in daylight, yet the moment Vargas climbed out of the truck and stood in front of the house, something cold and dry crawled up his spine.

A sense of anticipation. And dread.

The place was fairly typical for this part of the country. A large crumbling rectangle of sun-dried clay that had undoubtedly once housed the family who ran the gas station near the highway.

Its walls were adorned with more graffiti. One of the newer additions read, CASA DE LA MUERTE.

House of Death.

Despite the missing chunks of roof tiles that let in swaths of mottled sunlight, there was a darkness of spirit here. A malevolence. The entrance was a doorless hole that reminded Vargas of an open maw. And stepping past its threshold was to risk being swallowed alive.

Apparently he wasn't the only one who felt this way.

'I'm not goin' in there again,' Junior said. He was still in the F150, uncertainty in his eyes.

Ainsworth spat into the dirt, then squinted at him through the open driver's door.

'What did I just tell you, boy?'

'I don't like this place.'

'It's a goddamn house. It's not gonna bite you.' Ainsworth lowered his voice, but there was no softness or warmth this time. 'Now you can sit in there like a friggin' faggot, or you can paint that sorry butt white and start runnin' with the antelope. Which is it gonna be?'

Junior was quiet for a moment, then finally wilted under the heat of his father's gaze.

'Okay,' he said quietly.

'Okay *what*?'

'I'll come out.'

Ainsworth's gaze didn't waver. 'You're gonna do a helluva lot more than that, Kimo Sabe. You're gonna lead the way. Take us inside, show Nick here where we found the rest of those bodies.'

Junior solemnly nodded his head. 'Yessir.'

Climbing out of the truck, he stared at the house a long moment before moving up to its crumbling doorway.

Pausing at the threshold, he shot his father a nervous glance, then gestured for Vargas to follow him inside.

8

Vargas didn't believe in ghosts. His childhood had been full of the usual stories, like the tale of La Llorona, the inconsolable widow who wandered the countryside crying for her dead children. Or the shuffling spectre of a murdered husband in search of his golden arm.

But Vargas had always taken such tales for exactly what they were: harmless folklore. Make-believe stories told in hushed tones by his older brother Manny, who was always trying to get a rise out of little Nick as they huddled in the darkness of their bedroom.

Yet there was something about this place – a sense of foreboding – that brought the memory of those nights flooding back to him, and he knew that if his brother were still alive he'd be milking it for all it was worth.

He followed Junior through the doorway into a small room with a dusty plank floor and faded yellow walls. More graffiti. The word, *paraíso* – paradise – was spray-painted above it all in bold red letters.

A decades-old sofa sat against one wall, its upholstery ripped to shreds, its stuffing long gone. There were a couple of tattered aluminium patio chairs next to it, probably brought in by squatters long after the house had been abandoned. A few used syringes and crushed cigarette butts were scattered around them.

'This room was empty,' Ainsworth said as he stepped inside behind Vargas. 'We found it pretty much like it is now.'

'Through here,' Junior said, then crossed to a doorway on his left. Vargas followed, moving with him down a narrow, litter-strewn hallway to a large room with a sink and overturned ice box. Obviously the kitchen. Beyond it was another short hallway that ended at what seemed to be the only door left in the place, a dilapidated slab of wood with peeling blue paint and a hole where the knob should be.

Junior came to a stop just short of the second hallway.

'In there,' he said, gesturing to the door. 'That's where we found 'em. Me and Big Papa.'

'All four?'

'Five,' Ainsworth said behind him.

Vargas turned. 'Four in there and the one outside, right?'

Ainsworth shook his head. 'There were six bodies altogether.'

'But the police said—'

'I don't give a good goddamn what those bastards told you. We found one outside and five in the room. Even Junior can do the math on that one.'

'But I spoke to the investigating officer. He said there were only five bodies.'

'Cops say a lot of things. Don't mean it's true. Especially down here.'

'Why would he lie?'

Ainsworth shrugged. 'My guess is he doesn't want anyone to know about the American gal.'

Vargas paused. 'The what?'

'You heard me.'

Vargas frowned. He had personally gone over the police file and there was never any mention that one of the victims was an American, female or otherwise. It was true that the lead detective, Rojas, had declined to show him the crime scene photos, but that had merely been a gesture to protect the dignity of the victims.

At least that's what Rojas had said.

But could the police files have been sanitized before Vargas got hold of them?

If Ainsworth was telling the truth, this put a whole new spin on things. And maybe all the time Vargas had spent on this story so far would turn out not to be a waste. Far from it.

Ainsworth grinned. 'You ain't exactly an ace reporter, are you, son?'

'Cut the bullshit,' Vargas said. 'Did you really find an American?'

With an impatient gesture, Ainsworth pushed past Junior and moved to the dilapidated blue door.

'Let me show you,' he said, then pushed it open and stepped inside.

9

Vargas followed Ainsworth, with Junior now bringing up the rear. He wasn't sure why, but he suddenly felt uncomfortable being sandwiched between these two men.

Pushing the thought aside, he stepped into a large room, what must have been the master bedroom. A single, paneless window looked out onto the desert landscape, the late afternoon sun streaming in, falling across a ruined old queen-sized mattress.

The mattress was caked with grime and dried blood.

Lots of it.

Soaked in deep.

The floor was also painted with the stuff, the graffiti-laden walls covered with splashes of arterial spray, now darkened with age.

Vargas felt the chill again. Stronger than before. Accompanied by a wave of revulsion.

This was where it had happened. The massacre he'd first heard about on Channel Z, then read about in *El Diario de Chihuahua*. The house full of butchered nuns. A story that, for reasons he couldn't explain, had grabbed hold of him and refused to leave him in peace.

Looking around the room, he could imagine the screams of horror, the cries of pain, echoing through the desert. Heard by no one.

Except the killers.

Ainsworth pointed to the floor.

'There were three of 'em right here.' He stood in the centre of the room, an odd half-smile on his face. He looked a lot like his son. 'Three women. All Mex. Two of 'em with their throats slit and the third shot straight through the heart.'

'What about the American?'

'On the bed. Pretty little white gal and another local. The Mexican had been gutted, and the American had taken at least two bullets to the chest.' He shook his head. 'Whatever happened in here, it musta been one helluva party.'

Vargas nodded. 'How do you know the white girl was an American?'

Something shifted in Ainsworth's eyes. As if he'd been thrown off guard by the question.

'I just know, is all.'

'How?'

'She looked it, for one. Had that well-tended thing going. Never seen a hard day's work in her life. Plus she was wearing a USC sweatshirt. Go Trojans.'

'That doesn't mean much. Did she have any kind of identification on her? Driver's licence?'

Junior, who stood in the doorway, said, 'We didn't touch anything. We didn't take—'

'Shut your tamale trap,' Ainsworth snapped. Then he turned again to Vargas. 'You think we find a bunch of dead bodies we start checking IDs? You're just gonna have to take my word for it on the American thing.'

And all at once Vargas understood. These two Texas shit kickers had not only found the bodies, they'd ransacked them, too. Cash, jewellery. Anything they could find. It wasn't likely they'd got much for their effort, but Vargas had no doubt they'd done it.

But why, then, call the local police and report their discovery? That part didn't make sense.

'If she really was an American,' he said, 'then why is this the first time I'm hearing about it?'

Ainsworth shrugged. 'Try looking at it from Chihuahua's point of view. You find a bunch of dead wetbacks, it's nothing really new. It makes the papers, maybe a couple of local news shows. They do their Casa de la Muerte bit, but in the end it's the same old, same old. A run for the border gone wrong.'

'Except these were nuns.'

Another shrug. 'So that adds a juicy little twist to the story, maybe gets a little traction north of the border, gets the Jesus huggers all in a bind. But in the end, it's something you can contain because, let's face it, a dead wetback's a dead wetback.'

He paused, scratching his chin. 'But think about it. You throw a nice, creamy white American gal into the soup, and all of a sudden you've gone international. You've got the US embassy involved, the family, maybe the FBI, a shitload of press and a lot of angry goddamn Texans coming down into Juarez and Tolentino and shootin' at citizens. It's a national fuckin' nightmare.'

'So you're saying the police covered it up?'

'You're a bona fide genius, you know that?'

'I'm just trying to get it all straight,' Vargas said. 'You have any idea who this American was?'

'Why would I?'

'Angie,' Junior blurted out. 'Her name was Angie.'

Ainsworth turned sharply, eyes blazing. 'Didn't I just tell you to shut the fuck up?'

'But I heard her say it, Pa.'

Vargas felt another chill slice through him.

He glanced at the blood on the mattress, then looked at Ainsworth. 'She was alive?'

Ainsworth shook his head.

'He's just imagining things. He does that sometimes. Engine's runnin' but nobody's drivin'.'

'But I heard her, Pa. She said it when—'

'Goddammit, Junior!' Ainsworth shot past Vargas, grabbing the front of Junior's shirt, and shoved him through the doorway, into the hall. 'Get back outside. Go see if Sergio's here yet.'

Vargas felt something tighten inside his chest.

'Who's Sergio?'

Ainsworth turned. 'Friend of ours. Wants to meet you.'

'Me?' Vargas said. 'Why?'

'I don't ask questions, Poncho. I just do what I'm told.'

And before Vargas could say anything more, Ainsworth put a fist in his face.

BETH

10

Beth stood at the ship's bow, looking out at the moon dappled Pacific, and at that moment, she could think of no sight more beautiful.

They were rolling along at a fairly good clip, the sound of the roaring ocean rising towards her. The cool, damp wind felt wonderful against her skin. Made her feel alive.

She was alone out here, Jen fast asleep in their stateroom, the rest of the passengers inside at the casino, the variety shows, the late-night buffets, the dance club – no doubt still buzzing about the crazy girl who flashed her boobs in the middle of the dining room. And despite her initial disappointment that she and Jen wouldn't be partying along with them, Beth now realized that she was, in some small way, relieved that Jen had passed out.

Life was safer that way. Easier.

Beth loved her sister. She really did. But sometimes she could be so . . . taxing. Twenty-nine years old and still a child.

Peter Pan on an endless spring break.

Beth herself had matured fairly quickly. A matter of necessity, really, after their parents died in a plane crash in Brazil. They had moved in with their grand-mother at the time, but Gramma Jean hadn't been in the best of health, so it was up to Beth to take charge of the wild one.

It was a familiar story, and not a particularly earth-shattering one at that, and Beth did her best with the meagre skills she had. But it had never been enough to tame the girl.

Jen hadn't always been such a handful. In fact, in her younger years, long before the crash, she'd been considered the 'quiet' one. She was so shy that she couldn't muster up the courage to buy a candy bar in a convenience store, and big sister Beth was always forced to come to the rescue. Even as they got into their teen years, Jen kept mostly to herself, spending her time with books and schoolwork.

But the crash had changed that.

They got the news from their school headmistress, Mrs Llewellyn. A chartered jet had gone down in the Brazilian jungle, no survivors found. At first, Beth and Jen had grabbed onto the hope that there'd been a mis-take, a mix-up of some kind, but that hope was shattered when their parents' bodies were shipped back to Santa Barbara.

After the funeral, it seemed as if some foreign entity had invaded Jen's body. Her shyness gene receded and died. And back at school, she began sneaking away with the older girls to smoke cigarettes in the woods. And God knows what else. She openly flirted with the school gardener, a part-timer from the local college, who was a good six years older than her.

Jen was possessed, Beth often thought, by some crazed demon who looked and sounded a lot like the old Jennifer, but was most certainly an impostor.

When Mrs Llewellyn told them that they'd be leaving the academy at the end of the school year to live with their grandmother up in San Luis Obispo, Jen screamed and went running from the room, and kept on running, only to be found, hours later, sitting in the academy clock tower, threatening to do a swan dive into the shallow waters of the school fountain.

A crowd gathered, their classmates snickering, Mrs Llewellyn shouting for Jen to come down, but Jen refused, and it was up to Beth to climb into the tower and talk her out of this silliness. This hadn't been Mrs Llewellyn's idea, of course, but Beth the Dutiful had known what she needed to do, so she did it, despite the headmistress's commands for her to stop.

By the time she climbed out onto the ledge and sat next to Jen, she could hear sirens approaching.

'What are you doing?' she asked softly. 'Why are you up here?'

'It's all their fault,' Jen said. She was fifteen at the time, just two years younger than Beth. Tears in her eyes.

'Mom and Dad?'

Jen nodded. 'If they loved us, they wouldn't have gone. Or they would've taken us with them and we could all be in Heaven together.'

'It was a business trip. They couldn't take us.'

Jen looked at her, defiance in her gaze.

'And what about the week in Paris? The cruise

around the Greek islands? Were those business trips, too?'

Beth didn't respond.

'Face it, sis, they didn't want us around. This school is more of a family to us than they ever were.'

'They had a business to run.'

'And kids to raise. But what did we ever get out of them besides holidays and summer vacation? I'm almost glad they're dead.'

'Stop it,' Beth said.

Jen was quiet for a long moment.

Then: 'I don't want to live with Gramma Jean. I don't want to leave school.'

'I know. Neither do I.'

'And Gramma Jean's not gonna be too happy when she finds out about . . .'

Her voice trailed.

'About what?' Beth asked.

The tears welled up in Jen's eyes.

'I think I'm pregnant.'

11

It turned out to be a false alarm.

Thank God.

Jen's menstrual cycle had merely been thrown off-kilter by the emotions of the last few weeks, and after three days of panic she began to bleed and told Beth she'd never been happier in her life to use a tampon.

But just the fact that Jen was having sex was shocking enough to Beth, who herself had not yet met a boy she was willing to lose her virginity to. And although Beth wanted to stay at the academy as much as Jen did, she thought that moving in with Gramma Jean might turn out to be a good thing.

It didn't. But they did their best to cope.

Besides her health troubles, Gramma Jean was not the most loving grandparent in the universe, and Beth began to understand why their own mother had been so aloof.

Beth made a vow to herself that if she ever had kids – and she fully intended to one day – then she would love them like nobody's business. And when she died, you'd never hear a single one of them say they were almost glad it had happened.

*

The two girls settled into life at San Lucas High, Jen immediately carrying on where she had left off at the academy. Instead of the woods, cigarette breaks were taken behind the band building. A quick way to make friends. And because the school was co-ed, Jen was never short of potential boy toys. It didn't help that she'd developed into a first-class stunner, with nearly every male in school lusting after her. Including some of her teachers.

'Just remember how scared you were when you were sitting up on that ledge,' Beth warned.

'I don't think anyone ever got pregnant giving blow jobs,' Jen said.

Beth certainly couldn't argue with that.

Now, standing at the rail, she let the ocean breeze wash over her, thinking about the last ten years. Ten years that felt like a hundred.

While Beth went off to college and law school, Jen stayed true to her nature and continued to play wild child, eventually getting married to a tattooed motor-cycle mechanic named Bradley – who was a sweet enough guy, but no match for Jen. When he wanted to stay in, she wanted to party. When he wanted to go for a Sunday ride, she was too hungover to climb onto the back of his bike.

The marriage lasted three years. And only that long, Jen explained, because of their 'monster' sex life.

Beth herself had used her time a bit more productively. She graduated from law school, spent a year clerking for a Santa Barbara Circuit Court judge, then snagged a job as assistant district attorney with the Los Angeles district attorney's office.

And fell in love.

His name was Peter, a young assistant prosecutor, and there was a time she thought he could do no wrong.

But, oh, how times change.

Thinking about Peter, however, was too painful right now, and as much as she loved looking out at the ocean, she was still wearing her dinner dress and starting to get cold. Better to go back to the cabin, slide into bed for the night and hope that Jen had learned her lesson.

Tomorrow would be a better day.

At least Beth was determined to make it one.

She was about to head for the door or hatch or whatever the hell you called it, when—

'Beautiful night, isn't it?'

Startled, Beth turned and saw the silhouette of a man sitting in the shadows behind her on one of the deck chairs.

Had he been there all along?

Her face must have shown her surprise, because he said, 'I'm sorry, did I frighten you?'

An accent. Slight but unmistakable.

Then he rose, moving into the moonlight – one of those big movie moments, where time seems to momentarily stand still. He was in his mid-thirties. Hispanic. Dark hair pulled into a pony-tail – not a style

42

Beth particularly liked, but that didn't much matter, because he was so damn gorgeous he had no trouble pulling it off.

Buffeted by his presence, she felt herself take a slight step backwards.

'I *did* frighten you.'

'No,' she said. 'I mean . . . a little, I guess.'

She tried a smile, but it was an awkward one at best. Thirty-one years old, a prosecuting attorney for one of the biggest cities in the world and here she was, suddenly acting like a complete spaz.

Get a grip, girl.

'You thought you were alone out here. It was rude of me to sit in the dark and watch you. Even worse to interrupt.'

Beth shook her head. 'It's no big deal. I was headed back inside, anyway.'

'Oh? Then let me apologize by buying you a drink.'

Beth hesitated. After four years with the DA's office, she was naturally suspicious, but such an offer didn't exactly fall into the realm of criminal behaviour.

Still, at this point in her life, it was hard for her to believe that anyone would be even remotely interested in buying her a drink, let alone someone who looked like this. She couldn't help wondering what his angle was.

'That's kind of you,' she said, 'but there's nothing to apologize for.'

He nodded. 'No apologies, then. Just the drink.' He held out a hand to shake. 'My name is Rafael Santiago.'

Beth hesitated again, then took the hand.

43

VARGAS

12

'Where the hell you been?'

'His car wouldn't start,' the one called Sergio said. 'Thing's a piece of shit.'

Vargas was barely conscious. Head throbbing. Wrists bound with a rough piece of rope. He could feel himself being half-carried, half-dragged somewhere, but was afraid to open his eyes. Opening his eyes might mean another fist to the face – or worse, a fresh new blow to the head – and he sure as hell didn't want that.

But then he didn't want any of this, did he?

'You find out what he knows?' Sergio asked.

'Peckerwood comes on like he's the beaner answer to Woodward and Bernstein, but I don't think he really knows squat. I mentioned the American gal and he was completely clueless.'

'Who the hell are Woodward and Bernstein?'

They came to a stop.

'Forget it,' Ainsworth said. 'Where's Junior?'

'Right behind you, Pa.'

'Here, take these and open the trunk.'

Vargas heard the jangle of car keys as Junior did what he was told. There was the faint but unmistakable *thunk* of his own trunk latch being released, the groan of its hinges, then he was hoisted upwards and dropped inside as if he were nothing more than a bag full of rocks.

Pain shot through him as his tailbone came into contact with something solid – the spare tyre, which was hidden in a well beneath the carpeted lining that served as the trunk floor. There had once been a thin particle-board divider covering the well, but somewhere in the last several months it had broken in two and he'd tossed it aside. He couldn't remember when.

It took everything he had to keep from groaning. Then the hands grabbed him again, taking hold of his legs and bending them so he'd fit all the way inside.

'We'd better wrap some tape around his mouth,' Sergio said. 'And truss up his ankles, too. In case the asshole wakes up halfway there.'

'Where you headed?'

'Safe house in Juarez. He's waiting for us.'

'He? You mean the man himself?'

'That's what they tell me.'

'Well, I'll be damned. I thought he only came out on special occasions.'

'I guess this is special.'

'Doesn't sound like they're planning a prayer meeting. What the hell does he want with this idiot, anyway?'

'Why do you care? You got problems of your own.'

'What do you mean?'

'He's pretty pissed at you and the retard.'

There was a shuffle of movement, then Sergio squealed.

'What the hell are you doing?'

'Call him that again, you little shit, and I'll gut you right here.'

'All right, all right! Jesus, I didn't mean nothin' by it.'

There was a beat of silence, more shuffling. Vargas fought the temptation to open his eyes.

Then Ainsworth said, 'I don't know what he's so upset about. Me and Junior did what we were told. Wasn't even our mess to begin with, and he got what he wanted, didn't he?'

'What he wanted was this whole thing erased. But you two blew it.'

'Like it's our fault the only honest cop in Chihuahua decides to get curious before we can finish.'

'And you think calling out to the guy made it any better?'

'He saw our truck, asshole. Was staring right at the plate. Besides, we signed on as couriers, not garbage collectors.'

'Maybe, but even you've gotta admit it was pretty stupid leaving the American woman alive.'

'We ain't killers, either. Shape she was in, it was only a matter of time, anyway. And it all worked out in the end. So you tell the man: he's not happy with us, he can shove the whole goddamn arrangement. We'll go back to raising chickens for a living.'

'Are you sure that's what you want me to say?'

'I'm not afraid of him.'

'You should be, *mi amigo*.'

'You ask me, only a coward leaves a mess and tells

somebody else to clean it up. And cowards don't scare me.' A pause. 'Besides, the way he's been pissing his pants over our boy here, tells me *he's* the one who . . .'

Another pause, and Vargas knew instinctively that he was being stared at.

'What?' Sergio asked. 'What's wrong?'

'Might be my imagination, but I think this son of a bitch is awake.'

And before Vargas could assess what had given him away, he felt something thud against the side of his head, followed by an intense, hot white pain.

Then darkness.

13

When he came to, he had to fight his way through a hazy field of cobwebs and cotton before he remembered where he was and what had happened to him. But the rope around his wrists and ankles and the layers of duct tape wrapped around his head and covering his mouth were fairly good reminders.

And the heat.

Jesus, it was hot.

The Corolla was moving, and he was now locked inside the trunk, his body screwed up into an impossible position, the road bumping beneath him, sending little jolts of pain through his tailbone and along his spine.

His head throbbed worse than ever, blood and sweat trickling along his temple, across his cheek, then down past the tape and into his mouth.

He recognized the taste.

When he was six years old, his father had fashioned a toy parachute for him using some string, a handkerchief and a small lead weight. For hours, he had delighted in tossing it into the air and watching it float to the ground like a miniature paratrooper about to land on some foreign beach.

One time, however, he threw it high and into the sun and immediately lost track of it. Spinning in a circle to see where it would come down, he couldn't for the life of him find it. Then something hit his head, pain shooting through him, and what seemed like a bucket of blood began to flow into his eyes and mouth.

Horrified, he ran into the house, screaming for help. And after his father had washed and treated what turned out to be a fairly insignificant wound, Vargas had asked how such a small piece of lead could have caused so much blood.

'The head is very sensitive, *mijo*. Even the tiniest of cuts will bring on the blood of a hundred more.' Then his father smiled. 'Just be thankful that none of your brains leaked out along with it.'

Vargas wasn't sure he could be so thankful this time. Ainsworth had thumped him pretty good – twice – and he had no doubt that he'd need stitches to repair the damage.

He lay there, fighting off the urge to panic, and tried to assess his predicament.

There was no sound of conversation in the car. A song played on the radio – an old *corrido* that had always been one of his grandmother's favourites. But other than that and the hum of the tyres, there was silence.

Which meant that either no one felt like talking, or the driver was alone. And based on the conversation he'd overheard earlier, he figured the one called Sergio was behind the wheel.

Where Ainsworth and son might be was anyone's guess, but he didn't think they were here. Ainsworth liked to talk too much. Enjoyed listening to himself. And Vargas couldn't imagine he'd leave the F150 behind.

So it was just Vargas and Sergio.

Better odds, but still not good.

Where you headed?

The safe house in Juarez. He's waiting for us.

Vargas had no idea who they'd been talking about – that was a question for another time – but he was pretty sure that if he didn't do something, right now, he wouldn't be getting out of this little rendezvous alive.

And since Juarez was less than an hour's drive from Dead Man's Dunes, chances were good that he and Sergio would soon be arriving at their destination.

Too soon.

So Vargas had only one goal in mind: to get out of this trunk.

As fast as humanly possible.

BETH

14

It took them three tries to find a bar they liked.

The first was close to the bow of the ship – the Seafarer's Lounge – a large, glow-in-the-dark cave that was packed to the gills with drunken karaoke-lovers.

Beth told him she'd rather eat ground glass than go inside.

Taking the elevator to Deck 11, they were halfway to the next one, a place called the Vibe, when the sound of raucous laughter and a pounding bass beat assaulted them.

Without a word, Rafael took her by the elbow and steered her away – winning points in the process – then led her through a long hallway to a set of wrought-iron steps that wound downward to a small, enclosed piano bar.

This was more like it.

The place was sparsely populated, a slightly elevated stage featuring a solo pianist playing a slow jazz tune, Bill Evans or Herbie Hancock or – Beth wasn't sure who. Peter had been the jazz buff in the family.

Rafael's hand touched the small of her back, gently

guiding her towards the bar itself, a wide semi-circle that dominated the place.

She had to admit she liked the feel of that hand.

'Shall we sit here?' he asked.

'Wherever you want.'

The bartender, a tall Norwegian whose name tag read 'Edvard', nodded to them as they slid onto stools.

Beth was carrying nothing but a small clutch purse that held her cell phone, a packet of gum, lipstick, a couple of Bandaids, and her Seafarer card. The cards were given to passengers as they checked in at port, and not only unlocked their stateroom doors, but were linked to their identification.

And, more importantly, to their credit cards. They were used as cash aboard ship for buying paperbacks and trinkets and toiletry kits and drinks. Mostly drinks. Beth imagined that quite a few guests would be in for a shock when the final bill was tallied.

As she lay her purse on the bar, Rafael brought out his own Seafarer card and handed it to Edvard.

'Tequila tonic,' he said, then turned to Beth and waited.

She smiled. 'Long Island Iced Tea.'

It was a strong drink – what her boss had once called, dollar for dollar, the best value in booze – but she knew her limits, and didn't imagine she'd be flashing her boobs anytime soon.

Edvard nodded, carried the card to the register, passed it under a scanner, then handed it back to Rafael and began mixing their drinks.

'For the record,' Rafael said, 'I don't normally skulk around in the dark, spying on beautiful women.'

It took Beth a moment to realize she'd been complimented – something she wasn't used to these days – but she said nothing.

'You know that, *si*? That you're beautiful?'

She smiled again. 'I'm sure that kind of flattery works on your typical tourist. Unfortunately, I have a mirror. More than one, in fact.'

Not that she considered herself ugly, by any means. Or even plain. But when she looked into those mirrors, what she saw staring back at her was no movie star. She was a slightly above average woman who could stand to lose five pounds. At the very least. And when she wore the right make-up, the right outfit, the right shoes, she might even lean towards attractive.

But beautiful? That was Jen's territory, not hers.

'True beauty,' Rafael said, 'has little to do with the surface of the skin.'

Oh, brother. Deduct a boatload of points for that one. Pun intended.

She touched her heart. 'Let me guess. It's what's in here that counts.'

He frowned. 'Why do you mock me?'

'Sorry. But I know a line when I hear it. Especially when it's not all that original.'

'I don't claim originality. Only sincerity.'

'That's sweet, Rafael, it really is, but you just met me. For all you know, I've got the heart of a Gila monster.'

'I know people,' he said. 'Or perhaps I should say I sense them.'

'Sense them?'

'I am a student of the soul. I see things that most people overlook.'

Beth studied him. Was this more bullshit on top of the previous shovelful, or did he actually believe what he was saying?

Determined not to let the surface of *his* skin cloud her judgement – God, he was gorgeous – she decided to keep the red flag flying.

For now, at least.

She was not, after all, merely Beth the Dutiful. She was also Beth the Cautious. It was a trait that had served her well over the years. If you didn't count her ex-husband, that is.

Of course, none of this kept her from thinking about that hand on her back. Or those eyes.

Edvard set their drinks in front of them and Beth reached for hers, took a sip.

Strong as predicted, but manageable.

'I've offended you,' Rafael said. 'That certainly wasn't my intention.'

'Just call me a sceptic. I make a living at it.'

'Oh? What do you do?'

She shook her head, suddenly sorry she'd brought it up. The last thing she wanted to think about was prosecuting rapists and paedophiles. That was buzz kill of the worst kind.

'Let's talk about you instead.'

He smiled. 'I'm afraid I am not very interesting, but what would you like to know?'

'Where you're from would be a start. Why you're here.'

He took a sip of his tequila.

'My home is a place called Ciudad de Almas. But I do not spend much time there.'

'Why not?'

'My work requires me to travel: Mexico City; San Antonio; El Paso.' He gestured to their surroundings. 'And sometimes I like to get away. Have some fun.'

'Alone?'

'That would be unusual?'

'Cruising doesn't strike me as a solo sport.'

He smiled again. 'You are right. I am travelling with someone.'

She knew he was too good to be true. But before she could give this too much thought, the lights began to dim and Rafael quickly checked his watch.

'Speak of the devil. We're here just in time.'

'For what?'

He nodded towards the stage. 'To meet my travelling companion.'

15

Beth turned as a spotlight came to life near the piano and a woman stepped on stage.

Tall. Brown. Exotic.

A cascade of raven hair. Dark eyes. A killer body in a black satin dress. A perfect combination of genes and breeding that sucked the life out of every female in a room the moment she entered it. Including Beth.

In short, she was stunning.

Moving up to a microphone, she waited as the piano player tinkled a few keys, then she launched into a smoky Latin jazz tune – singing in Spanish – wrapping her voice around the words and melody in a way that Beth hadn't quite heard before. Low, sultry, but with phrasing just unique enough to take her beyond the average lounge singer, into the realm of the anointed.

The cliché *oozes charisma* popped into Beth's mind. And it was an accurate one.

Except for the piano and the sound of that voice, the bar was silent, all eyes riveted to the creature on stage. And Beth knew that the men in the bar – and possibly a few of their wives or girlfriends – were suddenly re-evaluating their lives, wishing they could steal just a few moments away from their current entanglements to pursue this woman, no matter how futile such a pursuit might be.

Beth watched and listened, glancing at Rafael, thinking how well matched the two were. Perfect specimens – mirror images really – who belonged together.

As the song came to an end, the bar erupted into applause and whistles. The woman said a throaty '*gracias*,' then nodded to the piano player and launched into another tune, this one a bit more uptempo than the first.

As Beth listened, she felt a hand graze her shoulder, then turned to find Rafael holding her drink.

'Don't forget this,' he said.

She thanked him as he handed it to her, then took a long sip and returned her attention to the stage, where the woman was proving that she wasn't a one-hit wonder.

But Beth didn't really feel like drinking any more. The pre-Rafael, low-grade depression she had been battling as she stood at the ship's rail was starting to return. Whatever adolescent fantasy she had been harbouring had become instantly laughable. With someone like this woman to keep him company, why would Rafael be even remotely interested in her? Not that she'd ever really believed he was anyway.

The wisest thing she could do right now was to thank him for the drink, then wish him a goodnight and go to bed.

She was about to do just that, when the second song came to an end, followed by another burst of applause.

Apparently believing in the motto, leave them wanting more, the woman thanked the audience, then stepped off the stage as the piano player launched into another solo.

A moment later, she was at Rafael's side, kissing his cheek, murmuring something in Spanish. Then she turned, assessing Beth. A mildly aggressive look, but not hostile.

'Who is your friend?' she asked Rafael.

He gestured, said, 'Beth, I'd like you to meet Marta Santiago. My sister.'

Sister?

Beth almost laughed.

Of course. As they stood side by side it was obvious now that they came from the same gene pool. And a fairly exclusive one at that.

Marta continued to assess Beth. 'I remember you from dinner.'

'Oh?'

'We were dining at a table near yours.' She turned to her brother. 'You remember, don't you, Rafael?'

Rafael said nothing, avoiding Beth's gaze.

Oh, crap, Beth thought, they saw Jen's spontaneous unveiling. And apparently Rafael had been too polite to bring it up.

Marta said, 'Is something wrong?'

Beth smiled weakly. 'My sister has a few issues. I sometimes think of her as my evil twin.'

'Ah, *si*,' Rafael said with a sly smile. 'I can see the resemblance.'

'But only from the neck up, right?'

58

They both looked at Beth, surprised, then burst into laughter.

Beth joined in, the ice broken.

After a moment, Rafael lifted his tequila tonic in toast.

'To sisters,' he said. 'A blessing and a curse.'

Marta shot him a quick look, then they laughed again as Beth clinked Rafael's glass with hers and took another long sip. Not that she needed it. She was already starting to feel a little woozy.

She said to Marta, 'So you work for the cruise line?'

Marta shook her head, gesturing towards the piano player. 'Actually, I met Miguel in the food court this afternoon and he was kind enough to let me have some fun.'

What a surprise, Beth thought. Most guys would let this woman do anything she wanted. Join me on stage? Sure, why not.

'You have a remarkable voice.'

'Thank you. I don't often have an opportunity to show it off.'

'Oh? You're not a professional?'

'Singing is more of an avocation for me. A form of release.'

'With a voice like that, I'm surprised you don't have a record deal.'

Marta shrugged. 'Such things don't interest me.' She glanced at her watch. 'And I don't mean to be rude, but Rafael, we need to talk.'

Rafael's eyebrows rose. 'What is it?'

She looked at Beth. 'Do mind if I steal him for a moment?'

'No, not at all.'

'It was nice meeting you.' She took Rafael by the hand, and he shrugged at Beth, saying, '*Una momento*,' as his sister led him across the floor to a spot near the wrought-iron staircase. They huddled together, speaking into each other's ear, Marta doing most of the talking.

Beth tried not to watch them, tried instead to concentrate on Miguel, the piano player, but she couldn't help herself. Their conversation seemed to be growing heated – a fiery look in Marta's eyes – and Beth had a feeling they were arguing about *her*.

Which made no sense at all.

As if to confirm it, however, Rafael glanced in her direction – forcing Beth to momentarily avert her gaze.

Then Marta touched his cheek, looking apologetic, and Beth got the sense that something more was going on here than a simple spat between siblings. Something in their body language that went beyond the bond of brother and sister.

With a quick look around, Marta pulled Rafael into the shadows beneath the staircase. Beth could barely see them now, but what she *could* see made her stomach turn.

Marta leaned into him, kissed him.

Full on the mouth.

And this was no sisterly kiss. At least not where Beth came from.

Worse yet, Rafael seemed to be kissing her back, neither of them even remotely close to coming up for air.

Oh. My. God.

Turning away from the spectacle, Beth took a nice big gulp of her drink, then set it on the counter. Waited for her stomach to settle.

This was obviously her cue to exit. She had no interest in hanging around with Mexico's answer to the Appalachia twins. And from all appearances, they seemed to be getting on just fine without her.

Ugh.

Scooping up her purse, she crossed for a doorway on the opposite side of the bar and fled.

16

When she got back to their stateroom, Jen was gone. A note on her bunk said:

Got my second wind. Went dancing.

Beth sighed. Only Jen could be throwing up one minute and raring to go the next. She never ceased to amaze.

Pulling off her dress, Beth crawled onto her bunk, grabbed the remote from her nightstand and flicked on the TV. Not that there was anything playing that could top what she'd witnessed tonight.

She was no stranger to incest. In her work at the prosecutor's office she'd seen more cases of father–daughter couplings than she'd wanted to, but those were always crimes of abuse. Some twisted fuck taking advantage of his parental authority, perverting a child's love.

What she'd seen between Rafael and Marta, however, was obviously consensual. But that didn't make it any more palatable. Some might argue that Beth's objection to it was both morally and intellectually empty

– they were adults, after all – but that didn't keep it from creeping her out. The 'ick' factor was almost too much to bear. And the image of two his-and-her beauty queens macking on one another was not likely to go away anytime soon.

Beth shivered, trying to concentrate on the TV, which was showing a remake of *The Day the Earth Stood Still* with Keanu Reeves. She managed to stare at it for a full thirty minutes, but would be hard pressed to tell anyone what she'd seen.

This was turning out to be one hell of a vacation.

But if Jen could recover so quickly, why couldn't *she*? The original plan was to go dancing together, and late was better than never.

Flicking off the screen, she got up, pulled on some jeans, a T-shirt and a pair of shoes, then grabbed her purse and headed out of the door.

Two staircases and an elevator ride later, she was back on Deck 11, standing outside the Vibe, the pounding beat vibrating beneath her feet as the bodies inside moved to the rhythm – a sea of bobbing heads and waving arms and drunken, smiling faces.

Jen was bound to be in there somewhere.

Pushing past a couple locked in an embrace, Beth squeezed into the room and searched the crowded dance floor.

It was dark, except for swirling, multicoloured lights and a spotlight on the DJ, who looked a little lame wearing his ship's uniform. At least he played good music.

But there was no sign of Jen.

Anywhere.

Shit.

Thinking she may have made a mistake, Beth was about to turn and head back out the door when she heard a familiar peal of laughter rise above the din. Spinning around, she saw a cluster of bodies move from the shadows onto the dance floor, Jen at the very centre, head thrown back, hair wild and flowing.

Beth called out to her and waved, but was drowned out by the music. Stepping onto the dance floor, she squeezed past several dancers, pushing towards Jen—

—then stopped cold, a ball of bile rising straight to her throat.

Jen was dancing with a man and a woman.

But not just any man and woman.

Rafael and Marta Santiago.

And on closer inspection, it was much more than dancing. Jen was sandwiched between the two, Rafael behind, Marta facing her, breast to breast, all three rubbing their bodies against each other. Rafael's hands roamed Jen's ass as Marta kept her arms around her neck, staring intently into her eyes.

Beth watched them in utter amazement, unable to quite understand what she was looking at, trying to convince herself that she'd made a mistake, that this wasn't Jen at all, that the flashing lights were playing tricks on her eyes.

But of course that was only wishful thinking.

It was Jen all right.

Her little sister.

And like any protective mother, Beth waded

into the crowd towards them with only rescue on her mind.

Jen turned as she approached, let loose a squeal. 'Beth! We were just talking about you.'

Rafael and Marta also turned, smiling at her, as Jen reached out and tried to pull her into an embrace. She was drunk again – or still – and judging by her glazed eyes, was high on more than booze. God only knew where it had come from, but Beth had her suspicions.

Avoiding the embrace, she shouted above the music: 'Jen, what the hell are you doing?'

'Didn't you get my note?'

'That's not what I'm talking about. What are you doing with *them*?'

Jen frowned, glancing at Rafael and Marta. 'What does it look like I'm doing?'

'Whatever it is, it's making me sick to my stomach.' She grabbed Jen's arm. 'Come on, let's go.'

'Hey, I just got here.'

'Do you know anything about these people?'

A shrug. 'They're hot, they can dance and they've got really good drugs. What else is there to know?'

Rafael broke in. 'Is there a problem, Beth?'

She shot him a look. 'Fuck off, perv.'

'You disappeared without a word. If I've offended you in some—'

'Spare me, asshole. I don't care what you and your sister do when nobody's looking, but keep *my* sister out of it.' She tugged on Jen's arm. 'Come on.'

Angry now, Jen yanked free. 'Do you mind?'

'These people are sick. You don't know what I saw them—'

'Oh, for godsakes, Beth, get a goddamn life, will you? And leave me alone.'

'Come on, Jen, you can't do this.'

'Do what? Have fun? I'm sorry I don't live in Beth land, where everybody sits around moping all the time, but I didn't come on this cruise to play shuffleboard. So kindly fuck off, okay?'

'Jen, I—'

'Leave. Me. Alone.'

And with that, Jen turned abruptly, grabbing hold of Rafael and Marta and pulling them with her, deeper into the crowd.

Beth stood there a moment, stung, a motionless figure amid all the writhing bodies.

Feeling tears well up, she quickly backed away.

Then headed for the door.

VARGAS

17

Vargas had never been much of a car guy. If it got you from point A to point B, he'd drive it, no matter how battered. And if you were expecting any upkeep other than the occasional service and tyre change, you'd be sorely disappointed.

He rarely looked under the hood of his Corolla, and couldn't remember ever picking up the manual, which had been stashed in his glovebox since the day he bought the car, used, a year and a half ago.

If you'd told him then that he would one day be bludgeoned and gagged and tied up and locked inside his own goddamned trunk, he would have looked at you as if you were a candidate for a straitjacket.

Yet here he was. And it occurred to him that if he'd ever bothered to crack open that manual, he might know how to get himself out of this mess. There had to be an emergency lever or something, right?

Maybe. But he was thinking too far ahead.

He wouldn't be pulling any levers, emergency or otherwise, if he couldn't manoeuvre. And he couldn't manoeuvre with his wrists and ankles bound. Whoever had tied them – Ainsworth, no doubt – had done a damn good job, leaving him very little wriggle room.

His fingers were starting to go numb.

Reaching his ankles would be impossible at this point, and every time he tried to move his hands, to get a little air between his wrists, the rope cut deep, digging into his flesh – a rough, burning sensation that he could have happily avoided his entire life without feeling he'd missed out on something.

His only solution, he decided, was a sharp surface of some kind, and there was bound to be one in here somewhere. The last time he'd bothered to pay any attention to the underside of his trunk lid (during a move to a new apartment, when he'd overloaded the trunk and was forced to tie the lid down with bungee cords), he'd noticed all kinds of exposed metal. But would any of it do the trick?

Hard to tell, when you've got no light.

He'd have to feel his way through this.

Twisting his body slightly, he tried to roll over onto his back and managed to get only halfway there before the base of his spine once again made contact with the spare tyre lodged beneath him.

Making a mental note to rip the thing out of there and roll it off the nearest cliff – just in case he should find himself in this predicament again – he readjusted his body, then took it slower this time.

And hit his head on the trunk hinge.

Fuck.

A bullet of pain shot through his skull and he cried out, the sound muffled by the layers of duct tape. Taking a moment to let the pain settle into a dull throb, he carefully ducked his head, rolled slightly, then shifted around until he was more or less facing upwards, his legs twisted awkwardly beneath him.

All of this took him a hell of a lot longer than he'd expected it to and he could tell by the growing sound of traffic around them that they'd reached civilization. Which meant their destination might not be as far away as he needed it to be.

Reaching out, he ran his hands along the surface of the trunk lid, finding nooks and crannies and metallic edges, but nothing sharp enough to do the trick. Everything was as smooth as the backside of a butter knife.

Then he hit something, almost stabbing himself in the process.

A screw.

Holy shit.

A fucking screw.

It wasn't just any screw, however, but a long, sharp one, probably rusted, protruding through the metal next to a circular hollow spot just above his head, on the far left side of the trunk.

Vargas had no idea how it had got there, but he knew it couldn't be part of the car's original design – too much of a hazard – so it had to be the handiwork of the previous owner, an old navy veteran named Harry 'Jackhammer' Bridger. A handyman's handyman, Harry had worked maintenance at the LA Tribune building until throat cancer forced him to retire, then killed him less than six months later. God only knew what he'd attached to the inside of the trunk, but when he'd ripped it out, he'd left behind this screw.

Thanks, old buddy. Rest in peace.

Readjusting his hands, Vargas brought his wrists up to the tip of the screw and began scraping the rope against it.

It wasn't quiet work, especially in the confines of the trunk, but he figured the hum of the tyres and the blasting radio would mask the noise from Sergio's ears. He moved as quickly as he could, feeling the screw snag and grab hold, then cut through the fibres, a nanometre at a time, each move of his hands forcing the rope to dig deeper into his wrists.

Then the brakes squeaked and the car came to a sudden halt.

Vargas's hands slipped, jerking upward, and the screw pierced flesh, driving deep. Hot pain shot through the left side of his hand, radiating up into the pinky.

It took everything he had to keep from screaming.

Yanking his hands free, he brought them down to his thigh, pressing the wound against it, and squeezed his eyes shut, as if this would somehow put out the fire.

No such luck.

He could still hear cars around him, their engines idling, which meant they were at a traffic light. Inside the Corolla, Sergio started singing along with the tune on the radio.

But these were only peripheral observations. Most of Vargas's concentration was centred on the one small part of his body that stung like a motherfucker. And he felt like singing, too – but it wouldn't be a happy tune.

Wondering how much more damage he could do to himself, he waited for the pain to subside, and when the car lurched into motion again, he quickly raised his hands to the trunk lid and resumed his task.

But he'd have to make it fast. He had a feeling that the next time this car stopped, it wouldn't be for something as insignificant as a traffic light.

18

Five minutes later, Vargas felt something give, and the rope loosened.

It wasn't much, but it might be enough.

Twisting his hands back and forth, feeling the burn and not giving a damn, he worked the rope, forcing it to give again, and then again, until finally, thankfully, he pulled his wrists free.

He let out a breath. Felt exhausted. But he couldn't quit now.

Carefully rolling onto his side, he brought his knees up towards his chest, then reached down to his ankles with his right hand, found the knot in the rope and started tugging at it. It was tight and rock hard, but Vargas wasn't about to let that stop him. He kept working at it, wriggling it back and forth until it, too, loosened and came free.

He didn't bother with the tape across his mouth. That could be taken care of later.

Instead, he shifted his body again and let his hands roam the trunk, searching for an emergency lever, or cable, or anything that might pop the lid.

Then he found one, near the rear of the trunk, next

to the panel behind the back seat, where the rear speakers were supposed to be mounted.

A small knob.

He had no idea if this was the emergency trunk release, or simply a lever that allowed the back seats to be lowered. But it didn't matter. Either way, it was his ticket out. Escaping through the back seat might be more problematic, with Sergio up there, but it was a chance he'd have to take.

Grabbing hold of the knob with his good hand, he pulled on it as hard as he could.

Nothing happened.

What the hell?

Muttering into the duct tape, he tried again, and this time got something in return for his efforts.

With a sharp, snapping sound – snapping cable, that is – the knob came loose in his fingers.

Broken. Useless.

Sonofabitch.

Vargas dropped the knob and lay still for a moment, feeling the hump of that goddamned tyre beneath him, wondering what his next move should be. He could search for another knob, another lever, but he had a feeling he'd pretty much shot his wad on that front.

So what now, genius?

Time isn't exactly on your side.

He was searching desperately for a Plan B, when a sudden thought occurred to him.

The tyre.

The goddamned tyre.

Where there's a spare, there's bound to be a tyre iron, right?

Why hadn't he thought of that before?

Every car came equipped with one. And it may be true that he was a pitiful excuse for a car owner, but the previous owner, good old Harry, would be the last person in the world to leave his trunk without the proper emergency gear.

At least Vargas hoped so.

Harry hadn't been too diligent about cable replacement, had he?

Still, Vargas had a feeling that somewhere down in that tyre well there was a jack, some flares and a tyre iron, which, like the manual in his glovebox, had lay untouched for at least a year and a half.

Finding the edge of the carpet, he peeled it back and reached down into the well, rooting around down there until he found a bulky cloth sack with a drawstring on top. The tools inside clanked as he picked it up.

Bingo.

Pulling it out, he loosened the string, opened the sack and found the tyre iron – at least what felt like a tyre iron – nestled up against the jack. He grabbed it, set the sack aside, then ran his fingers along the rim of the trunk lid until he found the latch.

Shifting his weight for leverage, he shoved the sharp side of the tyre iron between the latch and the lid and levered it back with a quick, hard jerk.

The latch snapped and the lid flew open, Vargas scrabbling up to the edge, looking down at the road passing beneath him. His only choice was to jump, but he knew he'd do some damage in the process.

Then the Corolla began to slow, Sergio apparently aware that something was up, and Vargas started over the side—

—only to hear the loud, long honk of a horn.

Snapping his head up, he saw a familiar F150 headed straight for him. Fast.

Shit.

Ainsworth.

He'd forgotten about him.

Vargas pulled back just as the F150 smashed into the rear of the Corolla, the impact throwing him forwards again. Grabbing onto the lip of the trunk, he held tight, trying to avoid becoming part of the truck's grill, just as Sergio put on the brakes.

Ainsworth braked, too, getting some distance between them, then sped up again, about to ram the Corolla a second time.

Knowing it was now or never, Vargas scrambled over the edge, then dived sideways towards the road, tucking his head as he went.

He hit the road hard, tumbling like a cat caught in a dryer, feeling his shoulder give, another stab of pain. The world swirled around him, quick flashes of colour, as he rolled into the dirt at the side of the road and lay still.

Hearing the screech of tyres, he willed himself to sit up, saw Ainsworth and Junior and a squat, muscular Mexican guy – Sergio – emerging from their vehicles, shouting at him, and he knew he had to get to his feet, fast.

Glancing around, he saw that he was on a main drag, a cluster of buildings in the distance. And beyond that –

– the border station –

– the fucking border station –

– where several rows of cars were lined up for passage into El Paso.

Vargas jumped to his feet, his body protesting, then turned towards the station and ran, not looking back, not thinking about how close the others might be.

Someone shouted his name again – Sergio this time – and he picked up speed, forcing his legs to move faster than they'd ever moved before, feeling as if they could give out on him at any moment.

Approaching the line of cars, he began to weave through them, not slowing down, doing his best to make himself a difficult target. Grabbing hold of the duct tape plastered over his mouth, he yanked it free.

'Help me!' he shouted. 'Somebody help me!'

All around him drivers rolled down their windows and craned their necks, trying to get a look at what was going on. Trying to get a glimpse of the shouting mad man.

Up ahead, a guard came scrambling out of his booth, drawing his sidearm as he went.

He pointed it directly at Vargas. '*Alto! Manos arriba!*'

Chancing a look behind him, Vargas saw that Ainsworth and crew had stopped short at the sight of the guard, their gazes unwavering. And none of them looked happy.

'*Alto o disparo!*' the guard shouted, and Vargas snapped his head around. There were two more of them now, guns trained on Vargas.

Coming to an abrupt halt, he dropped to his knees and threw his hands into the air as the guards ran towards him.

'I'm an American!' he shouted. '*Soy Americano!*'

And a moment later, as they pulled him to his feet, he repeated the words, much softer this time.

'*Soy Americano . . .*'

BETH

19

Beth didn't have much of an appetite, but she went to breakfast anyway. After tossing and turning all night, she awoke early, only to find that Jen hadn't returned, her bunk empty.

But Beth wasn't surprised. Why should she be?

This was typical Jen behaviour. A symptom, Beth believed, of her sister's unending restlessness. And the unhappiness that had plagued her since the death of their parents.

Beth chose the dining room rather than fight the crowd at the food court. It was a risky choice, considering what had happened there last night, but she decided to take her chances.

Heading to the fifth deck, she made her way inside and went straight to her assigned table, which was, thankfully, as empty as Jen's bunk. Maybe she could eat in peace.

As she sat, their waiter, Timothy – who, according to his name badge, hailed from Germany – came over and put a menu in front of her.

'And how are we this morning?'

His English was very good, with only a trace of an accent.

'We,' Beth said, 'are seriously considering retiring to a convent.'

Timothy smiled. 'And what fun would that be?'

'Apparently I'm not allowed to have fun.'

'Oh? Why is that?'

'Long story,' she said, then gave the menu a quick scan and closed it. 'I'll have the lox and bagel with extra cream cheese and a cup of coffee. Black.'

'Would you like capers with that?'

'Sure. Why not live a little.' She handed him the menu. 'My sister didn't happen to drop by this morning, did she?'

'Sister?'

'The girl I was sitting with last night. The one who thought she was at a rock concert?'

He smiled slightly. 'Yes, I remember.'

'How could you forget? I'm still mortified at the thought.'

Timothy shook his head. 'You shouldn't let such things bother you. People drink, they go a little crazy. It's nothing new. We see it all the time.'

Beth nodded. 'One of the perks of the job, I guess.'

These people lived and worked on this ship 24/7 for weeks on end, so she imagined they did see quite a lot of crazy behaviour. Enough to make Jen's display last night fairly innocu—

'Hey, sis.'

Beth snapped her head around and saw Jen crossing the dining room towards her.

Jen looked – in one of Peter's favourite phrases – as if she'd been rode hard and put away wet. 'I was hoping I'd find you here.'

She pulled out a chair and sat, leaning her elbows on the table. Her eyelids were drooping. Not that this made her any less beautiful.

'Just coffee for me,' she said to Timothy.

Timothy gave Beth a quick look, then with a small bow said, 'I'll put in your order,' before disappearing into the kitchen.

'If I were alive,' Jen said, 'I'd say he's kinda cute. Is he the same one from last night?'

'You don't remember?'

'They all wear those gold tunics, it's hard to keep them straight. Besides, I think I've lived about three lifetimes since then. Are you still mad at me?'

'Mad?' Beth said. 'I wasn't the one screaming to be left alone.'

'I'm sorry, okay? You know how I get when I'm high.'

'Unfortunately, yes.'

Jen frowned. 'Look at you, still in mom mode. You really have to find a new hobby, Beth. I can't keep you entertained forever.'

Beth just stared at her. 'You're about as entertaining as a train wreck.'

'Nice. Tell me how you really feel.'

'I'm sick of it, Jen. You only invited me on this trip because Debbie flaked out. You give me all this bull-shit about wanting to help me work through the divorce, and the first chance you get, you're off fucking

Bob and Betty Beautiful – who, I might add, are brother and sister – and I'm stuck watching Keanu Reeves stand in for Michael Rennie.'

'In other words, you *are* still mad.'

Beth shook her head, exasperated.

'I give up,' she said, then pushed her chair back and rose. 'I want off this goddamn ship. And once we get into port, I'm catching the next plane back home.'

'Oh, for godsakes, don't be so dramatic.'

'Dramatic?'

'I told you I was going to get laid, so I got laid.'

'You're disgusting, you know that?'

'Look, I don't know what you think happened last night, but you're wrong.'

'Am I? It didn't look that way to me.'

'We were *dancing*, okay? Just messing around. If it makes you feel any better, when it came time to do the dirty deed, it was just me and Rafael. Marta didn't come to the room until later.' She smiled. 'Not that I would've minded a little extra attention . . .'

Beth eyed her dully. 'Enjoy the rest of the cruise. I'm out of here.'

She started to walk away, then Jen said, 'You're just jealous.'

Beth stopped in her tracks, spun around. '*What?*'

'You've always been jealous. You were in – what – your second year of college before you lost your virginity? I was already working on orgasm number two thousand and fourteen by then.'

It took everything Beth had to keep her jaw from dropping. 'Are you even listening to yourself?'

'You want to know the real reason I hung out with the Santiagos last night? Because they make me feel good. Like someone special. They let me be me, without apology. And all I ever get from you is disapproval. Do you know how many times in our life you've treated me like an adult? Zero.'

Beth squinted at her. 'So what exactly are you saying? You don't feel special because I don't pump you full of drugs and use you for a sex toy? You need therapy, Jen. The sooner the better.'

'That's not what I mean, and you know it.'

'All I know,' Beth said, 'is that we dock in Playa Azul in less than twenty minutes. And as soon as we get there, I'm gone.'

And with this, she turned on her heels and headed for the exit.

20

She was navigating the narrow hallway to their state-room when Jen caught up with her.

'Beth, wait!'

Beth waved a hand at her. 'Enough. I've had enough.'

'Look, I'm sorry for being so cranky. I'm hungover and haven't had any—'

'There's always an excuse.'

'It's not an excuse, it's a reason.'

Beth said nothing. Just shook her head, then shoved her card key into the slot and opened their stateroom door.

Jen grabbed her arm. 'Beth, please. Don't be mad. We're family for godsakes. We're not supposed to be pissed at each other. At least not to the point that you're ready to hop on a plane.'

'Oh, I'm not mad. I'm just jealous, remember?'

Jen sighed. 'And I'm an idiot, okay?'

Beth didn't want to cry, but felt the tears start to well up.

'You're just like Peter, you know that? One minute

you treat me like shit, the next you're trying to make nice. I can't take it any more.'

'Oh, come on, sis, don't cry. I . . .' She stood back suddenly and patted her chest. 'Go ahead, punch me. Right in the boob job. I deserve it.'

'I don't want to punch you.'

'I'm serious. I'm a complete bitch and you're right about everything and I deserve to be punched.'

'Now you're being ridiculous.'

Beth pushed through the doorway and stepped inside, flicking on the light.

Jen followed her. 'Are you really leaving?'

'Yes.'

'Why?'

Beth moved to the closet, slid open the door and started pulling her clothes off the hangers. 'Because I shouldn't have come in the first place.'

'How can you say that?'

Beth looked at her. 'You were right about me. I *am* jealous. I'm jealous of your ability to say fuck you to everyone around you and never take responsibility for a goddamn thing.'

'That isn't fair.'

Beth pulled her suitcase out and threw it on her bunk. 'No, it isn't fair. I've spent my entire life trying to be the rational one. The stable one. I thought coming on this trip might be my chance to let go for once, but as usual, I wind up playing babysitter.'

'You *choose* that role. I've never asked you to watch over me.'

Beth opened the suitcase and threw her clothes in,

not bothering to fold them. 'But I'm the first one you come running to whenever you screw up, aren't I?'

'Who am I supposed to go to? Mom and Dad?'

'Very funny.'

She returned to the closet and bent down, gathering up her shoes. She'd spent fifteen minutes washing Jen's vomit off her Kenneth Coles last night, but just the sight of them made her stomach turn, so she left them behind.

Jen watched her dump the rest of the shoes into her suitcase. 'You're really doing this, aren't you?'

'Yes,' Beth said. 'I told you, I shouldn't have come. I've got cases piling up – I don't know why I let you talk me into this trip in the first place.'

Jen said nothing. Just stared at her a moment, then moved to her bunk and sat, looking down at her hands.

Then she said, 'You know what next week is, right? Next Wednesday?'

'What?'

'The twenty-seventh. Fourteen years since they died.'

Beth felt her gut tighten.

Jen turned her left hand palm up and began tracing the lines with a finger.

'I remember once, a long time ago, I read a book about palmistry, and all I wanted to do when I grew up was be a fortune teller. How stupid is that?'

'Pretty stupid,' Beth said.

'I learned about the head line, the life line, the heart line . . . and one day, when we were home for the weekend, I asked Dad if I could read his palm.' She smiled at the memory. 'He had really strong hands, you know that?'

Beth sat on her own bunk, nodded. 'I know.'

Jen's smile faded. 'When I started to do the reading, the first thing I noticed was his life line. It was really short. And I thought, this is not good. This is not good at all.' She paused, looked up at Beth. 'But then I told myself I must've misunderstood what I'd read. So I didn't say anything to him. I just made up some bull- shit prediction about his future, then went off to watch *Saved by the Bell*.'

'What are you saying?' Beth asked.

'That I knew he was going to die. I knew he was going to die and I didn't tell him. I didn't warn him.'

Beth shook her head. 'They died in a plane crash, Jen. How could you warn him about that?'

'I don't know. But maybe if I'd told him to be careful, if I'd shown him his life line and told him what it meant, maybe they wouldn't have chartered that plane.'

'That's ridiculous.'

'I know,' Jen said. 'I know it is. But I can't help it. I think about it almost every day. And I know none of it's my fault, but that doesn't stop me from feeling like it is.'

'Let me say it again,' Beth told her. 'They died in a plane crash. So unless you performed a Vulcan mind meld and told that pilot to fly into a mountain, what happened to Mom and Dad was purely accidental.'

Jen nodded, was quiet for a moment.

Then: 'I tried to contact them last night.'

Beth frowned. 'Contact who?'

'Who do you think, dummy? Mom and Dad.'

'What the hell are you talking about?'

Jen paused before answering. 'I know you can't stand Rafael and Marta, but contrary to what you might think, I didn't spend all my time fucking last night.'

'Oh, brother.' Beth rose again, moved to the dresser and started pulling out her underwear.

'I'm trying to tell you something here, Beth. Can you at least give me the courtesy of listening?'

'I have absolutely no interest in anything remotely related to those two.'

'Just listen, okay?'

Beth sighed, threw a fistful of bras and panties into the suitcase and sat again.

'Okay, I'm listening.'

'Promise not to laugh?'

'I promise,' Beth said, and waited for Jen to tell her story.

21

Jen took a breath.

'By the time Marta showed up, Rafael was pretty much passed out, so she and I spent a lot of time talking. She told me she's what they call a *bruja*.'

'A what?'

'A *bruja*. A witch.'

'You're kidding me, right?'

Jen shook her head. 'She says she has powers, including the ability to communicate with the dead.'

'I'll bet that comes in handy.'

Jen frowned. 'It's not a joke, Beth. After last night I'm convinced it's true. She's psychic. Knows things that are impossible for her to know.'

'Like what?'

'Stuff about my love life. About Mom and Dad. About me being . . .' She paused. 'About a lot of things. Like she was inside my head.'

Beth stared at her. It took everything she had to keep from rolling her eyes. Over the years she'd run across more than a few so-called psychics. Every one of them had been a con artist.

'Have you ever heard of a cold reading?'

Jen shook her head again.

'It's a technique used by people who claim to be psychic,' Beth said. 'They extract information from you without you realizing it. Ask leading questions. Study your body language. It's all designed to make you think they have special powers. But the only real power they have is the ability to extract money from your wallet.'

'That's not true. Marta didn't ask me for a cent.'

'Not yet. But if you keep hanging around with her, it'll happen. Believe me.'

'Why are you always such a cynic?'

'Not a cynic,' Beth said. 'A realist.' She reached across and took Jen's hands in hers. 'I know you miss them. Mom and Dad. I do, too. But Marta can no more communicate with them than we can. And if you let her convince you that she has some supernatural power, you're only gonna be dis—'

A bell rang over the loudspeaker in the hallway.

'Good morning, ladies and gentlemen, this is your purser speaking. We have now docked in Playa Azul, Mexico and will begin debarking in five minutes.'

Beth released Jen's hands and stood. 'That's my cue.'

Jen grabbed her arm. 'Don't go, Beth. Please don't go.'

'I have to,' Beth said. 'I'm sorry. But I can't deal with—'

'I promise to be good. No more me, me, me. From now on this vacation is all about you.'

'We both know that won't happen.'

'I promise. I swear to God. And if I step out of line, you can kick my ass.'

'Punching, kicking – what's got into you?'

'I just want you to stay, okay? Leave your suitcase here and we'll go into town and do some shopping. You love to shop.'

Beth sighed. 'I also hate it when you beg.'

'Does that mean you'll stay?'

Beth thought it over and, against her better judgement, nodded. 'All right. One last chance.'

'Hooray!' Jen said, pulling her into a hug. 'And when we're done shopping, let's go to Armando's for some Jello and tequila shots.'

Beth pulled away abruptly, glared at her.

Jen grinned. 'I'm *kidding*,' she said. 'Just kidding.'

VARGAS

22

According to the placard on his chest, the border patrol agent's name was S. Harmon.

Sam? Steven? Stan?

It didn't much matter. He was a fastidious-looking guy in a crisp army-green uniform, with neatly trimmed greying hair and a pleasant but cautious smile.

He was hard to read, and Vargas got the impression that he was the type of guy who liked to play his cards close, and would only raise a bet when he was looking at a sure thing.

'You've managed to make a routine day pretty interesting,' he said. 'I'll give you that.'

He stood just inside the doorway to the examination room at the local emergency clinic, a few blocks north of the border station.

After a brief interrogation, the extent of Vargas's head wound was assessed and he'd been brought here by ambulance. The wound was cleaned and stitched, his shoulder examined and found to be bruised but not dislocated, the puncture and wrist burns treated with antiseptic ointment, his hand bandaged – all followed by a tetanus shot and a CT scan to make sure his brain wasn't bleeding. The nurse who administered them all had the warmth and personality of a motel room curtain.

Fortunately, Ainsworth and company had neglected to steal Vargas's wallet and passport, so he'd had no trouble proving his American citizenship. And he'd had the foresight to buy a SENTRI card, which afforded him easy entry into the US.

None of this had done much to allay the suspicions of the border guards, however, who seemed ready to toss him into a cell as a suspected terrorist or drug smuggler. Fortunately, they didn't have any evidence to back up their suspicions, and word came down from on high – Harmon, no doubt – to cut him loose.

So, they'd transported him to the clinic. Vargas had been on concussion watch for a good two hours and had spent a large portion of that time trying to figure out what the hell he'd stumbled into.

He'd obviously been set up, but why? He was pretty sure he'd been right about the looting of the bodies in the House of Death, but there was something much more sinister going on here than simple robbery, and he'd be damned if he could figure out what it was.

Ainsworth had complained of having to clean up someone else's mess – the someone that Vargas had been on his way to see before his escape.

But who?

The man who had slaughtered the people in that house?

And what did he want from *Vargas*?

It occurred to him that maybe the border patrol was onto something here. Maybe this *was* about smuggling. Hadn't Ainsworth referred to himself as a courier?

And then, of course, there was his story about the American woman. But was it even true?

Vargas didn't imagine Ainsworth would have any trouble lying, but Junior didn't seem capable of it.

So who was this American woman? And how did she fit into the equation?

Harmon approached the gurney where Vargas lay. Vargas had no idea why he was here, but figured he was about to find out.

'My crew tells me you're claiming somebody's after you. That you were trussed up and thrown into the trunk of your own car.'

'Not a claim,' Vargas said. 'A fact.'

Harmon nodded. 'They showed me the duct tape.' He glanced at Vargas's wrists. 'And I've seen rope burns before. Unfortunately, your car's nowhere in the vicinity.'

'I gave them a statement. Names.'

'That you did. And I have to admit I was pretty surprised when I heard those names.'

'What do you mean?'

'I'm not familiar with this Sergio fella, but Jim Ainsworth happens to be an old family friend of mine. And I've known Junior since he was just a gleam in his daddy's eye.'

Oh, Christ, Vargas thought.

'Hard to believe, I know. Over half a million people in El Paso proper, and I just happen to know the ones

93

you say jumped you.' He paused. 'And I suppose you think that means I won't be fair and impartial, but there's not much I can do about that.'

'You could be fair and impartial,' Vargas said.

Another nod. 'Just remember it cuts both ways. Thing is, the crime you're alleging took place on Mexican soil, so we're not really in a position to claim jurisdiction. And I'm not sure we need to get the FBI involved.'

'You want me to go to the Chihuahua state police. Is that what you're saying?'

'That's entirely up to you.'

Vargas chuckled and shook his head. Which was a mistake. His brain felt like the business end of a battering ram floating in a thick, soupy liquid.

He waited for it to stop sloshing around inside his skull.

'So that's why you're here? To more or less tell me to fuck off?'

'No,' Harmon said. 'You live this close to another country, there tends to be a lot of spillover when it comes to crime. These are nasty times, and we'd like to keep the less desirable elements of Juarez from contaminating our water, so to speak.'

'That's understandable.'

'Problem is, I don't put Jim and Junior in that category. So the question I have to ask is, why? Why would they want to hurt you?'

'I've been wondering the same thing. But you must've read my statement.'

'That I did.'

'So then you know I think they're involved in those murders down in Dead Man's Dunes.'

'Of course they're involved,' Harmon said. 'They found the bodies. That's no secret. Isn't that why you contacted them in the first place? To give you the dollar tour?'

'Yes, but—'

'So here's my problem: I happen to know that Jim Ainsworth is a simple egg rancher who may be a bit too arrogant for his own good, but he doesn't have a violent bone in his body.'

Vargas gestured to the stitches in his scalp. 'I beg to differ.'

'I gave Jim a call, asked him about it, and you know what I heard in the background?'

'What?' Vargas asked.

'A dirt bike. That annoying little insect buzz? Turns out he and Junior have been riding all afternoon. Says they showed you the house, then dropped you off at the Cafe Tecuba.'

'He's lying.'

'I had a feeling you'd say that.'

Vargas gestured to his head again. 'Are you suggesting I did this to myself?'

'I'm not suggesting anything. Just trying to be fair and impartial.'

It was Vargas's experience that people who said such things were usually anything but.

'I got on the computer,' Harmon continued, 'ran your name through the law enforcement databases and didn't get any significant hits.'

'Because I'm a law-abiding citizen.'

'That you are. But imagine my surprise when I Googled you.'

Vargas's gut tightened.

Uh-oh. Here it comes.

'That's right, sunshine. Turns out *you're* the one knows a lot about lying.'

23

'That was blown out of proportion,' Vargas said.

'Not according to the *LA Tribune*. Seems your former editor doesn't think too highly of you. I called him, too, and he told me I shouldn't believe a word you say.'

'That was one isolated incident. I was under a lot of stress.'

'Is that what you call it?' He paused. 'Look, son, I don't give a flying fart about what kind of drugs you use any more than I care about you phoneying up a couple of newspaper stories. You're probably not the first, and you sure as hell won't be the last. But I think you understand why you might have a bit of a credibility problem.'

'I'm past all that. I went to rehab. And I wouldn't even let them give me painkillers for my head.'

It had been two years since the incident in question, a foolish wrong turn by Vargas that he'd been paying for ever since. Due to a confluence of circumstances, he'd managed to get himself hooked on Rush Limbaugh's drug of choice – Oxycontin – and had paid the price. His story output had dwindled to almost nothing, and in his zeal to remain employed he'd done a series of articles about the Mexican Mafia called 'El Asesino: Confessions of a Hit Man'. The series was hard hitting and dramatic, but with one small problem: it was based on interviews he'd conducted with a man who existed wholly within his imagination.

He'd faked it all.

And was nominated for a Pulitzer in the process.

Not something he was proud of.

After the publicity started getting out of hand, he'd offered a drug-addled confession to his now ex-girlfriend – a fellow reporter – who was so appalled by his behaviour that she went straight to his editor. Then the world Vargas once knew abruptly imploded, sucking him straight into its vortex.

It had taken him nearly two years and three stints in rehab to climb his way out. But the only publisher willing to risk an advance on anything other than a confessional memoir (which Vargas refused to write) was a small, regional house that thought the controversy surrounding his name might actually sell a few books and help push them into the mainstream. It had taken Vargas a considerable amount of salesmanship to convince them to let him pursue what appeared to be a routine story, but his enthusiasm – and notoriety – had finally won them over. Especially after he agreed to take a low-ball advance.

He didn't know if he'd ever be able to repair the damage to his reputation, but it wouldn't be for lack of trying.

'I've met a lot of fellas gone to rehab,' Harmon said. 'Doesn't mean all that much.'

'Everything in my statement is true.'

'I'll bet that's what you told your editor, too.'

'Fuck you.'

Harmon frowned. 'Is that kind of language really necessary? I've got conflicting stories here and I'm afraid right now you're looking like a monkey up to his old tricks. I've seen a few attention whores in my time, and I know the lengths some people will go to to get it.'

This guy was a first-class asshole. But Vargas saw no point in antagonizing him any further.

'There's one way to settle this,' he said.

Harmon raised his eyebrows. 'And that is?'

'Look at the truck. Look at Ainsworth's F150. He did a job on the bumper when he rear-ended my car.'

Harmon thought about this a moment. 'Doesn't necessarily mean anything. Could be pre-existing damage for all I know.'

'You also know there are ways of proving it. Check for paint. Some of it may have rubbed off.'

Harmon looked at him. Seemed to be weighing the pros and cons of such an undertaking.

Mostly the cons, no doubt.

'Like I told you, CPB doesn't really have jurisdiction. But I have to admit, I'm curious.' He paused, thinking it over. 'So I'll tell you what. I don't expect Jim and Junior back until later tonight, but maybe I'll stop by for a friendly chat before bedtime. Give his truck a little look-see.'

'And if it turns out I'm telling the truth?'

'I'll personally call a friend of mine with the

Mexican state police tomorrow morning. Make sure they take a look into the matter.'

'Doesn't sound very promising,' Vargas said.

Harmon snorted. 'Welcome to life in a border town. Nothing promising about it.'

24

They kicked him out of the clinic at about 9 p.m., telling him to make sure he got plenty of sleep, with a suggestion that he not be alone for the next twenty-four hours in case his symptoms worsened.

Vargas had been alone for much of his life, and didn't expect that to change anytime soon. He'd always thought that victims of concussion were supposed to stay awake, but was assured by the doctor that this was a complete myth. Sleep, he was told, would help him mend.

Which was a relief. A nice, comfortable bed sounded awfully good to him right now.

His base of operations was a Western Suites Express about five miles north of the emergency clinic. He caught a cab, moving slowly as he climbed in, and for one brief, terrifying moment thought it was Sergio behind the wheel.

It wasn't.

The driver, who remained mercifully quiet during the ride, dropped him off at the kerb in front of the motel. The charge was six bucks – highway robbery – and as Vargas paid the fee, he worried that his advance was almost gone. He'd have to start dipping into his savings to fund this little outing and wondered if it was all worth it. The visit to the clinic alone was going to cost him a bundle, even with the emergency medical insurance he'd been paying every month. His deductible was high and would take a large, painful chunk out of his net worth.

In the movies, he would've walked away from this without spending a dime. He would also be driving a sleek Jaguar or a refurbished Mustang – something with a roomier trunk at least – and would have an annoying but affable sidekick, along with enough clues right now to know he'd just hit the jackpot with the story of the decade.

Oh, and a girl. There was always a beautiful girl in the movies, and a nice semi-nude encounter on the motel room sheets, concussion be damned.

Maybe that's where the American woman came in.

Whoever she might be.

Being the big spender he was, Vargas tipped the cabbie a buck, then headed around the corner past the lobby entrance until he was in the motel's parking lot, where about a dozen cars were parked.

He stopped short when he saw it.

His Corolla.

He didn't know how the hell they'd managed to get it across the border, but there it was, parked under a light in a slot close to the building, its busted trunk lid tied down with a bungee cord.

Vargas's gut tightened. Quickly scanning the area, he searched for any sign of trouble in the darkest pockets

102

of the building – Ainsworth or Junior or Sergio waiting for him to come home.

Except for a lone woman crossing to her car, the place seemed deserted. And there was no sign of Ainsworth's F150.

Which didn't mean a damn thing.

His car hadn't gotten here on its own, and he didn't imagine that anyone who was willing to set him up in the first place would be likely to back down easily.

They knew where he was staying. Worse yet, they might even be sitting in his room right now.

So, what, he wondered, was his next move?

BETH

25

Playa Azul. Baja Norte.

Just another harbour town full of bars and trinket shops, as far as Beth could tell. People and cars crowded the sidewalks and streets, competing for room among the vendors and open-air restaurants that dominated the place.

Small children hawked Chiclets to unsuspecting tourists, as their mothers sat nearby, selling colourful bead necklaces. Kerbside stands offered painted plates and jewellery and Mexican blankets and T-shirts and sunglasses and lighters and knives and ornately carved ivory figurines.

And horse-shit cigarettes.

There were signs everywhere advertising them. GENUINE HORSE SHIT! they proclaimed. Beth was no smoker, but even if she were, she'd have no desire to find out if this proclamation was true.

The first thing they'd seen as they strolled off the ship was a red, white and green flag flapping in the breeze above the harbour. It was massive. The size of a building – leaving no question that they were on Mexican soil.

They travelled on foot, navigating the few short blocks past the fish markets and taco stands to the centre of town, Jen getting appreciative stares along the way, thanks largely to a pair of cut-off jeans and a halterneck top.

She was, of course, just another crazy Americano tourista, one of thousands who circulated through Playa Azul on a weekly basis. But Beth was pretty sure that this didn't keep some of the locals – particularly the gangbangers who cruised the streets in souped-up import cars – from fantasizing about her.

Images of Jen cavorting with Rafael on a rumpled stateroom bed suddenly popped uninvited into Beth's mind, and she reeled them back quickly, doing her best to ban them from her consciousness.

But setting aside the 'ick' factor for just a moment, she had to wonder if Jen was right about her.

Maybe she *was* a Pollyanna.

She hadn't been lying earlier when she said that she sometimes envied Jen's freedom. Even if much of her sister's fearlessness was a mask for insecurity, maybe it was better than the one Beth herself had chosen.

She was, she had decided – long before today, in fact – a boring woman who led a structured, predictable life. She had taken the job with the district attorney because it had promised to be exciting, but she soon discovered that it held no real surprises.

There were laws; they were broken. You broke the law; you went to jail. Prosecutors rarely dealt in shades of grey.

The position was more about stats than truth and

justice, about keeping your conviction rate high, and Beth was long past the thrill of winning a case. She couldn't remember the last time she'd felt butterflies before a closing argument. It was a job, plain and simple. And it didn't fulfil her any more than her marriage had.

Or her sex life, for that matter.

While Jen was working towards orgasm number two thousand whatever, Beth was still working on number one.

And, who knows? Maybe that was why Peter had cheated on her.

'Oh my God,' Jen said, 'look at these.'

They had been wandering the streets for what seemed like hours now, moving from shop to shop, finding a lot of interesting little trinkets, but nothing they'd felt like spending actual cash on. The latest stop had been a right turn down a narrow alleyway lined with street vendors.

Beth, who had been pretending to admire a stack of Mexican blankets as she ruminated on her humdrum life, turned and saw Jen stopped at a small table lined with jewellery.

'What did you find?'

Jen held up two thin silvertone rings, each with a small, flat, black and silver carving of a hooded skull in place of the stone. The workmanship was bordering on crude, but oddly affecting.

'They're wonderful,' Beth said.

Jen nodded and gestured. 'Put out your hand.'

Beth obliged, offering the left one, and Jen slipped the ring onto her newly bare fourth finger.

'Perfect.' Jen took the second ring and slid it onto her own finger. 'We're officially best friends forever,' she said, then smiled. 'With the devil.'

Beth laughed. 'Been there, done that.'

She started to pull the ring off, but Jen stopped her.

'Consider it my way of apologizing for being such a bitch.'

'Jen, you don't have to keep—'

'It's either this or a pack of horse-shit cigarettes. Which would you prefer?'

Beth smiled. 'The cigarettes might be more appropriate.'

Jen stuck her tongue out, then turned to the vendor, a slender man in a T-shirt, jeans and sunglasses.

'*Cuánto cuesta esto?*'

She'd told Beth earlier that she only knew two phrases in Spanish: How much does this cost? and Where's the bathroom?

Beth suspected she butchered them both.

The vendor's accent was thick, but at least his English was better than Jen's Spanish.

'Sixty dollar for two,' he said.

'Seriously?'

'On especial today. Forty-five.'

'I was thinking more like ten bucks each,' Jen said, and started to take hers off.

'Thirty dollar,' the vendor told her.

'Make it twenty-five and you've got a deal.'

He nodded, and Jen dug into her purse for the cash. She rooted around for a while then said, 'Shit.'

'What?' Beth asked.

'I must've left my wallet in the cabin.'

'You're kidding, right?'

'I could've sworn I had it, but all I've got is my Seafarer card and a bunch of loose change. Can I borrow a few bucks?'

Beth rolled her eyes.

'Come on,' Jen said. 'I'm good for it, I swear. Soon as we get back onboard.'

Beth looked at the ring on her finger, the tiny hooded skull staring up at her. It belonged on the hand of a punk rocker or a Goth girl or a wild child like Jen. Certainly not her. But she liked it and thought, what the hell, why not do something unpredictable for once. Maybe she'd even wear it for her next opening argument, see what the jury made of it.

Reaching into her purse, she pulled out her wallet, opened it and extracted a twenty and a five, handing it across to the vendor. He quickly stuffed it into his pocket, then turned his attention to an elderly couple who had just approached.

Jen grinned at Beth and held up her hand, admiring the ring. 'Big sis to the rescue again.'

'Don't even start.'

'Yes, ma'am.'

Beth heard a faint gurgling sound and Jen frowned, patting her stomach.

'You hear that? I've got the growlies. Let's find some food.'

'I'm tired,' Beth said. 'Why don't we just go back to the ship and eat there?'

'Now why would we want to eat assembly-line hamburgers when we can go for some authentic local food? Come on, you can pick the place.'

'And pay the bill?'

Jen offered her a sheepish smile. 'Don't you still have a couple of Peter's credit cards?'

'Ha ha,' Beth said. 'You're hilarious.'

26

They chose an outdoor cafe called Taqueria Tapatia, an oblong, open-air enclosure that ran the length of the sidewalk, the chef's station smack in the middle of half a dozen tables.

Jen, being Jen, became immediately enamoured with the chef, a curly-haired twenty-something hunk with a nice body and an even nicer smile. But to her credit, she kept it low key, in an effort, Beth supposed, to avoid upsetting the prude. And Beth suddenly felt guilty for always trying to suppress what came naturally to Jen.

Why couldn't she just accept her sister for who she was?

'I'm thinking about going back to school,' Jen said as their waitress set their taco plates in front of them.

Beth was surprised. 'Since when?'

Jen took a bite of taco, then took a moment to chew and swallow. 'I know this'll sound like b.s., but you're not the only one who's jealous. A lot of times I look at you, look at what you've accomplished and I think, what the hell? Why am I such a loser?'

'You're not a loser.'

'What else do you call it, then? I've spent the last decade bouncing from guy to guy, job to job, party to party and I've got nothing to show for it but a failed marriage, an empty bank account and a constant hangover.'

Beth had to admit she had a point.

'It could be worse,' she said. 'You could be crippled. Or blind.'

Jen laughed and shook her head. 'I don't know what's wrong with me. No direction, no ambition. And I can only blame so much of it on Mom and Dad.' She paused, took another bite of taco. 'I know you don't want to hear this, but last night kinda opened my eyes.'

Beth stiffened. 'Meaning?'

'Marta and I spent a lot of time talking about things I don't usually bother thinking about. It might be hard to believe, but she and Rafael are very spiritual people.'

'If you consider witchcraft and phony psychics spiritual, sure.'

Jen shook her head. 'I really wish you could be a little more open minded. Some people believe there's a man in the sky watching over us. Does that make them con artists?'

'Not all of them. No.'

Beth wasn't the most religious person in the world, but she did believe in God. A belief that was based on gut, not intellect. But she also knew that there was no shortage of people in this world who would try to exploit that belief.

'Despite what you think of her,' Jen said, 'Marta really believes the things she talks about.'

'Like what?'

'Like the power of the dead, for one. She says they're always among us, ready to guide us, advise us when we ask for help. And I know this'll sound stupid, but when she told me that, it was the first time I've actually felt like there might be some hope for me after all. Like maybe since they died, Mom and Dad have been watching over us. Maybe it's time for me to stop disappointing them.'

'Is that Marta talking, or you?'

Jen frowned. 'I do have a brain, you know. I can think for myself.'

She went inward for a moment, seemed to be struggling with a thought. Then she said, 'I cried like a baby last night. Right there in their cabin.'

'What happened?'

'Marta and I were talking and all of a sudden I started crying. It just came over me.'

Beth nodded. 'You were in over your head with those two. Finally realized you'd gone too far.'

'No,' Jen said, looking annoyed. 'That's not it at all.'

'Then what?'

'I already told you, Rafael and Marta made me feel special. Wanted. Like this was much more than some random hook-up. It felt like they'd both somehow managed to channel my thoughts and feelings and were speaking to me in a language only I could understand.'

'Was this before or after you all took Ecstasy?'

Jen's eyes hardened. 'It wasn't the drugs, Beth. Or

the booze. Besides, I'm done with all that stuff. As sappy as it sounds, I started crying because I felt . . . I don't know . . . *loved*. Unconditionally. By two people who barely even know me.'

Beth bit her tongue. Her immediate instinct was to dismiss Jen's talk as nonsense, to explain that that was exactly what Ecstasy, or MDMA, does to you – something Jen should well know. But there was a sincerity in her sister's voice that couldn't be ignored. She was vulnerable. And hurting. And Beth knew that, in many ways, and for many years, she had contributed to that hurt, just as Jen had contributed to hers.

But none of this changed her opinion of the Santiagos. The more she heard about them, the less she trusted them. And if they were taking advantage of Jen's vulnerability, she might just have to kick their perfect little backsides.

'So this is what got you thinking about the direction of your life? About going to school?'

'Partly,' Jen said, 'but there's something else I've been wanting to tell you. Something . . .'

Jen paused, looking anguished. Guilty.

'What?' Beth asked. 'What's wrong?'

Jen thought a moment, then shook her head. 'We'll talk about it later. And this whole school thing is just an idea. I'm not really sure *what* I want.'

'That's true for about ninety per cent of the people who walk this planet. Even the dead ones.'

Jen frowned again. 'Are you making fun of me?'

'No,' Beth said, immediately regretting her words. 'Just a joke. And a bad one at that.'

Jen sighed. 'You're never going to take me seriously, are you?'

'Look, I didn't mean anything by it. It was just a stupid—'

'I've gotta pee,' Jen said abruptly, then threw her napkin on the table and turned to the waitress, whose command of English was halting at best. Fortunately, they'd been able to point to their choices on the menu. '*Adónde está el baño?*'

Phrase number two.

'*Disculpa, esta fuera de servicio,*' the waitress said, then gestured to a leather goods shop across the street. '*Puedes usar el que esta al otro lado de la calle.*'

Jen pushed her chair back and stood. 'I hope that means they have a toilet.'

'Jen, wait . . .'

'Don't worry, I'm not gonna go mental on you. I just can't hold it any more.'

Then she crossed the street and disappeared into the leather goods shop without a backward glance.

And that was the last time Beth saw her.

VARGAS

27

Nobody could ever accuse Vargas of being smart.

The smart thing to do would be to go back to the motel office, ask to use the phone (his cell phone had been stolen along with his car keys), and call Agent Harmon.

The problem with this idea was that Harmon already thought he was a drug-addicted, attention-mongering crackpot, and the presence of his car in the Western Suites parking lot would more than likely bolster that opinion.

Vargas still had no idea how they'd managed to get the thing across the border – seeing as how the border patrol was reportedly on the lookout for it – but that didn't much matter, did it?

Whoever he'd got himself involved with was not playing around. And if they were somehow associated with what had happened in the House of Death, a story that had gone through the usual news cycle then faded away, they might be a bit concerned about some Americano reporter starting to dig it all up again.

How much did he know? Who had he told?

That, if his jangled brain was remembering properly, had seemed to be Sergio's concern. A concern that was no doubt shared by 'the man himself'.

Part of Vargas wanted simply to jump into his Corolla, head straight back to California and pretend he'd never gotten involved in any of this nonsense in the first place. But, besides coming up a bit short in the smarts department, under the right set of circumstances Vargas was also insanely curious. And he could think of no better set of circumstances than the one he'd stumbled into today.

One of his old story sources, an ex-cop in Las Vegas who had a serious obsession with cards, had once described his addiction to Vargas as an itch. One that just had to be scratched. But once you scratched it, he'd said, the itch only got worse and worse until it was all you thought about.

Vargas had had his doubts about pursuing this story before today, but now the itch was setting in. And despite his encounter with Ainsworth and Sergio – an encounter he was convinced would have led to his interrogation and possible death – he knew his only choice was to start scratching.

So, instead of calling Harmon, he decided to chance going back to his room. His laptop was there, along with the notes from his interviews with the Chihuahua police and the information he'd gotten from the murder file. Much of this had been transferred to the SD card he always kept in his wallet, but he hadn't managed to do a full backup before his meeting with Ainsworth.

Going inside was a stupid move, sure, especially with his head feeling the way it did.

But he was stupid enough to make the move anyway.

28

Unlike many motels Vargas had stayed in over the years, the Western Suites Express was an enclosed two-storey structure with its hallways and room entrances on the inside. It was a design that fed the illusion that you were staying at a higher-class establishment than you were actually paying for. But the illusion was shattered the moment you stepped inside to find hallway carpet made of thin, replaceable squares, and wallpaper a shade too cheap and adorned with art mart reproductions in plastic frames.

Not that any of this mattered to Vargas. But it occurred to him that if the motel charged just a couple of bucks more a night, they might be able to sustain the bullshit at least until the guests got to their rooms.

He went in through a set of double doors at the back of the building. There were entrances on either end as well, but he'd noticed shortly after he checked in that the rear doors were used almost exclusively by the maids. If anyone was waiting for him inside, they'd more than likely concentrate on the main points of entry.

It was possible that he was being overly cautious.

If someone really *was* waiting for him, why would they telegraph their presence by parking his Corolla in plain view? Unless they were just as stupid as he was. And neither Ainsworth nor Sergio struck him as mental giants.

Closing the double doors behind him, he made his way down a narrow corridor past a small alcove that housed a gurgling ice machine.

His room was on the first floor. Up ahead, on the left, was a door marked STAIRS. He was about to cross towards it when a faint bell rang, and somewhere around the corner an elevator door rolled open, voices filling the adjoining hallway.

'So what did you do?'

'What do you think I did? I fragged the mother-fucker right there in the alleyway.'

Shit.

Picking up speed, Vargas lurched for the stairwell door, quickly pushed it open, then closed himself inside.

Sucking in a breath, he held it. Waited. The sudden movement had jangled his brain again and he felt a slight burning sensation under the bandage on his scalp – not to mention the hundred and fifty thousand other protests his body was making right now.

But had they seen him?

Doubtful.

And as the voices rounded the corner, Vargas realized with relief that the rush to get out of sight hadn't even been necessary.

They weren't a threat. They sounded like a couple of college kids talking about a video game, in which fragging motherfuckers was apparently routine procedure. Probably spending the night on the border before a trip into Juarez the next day in search of cheap booze and cheaper women.

Vargas let out the breath. Relaxed. Waited a few moments for his body to recover.

Then he hit the stairs.

The first floor looked empty. So quiet you'd think it was three in the morning instead of 9.30 on a Friday night.

Vargas left the stairwell and started for his room – which, of course, was all the way at the far end of a corridor about the length of a football field.

He took his time, not rushing it, but bracing himself, just in case he had to move quickly. He felt a little silly for being so paranoid, but then his scalp began to burn again, reminding him that his paranoia was well founded.

He was staying in room 219. He moved past the elevator, mentally counting the numbers on the doors as he walked.

252, 251, 250 . . .

He'd found himself doing that a lot lately. Counting. Wondered if he suffered from some low-grade form of obsessive compulsive disorder.

But that was the least of his worries right now.

246, 245, 244 . . .

The elevator bell rang behind him and he tensed slightly, knowing it was probably the college students returning with a bucket of ice, but worried that he might be wrong. There was nowhere to hide up here, so he picked up his pace.

238, 237, 236 . . .

The elevator door rolled open and his shoulders bunched up, in anticipation of the worst.

Then the college kids' voices filled the hallway, still talking about fragging and what Vargas assumed was game strategy. He'd never been a big video-game fan and it all sounded like Greek to him.

But he relaxed a little, continued on.

231, 230, 229 . . .

Ten doors to go.

He reached into his back pocket, pulled out his wallet, found his key card.

224, 223, 222 . . .

He was a few steps from the door when he stopped in his tracks.

If someone had managed to circumvent the lock and was waiting inside his room, then sticking a key card in the slot and just pushing the door open was probably not a terrific idea. In fact, it was one of his worst ideas ever.

In his imaginary movie, he'd find a way to break into the adjoining room instead, sneak out onto the balcony and come in through the sliding door at the rear of the suite, surprising any intruders. This would undoubtedly involve seducing his next-door neighbour, who was in town for a cosmetics convention and just happened to look like Selma Hayek or Angelina Jolie.

Unfortunately, this wasn't a movie. And his room

didn't even have a balcony. So he had no choice but to take the traditional route and hope for the best.

He could, however, try a ruse.

An obvious one, sure, but simple and effective.

Stepping up to the door, Vargas rapped on it sharply and called out in his best imitation of his Aunt Cecilia, a talent he had perfected at the age of nine.

'*Hola*. Housekeeping.'

Silence. No sound of movement inside. Nothing.

It was a little late for a maid to be showing up, but certainly plausible.

He knocked again. 'Housekeeping. *Es cualquier persona casero?*'

Still nothing.

Vargas slipped the key card into the slot, waited for the green light to flash, then grabbed the knob and turned it, pushing the door open just a crack.

'*Hola*,' he said again. 'Housekeeping.'

There was a chance he was overdoing it. He was a lot older than nine now, and his falsetto wasn't what it used to be, but as he stood there, listening to the sound of the room, he felt pretty confident that he'd pulled it off.

He was also pretty confident that the room was empty.

Sucking in another breath, he pushed the door wide, staring into the darkness. He knew he was silhouetted in the hall light, his ruse now blown, but decided to trust his instincts and continued inside.

He ran his fingers along the wall until he found the light switch.

When he flicked it on, the lamp on top of the dresser came to life, throwing dim yellow light across the room, and all the tension drained from his body.

Just as he had suspected, the room was empty.

The queen-sized bed was made. The towels he'd thrown on the floor had been cleared away. The dollar tip on the bedside table was gone.

But as he moved deeper into the room, he realized that someone beside the maid had definitely been here. His suitcase lay open on the floor near the bed, half of its contents scattered around it. Shirts. Socks. Underwear.

The stack of notes he'd left on the small round table near the window were gone. Along with his laptop.

And in their place was a set of keys.

His car keys.

Along with his cell phone.

Vargas stiffened. Took a quick look around the room again, half expecting someone to step out of the closet with a gun in his hand.

But the room was empty. No surprises waiting.

Letting out a breath, he crossed to the table and started to pick up his keys, flinching slightly when he felt something sticky.

Pulling his hand away, he stared down at his fingers, and what he saw there sent a chill through him.

Blood.

They were covered with blood.

He was contemplating the significance of this when his cell phone rang. Vibrated on the table.

Vargas flinched, then squinted down at the screen: *Unknown caller.*

Wiping his hand on his shirt, he pushed the keys aside, picked up the phone, then put it against his ear and pressed the receive button.

'Hello?'

'Welcome back, Mr Vargas.' The voice on the other end was calm, direct, vaguely Hispanic. 'We trust you are feeling better now?'

Vargas's first instinct was to throw the phone down and run.

Instead, he gripped it tighter, steadied himself. 'Who is this?'

'That isn't important at the moment. We simply wanted to apologize to you for the behaviour of our associates, and to give you a piece of advice.'

'Which is?'

'We are a family that is very protective of its privacy. As you may have noticed, your laptop and notes are gone. We took the liberty of going over them and discovered, to our satisfaction, that you are quite unaware of what you've stumbled into here.'

'So, in other words, you jumped the gun. Sent your goons after me too soon.'

A pause. 'I hope you'll forgive their enthusiasm. We merely wanted to speak to you.'

'Why do I have a hard time believing that?'

'If it weren't true, we wouldn't be having this conversation.'

Vargas felt his gut tighten. 'So are you the one that Ainsworth and Sergio were talking about? The big man? Did you have something to do with the people in that house?'

'You don't want to be asking such questions.'

'All right, fine. What's this piece of advice you have for me?'

'Simply this: go home. Back to California. Find another story. We have no desire to punish the innocent, and who we are and what we do is none of your concern. I hope you'll decide to keep it that way.'

'And if I don't?'

Another pause. 'Check your trunk, Mr Vargas. We think the message is clear.'

Then the line clicked.

BETH

29

Fifteen minutes after Jen left, Beth started to worry.

What was taking her so long?

She supposed the restroom could have been occupied and that Jen had had to wait her turn. If it were like the restrooms in the States, there might even be a line. A long one. But fifteen minutes seemed a bit much.

Beth had already finished her lunch – not that she'd eaten a whole lot – and had watched as the waitress cleared their dishes away.

About five minutes in, she noticed some of the people from their ship wandering by across the street. First, the grey-haired man and his wife, the ones who had been the direct recipients of Jen's boob flash. Then later, the young newlywed couple, who had managed to weather the storm and were smiling happily, walking hand in hand.

Pulling out her wallet, Beth dropped some bills on the table, leaving a generous tip. She was about to rise when she heard a silky Hispanic voice behind her.

'Dining alone?'

She tensed at the sound of it. Turned and saw Rafael Santiago approaching, looking much less formal today in jeans and a long-sleeved off-white shirt. The effect was dazzling. He was even more handsome in daylight, and her complete disgust with him didn't diminish that fact.

'Not alone,' she said, 'and I'd appreciate it if you'd just keep on walking.'

He ignored the request, stopping in front of her table. 'Why so hostile, Beth?'

'I think you know.'

'Jennifer told us how protective you are. That's quite an admirable trait.'

'Did I ask for your opinion?'

'No,' he said. 'No, you didn't. And I have a terrible habit of offering them unsolicited. But Marta and I got to know Jennifer quite well last night and—'

'Don't say another word.'

Unwanted images flitted through her brain again and as she tried to shut them out, she silently cursed Rafael's very existence.

'You need to unburden yourself of this anger, Beth. I understand how someone such as you might have trouble accepting that Marta and I are free spirits, but we mean no harm.'

'Free spirits? Is that what you call what I saw in the bar last night?'

'What you saw was harmless.'

Beth scoffed. 'You practically had your tongue down your sister's throat.'

'And your thinking is clouded by a false sense of morality. We come from a family that doesn't believe in hiding our affection for one another.'

'Oh, Christ. There are more of you?'

He gestured at their surroundings. 'Everywhere you look.'

Beth frowned. 'What the hell does that mean?'

Rafael shook his head. 'Nothing you would under-stand. There are those who seek enlightenment and those who resist. When we first met last night, I thought you might be a seeker, but Marta is much more intuitive than I. She saw it the moment she met you, and I know now that she was right.'

'About what?'

'About the wall you've built. The one you've spent a lifetime building.'

'So let me get this straight,' Beth said. 'She's a witch *and* a clinical psychologist? How fascinating.'

He smiled. 'She is a child of La Santisima. As we all are.'

Beth just stared at him. La Santisima? She had no idea what this meant, and didn't really *want* to know. She was tired of this pretty boy and his unrepentant arrogance.

'I have five simple words for you,' she said. 'Stay away from my sister.'

His smile widened. 'Protective to the last.' His gaze shifted to her left hand. 'I like the ring.'

Then he turned and headed down the sidewalk.

Beth glanced at the tiny hooded skull on her finger, and when she looked up again, Rafael was gone, nowhere to be seen.

Good riddance to bad rubbish, she thought, hoping she could avoid running into him onboard ship.

Fortunately, it was a big place.

Offering up one last silent curse, she turned her attention to the leather goods shop.

Where the hell was Jen?

30

The shop's proprietor was a small, unkempt woman with a shock of grey-white hair. She sat on a stool behind a counter with a cash register, surrounded floor to ceiling by racks full of black, red and brown leather jackets and handbags.

The counter was made of scarred glass, and neatly laid out inside were wallets and chequebook covers with the words MEXICO and PLAYA AZUL burned into them.

The place wasn't exactly large, and Beth saw no sign of Jen anywhere. In fact, the proprietor seemed to be alone.

'Excuse me. I'm looking for my sister. She came in to use the restroom?'

The woman shook her head. '*No inglés.*'

Wonderful.

Beth's command of Spanish wasn't much better than Jen's, but, working in the Los Angeles criminal court system, she'd managed to pick up bits and pieces of a dozen different languages.

'*Mis hermana,*' she said. '*El baño.*'

The old woman held out a hand, palm up. 'One dollar.'

'No, I don't want to *use* the restroom. I'm looking for my sister. *Mis herm . . .*'

She suddenly realized that if using the facilities cost a dollar, Jen would've been out of luck. She'd forgotten her wallet. But she hadn't come to Beth, begging for more money, so it only made sense that she'd gone in search of a free toilet.

Beth wondered why she hadn't seen Jen leave the shop, but then it wasn't as if she'd been keeping constant vigil.

Nodding thanks to the old woman, she moved past the racks of jackets and stepped outside, scanning the street, hoping to see Jen headed back towards the restaurant.

No such luck.

She opened her purse, dug out her cell phone. Someone had told her that the wireless charges down here would cost her a fortune, but she was pretty sure a quick call wouldn't break her.

She hit speed dial, waited for it to ring. Instead it went straight to voicemail and Jen's greeting came on the line: 'Hi, this is Jen. If you're an old boyfriend, fuck off. Otherwise, leave a message at the beep.'

Beth hung up. Couldn't believe Jen was still using that greeting, but then why should she be surprised? No matter how many 'eye-opening' nights her sister had – whether it be with some biker bad boy or a couple of spiritual, incestuous whack jobs – Jen would always be Jen.

Beth looked across at the restaurant again, but saw no sign of her. At the top of the block, however, was a McDonald's, one of Jen's comfort zones, one that might just have a free public toilet. Beth dropped her cell into her purse and headed towards that familiar red-and-yellow sign.

A few moments later, she was standing inside, amid the usual mix of locals and tourists chowing on burgers and McNuggets. The restrooms were tucked into a corner near the back, and Beth crossed to them, pushing her way into the one marked *Mujeres*.

There was one stall. Empty.

Damn it.

Where the hell was she?

Turning, Beth headed back outside and pulled her cell phone out again, checking up and down the street as she dialled.

Again, no ring. Straight to voicemail. Which meant that Jen was either in a dead zone or had her cell phone off.

Beth waited for the beep.

'Hey, where are you? I went to the leather goods shop and you were gone. I'm at McDonald's now, but I'm going back to the restaurant. If you're there, don't move.'

Hanging up, she tucked the phone back into her purse and headed down the street, hoping she'd see Jen standing outside the restaurant.

But when she got there, there was still no sign of her.

Their waitress wasn't there either, so she flagged another one who stood nearby. 'Excuse me.'

'*Si, señorita?*'

'I'm sorry,' Beth said. 'Do you speak English?'

The waitress shook her head. '*No. No inglés.*' Then she turned and said something in Spanish to the chef, who had just finished preparing another taco plate.

The chef stepped out from behind his stove, wiped his hands on his apron and came over.

'Is something wrong, señorita?'

'No,' Beth said. 'I mean, yes, but not with the food or anything. I don't know if you noticed, but I had lunch here a little while ago with my sister.'

He nodded. '*Si*, I remember. But you were alone.'

'No, that was later. The girl I was with was about my height – a younger, prettier version of me – and she was wearing cut-off jeans and a halter-neck top. She asked the waitress if she could use the restroom.'

The chef shook his head. 'Our wash room is out of order. Most people use the one across the street.'

'Yes,' Beth said, trying to remain calm. 'Yes, I know. I went over there, but she's gone. I was hoping she came back here. Have you seen anyone around here in the last few minutes that looked like the girl I described?'

'No, señorita.'

'What about our waitress? Is she around?'

He shook his head. 'She go home early on Saturdays.'

Beth gestured to the other waitress. 'What about her? Could you ask if she's seen my sister?'

He nodded and called out, saying a few words in Spanish. The waitress, who was busy wiping a table, looked at him blankly, then shook her head and rattled off a reply that didn't sound promising.

The chef returned his gaze to Beth. 'I'm sorry, señorita, she hasn't seen anyone like that.'

'We just had lunch here.'

He shrugged. 'We serve many customers, most of them *touristas*. You come from the cruise ship, *si*?'

Beth nodded.

'Perhaps she was tired of shopping and went back there.'

'No,' Beth said. 'She wouldn't have gone without me. She wouldn't . . .'

Beth paused, thinking about it. Jen had been upset when she left. Maybe this was her way of punishing Beth for not taking her seriously. A classic ditch, straight out of junior high school.

In other words, typical Jen.

Still, if this wasn't a ditch, Jen could be looking for her right now. May have come back to the restaurant, seen that she was gone and started checking shops in the area.

But why no phone call?

And why had she turned off her phone?

Was the battery dead?

It wasn't time for panic. Much too early for that. There was undoubtedly a simple explanation for all of this, but that didn't keep a tiny tickle of fear from fluttering through Beth's stomach.

'Señorita?'

Beth focused, looking at the chef.

'I'm sorry,' she said. 'I'm keeping you from your work. Thanks for your help.'

He nodded, then tightened the strings on his apron and went back to his stove.

Beth decided the best thing to do was to stay put, in hopes that Jen would either return or call.

Twenty minutes later, she gave up and started back towards the ship.

31

'I'd like to check out.'

The night clerk was an elderly gentleman, just a few years shy of retirement. He looked up from his magazine and set it aside, his eyes widening slightly at the sight of the bandage on Vargas's head.

'Is there a problem with the room, sir?'

It was a wonder he couldn't hear Vargas's heart beating.

'No, the room's fine. I got some unexpected news and I have to leave.'

'I'm afraid you'll be charged for the entire night. Company policy.'

Vargas was expecting this and didn't object. He just wanted to get out of here.

The clerk quickly processed the check-out, gave him a receipt, and five minutes later, Vargas was rolling his suitcase towards the Corolla, heart still pounding, a knot the size of a fist in his stomach.

The battered, bungee-corded rear end of his car seemed to call out to him, a beacon for both his dread and his curiosity.

Check your trunk, Mr Vargas.

We think the message is clear.

After the phone call, he had resisted the urge to run down to the parking lot immediately. Had instead washed the blood off his keys, then taken a shower to wash the remaining blood and dirt off his body, before changing into a fresh set of clothes.

Repacking his suitcase, he'd checked the room for anything he might have forgotten, then closed the door behind him and went straight to the motel lobby.

He had considered abandoning the Corolla altogether, but it was the only transportation he had – or could afford – so his choice was clear no matter what might be waiting for him beneath that battered trunk lid.

But he couldn't check it here.

There were possibly dozens of eyes staring down on him in the motel parking lot. Not the place to try to satisfy his curiosity.

He needed to get somewhere private.

Throwing his suitcase in the back seat, he climbed behind the wheel, jammed the key into the ignition and started the engine.

Ten minutes later, he found himself driving through an industrial section of town, steering towards a dark cluster of warehouses.

Pulling into a narrow alley between a glass factory and an unfinished furniture wholesaler, he parked near a dumpster and waited a full half-hour to make sure that no night watchmen were about. He checked the high corners of the warehouses for any sign of surveillance cameras.

Satisfied that he was alone and not being recorded, he took his flashlight from the glove compartment, then opened his door, stepped around to the rear of the car. The knot in his stomach started to burn, and his heart seemed to have burrowed its way up into his throat.

Crouching down, he unhooked the bungee cord from his bumper and let the broken trunk lid rise, then stood up and shone the flashlight inside.

He had expected to find a body. But to his great relief, all that greeted him was a cardboard box. Just big enough to hold, say, a soccer ball.

What the hell?

He picked it up, felt something loose inside, banging against the sides of the box. The flaps were sealed shut by a strip of duct tape, not unlike the one he'd pulled from his mouth.

Setting the box back down, he peeled the tape away, opened the flaps, and pointed the flashlight beam inside.

What he saw made him step backwards involuntarily, a wave of revulsion rising in his chest.

It was a severed head.

Eyes wide. Frozen in horror.

Sergio?

Vargas stared down at it in disbelief and continued stepping backwards until his back met the wall of the glass factory. Feeling his legs start to give out, he leaned against it for support and tried to keep his breathing steady.

Then his cell phone rang.

Knowing instinctively who the caller was, he dug it out of his pocket, clicked it on.

'Across the street,' the voice said.

Vargas turned sharply, looking out through the mouth of the alley. There was a car parked on the far side of the street – a Lincoln Town Car – a man leaning casually against the driver's door, cell phone to his ear. He made no attempt to hide himself, clearly illuminated under a streetlight.

His dark hair was on the longish side, hanging loose around his collar. The left half of his face was mottled with red, blistery burn marks.

Vargas felt something cold and prickly skitter up his spine.

'There is only one question you need to answer, Mr Vargas: Has the message been received?'

Vargas tried to swallow. '. . . What?'

'Has the message . . . been . . . received.'

Vargas's voice wavered. 'Yes. Yes it has.'

'Excellent,' the man said. 'You had better go now. You have a long drive ahead of you.'

Vargas just nodded, unable to speak, then clicked off the phone.

32

He must have checked his rear-view mirror at least a hundred times before he hit the Interstate, but he saw no sign of the Town Car.

Not that this was any guarantee he wasn't being followed.

He left the way he came, shooting up the 10 towards Las Cruces, figuring he'd drive straight into Phoenix, take a rest, then continue on to Los Angeles. But by the time he reached New Mexico – a short, forty-minute drive from El Paso – he was feeling sick to his stomach and pulled into a truck stop to throw up.

Staggering out of the restroom, he sat in a booth near the windows of the truck stop cafe, searching the parking lot for any sign of the Town Car.

All he saw were half a dozen big rigs and his own battered Corolla.

This gave him some relief, but there was something else gnawing at him that just didn't seem to want to let go. It was, he thought, the thing that had made him sick. A feeling he'd had only once in the past, when confronted about his drug abuse and those accusations of fraud:

Shame.

He felt ashamed.

Vargas had been in tight situations before. Had seen his life in danger. Had been threatened and terrorized by gang members on the streets of East Los Angeles. Had gone up against striking teamsters who wanted to beat him senseless. Had even been shot by a psycho ex-cop whose career he had managed to destroy with a series of articles on police corruption.

But he'd never before backed down.

Never.

He knew it was a miracle that he was still alive. Whoever was behind this thing, this House of Death massacre, could easily have killed him and been done with it. He wasn't sure why he had been spared, but thought that it might have something to do with his profession, no matter how tarnished his reputation might be.

A dead or missing reporter – especially one as notorious as Vargas – was like a dead or missing whistleblower. It might raise more questions than these people could afford. So why not scare the everloving crap out of the guy and send him on his way?

And it had worked.

He was about as spooked as a man could get.

Despite all those past brushes with injury and death, despite all his thoughts of an itch needing to be scratched, Vargas had caved. And caved big time.

The sight of that severed head – which he'd left in the alleyway dumpster – had done exactly what it was intended to do.

And he felt ashamed.

Ashamed for letting them terrorize him. For letting them scare him away from a story that was looking to be much bigger than he had ever imagined. A story he had hoped would be the first step in salvaging a ruined career.

And he needed that career. Needed it desperately.

But he also liked breathing.

A waitress came over. She didn't look much older than a high-school kid, but she sounded like an old truck stop pro.

'What can I get you, hon?'

A backbone, Vargas almost told her, but he wasn't in the mood for conversation. 'Just coffee.'

'You look like you could use something stronger. Bad night?'

Vargas glanced at his reflection in the window. Was it that obvious?

'Bad enough,' he said.

She nodded. 'I know how that goes. How about a piece of cherry pie to cheer you up a bit?'

Vargas shook his head, feeling his stomach flip-flop. 'Just the coffee.'

She nodded again and went away and he returned his attention to the parking lot as another big rig pulled in. A beefy trucker wearing a cowboy hat climbed down from the driver's seat, eyeballing Vargas as he crossed towards the cafe entrance.

Vargas averted his gaze, then immediately regretted it, feeling like a spineless fool. Not that he gave a shit about macho stare downs, but Jesus, what the hell was the matter with him?

When had he lost his edge?

He sat there, waiting for his coffee, sinking deeper and deeper into the quicksand of depression, wondering where the old Nick Vargas had gone.

He thought about the men who had brutalized him, about the bodies in that desert house. About the American woman, who was probably long dead, but certainly deserved better than she'd gotten.

Deserved to have her story told.

Sure, he could forget about her and go back to California, maybe get a job writing technical manuals or working up travel brochures, and he might lead a safe, carefree life – maybe even a comfortable one.

But he'd never get another book deal, and he'd never again work for a major newspaper, would never feel the pride he'd once felt when he saw his byline above the fold.

And he would always be remembered as the hillbilly heroin addict who almost faked his way to a Pulitzer.

All because he had turned tail and run. Had let himself be intimidated by three border rats and a thug with a half-burnt face.

Mr Blister.

A voice on the phone.

And as the waitress brought his coffee, smiling warmly as she set it in front of him, he knew he was about to do something stupid again, if for no other reason than to rid himself of this feeling of shame.

He may have lost his edge, but he could get it back. He may well lose his life in the process, but what good was it if he lived it as a coward?

He had every right in the world to be afraid, but even the darkest of fears could be overcome.

He was, after all – as old-fashioned and corny as it might sound – a muckraker.

A truth seeker.

And maybe some of that truth was waiting for him on an egg ranch in El Paso.

BETH

33

The first thing she did was go back to their stateroom, hoping that Jen was either inside sulking, or getting some much needed sleep.

But it was empty.

As dark and uninviting as ever.

Not that she'd expected anything else.

Trying to convince herself that Jen's abrupt disappearance was just her way of saying fuck you, Beth took the elevator to the atrium, found an empty deck chair and sat, staring out the windows at the flat, unmoving ocean.

She could feel another headache coming on. One of several she'd had to fight off in the last couple of months. Probably stress from the job. And the divorce.

But a headache was the least of her concerns.

She knew she was often too quick to dismiss Jen's feelings, and the joke she'd made at lunch had been insensitive and maybe even a little cruel. So it made sense that Jen was mad at her.

But that didn't keep the uneasiness from rising in her chest. A feeling that something might be wrong.

Don't worry.

I'm not gonna go mental on you.

Beth took her phone out of her purse and tried calling again.

As before, she was transferred straight to voicemail. Which only compounded her uneasiness. She didn't bother waiting for the beep. Instead, she clicked off, then punched in a quick text message:

WTF?

It wasn't like her sister to shut off her phone or let the battery go dead. But then Beth had to remember that they were in Mexico and neither of them had expected to use their cell phones all that much.

Still, wouldn't Jen have found a way to call *her* by now?

When she couldn't take staring out at the ocean any more, Beth went back downstairs and checked their stateroom again.

Still empty.

Stepping into the corridor, she noticed that their steward, a young, pleasant-faced Ethiopian man, was busy cleaning the cabin three doors down from theirs.

Beth stuck her head in the doorway.

'Excuse me, I'm sorry to bother you, but I'm in cabin 829?'

He turned, trash basket in hand. Nodded politely.

'You need something, ma'am?'

'I'm looking for my sister. Have you seen her come by the room?'

'No, ma'am. I see her this morning, but she don't come again.'

'What time this morning?'

'Before breakfast. Right before we dock.'

Disappointed, Beth nodded thanks, letting him get back to work.

She was turning away when the steward said, 'Her name is Jennifer, yes?'

Beth stopped. 'Yes. How did you know?'

'She tell me last night when I come to turn down the beds. And earlier this morning, two people come knocking on your door, calling her name.'

'What two people?'

As if Beth had to guess.

'A man and woman.'

Ugh.

Why couldn't those sleazoids just *go away*?

'If I see her,' the steward said, 'I tell her you look for her.'

Beth thanked him a second time and moved back down the corridor. She went inside the stateroom again and flicked on the light, conscious for the first time that the place had been cleaned, and her suitcase, which she'd left open on her bunk, had been closed and tucked in a corner.

God, this place was small. Borderline claustrophobic. And she sure as hell didn't feel like hanging around in here, waiting for her phone to ring.

She was about to leave when she remembered that Jen had forgotten her wallet.

Closing the door behind her, Beth checked the

dresser top and the nightstand, but saw no sign of it. She opened Jen's dresser drawer and found three pairs of panties, some socks, two barely there bikinis, Jen's cruise line voucher and passport and nothing else.

Did that mean she'd come back to get the wallet? Or had she left it somewhere else – like the Santiagos' stateroom?

Maybe that was the reason they'd been knocking on the door.

But why, then, hadn't Rafael said anything about it when he saw Beth at the restaurant? Wouldn't he have given it to her?

Unless, of course, he had already given it to Jen.

Or Marta had.

Could they have run into her at the leather goods shop as Beth waited at the restaurant? Had Rafael merely been distracting Beth so Jen and Marta could sneak away for a date with some Jello shooters?

The notion seemed so goddamned juvenile it wasn't funny. But it was also within the realm of possibility. Maybe Beth's earlier thought had been right. She really *had* been ditched.

As she stood there, feeling anger start to boil up, her gaze drifted to her suitcase, and she had half a mind to scoop it up and follow through on the threat she'd made in the dining room. Find the nearest airport and go home.

The ultimate ditch.

The *quintessential* fuck you.

But what if she was wrong? What if this wasn't a junior-high prank at all?

What if Jen was in some kind of trouble?

They were, after all, in a foreign country. And while Beth had never had a xenophobic bone in her body, she'd be lying if she didn't admit that she'd felt just the slightest bit of trepidation as they'd walked the streets of Playa Azul.

She thought of the gangbangers who had been ogling Jen with undisguised lust.

Could one of them have followed her? Confronted her when she was alone?

Beth's anger dissipated as the uneasiness grew inside her stomach. She tried to talk herself down.

She was, after all, in a profession that examined the worst of people. Her natural instinct was to look at the dark side of human nature, simply because she was always surrounded by it. She'd interviewed enough rape victims and prosecuted enough of their assailants to colour her view of the world permanently.

She'd always tried not to let this carry over into her private life, but how could it not?

Yet she knew it was still too early for panic.

Much too early.

She considered heading back into town to have another look around, but decided to check the ship first, from top to bottom, stern to bow – every restaurant and bar and extracurricular activity in progress – in hopes that she'd find Jen hiding out.

Or getting drunk.

Because a drunk, unhappy Jen was better than no Jen at all.

34

'May I help you, ma'am?'

The purser was a grey-haired, distinguished-looking gentleman in a crisp white uniform. He stood behind a narrow counter, typing something into a computer.

Beth had waited five minutes to speak to him, but now that she was at the front of the line, she wasn't sure how to start without sounding melodramatic.

'I . . . I'm a little worried about my sister,' she said.

The purser continued typing, barely glanced up.

'Is she ill? Would you like some seasick tablets?'

He started to reach under the counter, but Beth put a hand up, stopping him.

'No, it's not that,' she said. 'We went into town this morning and . . . well . . . I guess you could say I've misplaced her.'

She followed this with a soft, embarrassed laugh. This whole situation had thrown her off her game and she felt more like a hapless victim than a seasoned prosecutor.

The purser frowned. 'Misplaced her?'

'She's missing.'

'And this happened onboard ship or in port?'

'I just told you,' Beth said. 'I lost her in Playa Azul.'

'How long ago?'

'About an hour and a half.' Beth had spent a good half of that time conducting her search of the ship, which had yielded a big fat doughnut. 'We were having lunch and she went across the street to use the restroom. I haven't seen her since.'

The purser shrugged. 'An hour and a half isn't long. There's a lot to do in town.'

'You aren't listening,' Beth said. 'She went to the restroom and never came back.'

'I'm sure there's an explanation. Maybe she got distracted, saw a shop she wanted to explore and lost track of you. It happens. She'll turn up.'

He shifted his attention to his computer screen again and, feeling her assertiveness return, Beth reached out, blocking his view with her hand.

The purser jerked his head back in surprise and irritation.

'I just told you,' Beth said, '*my sister is missing*. I think she may be in trouble. I've tried calling her half a dozen times, but her phone is turned off. I've searched every inch of this ship that's accessible to guests and—'

'Why search the ship if she disappeared in Playa Azul?'

Beth looked at him. It was certainly a reasonable question. 'I thought she might have come back here.'

'Well,' he said with another shrug. 'That's easy enough to find out.'

'How?'

'Her Seafarer card. You remember how security scanned your card when you came back onboard?'

Beth nodded. She'd been asked to push it into a slot so a ship's security officer could check the photo they had on file to make sure she was really who she claimed to be. The photos had been taken as they boarded the ship for the first time back in Long Beach. It had seemed a bit Big Brotherish to Beth, but she understood the reasons for it. Security at the district attorney's office was nearly as tight.

'If your sister came back to the ship,' the purser said, 'they would've scanned hers as well. In which case, we'll have a record of her return. Did you book your passage together?'

Beth nodded.

'What's your cabin number?'

Beth told him and he keyed it into the computer, then frowned.

'I have a note here that you were involved in an incident in the dining room last night.'

Beth felt herself redden. 'My sister,' she said. 'She had too much to drink. It won't happen again.'

He eyed her warily, then hit a few more keys and stared at the screen a moment.

'I'm afraid there's no record of her return. So she must still be in town. I can contact the Mexican authorities, if you like, but I'm pretty sure they'll agree that an hour and a half isn't all that much time.'

Beth thought about it, and despite her concern, she still wasn't absolutely sure Jen hadn't disappeared by choice.

Then an idea struck her.

'She's been hanging around with some friends of ours. Rafael and Marta Santiago. Maybe they know where she is. Do you think you could check to see if they've returned?'

The purser shook his head. 'We have strict guest privacy rules. Have you tried calling them yourself? Or checking their cabin?'

'I'm not sure what room they're in. We just met them last night.'

'Then I'm afraid you're out of luck. I will, however, be happy to have security stop by their cabin and ask them if they've seen her.'

'Thank you,' Beth said. 'I think I'll go back into town and look around some more.'

The purser nodded. Feigned a little empathy. 'Not to worry, I'm sure you'll find her. You might check some of the bars.'

Beth knew this was a backhanded reference to last night's embarrassment, but decided to let it go. No point in creating a scene.

Besides, he was probably right.

'And don't forget,' he continued, 'the gangplank closes at 5.30. We sail at 6 p.m.'

She hesitated, thinking about this, then thanked him again and went downstairs to the debarking station.

The first place she planned to hit when she got back into town was Armando's Cantina.

VARGAS

35

According to Google Maps, the Ainsworth ranch was located on three acres of dusty countryside just north of an El Paso suburb called Montoya.

Thanks to the phone's secure digital expansion slot, Vargas was able to access the laptop data he'd backed up to the SD card in his wallet. This included the witness contact information he'd copied from the Casa de la Muerte police file.

Not everything was there, but it was enough.

After transferring Ainsworth's address to the phone's Google navigation system, he called up the directions and started driving.

The ranch stood across the street from a housing tract still under construction, and was accessible by a narrow dirt road. A faded, beat-up sign at the top of the road said:

Have an *egg*-cellent meal
With Ainsworth family eggs

There were no streetlights out here, but there was enough moonlight to make out a distant cluster of small, dilapidated warehouses and an old, two-storey dwelling that could best be described as a fixer-upper, circa 1922.

Vargas had no intention of driving down that road. Instead, he turned into the housing tract and parked next to a vacant lot.

In the middle of the lot stood another, newer sign, announcing the impending construction of a luxury four-bedroom home, which, if it ever got built, would one day stand in stark contrast to the Ainsworth house across the street.

As he killed the engine, Vargas started having second thoughts about this little excursion. What exactly did he hope to accomplish out here?

He had no interest in confronting Ainsworth directly.

Been there, done that.

Considering his current physical condition, any attempt at face time would be an exercise in disaster. He couldn't just walk up to the guy and say, 'Hey, tell me everything you know about your psycho friends.' Not if he wanted to avoid winding up in a box in some warehouse district alleyway.

Instead, he was forced to go into stealth mode. Convinced that Ainsworth and Junior had ransacked those bodies back in the desert, he hoped that an uninvited tour of their house might yield some of their ill-gotten bounty. And if he was lucky, he might just find something that pointed to the American woman's identity.

A driver's licence. Credit card. Family photo.

Considering the amount of time that had passed, it was a long shot, sure.

But it was the only shot he had.

Still, as he sat there listening to the Corolla's engine rattle and die, he realized he'd been running on pure impulse and had no real plan of attack.

When he was a teenager, he and his brother Manny had spent a couple of summers breaking into houses in their neighbourhood to steal beer and cigarettes, which they sold to their friends at the local rec centre. They got so good at it that most of their victims never even knew they'd been there at all.

But that was a long time ago, and Vargas wasn't sure if he still had the skill – or the guts – to pull off a B & E. Breaking into a neighbour's house was one thing. If you got caught, they'd probably call your parents. But if Vargas were to get caught now, Ainsworth would likely blow his head off.

So his only hope was that Big Papa and Junior had taken a detour to a Mexican whorehouse and hadn't yet returned from Juarez.

Locking his car, he glanced around to make sure he was alone and unobserved. The housing tract had the feel of a ghost town – which, he assumed, was a fairly accurate description. Thanks to the failing economy, construction sites all over the country had stalled or gone bankrupt, and he didn't figure it was any different out here.

Checking up and down the street, he saw no people, no traffic, no Town Cars . . .

So he sucked in a breath and crossed towards Ainsworth's property.

36

If he stayed low, there was just enough brush to give him cover. Keeping about ten yards out from the access road, he moved parallel to it, working his way slowly towards the grouping of warehouses that sat a good distance from the main dwelling.

He assumed that one of them was a chicken coop, and had expected to hear clucking sounds coming from inside.

But the place was still and silent. Another ghost town. Which might explain why Ainsworth and Junior were working for the bad guys.

Reaching the first warehouse, Vargas pressed his back against the rusted aluminium siding. There was an open doorway about ten feet away, and nothing but darkness inside.

Vargas looked across the yard at the Ainsworth house.

No lights. No sign of the F150.

Maybe he'd been blessed with a bit of luck for once.

Still, it was wise to be cautious. His best approach, he decided, was from the rear of the place. If he continued to stay low and quiet, he could circle around with minimum risk, then put his burglary skills to the test on one of the rear windows.

He was about to make his move when he heard it. On the road behind him.

The sound of a truck approaching.

Shit.

So much for luck.

Headlights flashed in his direction and he dropped down, scurrying – as best as he could – through the open warehouse door. He watched from the shadows as not one, but two sets of headlights, one after the other, bounced along the road towards the house, and two familiar vehicles came to a stop out front:

Ainsworth's F150.

And the Lincoln Town Car.

Something cold and dead wrapped its fingers around Vargas's heart.

Check your trunk, Mr Vargas.

We think the message is clear.

Doors flew open and Ainsworth and the burnt-faced man, Mr Blister, emerged from their vehicles, Ainsworth looking a little less cocksure than normal.

Vargas waited for Junior to climb out also, but it didn't happen. Which was odd, considering that father and son seemed to be glued together at the hip.

He thought of Sergio's fate and wondered if Junior had joined him. That might explain Ainsworth's change of demeanour.

'Where is it?' Mr Blister asked.

Ainsworth gestured towards the side of the house. 'Still in the shed. We just got the bikes unloaded when you called and I figured it was best to get a move on. I know the boss man don't like to be kept waiting.'

'Show me,' Mr Blister said.

They walked towards the house, moving into the darkness along the right side. After a moment, a light came on, revealing a row of rabbit cages. The two men stepped past them to a small metal shed, its doors chained and padlocked.

Vargas's view was partially blocked by the vehicles. But that could work to his advantage. He needed a closer look and they'd give him cover.

Sucking in a breath, he moved forwards, running in a quick straight line to the rear of the Town Car and crouching behind it.

Much better view.

Ainsworth had opened the padlock and was pulling the chain from the door handles. Gesturing for Mr Blister to stand back a bit, he swung open the doors to reveal the two dusty red dirt bikes sitting inside.

Moving to the closest one, he grabbed hold of the seat and pried it upwards, then reached beneath it and brought out a tightly wrapped plastic bag.

He handed it across to Mr Blister. '*Seis burritos, amigo.*'

He wasn't talking about dinner.

Vargas had heard the term 'burrito' before. It referred to a rolled-up sheet of Ecstasy tablets. A thousand tabs, with a wholesale value of about five grand. Which meant that the bundle Mr Blister had in his hand was worth thirty thousand dollars, with a street value of at least double that.

But Ainsworth wasn't done yet. He moved to another part of the bike – a piece of plastic moulding just above the rear wheel – and prised it apart, revealing another hidden compartment, and another tightly wrapped plastic bag.

Mr Blister, in the meantime, brought out a switch-blade, flicked it open, then sliced through the first bag, checking its contents.

After tucking the new bundle under his arm, Ainsworth moved to the second bike and went to work. By the time he was done, he had two more bundles.

Vargas did some quick math and came up with a total street value of about two hundred and forty thousand dollars. Not bad, but not an earth-shattering figure in the world of drug smugglers.

Ainsworth and Junior were obviously small-run couriers, but Vargas figured that whoever they were working for had a variety of transport methods.

So much for the war on drugs.

But what did all this have to do with a house full of dead nuns?

Could they have been couriers, too?

'Where's Monday's run?' Mr Blister asked.

Ainsworth gestured with a thumb. 'Up in the house.'

'Show me,' Mr Blister said again, then added, 'And I'll need something to carry it all in.'

Ainsworth nodded and the two men turned, taking the plastic bundles with them to the front of the house.

Vargas crouched low, peeking around the bumper of the Town Car as they headed up a set of creaky porch steps and disappeared inside.

A light went on, illuminating the front room, which was clearly visible through the windows. Ainsworth handed his bundles to Mr Blister, then crossed to a door and opened it, revealing a closet full of coats. Bending down, he disappeared from view for a moment, then reappeared holding a black duffel bag.

Returning to Mr Blister, he held the bag open while the burnt-faced man started stuffing the bundles inside.

Vargas glanced down at the Town Car's licence plate. Alabama, of all places. Which didn't quite fit.

So was the car stolen?

It didn't hurt to check. Taking his cell phone from his pocket, he quickly snapped a photo of the plate.

Figuring he had a few moments before they came outside again, he moved to the open driver's door and leaned in across the seat, reaching for the glove compartment, hoping to find the registration.

But as he grabbed hold of the latch, something cold and hard touched the back of his head.

Then a quiet voice said:

'You're a dead man.'

37

Vargas froze. Felt his heart leap into his throat.

'Back out of there. Real slow.'

Despite the near-whisper, he knew exactly who it was. Doing as he was told, he said, 'Easy, Junior. Take it easy.'

The barrel of a shotgun nudged his cheek.

'Big Papa said you'd be here. Said you and the other ones want to hurt us.'

'You got it wrong. I'm not here to hurt anybody.'

'You think I'm stupid? That why you called me a retard?'

'I'm not the one who called you that, remember? That was Sergio.'

Junior was silent a moment, working it through.

'Yeah? Well, Sergio's just like you. That's what Big Papa said. You're one of the dead men. And he told me I shouldn't trust none of you guys. He said you'd be comin' after us. That's why he told me to hide.'

'Big Papa's a smart man. But you're wrong about me. I'm here to help.'

'Then why are you sneakin' around in the dark?'

'Same reason you are. Big Papa warned me, too.'

Junior hesitated. 'Bullshit.'

'It's true,' Vargas said. 'He called me on my cell phone. Told me to come out here and help you.'

'That don't make no sense. Big Papa put you in the trunk and you ran away.'

Vargas started to turn, but Junior stopped him with the barrel of the shotgun.

'Careful,' Vargas said. 'That thing goes off, the man who owns this car will shoot us both.'

'Why would he shoot you? You're a friend of his.'

Vargas shook his head. 'If I were, wouldn't I be in there with them? Would I be digging around in his glove compartment? I promised Big Papa I'd make sure you did what you were told.'

A pause. 'I don't believe you.'

'Believe what you want, then, but if we aren't careful, sooner or later they're gonna hear us and then we'll both be in a world of—'

Junior suddenly grabbed Vargas's collar and yanked him backwards. As his legs flew out from under him, Vargas glanced up to see Ainsworth and Mr Blister stepping onto the front porch.

Junior quickly dragged him across the yard, through the warehouse doors and into the darkness. Breathing hard, he released his grip then planted the barrel of the shotgun against Vargas's chest.

'Don't fuckin' move.'

He was silhouetted against the moonlight and Vargas could barely see him, but he could tell that the kid was confused and scared shitless, a hair trigger away from doing something foolish.

'It's okay, son. Everything's gonna be okay. Just be calm.'

But Junior said nothing, started pacing anxiously as Ainsworth and Mr Blister continued their conversation out on the porch.

Vargas sensed that he was about to blow. He needed to distract the kid, keep him from getting them both killed.

He kept his voice low. 'Tell me about the American girl.'

'Shut up,' Junior said. 'I gotta think.'

'You said she was still alive when you found her. That her name was Angie.'

Junior swivelled his head, looking at Vargas. 'I don't know nothin' about that. Keep your taco trap shut, Junior. That's what Big Papa said.'

'So you're a liar, then? Did Big Papa raise you to be a liar?'

'What the fuck are you talking about?'

'The whole thing was bullshit. There never was an American girl.'

'You're just trying to trick me, mister. You think I'm stupid and you can trick me. But I seen her plain as day. And I can prove it.'

'Oh? How?'

Vargas glanced towards the porch. The two men were coming down the steps now, moving out towards their vehicles.

'I got her necklace,' Junior said. 'I'm wearin' it right now.'

'Let me see it, then.'

'Why? So you can steal it? Why you so interested in her anyway?'

It was a good question.

'Because somebody shot her,' Vargas said. 'Somebody killed all those people and I want to find out who.'

'I told you already. The dead men. *They* done it. Left 'em to rot in that spooky old house. But Big Papa says we gotta do what they tell us or they're gonna hurt us, too.'

Vargas glanced towards the Town Car. The two men were standing at the trunk now, Mr Blister popping the lid, dumping the duffel bag inside. They were still out of range, but that didn't make Vargas feel any better.

'Easy, Junior, keep your voice down. They're gonna hear us.'

'You still think I'm lying, don't you? But I got her picture, too. I keep it in my drawer. I found it stuffed in her—'

A gunshot cracked the air, cutting him off.

Vargas jerked his head up just in time to see Ainsworth fall to the ground, his body quaking and quivering, as Mr Blister stepped over him and fired another shot, straight into his skull.

Then Mr Blister looked up, peering into the darkened warehouse doorway, his scarred face shining in the moonlight, the cold, black look of death in his eyes.

That was when Junior went ballistic.

38

The sound that rose from Junior's throat was more animal than human. A wounded, tortured cry that echoed through the still night air, full of palpable, untethered pain.

'You hurt Big Papa!' he sobbed, then lurched forwards towards the yard.

Towards Mr Blister.

Vargas jumped up, grabbing hold of his shoulder, but Junior spun around, jamming the stock of the shotgun into Vargas's chest, knocking the wind out of him. Vargas stumbled, landing on his backside as Junior barrelled through the doorway, his shotgun raised and ready to fire.

But Mr Blister was waiting for him, his own weapon raised. And the moment Junior stepped into view, he pulled the trigger, putting a bullet between the younger man's eyes.

Junior flew backwards, as if he'd been struck by a baseball bat, landing in the dirt just a few yards from Vargas's feet.

Vargas, meanwhile, was holding his chest, still trying to breathe—

—as Mr Blister stopped where he stood and stared into the darkness, looking for movement. Looking for any sign that Junior hadn't been alone.

Did he know that Vargas was in here?

Had he heard them talking?

Vargas didn't dare move. Not even a centimetre. For that moment in time, he ceased to exist, willing himself invisible as Mr Blister stared straight at him with those dark, dead eyes, suspicion on his disfigured face.

'You may as well come out,' he said.

Vargas felt his throat go dry. His heart kicked into high gear, pounding against his chest.

There was no way that Mr Blister could see him. Not from that distance.

It was a bluff. It had to be.

But that didn't keep Vargas from feeling as if he had a bright, white spotlight shining down on him.

'Come out now and I will be kind,' Mr Blister said. 'It is better to die quickly, no?'

No, Vargas thought.

It's better not to die at all.

And if he'd stayed on the goddamn Interstate, headed for California, the question would be irrelevant. But no, he had to suddenly decide to grow some balls.

Mr Blister stood there for a long moment, waiting. Watching. Listening.

Then, keeping his gaze on the warehouse doorway, he moved to the trunk of the Town Car, leaned in, and brought out a flashlight – one of those big industrial jobs, used for roadside emergencies.

Oh, Holy Christ.

Vargas didn't want to move, but he sure as hell wasn't about to stay put. The moment that flashlight was flicked on and its beam swept towards him, he'd be as dead as poor Junior.

Rolling onto his hands and knees, he quickly backed away, moving deeper into the darkness of the warehouse, trying to be as quiet as possible about it. He had no idea what was back here, and hoped to hell he didn't bump into something solid.

He kept his gaze on the doorway, waiting for Mr Blister to turn in his direction.

But then, out on the access road, a pair of headlights appeared.

Mr Blister swivelled around, his body stiffening slightly as he watched them approach. When the car drew closer, Vargas saw a light bar across the roof.

Law enforcement.

Some kind of police car.

Mr Blister relaxed, however, lowering his pistol as the car rolled up and parked behind the Lincoln.

A border patrol cruiser.

Then the door opened and Agent Harmon got out, and Vargas suddenly understood how his car had gotten across the border.

Harmon was one of them.

He looked at Ainsworth, then Junior. Slowly shook his head. 'Was this really necessary?'

Mr Blister shrugged. '*Qué diferencia?* I was told to clean up, so I'm cleaning up.'

Harmon nodded to Junior, a sadness in his voice. 'I watched that boy go through puberty, and he never hurt a soul in his life. Hell, he could've been mine for all I know. His mom and I had our moments.'

'I had no choice,' Mr Blister said. 'He came at me with that shotgun. But do not worry. El Santo will bless him.'

'Will he now. He gonna bless us, too?'

'Of course. He blesses us all.'

Harmon gave him a look, then crouched next to Junior, putting a hand over the kid's eyes, closing them. 'What about the reporter? You clean *him* up?'

Mr Blister shook his head. 'He was nothing. A scared little bunny. And he is less of a threat to us alive than dead.'

'Oh? How you figure?'

'Better he run away than someone come looking for him. Someone who knows what he was after. So El Santo showed him mercy, and like a good little boy, he went home.'

'Uh-huh,' Harmon said. 'So what happens now?'

'We have decided to suspend operations up here for a while. A cooling-off period. We will be re-routing our mules through New Mexico and Arizona.'

Harmon raised his eyebrows. 'And where does that leave me?'

'Nowhere,' Mr Blister said.

Then he raised the pistol again and shot him.

BETH

39

A flickering red and green neon sign out front read ARMANDO'S CANTINA.

It was a small place, with wooden floors and walls crowded with framed plaques and photographs celebrating Playa Azul's past. The bar ran the length of one side of the room, which was packed elbow to elbow with tourists and locals alike, clutching bottles of Tecate and laughing raucously.

The house band, wearing blue shirts and cowboy hats, played – of all things – a mariachi version of Pink Floyd's 'Another Brick in the Wall'. It was an odd choice, Beth thought, but it seemed to go over well with the tourists, who were too drunk to notice just how awful it sounded.

The moment she stepped into the bar, she felt as if she'd been assaulted. The noise and the music exacerbated her growing headache.

She studied the crowd, looking for Jen, but saw no one that even resembled her. She checked for Rafael and Marta as well, but came up empty handed.

Reaching into her purse, she pulled out Jen's passport, which she'd taken from the dresser drawer.

Crossing to the bar, she flagged the bartender – a busty woman in an Armando's T-shirt – hoping she spoke English.

'Excuse me.'

The bartender came over, wiping her hands with a small towel. '*Si*, señorita. Drink? *Cerveza?*'

'No,' Beth said. 'I'm looking for someone.'

She opened the passport, showing her Jen's photo. It was a couple of years old, but Jen hadn't changed much.

'My sister,' she said. 'She may have been here with two other people. A man and a woman, both Mexican. Very good looking.'

The bartender studied the photo, then shook her head. 'No, I don't see her. But I'm very busy today. I don't see everyone who comes.' She nodded towards a waitress, who stood near a table, taking an order. 'Try Isabella. She don't work as hard as me.'

Beth thanked her and crossed the room, waiting for the waitress to finish taking her order. When she turned, Beth stopped her.

'Excuse me, I'm sorry, but I'm looking for my sister, and I think she may have come in here this afternoon.' She showed her the passport photo. 'Have you seen her?'

The waitress looked at it. 'You are from the cruise ship, *si*?'

'Yes,' Beth said.

'I see many people from the ship. But not this one.'

Disappointed, Beth thanked her and was about to turn away, when someone nearby said:

'Maybe I can help.'

Beth focused on the source of the voice.

He was an American of about thirty, unshaven, sitting alone at a table close by. He was nursing a beer, and looked unhurried and unconcerned, just biding his time. Not a tourist, but not exactly a local either. He was wearing a T-shirt with a fish on front surrounded by the words, MEAT WITHOUT FEET.

A fisherman, apparently. Who looked like half the guys she'd prosecuted.

She went to him, wary, but optimistic.

'I'm something of a people watcher,' he said. 'And I've been here pretty much all day. Why don't you let me see that picture?'

Beth hesitated, then handed him the passport.

He squinted at Jen's photo, took a sip of beer. 'Now there's a face you don't forget.'

'So have you seen her?'

'Matter of fact, I have. She was in here about an hour ago. With some guy.'

Thank God, Beth thought. 'A Mexican man? Good looking? Wearing a pony tail?'

The fisherman nodded. 'That's the one. They hung out for a while, then they met up with a few other people. I heard one of them say they were headed up the street. To Emilio's.'

'Where's that?'

The fisherman took a long last sip of his beer, then set the bottle on the table and stood up.

'My name's Eric,' he said. 'Why don't you let me show you?'

Beth shook her head. 'That's okay. I'll find it.'

'I've gotta head back to my boat pretty soon anyway. And I need to walk off some of this *cerveza*.'

Turning, he headed for the door, weaving his way through the crowd, which seemed to have grown denser in just the few minutes Beth had been there. The mariachi band was now playing Santana. Badly.

When he got to the door, he gestured for Beth to follow him outside, showing her that he still had Jen's passport in his hand.

Shit, Beth thought, then went after him as he disappeared out the door.

When she got outside, he was already several steps up the street.

'Hey!' she shouted. 'Give that back.'

He stopped in his tracks, held out the passport. He was smiling slightly. Amused.

Beth caught up with him, snatched it away. 'I told you I'd find the place myself.'

'How long has it been?' he asked.

'I beg your pardon?'

'Since your sister disappeared.'

'A few hours,' Beth said.

He looked surprised. 'And you're already passing her picture around? Isn't that a little premature?'

'It's a long story,' she said. 'Just point me in the right direction, okay?'

He shrugged. 'Two blocks up, take a right, then a left into the alley. You can't miss it.'

Beth thanked him and headed up the street.

40

She was halfway up the first block before she realized she was angry again.

Now that she knew that Jen had been at Armando's – getting drunk and yucking it up with her new pervy friends – the worry that had plagued Beth for the last few hours had all but disappeared.

She'd had it with the girl.

All of the promises to behave, to devote this weekend to sisterly bonding, had been empty lies designed only to placate. To put out the fires before they burned her. Jen was all impulse and no brain. She was incapable of thinking beyond the moment. That whole life-sucks-I'm-thinking-about-going-to-school-I-miss-Mommy-and-Daddy-my-friends-talk-to-dead-people routine was a complete crock, and Beth's scepticism had now been officially validated.

This was the very last straw. Beth had devoted too much of her life and energy to Jen, and when she got back to Los Angeles – which would hopefully be soon – her sister's phone calls would no longer be returned, her emails deleted, the text messages ignored, just as Beth was being ignored right now.

She wondered why, at this point, she was even bothering with this little trek. So *what* if Jen and her friends had moved on to another bar? She obviously didn't care about Beth, so why should Beth care about her?

But before she headed back to the ship to grab her suitcase, she wanted to see Jen, just to let her know exactly what she thought of her. Right now Beth was savouring – was fuelled by – the thought of telling Jen off once and for all.

This was, of course, based on the assumption that she'd be able to find her. Jen's crowd seemed to be migrating, and just because Meat Without Feet had overheard them talking about going to this Emilio's place didn't mean they were still there.

But one could hope.

When she reached the top of the second block, she turned right as instructed, and found herself on a street that didn't quite jibe with the Playa Azul the tourists usually see. A simple turn and she seemed to have stepped into another world. A world that was a shade or two dingier, more rundown. Like some of the side streets in downtown Los Angeles.

One of the gangbanger cars, a souped-up Civic, was parked at the right-hand side of the road, a cluster of cigarette-smoking locals around it. Among them was a petulant-looking Mexican girl with bleach blonde hair and jeans pulled down so low that you could see the whale tail of her thong.

Beth crossed the street to avoid them, but she couldn't help thinking that the girl reminded her of Jen.

The alley leading to Emilio's was about half a block up, a faded, hand-painted sign pointing the way.

Beth hesitated as she approached.

Was this somewhere she really wanted to go?

Reaching the mouth of the narrow alleyway, she peered inside. The sun was blocked by the buildings, the lighting dim. She saw the entrance to the place at the far end, past a row of battered aluminium trash cans.

The door was closed, with an unlit neon sign above it that read EMILIO'S CANTINA.

Was it even open?

A muscular Mexican man in a white T-shirt – who looked as if he'd feel right at home with the gang-bangers across the street – was leaning on the wall near the trash cans, a cell phone glued to his ear.

He looked up when Beth appeared, assessing her in the same way Peter used to look at her whenever she stepped out of the shower in the morning.

Maybe this wasn't a good idea after all.

Stopping just inside the alley entrance, she pulled out her own cell phone, and dialled Jen one last time. But again it went straight to voicemail and she imme-diately hung up.

The guy near the trash cans was still staring at her. Smiling now as he continued to talk on the phone.

Beth quickly texted a message to Jen:

FUCK YOU. I'M GONE.

Thinking that that pretty much summed it all up, she turned to leave, but found Eric the fisherman standing directly behind her. He snapped his own cell phone shut and pocketed it.

'You find your sister?'

Startled, Beth stepped back. 'You scared the hell out of me.'

'Sorry,' he said. 'Bad habit.'

She didn't know what he meant by that, but didn't like the sound of it. 'Were you following me?'

'Didn't have to. I already knew where you were going.'

Beth studied him, suddenly realizing what this was about. 'You never saw my sister at Armando's. You made it all up.'

'A little bit of improv. I tend to go with what works.'

Frightened now, and feeling foolish for letting herself be duped – especially since she should know better – Beth tried to move around him, but he sidestepped and threw his hands out, blocking her way.

'What's your hurry, sweet stuff? You don't find me attractive?'

She glanced across the street at the gangbangers, but knew they wouldn't be any help. Without a word, she brought her knee up into the fisherman's crotch.

He grunted and doubled over and Beth started around him again, but before she could clear the alleyway, hands grabbed her from behind and swung her around, slamming her against the wall.

The impact knocked the wind out of her, and standing in front of her now was the Mexican man with the cell phone.

Without a word, he brought a fist up and smashed it against the side of her head.

She felt as if she'd been hit with a club.

Pain blossomed in her skull and her legs buckled. She sank to the alley floor as a whirlwind of darkness swirled inside her.

And although she fought as hard as she could to keep it at bay . . .

. . . a moment later, the darkness won.

41

For the next several minutes (hours?), she drifted in and out of consciousness, voices hovering somewhere above her.

Jesus, you really smacked the hell out of the bitch.

You still got your pelotas, *white boy?*

Fuck you.

She felt hands on her body, patting her down, checking the pockets of her jeans, and she tried to resist, but the darkness was pulling at her again.

She was gone for a while, then:

How much?

Hundred twenty bucks.

Shit.

Better than the last one. At least she's got some credit cards, too.

Then she was gone again, only to be awakened by hot breath in her face, a hand squeezing her right breast, finger flicking the nipple.

Looks like we'll have to take a rain check, sweet stuff.

She wanted to scream, but then the darkness came again and she floated there for a very long time.

*

The sun was down when she awoke.

Her head pounding.

She lay there a moment, trying to get her bearings, not sure where she was, then suddenly remembered the alleyway and Emilio's Cantina and the two men who had attacked her.

Meat Without Feet.

Bringing her hand to her chest, she discovered that her blouse had been ripped open, her bra askew.

Oh, Jesus.

She patted the rest of her body, and found that her jeans were still fastened, which meant (at least she hoped it did) that she hadn't been raped. She also didn't seem to be leaking anywhere. No blood or other fluids.

Another good sign.

But none of this kept her from feeling violated, and she started to cry.

How could she be so fucking stupid?

She dealt with victims of violent crime every day of her life and she couldn't believe she'd let herself fall prey to these bastards.

Wiping her face on her sleeve, she pulled herself upright and looked around, half afraid they might still be nearby.

But they were long gone.

She was alone in the alley, the sounds of the city like some distant, familiar tune filtered through a throbbing membrane.

She slowly got to her feet, wobbling slightly. Straightened her bra, buttoned her blouse.

She looked around at the grimy alley floor. It was dark in here, but there was enough light from the adjacent street that she could see that her purse was gone, along with her money and credit cards. The only thing they'd left behind was Jen's passport, which lay near the trash cans.

She crossed to them, bent down and picked it up, then opened it to the photo page and stared at Jen's smiling face.

Had they gotten to her, too?

Was that why she had disappeared?

Was she lying in an alleyway like this one, unconscious or worse, unable to call for help?

The police.

Beth had no choice but to go to the police.

Head still pounding, she moved out of the alleyway and searched the street, seeing nothing but parked cars.

The gangbangers were gone.

She headed towards the lights of the main drag, its sidewalks teeming with tourists. And when she reached the top of the block she saw one:

A blue-and-white police car, parked near a taco stand.

She moved towards it, waving her hands, signalling to the officer for help.

42

'*Cual es tu nombre?*'

'What is your name?'

The cop behind the desk didn't speak English, so he had pulled over a bilingual secretary to translate.

'Elizabeth Crawford,' Beth said. Her head was pounding worse than ever and she was convinced that she was on the verge of a fully fledged migraine.

The officer nodded and scribbled on the piece of paper in front of him. '*De dónde eres?*'

'Where are you from?'

Beth was no stranger to police stations. Her job required her to work closely with the Los Angeles police, and a week didn't go by without a visit to Parker Center, or one of the substations located throughout the city.

But this was her first experience with a Mexican station. And so far, it hadn't been good.

When she'd flagged the cop near the taco stand, his first reaction had been to tell her to move along. She was just another in a string of drunken American touristas who had interrupted his dinner.

It took her a while to convince him that she'd been attacked, and after a medic had been called and she'd been cleared of any major physical damage, he finally drove her to a nearby station.

Somewhere in the middle of it all, she heard the distant blast of the cruise ship's horn, and she knew it was leaving port, taking her suitcase and Jen's belongings with it.

She wondered for a moment if Jen was back onboard, partying with Rafael and Marta, but that didn't seem likely. After hours of battling her fluctuating emotions, she was convinced now that something terrible had happened. That, for once, Jen was in trouble not of her own making. She was also convinced that Rafael and Marta were behind it.

Beth had spent a good twenty minutes sitting on a bench in the police station next to a pair of hookers in handcuffs who had rattled on endlessly. Despite the language barrier, she figured they were complaining about what every hooker in the known universe complained about: asshole johns and abusive pimps.

Every once in a while, they'd glance in her direction and laugh, and she could only be thankful that at least somebody had something to laugh about on this godforsaken day.

She, on the other hand, had just wanted to cry, her face already streaked with dried tears.

But she hadn't let herself. It was time to be strong. Assertive. She might not have been in LA, but that was no reason to play the submissive victim.

Unable to take the wait any longer, she had got to her feet, gone over to the reception desk and demanded that she be seen immediately.

After being passed through three or four different people – most of whom spoke only broken English and had no idea what she was ranting about – she had finally landed at this desk, sitting across from an overweight man in a tight blue uniform shirt.

'*De dónde eres?*' the cop asked again.

Before the translator could speak, Beth held a hand up. She was tired and cranky and her vision was starting to double. She suddenly felt detached from the world, as if she were observing this moment through a dream of some kind.

'Is there any way we can get past all this and concentrate on finding my sister?'

The translator, a cute twentysomething with blood-red nails that were long enough to give Fu Manchu a run for his money, smiled politely, then did her job and came back with: 'Your sister was also attacked?'

Beth was at her wit's end. Tried to remain calm.

'How many times do I have to say this? She's been missing since just before noon. She went into a leather goods store and never came out. I think I may know who's behind it, and if you can just contact the cruise company, I'm sure we can get the information we need.'

After the translation, the cop nodded, then tapped the paper in front of him, as if it were the most important document in the world. '*De dónde eres?*'

This was going nowhere fast.

'California,' Beth said sharply. 'I'm from goddamn California. You happy now?'

Her head was killing her, and she needed to talk to someone who a) gave a damn about what she had to say; b) had some muscle around here; and c) spoke fucking English.

'Look,' she said to the translator, trying to keep the frustration out of her voice, 'is there someone else who can help me?'

The girl shook her head. 'You must understand, señorita, that we see many touristas who are missing loved ones.'

'Which means what?'

'People come here to drink and have fun. Sometimes they get lost, most times they are found. In between, there is paperwork.'

'In other words, I'm out of luck.'

'That is not what I said. I heard you talking to Eduardo at the front desk and I know you are worried about your sister, but it is our experience that such matters usually resolve themselves. You will see. She will be with you before the night is over.'

If only, Beth thought. But this was a waste of time. Without somebody lighting a fire under these people's asses, she might as well . . .

A sudden thought occurred to her.

Peter.

Peter had recently prosecuted a drug smuggling case that was brought to him by a joint American–Mexican task force. He was bound to know somebody with some pull down here. At least it was worth a shot.

She needed to call him.

She looked at the secretary. 'My cell phone was stolen. Is there a phone I can use?'

'*Si, señorita*.' The girl said, then pointed. 'You'll find a pay-phone around the corner and down the hall.'

The fat cop said something abrupt and nasty sounding and the secretary snapped her head towards him, giving it right back. Beth had no idea what they'd said, and figured that was probably for the best.

Thanking the girl, she stood up, and immediately felt a rush of dizziness. Had to grab the chair for support.

'Are you all right, señorita?'

'Yes,' Beth lied, then headed across the room in the direction of the phone.

43

The hallway around the corner seemed different than the rest of the station. Cleaner, better lit.

It almost looked like a hospital corridor.

But this could simply have been Beth's imagination. The migraine was in full blossom now and her vision kept going in and out of focus, making it difficult to see.

Down at the far end of the hall, a man in a bathrobe and pyjamas stood at the pay-phone, speaking quietly into the receiver.

That was a first. But then it was her experience that just about anything can happen in a police station.

As she approached, the man hung up and moved past her, nodding and smiling as he went.

Beth didn't return the smile. The anvil being hammered inside her head made it too difficult to think, let alone respond.

She stepped up to the phone on the wall and picked up the receiver. She was about to reach into her purse for some change, when she remembered it had been stolen.

Wonderful. Now what?

Then she realized she could hear a buzzing sound, a dial tone coming from the receiver. Maybe this wasn't a pay-phone, after all, but the Mexican *policía*'s version of a courtesy phone. That didn't explain the coin slot, but Beth wasn't about to look a gift horse in the mouth.

Putting the receiver to her ear, she dialled zero, and to her surprise, got a live operator instead of a recording. One who actually spoke English.

The operator asked for a number and Beth gave her Peter's cell phone number from memory.

It was a long-distance call from here, but the operator didn't seem concerned, and a moment later, the line began to ring.

At the third ring, a familiar voice answered.

'Hello?'

'Peter, it's Beth.'

There was silence on the line. And it went on too long.

'Peter?'

'I'm here. What do you want?'

She wasn't sure where to start. Over the past several months, things had become so strained between them, even a simple conversation was difficult. Her resentment towards him had been too hard to disguise.

But could anyone blame her?

It's a unique feeling to discover that you've been cheated on. A mix of hurt and rage and complete inadequacy. You feel as if you've somehow failed the relationship, you wonder about your ability to satisfy your mate both emotionally and physically, and every good memory you have of the two of you together is now tainted, filtered through a nightmare of stained sheets and writing bodies.

You have been betrayed. The trust is gone.

And in Beth and Peter's case, that trust was irretrievable.

So, whenever they spoke, her resentment was clear. But she had to tuck it away for now. There were more pressing things to think about, and her head was pounding so hard that she thought she might pass out before she finished telling him what was going on.

'Peter,' she said. 'I'm down in Mexico. Baja Norte. Jen and I took a cruise and after we docked in Playa Azul, she disappeared.' She started to cry now. 'She's gone, Peter. I don't know where she went, but I need your—'

'Beth, stop.'

His voice was a slap to the face.

'What?'

'You have to stop calling me like this.'

'What are you talking about? I hardly ever—'

'You're up to twice a week now. Do you realize that?' A pause. 'Of course you don't.'

Beth was at a loss. He wasn't making any sense. Other than curt hellos in the office – which was thankfully big enough for some distance – they hadn't spoken in over a month.

'Peter, listen to me. This isn't about us. It's Jen. I think someone may have—'

'Jen's dead, Beth.'

Another slap. Followed by a rolling wave of nausea.

'She's been missing for almost a year,' he said. 'And we all know what that means.'

'How can you say something like that? That's crazy.'

'Listen to me. Take a look around you. What do you see?'

'I—'

'Just do it, Beth. Look around.'

Thoroughly confused now, her migraine going into overdrive, Beth looked around the hallway, but it was the same as before. Clean, well lit . . .

Wait. No. Not the same.

Through doubling vision, she could see that on the far side of the corridor was what looked like a . . .

. . . A nurse's station.

What the hell?

How could she have missed that?

Turning back to the phone, she discovered that it wasn't a pay-phone at all. Just a small black box mounted on the wall, with no coin slot. A sign next to it read, PATIENT USE ONLY.

And when she glanced down at her clothes, she realized that she, too, was wearing a bathrobe.

She started to tremble.

'Peter, what . . . ?'

'You're not in Mexico, Beth. You're in a private rehabilitation clinic in Los Angeles. Jen disappeared almost a year ago and is presumed dead.'

'What?' Beth cried. 'That's impossible. I just saw her—'

'No. You need to focus. Concentrate on the here and now.'

'What are you talking about? Peter, what's going on?'

'You're hallucinating,' he said.

'How could that be? That's crazy.'

Then all at once she realized that it wasn't so crazy after all, as the corridor around her came into sharp focus, Playa Azul and the police station and the cruise ship and Jen all sliding down a dark memory hole.

And all she could hear was Peter.

'Someone shot you, Beth. Someone shot you in the head.'

PATIENT'S JOURNAL

Day 58?
10.20 a.m.

I don't remember the shooting, but I'll never forget the pain. That's what I wrote two days ago.

But I was wrong. I do forget.

And not just the pain, but about where I am. Why I'm here.

Thanks to the bullet fragments lodged in my brain, and the damage to the surrounding tissue, to the three haemorrhagic strokes that I'm lucky to have survived, I'm often whisked away to another place and time. A hallucination so real that I actually believe I'm living it.

Or *re*living it.

Those two days with Jen did happen.

I know that. They will forever be a part of me.

But for some reason, I can't seem to get beyond them. I live them over and over, each time as vivid as the last, and the only thing keeping me sane are these few lucid moments when I look around me and see a hospital room. When I can stare down at these words I've written and know that there is a part of me fighting this thing, struggling to push through the membrane, to move beyond the darkness into the light.

And while I can remember the pain at these moments, the spiked-heel, hot white pain in my head and the fire in my chest as I lay on wet pavement listening to a distant radio, I can't for the life of me remember how I got there.

Or how I wound up here.

The last real, fully formed memory I have is standing in that Mexican police station, nearly a year ago, feeling hurt and frustrated and angry.

But most of all worried.

About a girl I grew up with. A girl I took care of during the worst moments of our lives.

A girl I failed at the most crucial moment of all.

She wasn't perfect, but neither am I. She was family. The only family I had. And despite our differences, I loved her. I still love her.

And each time I learn that she's gone is as potent and as heartbreaking as the last.

The doctors tell me that their science is imperfect. That the study of the brain is still a work in progress and they can't be sure that I'll ever again be whole. Or that the nightmare I keep reliving will ever stop.

I am trapped, it seems, in my own private hell.

Alone.

Afraid.

And wanting to die.

TWO

LA SANTISIMA

VARGAS

44

Vargas breathed a sigh of relief when Mr Blister put the flashlight away.

He'd had visions of joining Harmon and the Ainsworths on the ground, but Mr Blister seemed to have either forgotten his suspicions or had simply dismissed them, and went about cleaning up his mess.

Taking hold of Harmon's arms, he dragged him out of view behind the cars, then reappeared on the steps, dropping him inside the house.

A moment later, he returned for Junior, then Ainsworth. After dragging them into the living room, he came back outside, climbed into Harmon's cruiser and started it, driving around towards the back of the house.

A good strategy, Vargas thought. Hide the bodies, get the cop's car out of sight, and the chances of anyone finding them within the next couple of days were pretty remote. This egg ranch had obviously long been out of business, and while Harmon's disappearance would eventually trigger a search, Vargas figured it would be a while before they thought of Ainsworth. Plenty enough time for Mr Blister and whoever he worked for to finish covering their tracks – which probably wouldn't be all that difficult.

What Vargas had learned in his years as a reporter is that in this country nearly forty per cent of all crimes go unsolved. And in a border town, cop murder or not, the percentage grows even higher.

The moment Harmon's cruiser rolled out of view, Vargas jumped to his feet, scrambled through the warehouse doorway and around the side of the building. A precautionary measure, just in case Mr Blister got suspicious again and decided to use his flashlight.

Vargas waited there for several minutes before he heard shuffling sounds in the yard, then the slam of a trunk lid. A moment later, an engine roared to life.

Chancing a peek around the corner, he saw the Town Car back up, then lurch forward down the drive towards the dirt road.

His first instinct was to follow the story. Wait for Mr Blister to reach the main drag, then sprint towards the construction site, jump into his Corolla and tail the guy.

But who was he kidding? He'd never get there in time. And he'd probably collapse from exhaustion before he even reached his car.

Besides, there was another part of the puzzle he needed. The real story.

And it was inside that house.

When the Town Car was gone, he crossed to the steps and went in through the front door.

Mr Blister had doused the lights, but Vargas could see the dark shapes of the bodies in the moonlight, laid out in a neat row, all three of the men well beyond help.

Looking down at Ainsworth and Junior, he thought about what they'd done to him and, despite this, he felt sorry for them. They'd gotten themselves caught up in something over their heads and he'd been the unfortunate victim of it. Junior, most of all, hadn't deserved to die this way. He'd been little more than a child in a man's body.

Harmon, however, was another story altogether. In Vargas's view, there was nothing worse than a corrupt cop – especially a border cop – and Harmon had obviously been a willing accessory to drug smugglers. Still, that didn't mean the punishment he'd received was justified.

Crouching next to Junior, Vargas unbuttoned the kid's shirt and found a thin rawhide string tied loosely around his neck.

I got her necklace, he'd said. *I'm wearin' it right now*.

Hanging from the string was a small, cheap ring. The kind you'd find at one of the street side jewellery stands down in Juarez, or at various tourist spots around Mexico. This one was a crude, black and silver carving of a hooded skull.

La Santisima.

Holy Death.

Vargas untied the string and moved to a lamp, flicking it on. He studied the ring more closely, but there was no sign of any engraving. Nothing that might clue him in to the identity of the American woman.

Pocketing the ring, he turned off the light, then found the stairs and climbed to the first floor. At the top of the landing were three open doorways.

Moving from one to the next, he flicked on the overhead light in each.

Two bedrooms and a TV room.

Figuring the one with posters of Elvis on the wall must be Junior's, he went inside.

I got her picture, too. I keep it in my drawer.

There was a three-drawer dresser in the corner, Jailhouse Rock Elvis pinned to the wall above it.

Vargas pulled open the top drawer. Socks and underwear.

He dug around a bit, but found nothing else.

He closed it, then moved on to the second drawer. T-shirts and jeans. Digging around again, he found a small metal box near the back.

Bingo.

He pulled it out, lifted the lid.

There wasn't much inside. Just a few childhood treasures: a small, sand-worn stone, a faded Elvis Aaron Presley baseball card, a wooden, dirt-encrusted baby's rattle, several Mexican coins, a tarnished silver bracelet—

—and a photo of a young white woman.

Vargas removed the photo from the box, studied it more closely, and realized it had been torn from a passport. No name, just an official seal and the image: a strikingly beautiful woman in her mid- to late twenties.

Was she the one? The one they'd found?

Angie?

If Vargas were a betting man, he'd put money on it. It was her all right. But what had she been doing in that abandoned desert house? And how was she related to the people who had threatened him?

There was only one way to find out. He'd have to return to Juarez and talk to the Mexican homicide investigator, Rojas. The one who had sanitized the murder file.

Ainsworth may have been right, that they were simply avoiding an international headache, but that didn't keep Vargas from wanting to know what had happened to this woman. If she was alive when they found her, had she survived?

And if she had, where was she now?

Confronting Rojas might be risky. For all Vargas knew, he could be part of all this.

But things were different now.

Too many people were dead.

A couple of hours ago, Vargas had almost turned tail and run. But now, this was more than an itch. More than curiosity. More than an attempt to suppress his shame.

And the only way you'd stop him from seeking out the truth . . .

. . . was with a well-placed bullet.

45

He spent the rest of the night in his car.

After leaving Ainsworth's ranch, he'd started to feel a little woozy, so he drove out of Montoya and found a nearly deserted WalMart parking lot in a neighbouring suburb.

He pulled into a spot near a brick wall, put his suitcase in the trunk (hesitating only slightly before lifting the lid), then curled up in the Toyota's back seat and shut his eyes.

By the time he opened them again, the sun was shining and the lot was full.

Vargas went into WalMart and bought himself an Egg McMuffin at the McDonald's inside. Around about his third bite, however, he started thinking about eggs and Ainsworth and the bodies in that living room, and felt a little queasy.

Before leaving Ainsworth's house, he had picked up the phone, dialled 911, then left the receiver off the hook.

He knew he should have done more, but that would only have resulted in a lot of questions from a lot of angry cops, and that wasn't a battle he could afford to get into. At least the bodies would be found a lot sooner than Mr Blister and his buddies had planned.

Tossing the McMuffin in the trash can, he went into the restroom and washed his face. The bandage on his head was getting bloody, so he removed it, soaked up some of the remaining blood with a few paper towels, then found the health and beauty section of the store and picked up some gauze and tape.

Before he hit the register, he searched the sporting goods section for a hat to cover the wound, and settled on a grey-and-red Texas Rangers baseball cap.

Back in his car, he did his best to tape himself up again, including a fresh new bandage on his hand, then pulled the Rangers cap down tight, started the engine and drove.

Heading back up to Las Cruces, he took the 10, driving two hundred and seventy miles to Tucson, Arizona, before cutting down through Green Valley and rolling on into Nogales.

He could probably have entered Mexico through El Paso again, but figured the farther away he stayed from that particular border station, the better off he'd be. There was no telling who might be working for Mr Blister's friends, and – assuming they were still alive – Vargas figured it was better to be safe than sorry.

He was, after all, the scared little bunny. And the longer Mr Blister believed that, the better off he'd be.

He was just about five miles out of Nogales when he heard a news report on his radio:

'Sources say a high-ranking border patrol agent and two unidentified men were found dead on a ranch in

El Paso, Texas, this morning. Police are investigating, and the source tells *Eyewitness News* that a motive for the crime has yet to be established.'

Vargas felt another wave of nausea as he listened. If he didn't know before just how lucky he was that they'd let him go, he certainly knew it now.

Getting through the border station in Nogales was an effortless enterprise. Nobody cares if you go into Mexico. The more money you spend, the more they'll love you. It's the reverse trip that creates all the headaches. America's racist paranoia clearly broadcast 24/7.

Once he was across, he found a motel and checked in for the rest of the day. He was feeling woozy again and needed to sleep. He bought a couple of quesadillas at a lunch wagon parked outside the motel, and washed them down with a bottle of lime Jarritos.

Then he crawled into bed, staring up at the rotating blades of the ceiling fan. Today was even hotter than yesterday, and he wondered if this heat wave would ever pass.

As he lay there, thinking about the house in the desert, he took the passport photo from his back pocket and studied it.

This American woman, whoever she was, had mischievous eyes and a million-dollar smile. The kind of woman men get in bar fights over. The kind who makes you regret you ever got involved with her in the first place, no matter how good she is in bed.

Maybe that's why she was in that house with a bullet in her chest.

Maybe she'd pushed someone too far.

Tomorrow morning – Monday – Vargas would get up well before dawn and take Highway 2 back into Ciudad Juarez. By the time he got there, the state police station would be open and Rojas was bound to be in his office.

But no whitewash this time. No missing crime scene photos or doctored police reports.

Vargas wasn't about to take any bullshit from Rojas. This time he wanted the fucking truth.

46

Rojas wasn't in his office.

Even though Vargas had gotten a 3 a.m. start, the drive to Juarez had been interminably long and almost unbearably hot, and by the time he reached the state police station, he felt as if he'd taken a bath in his own sweat.

The bandage on his head had become so drenched that he'd pulled it off and left it off, simply covering the damage with his new baseball cap. The bleeding seemed to have stopped, anyway.

Parking his car, he went inside to blessed air conditioning and found the homicide unit. The office looked the same as before: A reception counter adjacent to a waist-high entry gate. Dingy beige walls decorated with newspaper clippings and photos of wanted suspects. Half a dozen cluttered desks butted up against one another.

Today, they were all empty except one, where a young detective was leaning back in his chair, talking on a cell phone. Vargas remembered seeing him the last time he was here, but they'd never been introduced.

He waited, trying not to listen in on the conversation. The detective was speaking Spanish, but Vargas had no trouble understanding him. Growing up, he had been trapped in a kind of limbo between two cultures, raised in a country that spoke English by parents who rarely ever did. Much of the time he found himself thinking in Spanish, but in these last few days he'd been bouncing back and forth between the US and Mexico so frequently that he'd begun to blend the two languages, sometimes forgetting where he was.

'Come on, Carmelita,' the detective said. 'You know she means nothing to me. She asked for a ride, so I gave her one.'

He nodded to Vargas and held up a finger, indicating he'd be with him in a moment.

'No, baby, that's not true. If I wanted to be with her, I would have stayed married to her. Look, I gotta go. You still want me to come by tonight?' He listened a moment, then smiled. 'That's my girl. See you around 11.'

He clicked off, looked up at Vargas. He was a handsome kid with a wisp of hair above his lip that was supposed to be a moustache. He kept his piece in a shoulder holster, trying hard to look like Steve McQueen in *Bullitt*, but not quite pulling it off.

'You have a girlfriend?' he asked.

Vargas shook his head. 'Not lately.'

'Do yourself a favour and keep it that way. I give my ex a ride home, and now I'll be spending the night apologizing for it. Women are nothing but trouble.'

It was Vargas's experience – with few exceptions – that women were only trouble if you treated them that way, but he wasn't about to argue with the guy. Someone his age wouldn't get it anyway.

Instead, Vargas said, 'I'm looking for Rojas.'

The detective got to his feet, came over to the counter. 'You're the reporter, right? You were here last week.'

'That's right,' Vargas said. 'Is he around?'

'Not at the moment, no. You here about the Casa murders again?'

'Yes.'

'That case is as good as dead. Not one lead. I did some of the footwork on it, and we got nothing.'

'Maybe I can help you with that.'

The detective's eyebrows went up. 'You have information?'

'Yes,' Vargas said, 'but I'll only talk to Rojas.'

'I told you, he's not here. Why don't you tell me what you know and I'll—'

'Not gonna happen,' Vargas said, making it clear by the tone of his voice that he was leaving no wriggle room. It was Rojas or nothing.

The detective nodded, then held up a finger again. Moving back to his desk, he picked up his cell phone, dialled, then waited a few moments before speaking quietly into it.

Vargas couldn't hear him this time, but he knew what was being said.

After a few moments, the detective clicked off, then stuffed the phone into his back pocket.

'You hungry?'

Vargas shrugged. Truth was, he was famished, but he saw no reason to point that out. 'I could eat.'

'Good,' the detective said. 'Rojas has invited us to breakfast.'

47

The restaurant was in the heart of Juarez, a tiny hole-in-the-wall with a walk-up ordering counter and a backyard patio sheltered by trees.

Rojas sat at a table in the shade of a laurel, a large man with a short, military haircut, looking very much like the Mexican Army general he once was. He was halfway through a plate of chorizo and eggs when Vargas and the young detective – whose name was Garcia – approached.

'Have you ordered something?' he asked.

'Not yet,' Garcia told him.

Rojas frowned and gestured to a young woman nearby who was pouring water for another customer. 'Anna, bring my two associates some breakfast. And I'll have another plate as well.'

The woman nodded and, like an obedient servant, quickly disappeared inside.

Rojas gestured for them to sit.

'Best homemade chorizo you'll ever eat,' he said to Vargas. 'My promise to you.'

Vargas sank into a chair. 'I don't know. My mother's was hard to beat.'

'Was? She's no longer with us?'

Vargas shook his head. 'Cancer.'

Rojas crossed himself and raised a glass of water in toast. 'May Jesus smile upon her.' He took a sip and set the glass down. 'Let me revise my promise. What you're about to experience is the second-best chorizo you'll ever eat.'

Vargas wasn't quite sure why it mattered – but then it dawned on him. 'This is your restaurant?'

'It is,' Rojas said. 'Been in the family for over sixty years. People come from miles away to eat here.'

'An institution,' Garcia said.

Rojas shot him a look, as if he were an annoying fly, then smiled at Vargas. 'We'll eat first. Then talk.'

So they ate, Rojas telling them stories of his child-hood, working like a dog in the kitchen and wanting nothing more than to escape its hell. Then, once he joined the military, he found that he missed the place and, years later, when his older brother decided against taking the reins from their father, Rojas had agreed to run the business.

His version of running it, however, seemed to be to bark the occasional order to one of the staff as he chowed down on his second plate of sausage.

Vargas paid little attention to it all, merely nodding politely as he ate the chorizo, which, it turned out, was not the second-best he had ever tasted.

It was *better* than his mother's, God rest her soul, and as he shovelled it down, he realized he'd been more than famished. Although he had stopped for food along the way, he felt as if he hadn't had a bite to eat in days.

When they were finally done, Rojas said, 'What happened to your hand?'

Vargas glanced at the bandage covering the puncture wound, which was starting to look a little haggard.

'Long story.'

'But that's why you're here, yes? To tell it? Garcia says you have information about the Casa de la Muerte murders.'

Vargas nodded. He had been wondering all through breakfast how to broach the subject, and had decided that the direct approach was best.

'I'm offering an exchange.'

Rojas hesitated. This obviously wasn't what he had expected to hear. 'What sort of exchange?'

'I'll tell you what I know,' Vargas said. 'And you tell me the truth about what happened in that house.'

'Truth? I gave you unfettered access to my case files. Names, dates, all of it. What more could you want?'

Vargas reached into his back pocket and brought out the passport photo, laying it on the table in front of Rojas.

'You forgot to tell me about her,' he said.

He couldn't be sure, but he thought he heard Garcia involuntarily suck in a breath. He glanced at him, but Garcia had quickly recovered, his expression blank and oddly incurious as he looked at the photo.

Rojas, however, didn't flinch.

'What's to tell? I've never seen her before. Is she a friend of yours?'

'Come on, Rojas, I know she was in that house. And she was still alive when the Ainsworths found her.'

'Ahhh,' Rojas said. 'The Ainsworths. You take the word of a couple of *gabachos* over mine?' He looked at his associate. 'Garcia, I believe I've just been insulted. In my own place of business, no less.'

Garcia nodded, but said nothing.

'You were at the crime scene,' Rojas continued. 'Tell Mr Vargas what we found that night.'

It may have been Vargas's imagination, but Garcia seemed a bit stiff, as if he were about to lie and wasn't quite comfortable doing it.

'Five bodies,' he said. 'All of them nuns from the Iglesia del Corazón Sagrado in Ciudad de Almas.'

The words were spoken with about as much passion as a campaign worker who doesn't really believe in his candidate.

'You see?' Rojas said to Vargas. 'Your American friends are mistaken.' He wiped his mouth with his napkin. 'There's no doubting that the case is unusual, considering who the victims were, but as I told you before, our investigation has established that they were simply trying to get across the border and fell prey to bandits.'

'So then the name Angie means nothing to you?'

Vargas made a point to watch Garcia, whose poker game didn't even come close to the level of Rojas's. But this time the younger detective betrayed nothing.

'I'm afraid not,' Rojas said. 'And while I'd never presume to tell you your job, I can assure you that pursuing this particular angle will only result in disappointment.'

Was that a threat? Vargas couldn't be sure.

For a moment he wondered if Rojas was Juarez's

answer to Harmon, but the guy didn't strike him as someone who would be willing to take orders from anyone, let alone Mr Blister and his friends. But money was a different story. There was no doubt that in one way or another, the man was dirty. Vargas could see it in his eyes.

Rojas dropped his napkin to the table and leaned back. 'You mentioned an exchange. And now that I've lived up to my end of the deal, it's time for you to tell me what you know.'

'I asked for the truth,' Vargas said.

'And that's what I've given you. I even included a wonderful breakfast.' He smiled. 'Now it's your turn.'

There was something in that smile that said refusal was not an option, and Vargas knew he was on dangerous ground here. Mess with a cop in Juarez – especially one as powerful as Rojas – and you might find yourself in a very confined space, sharing your body heat with a new roommate.

But if Rojas and Garcia could lie, so could Vargas. And his poker game was pretty damn good.

'You caught me,' he said. 'I've got nothing. I was bluffing.'

Rojas's smile abruptly disappeared, his voice flat and unamused. 'Then I believe we're done.'

Vargas didn't move. Nodded to the photo. 'Not until you tell me who she is.'

Rojas took it from the table and without looking at it, ripped it in two pieces and tossed them at Vargas.

'A product of your imagination,' he said. 'And we both know what kind of trouble that will bring you.'

48

'You shouldn't have provoked him,' Garcia said. 'He's as bad as Carmelita. He'll blame me for ruining his breakfast.'

They were in Vargas's car, driving back to the station.

'All he had to do was tell me the truth.'

Garcia laughed. 'You don't know Rojas.'

'Then educate me.'

Garcia looked at him a moment, weighing the request. Then he said, 'The man is a pig. That story he told you about taking over the family business? He didn't mention that he stabbed his brother twice to convince him to step aside.'

'So why wasn't he arrested?'

'His brother denied it. Blamed the attack on a gang of teenagers. Three of them are still in jail.'

'Why are you telling me this?'

Garcia shrugged. 'Probably because I despise the man. Believe it or not, not all Mexican cops are corrupt. We're hard-working people, trying to do good and make a living at the same time. The drug cartels are out of control down here, treating people as if they're disposable. And trying to stop them is hard enough without *pendejos* like Rojas tainting the department.' He paused. 'But Rojas also has a lot of friends, so if you ever repeat what I've just said, I'll deny it.'

'Tell me about the girl in the photo.'

Garcia shifted his gaze to the street, which was filled with the passing hustle and bustle of downtown Juarez. 'That subject is off limits.'

'Then it's true. She *was* there.'

'Did I say that?' He shook his head, then pointed at the road. 'Drop me off around the corner. I want to get my hair cut for Carmelita.'

'I'll keep your name out of it,' Vargas said. 'An anonymous source.'

Garcia laughed again. 'You know even less about this city than you do about Rojas. No one is anonymous here. Not for long. And it doesn't help that I'm riding in your car.'

Vargas made a left at the next corner and pulled up alongside a shop with the word PELUQUERIA painted on the window. Inside, a barber was busy cleaning the hair out of his electric clippers.

'It must kill you,' Vargas said.

'What?'

'Seeing a man like Rojas in power. You say he taints the department, but what he carries is more like a virus that grows and spreads, infecting everyone who comes in contact with it. You'd better watch out, or you'll catch it, too.'

Garcia frowned at him, then opened his door and got out. Turning, he leaned in through the open passenger window. 'I don't think you were bluffing,' he said. 'You have more than a photograph to share.'

'Maybe. But there's only one way to find out. You know my terms.'

'This book you're writing. How many people will see it?'

'As many as it takes.'

Garcia thought about this a moment, then said, 'You like dancing?'

Vargas shrugged. 'Depends on what kind.'

'The kind where beautiful women show you only what their mothers and boyfriends should see.'

'One of my favourites,' Vargas said.

Garcia reached into his shirt pocket and handed a book of matches across to Vargas. 'Come watch Carmelita tonight. And if you buy me enough tequila, I might forget what it means to be cautious.'

And with that, he slapped a hand on top of the car and disappeared into the barber's shop.

49

Vargas wasn't ten minutes into his visit to the Velvet Glove when he learned what a woman can do with a simple ice cube. The dancer on stage was showing far more than what Garcia had promised, something no mother or boyfriend should *ever* see.

He had arrived shortly past 11, after spending another day in a motel room, trying to recover from his wounds. In his imaginary movie he would have bounced back by now, but this, unfortunately, was real life and sleep was his only cure.

When he wasn't sleeping, he watched Mexican TV, at one point finding himself caught up in an old black-and-white *lucha libre* movie.

One of the masked wrestlers reminded him of Rojas.

After grabbing a bite to eat at a restaurant next to his motel, Vargas checked the address on the matchbook Garcia had given him, asked the waiter for directions, and drove across town to a street lined with bars and nightclubs.

The Velvet Glove sat smack in the middle of the block, its darkened windows ringed in bright pink and purple neon.

Vargas paid an entrance fee, found a stool at the bar and ordered a beer. And as the dancer on stage finished demonstrating her amazing muscle control – the ice cube now a puddle of water beneath her – he felt a presence on the stool next to him.

'I'm supposed to be following you,' Garcia said.

'Oh?'

'Rojas wants to know what you're up to.'

Vargas nodded. 'Further proof that Ainsworth wasn't lying. He had a theory that the police were covering up about the American woman for fear of an international scandal.'

'Had?'

'He's dead. Along with his son, a guy named Sergio, and a border patrol agent who was working with them. They were all part of some anonymous drug ring.'

Garcia looked at him. 'Is this the information you were keeping from Rojas? Your so-called bluff?'

'More or less.'

'You've been busy this week.'

'You don't know the half of it.'

Garcia signalled to the bartender, holding up a finger. The Velvet Glove was an upscale establishment, and the bartender reflected this with her perfectly coiffed hair and her crisp white shirt, showing ample cleavage. She took a bottle of Patron from the shelf behind her, filled a shot glass and set it on the counter in front of Garcia.

When she was gone, he said, 'Rojas doesn't give a damn about international scandals.'

'Then why the whitewash?'

'To cover his backside. He's a powerful man and he uses that power to fatten his wallet. He doesn't want anyone from the outside poking around in his business and a dead American girl means *federales* and maybe even the FBI.'

'Does that business have anything to do with drug smugglers?'

Garcia snorted. 'Smugglers, thieves, politicians, extortionists. Rojas gets a taste of it all and offers allegiance to no one. But there have been a lot of kidnappings here in Juarez and all across Mexico in the past few years. Young women disappearing. Mostly factory workers and prostitutes, but quite a few touristas as well. Rojas has been under pressure to solve these cases, but he's as incompetent as he is corrupt. And his job is on the line. One more victimized tourista is more than he can afford.'

'The Ainsworths said she was alive when they found her.'

Garcia nodded. 'I'm surprised they said anything at all. Rojas paid them off to keep them quiet. Let them keep the treasures they'd looted and even gave them a few more.'

Vargas thought of the things he'd found in Junior's treasure box. Had any more of those treasures come from the crime scene?

'The Ainsworths didn't strike me as particularly trustworthy people.'

Garcia hadn't touched his drink, but he looked as

if he had just swallowed something hot and bitter. 'That virus you spoke of? It's about as virulent a strain as you're ever likely to see.'

'So what happened to her?'

'I was only at the crime scene at the very beginning. So I only know the rumours.'

'Which are?'

'When they first went in, they thought she was like the others. But then she moaned and they realized she was alive, but badly hurt. Two bullets in the chest. Rojas didn't wait for an ambulance. He put her in the back of his car and drove her to the hospital. Except he never got there.'

'Where did he take her?'

'Across the border into New Mexico. Dumped her in a parking lot, in a pool of her own blood – another victim of those degenerate Americans. And someone else's headache.'

'Where?'

'I'm not sure, but he was gone all night.'

'Is she alive?'

Garcia snorted again. 'Rojas may be incompetent, but he's thorough. The story goes that before he left her, he finished the job her attackers failed to complete.'

'He shot her.'

Garcia picked up the shot glass full of tequila now and drained it, his eyes flooded with contempt.

'He didn't just shoot her,' he said, then tapped a finger against his temple. 'He put a bullet in her brain.'

50

'So, in other words,' Vargas said, 'Rojas is a thug.'

Garcia signalled to the bartender for a refill. 'A well-protected thug. But that protection is wearing thin and he's worried. Which is why he ordered me to follow you.'

Vargas thought about this. If Rojas was directly connected to Mr Blister and friends, this conversation wouldn't be taking place and Vargas would probably be lying in his motel room just entering the early stages of rigor mortis.

But it didn't hurt to ask.

'So, tell me,' he said, 'have you ever seen him hanging around with a guy with a burnt face? Six one, Hispanic, long black hair?'

Before answering, Garcia waited for the bartender to pour his refill, his gaze lingering unapologetically on her chest.

When she was gone again, he said, 'Not that I remember. Is this someone I should know about?'

'A person of interest for the Casa murders. If he didn't do them himself, he's definitely connected to the people who did.'

Vargas took a folded square of paper from his shirt pocket and handed it to Garcia. He had written down the licence plate number of Mr Blister's car.

Garcia unfolded and read it. 'This is his?'

'A Lincoln Town Car. Probably stolen, but you never know.'

'Maybe you should be the one wearing the badge.'

'Just dumb luck, amigo. A matter of being in the wrong place at the right time.'

'We should all be so lucky,' Garcia said, then picked up his drink and drained it.

As he set the glass on the counter, a spotlight flashed on stage and Spanish rap music began to blast over the speakers. The curtain parted and a woman of about twenty stepped into the light wearing only flimsy lingerie – on a body that should have been declared illegal.

Turning, Garcia grinned. 'Carmelita,' he said. 'You see a creature like that and suddenly the world doesn't seem so bad after all.'

Vargas said nothing. Just nodded as Garcia's girlfriend launched into her act, a combination of dancing and acrobatics that put the ice-cube girl to shame.

When she was done, Garcia whistled and clapped loudly, and she gave him an appreciative smile as she gathered up her discarded clothes and a mountain of hundred-peso notes and dollar bills, then disappeared behind the curtain.

'Let's find a booth,' he said to Vargas. 'I have something I want you to see.'

Sliding off his stool, he reached to the floor and picked up a cheap leather satchel. Nodding towards the far side of the room, he gestured for Vargas to follow and they moved to a dark booth.

They slid in and Garcia placed the satchel on the table, then quickly unzipped it. He reached inside, pulled out a manila envelope and handed it across to Vargas.

Vargas turned it in his hands, then unfastened the flap and opened the envelope, taking out its contents.

Three photographs.

There was a domed candle on the tabletop. Vargas slid it over close and studied them in the flickering light.

Crime scene photos. Shots of the Casa de la Muerte bedroom, overlooking the blood-soaked mattress where two bodies lay, one of them a woman in a USC sweatshirt.

Angie.

Vargas took out the pieces of the passport photo he'd retrieved from Rojas's restaurant floor and laid them next to the crime scene photos.

Was it the same woman?

Hard to say. They looked similar, but the one in the crime scene photos was slightly older. Of course, the passport photo could be old, and two bullets in the chest has a way of ageing you. Hell, a couple of raps on the head had done a pretty good job on Vargas.

He looked up at Garcia. 'Have you tried to identify her?'

Garcia shook his head. 'Rojas doesn't even know I have these. If I start digging, asking questions, he's bound to find out and I'd just as soon keep them to myself. My own form of protection, you might say.'

He gathered up the crime scene photos, returned them to the envelope, then zipped it inside the satchel and slid it across to Vargas. 'My gift to you.'

'I assume you have copies?'

'Digitized and stored on three different thumb drives. Rojas is computer illiterate, so they're safe.'

'I take it this case will stay cold forever.'

'Only as long as Rojas is running things. But nothing is forever. He may be worried about you, but it's me and my thumb drives he should be watching for.'

Vargas nodded.

'Just one last question,' he said. 'Something I overheard that I've been curious about ever since.'

'Okay.'

'Have you ever heard of someone called El Santo?'

Garcia looked at him blankly, but as the name sank in, his face began to drain of colour. He said nothing for a long moment as another dancer took the stage and started stripping off her clothes to the cheers and applause of the regular patrons.

'Where did you hear this?' he asked.

'From the man with the burnt face. He said, "El Santo will bless him. El Santo will bless us all." And then there's this . . .' Vargas reached into his shirt pocket and pulled out the rawhide string with the ring attached. 'Ainsworth's son told me that the American woman was wearing it when they found her. It's only a cheap trinket, but it might have some significance.'

Garcia looked at it. His colour didn't return.

'La Santisima. What the hell have you gotten yourself involved in?'

'I'm not sure. That's why I'm asking.'

Garcia was quiet again. Then he said, 'You probably already know this, but worship of La Santisima is pretty common down here.'

Vargas nodded. His own parents, who were both Catholic and immigrants from Nuevo Laredo, had spoken of her. Known by many different names – La Santisima, Santa Muerte, Doña Sebastiana – she was a grim-reaper-like figure that many Latin Americans believed could perform miracles. All throughout Mexico you could find shrines to Saint Death, hooded statuettes surrounded by offerings of beads and flowers and bottles of tequila.

And while the Catholic Church frowned on such worship as counter to its beliefs, this didn't stop many of its followers from praying to her.

As far as Vargas knew, there was nothing sinister in any of this, but the discovery of this ring, coupled with Mr Blister's mention of El Santo – the Holy One – had raised a red flag.

It might be nothing. But then again it might be everything.

'Most of the time, this stuff is harmless,' Garcia said. 'Simple people praying for their health or their dying loved ones. But El Santo . . . that's a different matter altogether.'

'So who is he? Some kind of pagan god?'

'We're dealing in rumours again. Rumours that are far less reliable than the ones about Rojas. But it's said that there is a cult of La Santisima's followers, a cult that has distorted these simple beliefs and offers blood sacrifices in her honour. Led by someone known only as El Santo.'

'Blood sacrifices,' Vargas said. 'These don't sound like friendly people.'

'Just the opposite. El Santo is believed to be a messiah – the direct descendant of their god. And his followers will do anything he asks of them. Including kill.'

'Shades of Charlie Manson.'

'Some say they've been trafficking in drugs, but if that's true, they've managed to avoid territorial disputes with the other cartels. Not an easy thing to do.'

'Does this cult have a name?'

'I've heard it called by many different names. But the one that seems to stick is La Santa Muerte.'

The Holy Dead.

Vargas felt his gut tighten. The words triggered a memory. Something Junior had said.

You're a dead man.

You're one of the dead men.

Vargas thought about this a moment, then looked at Garcia.

'Thanks for your hospitality,' he said, 'but it's time for me to go.'

51

It took him nearly two hours to find it.

It was little more than a paragraph in the 14 August edition of the *Albuquerque Examiner*, a short blurb about the body of a female being discovered in the parking lot of a Taco Bell.

No identification, no description, but she'd been found by a security guard who was making his rounds.

The victim had 'multiple gunshot wounds', but was still alive and had been taken to Burke Memorial Hospital.

Albuquerque was nearly a four-hour drive from Juarez, but not beyond the bounds of possibility. If Rojas had been concerned enough about his career to commit murder, he surely wouldn't have hesitated to make the drive. The farther away from his jurisdiction, the better.

There were no follow-up stories. Nothing more about the victim – which, in Vargas's experience, was not unusual. There was a time when multiple gunshot wounds would have been big news, but nowadays such things were an everyday occurrence. Fresh new stories of violence popped up so frequently that the old ones were quickly forgotten.

Vargas stared at the computer screen and wondered what his next move should be.

He sat in an Internet cafe located in a strip mall on Triunfo de la Republica. After leaving the Velvet Glove, he had gone back to his motel and slept fitfully through the rest of the night, dreaming about Mexican wrestlers who looked like Rojas and Mr Blister and Charles Manson.

At one point, Carmelita entered the dream, buck naked, carrying a wad of cash in one hand and a tray of ice cubes in the other. But before she got three feet into the room, she morphed into La Santisima, a grinning skull in a red satin hood and, like something from one of his brother Manny's ghost stories, said, 'I want my ring. Give me my beautiful ring . . .'

Vargas had awakened at the crack of dawn, relieved to discover he was still in his motel room. He took a quick shower, checked his head wound and found it healing satisfactorily, then pulled on some fresh clothes, his baseball cap, and started driving, looking for an Internet cafe that opened early.

He'd found this one almost immediately.

After paying his fee, he went to a cubicle near the back, then fired up the computer and began his search. He had accounts with several newspaper archival services – expensive, but a professional necessity – and after two hours of searching had finally struck gold.

At least what he hoped was gold.

Pulling out his cell phone, he cycled through his address book and found the number of a guy named

William Brett, a reporter he'd met back in the old days who – if he recalled correctly – worked for the *Albuquerque Examiner*. He got him on the phone, reminded him who he was and discovered that Brett didn't need reminding.

'What do you want?' he asked.

As with many of Vargas's colleagues these days, there was unmistakable resentment in the guy's voice. Vargas had, after all, betrayed their profession and had tainted everyone in the process – much like Rojas had tainted the Chihuahua state police.

'I need a favour,' he said.

'Please don't tell me you're looking for a job.'

Vargas paused. 'No, I need information on a story your paper carried back in August. No byline.'

'You're actually working again?'

There was just enough incredulity in his voice to irritate Vargas, but he kept his cool.

'Strictly freelance,' he said. 'The story is dated 14 August this year, a woman with multiple gunshot wounds found in a Taco Bell parking lot. She was taken to Burke Memorial.'

'Doesn't sound familiar.'

Vargas hadn't expected it to, but pressed on.

'I'm hoping you can find out who worked it and see if they have any follow-up notes. She may be connected to a story I'm working on.'

'That's a tall fuckin' order,' Brett said. 'What's in it for me?'

'If it pans out, I'll give you first shot. An exclusive.

Drug smuggling, murder and the possible involvement of a Mexican religious cult. I'm working on a book, so anything you print is bound to help me down the road.'

'Yeah? And how do I know you aren't making all this shit up? I mention your name to my editor and he'll laugh me out of his office.'

'Fuck you,' Vargas said. 'You don't have to source me. You want in or not?'

There was a pause on the line as Brett thought it over.

'I'll call you back,' he said, then hung up.

The call came forty minutes later.

Vargas was on the road again, travelling back along Highway 2, this time headed towards Columbus, New Mexico, where he hoped to cross the border without incident. Grabbing his phone from the passenger seat, he clicked it on. 'Hey, Bill. Any luck?'

'Your victim was a Jane Doe. Spent seven hours in surgery for gunshot wounds to the head and chest, almost died twice on the table. She was comatose for three days, but finally managed to pull through.'

'Jesus Christ. She's alive?'

'Isn't that what I just told you?'

'Right, right,' Vargas said. 'So what happened to her?'

'Don't know, didn't ask. And that's all the charity work you're getting out of me.'

'What are you talking about? I told you, you could have an exclu—'

'Dream on, Nicky boy. You've got about as much chance of anyone taking you seriously as I do of getting a blowjob from an Argentinian whore. So I'm giving you this one because I'm a nice guy, but that's it. Don't call me again.'

Then he hung up.

Vargas dropped his phone onto the seat, feeling heat rise in his cheeks, wanting to put a fist into the dashboard.

Fucking prick.

But the sad sorry fact was that Brett was right. Getting anyone to take him seriously would be an uphill battle.

But then he'd known that for a couple of years now and that hadn't stopped him. Might even have fuelled him.

Whatever the case, he had new fuel now.

The American woman was alive.

BETH

52

'You're making remarkable progress, Elizabeth.'

Beth sat before a computer in a small examination room, the last of her cognitive regeneration exercises on screen. She had just finished alphabetizing twenty words in less than sixty seconds. A new record for her.

Or so she'd been told.

'Four weeks ago, you could barely walk and talk and look at you now.'

She had also aced a six-colour pattern sequence, and had correctly identified seven Central American countries randomly highlighted on a map. The stumbling block had always been Honduras, but this time she'd recognized it immediately.

Yet, despite these small victories, and the ever-expanding moments of lucidity, she often felt confused and disoriented.

Without looking up at Dr Stanley – who stood at her shoulder – she said, 'It's not the walking and talking I'm worried about. It's the remembering.'

Stanley was her neuropsychologist, a bear of a man who never pulled punches.

'I've told you before, there's no guarantee that

you'll ever get it all back. You've had significant tissue damage and there are still bullet fragments in your brain.'

'And the hallucinations?'

Stanley moved around to the other side of the table and sank into a chair, looking directly at her.

'I'm not convinced that what you're experiencing can really be classified as hallucinations. You're more than likely a victim of what we call confabulation.'

'Have you told me this before, too?'

Stanley nodded. 'Hallucinations exist in the present. For example, you might look down at this table and imagine there are a hundred spiders crawling across it.

'Confabulation, on the other hand, although rare, is simply the mind filling in the details of a memory where none exists. Some of those details might be false, while others might come from some other past event. If I were to ask you what you had for dinner last night, you might tell me you dined with the President of the United States and be entirely convinced that it's true.'

'But I know I was on that cruise. And I also know that Jen's missing.'

'Unfortunately, that's about all we can verify. You were missing, too, Beth, for nearly ten months. And no one knows what happened during that time. But a lot of what you remember about Playa Azul could well be a product of the dysfunction.'

'No,' Beth said. 'It happened. Rafael and Marta, Meat Without Feet, the mugging, every bit of it.'

'According to your ex-husband, the cruise company insists that they have no record of the Santiagos.'

'Then they must have been using false identities.'

'The Playa Azul police have discounted your story as well.'

'They're wrong,' Beth insisted. 'I . . . I just wish I could get my head past that police station and remember it all. Then I might be able to find her.'

Dr Stanley smiled. A gentle smile. Beth sensed he must be a man of infinite patience.

'I once worked on a case similar to yours. A young man who was convinced that his brain injury was the result of being mauled by a grizzly bear. He remembered it clearly. But the truth was, he was the victim of a bus accident and had never seen a bear in his life, grizzly or otherwise.'

'I'm not him,' Beth said.

'No, you're not. And every patient presents differently. But there are certain symptoms that we recognize and—'

'I was *shot*, doctor. How do you explain that?'

'I can't. Any more than I can tell you how you wound up in New Mexico.'

'I just want to remember. Why the hell can't I remember?'

'With any luck,' Stanley said, 'we'll one day know the truth. But I'd be lying to you if I told you you'll ever be completely back to normal. No matter how much progress you make, there will always be some brain dysfunction. How that will affect your life or your memory, is hard to say.'

He leaned forward, smiling again.

'But the good news is that you *are* improving. Much faster than we expected. Your CT scans are looking better, and while these cognitive tests can't really tell us how you'll function in the outside world, they do give us some reason to celebrate.'

'And these hallucinations or confabulations or whatever the hell they are. Will I ever be rid of them?'

Stanley raised his hands in a gesture that made it clear that he had no answer for her.

'Our research is spotty in that regard. In most cases, the confabulation is short term, but again, there are no guarantees.'

'Christ,' Beth said, 'I feel like I'm stuck in that fucking Bill Murray movie. How many times do I have to relive this stuff before I go bat-shit crazy?'

'Crazy is not a word I'd encourage you to use. It's demeaning and not even remotely accurate.'

'What the hell else do you call it, then?'

'You were severely injured, Beth. An injury that often leads to confusion. And while I know these episodes are taking their emotional toll, I'm as optimistic about your prognosis as a man in my profession can be.'

'That's not saying a whole lot.'

Another smile. 'Just the fact that we're having this conversation should give you reason to hope.'

Beth almost laughed.

Hope was a nice sentiment, but not much more than that.

And she couldn't help wishing that whoever had shot her had actually finished the job.

VARGAS

53

The woman behind the counter wasn't having any of it.

'I'm sorry, sir, but we can't give out patient information.'

She was Burke Memorial Hospital's custodian of records, a rotund African-American woman with startling brown eyes.

'Look,' Vargas said, 'I know you have rules, but maybe you can bend them a little. I don't care about her medical records. All I need is a name.'

'And all I need are some comfortable slippers, a bottle of wine, and a night with Barack Obama.'

'I'll *buy* you the damn wine if you give me that name. The slippers, too.'

The woman frowned. 'Is that a bribe? Do I look like somebody who can be bought?'

'I was joking.'

'Well, I'm not laughing, mister. I don't know where you went to school, but I think you must've skipped out on Ethics 101. That young lady was a patient at this hospital and it's not only against the law, but against my personal sense of responsibility to hand over private information to anyone, especially the likes of you.'

'Can't you at least tell me whether or not you were able to identify her?'

'No, I cannot,' the woman said. 'Both the police and the family have asked us to keep anything involving her case confidential, pending investigation of the incident that put her in here. For all I know, I've already breached that confidence just by opening my big fat mouth.'

'So you *do* know who she is. You just said family.'

She scowled at him. 'See what I mean? I think we're done here.'

With this, she turned away and disappeared behind her office door.

Vargas knew this had been a long shot. You don't often run across medical professionals willing to risk their careers to help make life easier for a reporter, but he'd had to try. And at least he knew that the American woman had been identified.

The logical next step would be to contact the Albuquerque police, but it sounded to Vargas as if they weren't likely to be cooperative either. His only choice, he decided, was to call in another favour and hope he got a better reception this time.

Several years ago, he'd done a story on a grisly string of murders stretching from California to Nevada and had struck up a friendship with a Las Vegas homicide cop by the name of Jennings – the guy who had told him about the 'itch'. After suffering a devastating loss, Jennings had flamed out and retired, then wound up doing half-assed magic gigs at a local casino to feed his gambling habit.

Jennings had an ex-wife in the Las Vegas police department and a lot of connections, and was one of the few people that Vargas knew who hadn't condemned him to his ignore list. In fact, when Vargas's humiliation went public in a very big way, Jennings had sent him a card with a Joker on the front, and a one-line message scribbled inside:

You'll soon be drawing aces

That hadn't happened quite yet, but Vargas knew that Jennings would help him if he asked. And a call to the Albuquerque police from one of their south-western brethren was likely to receive more attention than a visit from Vargas. Short of that, Jennings was bound to have a connection with access to just the right database. He'd always been a master at getting things done.

So Vargas went outside to his car, checked his cell phone's address book again and dialled.

After several rings, the line came to life. 'Hey, hey, Number Two, it's been a while.'

Jennings called him Number Two because they shared the same first name, and because the first time they met, Vargas was 'Just another reporter come to take a dump on the cops.' When that turned out not to be true, a friendship – and a nickname – were born.

'I need a favour,' Vargas said.

'So what else is new? Give me a minute or two to win this hand and I'll get back to you. I just went all in.'

'You're a brave man.'

'Tell that to my ex. In the meantime, I'm putting you on hold.'

Vargas heard the line click and waited.

A minute or two later, it came to life again and Jennings said, 'I just won a monster pot, my friend, so you caught me in a good mood. What do you want and who do I have to kill to get it?'

'No killing necessary,' Vargas said, then gave him just enough details to convince him to help.

There was a pause on the line. 'You sure this is something you want to get involved in?'

'No choice at this point,' Vargas said. 'I've gotta know who she is.'

'Sounds to me like you're developing a crush on the victim.'

'Hardly. I just found out she's alive.'

'Yeah, and I'd lay odds your hardened little heart skipped a beat or two when you did.'

'Are you gonna help me or give me grief?'

'Both,' Jennings said. 'The bad news is, nobody's all that anxious to talk to a brokendown ex-cop. But the good news is that I know a couple of Albuquerque major crime investigators who still owe me a favour. Maybe I can get one of them to pony up.'

'I knew I could count on you.'

'Yeah, that's me, *hombre*. Mr Reliable.'

54

The detective's name was Pasternak, an old-school Jack Webb clone, crew cut and all, a just-the-facts-ma'am kind of guy you wouldn't want to meet on the wrong side of a police baton. He looked about as at home in a Starbucks as a bulldog at a Japanese tea ceremony.

'Jennings tells me you're a good guy,' he said.

They were sitting at a corner table, nursing cups of coffee, Pasternak black, Vargas cream and sugar. Vargas didn't particularly like Starbucks coffee, but Pasternak had chosen the meeting place. It was several blocks away from the Albuquerque police station, and he figured the chances of running into one of Pasternak's colleagues was unlikely.

Which, he supposed, was the point.

'But I just want you to know,' Pasternak continued, 'that that don't mean jack to me. I learned a long time ago to make my own judgement about people. So until I know what your interest in this case is, you ain't gettin' squat.'

'Jennings didn't tell you?'

'Just enough to pique my curiosity and get you an

introduction.' He sipped his coffee. 'So what's on your mind?'

Vargas cut straight to it. 'Mexico.'

'And what exactly does that mean?'

'I just got back from Juarez. That's where your vic was shot the first time.'

Pasternak stared at him. 'The first time?'

'Come on,' Vargas said. 'You've done the ballistics, talked to the medical examiner. You know she was shot three times, by two different guns. And since the third one was a head shot, I'm guessing she still hasn't made much of a statement.'

Pasternak tried and failed to hide his surprise. 'Know about head wounds, do you?'

'My brother was shot point-blank by a gangbanger when he was seventeen. He was never the same again.'

'Tough break.'

'Especially the part when he killed himself fifteen years later.'

Manny had led a tortured life for those fifteen years. Unpredictable motor functions, slurred speech, a diminished IQ. No more ghost stories. No more smiles. A lonely man who had decided that life just wasn't worth living. So about two and half years ago, he had repeated what the gangbanger had done, and got it right this time.

Not that Vargas could blame him. As low as he himself had gotten after the suicide, he couldn't even imagine the shit his brother had been going through.

But then this wasn't the time and place to be dwelling on such things, was it?

Apparently Pasternak didn't think so either.

'So, tell me,' he said. 'Do we have a leak in the department or are you getting your information from somewhere else?'

'If you had a leak, we wouldn't be talking. And, believe me, there's a lot more.'

Pasternak stared down at the dark liquid in his cup, taking a moment to process this.

'Okay,' he said. 'I'm on the hook. What do you want from me?'

'Just the basic facts of the case.'

'That's it?'

'That's all I really need.'

'You're a cheap date,' Pasternak said. 'Maybe Jennings was right about you.' He took a sip of the coffee. 'Her name is Elizabeth Crawford.'

Vargas was surprised and must have shown it, because Pasternak said, 'Not what you were expecting?'

'The name I heard was Angie.'

Pasternak's eyes widened slightly. 'Who's your source?'

'Not until I get the rest.'

'The only people who could possibly know that name are people who had direct contact with her.'

'Exactly,' Vargas said. 'So finish what you were saying.'

Pasternak nodded. 'Like I told you, her name is Elizabeth Crawford. First few days she was at Burke Memorial in intensive care and we got nothing from her. Paramedics reported that she kept saying the name

Angie over and over again, but her speech was slurred and nobody was even sure if that was accurate. Whatever the case, she wasn't much help with the identification. They almost lost her a few times and I gotta say, it's a miracle she pulled through. Somebody fights that hard to survive, you figure they must have a real good reason to live.'

'Did you fingerprint her?'

Another nod. 'That's what did it for us. We put her in the database and got a hit out of Los Angeles. We contacted her place of employment, wound up talking to her ex-husband and he told us she'd been missing for several months. Went on vacation and never came back. And guess where she went?'

'Where?'

'Mexico.'

'Juarez?'

Pasternak shook his head. 'Baja Norte. She and her sister went on a Mexican Riviera cruise and disappeared off the face of the earth. Cruise line reported it when their room steward realized they hadn't returned in a while. And the purser said Crawford had mentioned she had "misplaced her sister". '

'So then Angie's the sister?'

'Nope. Her name is Jennifer. Angie's still a mystery to us.'

'I assume the FBI was called in?'

'FBI, Homeland Security, the whole ball of wax. They checked activity on their credit cards, tried tracing their cell phones and got nada.'

'Until Taco Bell.'

'That's right. And, believe me, they threw everything they had into it, since Crawford was practically one of their own.'

'What do you mean?'

'She's an assistant district attorney. Or was. Just like her ex. They thought maybe the disappearances might've had something to do with one of her cases, but they could never connect anything. She dealt mostly with domestic crimes and special victims.'

Vargas felt a small bump in his heart rate. This story just kept getting better and better. But he wondered why he hadn't heard about this.

Then he realized that it had happened around the time he was up in Vancouver, going through his third stint of rehab. The one that finally stuck. And he hadn't exactly been paying much attention to the world before that.

'So what's her condition now?'

'Last I heard, not so good. Once she was physically able, she was transferred to a traumatic brain injury facility in LA. The ex tells me the lucid periods are few and far between. She managed to give us a couple of names that we looked into, but we got nothing. Her doctor thinks they might be a product of the brain injury.'

'Jesus.'

'Tell me about it. The ex says she keeps calling him, thinking it's a year ago and that she's still down in Playa Azul.'

'You're kidding me.'

'According to him, she's completely fucked.'

Pasternak lifted his cup, took another sip, then set it down and gave Vargas a hard stare.

'Okay, hot shot, now it's your turn. Tell me about Juarez.'

55

Vargas reached into the satchel under the table, brought out the manila envelope and handed it to Pasternak.

Pasternak said nothing as he pulled out the three photographs.

'She look familiar?' Vargas asked.

Pasternak was leafing through them now, staring at them with undisguised surprise. 'What the hell *is* this?'

'I'll tell you what it isn't,' Vargas said. 'It isn't a Taco Bell parking lot.'

'I can see that. I assume this is in Juarez?'

'About a half hour or so south. Place called Dead Man's Dunes.'

'And the woman with her?'

'A nun. There were four more found nearby and a fifth outside.'

It took Pasternak about two seconds to put it together.

'Holy . . . fucking . . . shit. The Casa de la Muerte murders?'

He'd said it fairly loud and several of the other customers turned and stared at him. But he was either oblivious or didn't give a damn.

'I don't fucking believe it. We got a couple of bulletins on this, but nobody ever said anything about an American woman, let alone Crawford. Where'd you get these?'

'I'm afraid I can't tell you that, but there's a Chihuahua state police homicide investigator you might want to take a look into. Guy by the name of Rojas. He removed these photos and every other trace of Crawford from the official file.'

'Wait, wait, now,' Pasternak said. 'Back up a bit. Start at the top.'

So Vargas did, telling him about the trip to Juarez and the tour of the Casa de la Muerte crime scene. About the Ainsworths letting it slip that there was an American woman named Angie, and about Rojas's cover-up, including what Rojas had thought was a fatal shot to the head.

He didn't mention the ride in the trunk of his car, or the executions at the egg ranch. No point in getting caught up in this thing as a material witness. Not right now, at least.

Pasternak would probably find out about it all himself – probably with Garcia's help, once Operation Rojas kicked into gear – but Vargas planned to be long gone when that happened.

'You have anything in your files on a hit man with a half-burnt face?'

Pasternak shook his head. 'I'm pretty sure I'd know if we did.'

'What about a religious cult called La Santa Muerte?'

'Doesn't sound familiar.' Pasternak pointed to the photos. 'They have something to do with this?'

'I can't be sure, but it's come up in conversation.'

'You wanna clue me in?'

'Apparently the cult is run by someone called El Santo,' Vargas said. 'They're into drug smuggling and God knows what else, and the guy with the burnt face seems to be their enforcer. I did a quick Internet search when I was down in Juarez and got zero hits. Which means they're about as far under the radar as you can get.'

'And Juarez is so far out of our jurisdiction it might as well be Mars,' Pasternak said. 'But since this is all directly connected to my case, it warrants a road trip, and I have a feeling the FBI's gonna want to ride shotgun.'

'I have a feeling you're right,' Vargas told him. 'But all we've got so far is a rumoured cover-up. We still don't know how Elizabeth Crawford wound up in that house, surrounded by five dead nuns.'

'True, but what you've given me here puts me a step closer to closing an attempted murder case, and if this fucker Rojas is as bent as you say he is, he's going down.'

'You manage that one, you'll make my source a happy man.'

Pasternak looked at the photos again. 'I assume you're gonna let me keep these?'

Vargas nodded. While he was at the Internet cafe, he'd paid a few extra pesos to use the scanner and had transferred the images to his SD card.

Pasternak said, 'I've gotta admit you managed to root out one helluva story.'

'That's what I keep telling myself.'

'So what's your next step?'

Vargas didn't even have to think about it.

'California,' he said. 'I'm headed back to California.'

BETH

56

Everyone kept telling her how remarkable her progress was, but Beth didn't see it.

Physically, perhaps. Her motor skills had improved to the point that she could now walk unassisted for long periods of time, was able to eat on her own, and even write passages in her journal – a journal Dr Stanley had encouraged her to keep. But the inability to remember clearly was driving her mad. That, to her mind (such as it was), was much more debilitating than not being able to clench a fist or stand without assistance. She'd gladly give up her mobility for a day free of confusion. A day in which her long- and short-term memory were both fully functioning, all synapses firing properly and glitch free.

A day in which she stayed put. No more imaginary trips to the Mexican Riviera.

In these welcome moments of clarity, however, all she could think about was Jen. Those last few minutes she'd spent with her sister didn't seem to want to leave her alone.

Lunch. Fight. Bathroom break.

Gone.

And far from being a figment of her imagination, Rafael and Marta Santiago had been very real. Just because the cruise line had no record of them didn't mean they weren't there. Maybe they were stowaways. Maybe they had signed on under fake names, using false identification. It certainly wouldn't be the first time that had happened.

And the fact that there *wasn't* a record of them led Beth to believe that they had, indeed, been somehow involved in what had happened to Jen.

And to her.

In one of her brief, uncomfortable phone conversations with Peter, he'd told her that the FBI and the Albuquerque police were now convinced that the two didn't exist. But Beth didn't care what they said, she knew in her gut that these weren't false memories.

No White House dinners or grizzly bears for her, thank you.

'You ready for your walk now, Elizabeth?'

It annoyed her that everyone around here called her Elizabeth. At first she had accepted it. They were simply reading the name off a chart. But she was pretty sure that she had finally told them that most people called her Beth.

This was not, she decided, a particularly friendly place. Everyone was nice enough, sure, but they were just people doing their jobs, smiling professional smiles, offering professional sympathies and encouragement.

She'd done enough of that in her own job to know when it was happening to her.

But the people here always treated you as if you

were a child. That *they* were the ones who knew best, no questions asked. A little pat on the head when you forgot your words or a face or a name.

Isn't she cute?

She'll do better next time.

But they couldn't even remember Beth's name. So who was the one with the brain damage?

'Did you hear me, Elizabeth? Time for your walk.'

Ever since Beth had learned not to rely on her wheelchair, her physical therapist had been taking her for regular walks. Not far. Just out to the courtyard and around the field, a small stretch of land bordered by trees and a chain-link fence.

Every time they walked the perimeter, Beth would look out at the city streets and wish that she could close her eyes and will herself back into her old life. Back to the days when she would slip behind the wheel of her BMW, drive down the 101 to the building on Spring Street, then settle into her office chair, ready to take on the new morning.

Back when Jen was still here. And Peter had not yet been exposed as an unrepentant philanderer. Before his late-night meetings with 'clients', the faint but unmistakable lipstick stains, the condoms in his wallet.

Beth had been blissfully ignorant of his cheating before then, and maybe she was better off that way.

Growing up, she'd thought that the worst that could ever happen to her already had: the death of her parents.

But she'd been wrong about that, hadn't she?

Very wrong.

A hand touched her shoulder and she turned with a start, looking up from her wheelchair into the pleasant but rather bland face of her physical therapist.

David?

Danny?

'Time to go,' he said, then helped her to her feet and guided her towards the courtyard door.

When they got outside, Beth was happy to see that the sky was clearer than usual. The smog had decided to take an unscheduled holiday. The morning was bright and clean and she drank it in, wishing every day in Los Angeles could be so beautiful.

She remembered the first morning after the break-up, when she had moved into her own apartment. It had been a day a lot like this one, the sky clean, sunlight slanting through her bedroom window, and she had hoped it would be the start of a new life.

Apparently it was. Just not the one she'd bargained for.

Now, that apartment was gone. Given up after she went missing. Peter had had all of her things sent to a storage facility, then, later, some of it was transferred here.

Clothes. Family photos. A box full of her favourite books. Her entire life summed up by a few meagre possessions.

Pretty pathetic, when you thought about it.

As David or Danny guided her towards their usual starting point at the edge of the field, Beth looked out at the street again, at the rows of cars parked on either side.

She couldn't tell you why, but something drew her attention to the distant street corner. A sense that she was . . . what?

Being watched?

Yes, that was it.

There was no rational explanation for this feeling, of course. Something Dr Stanley would have a field day with. All she saw there was a parked car, covered with dust, as if it had just travelled a long distance.

She couldn't even see the driver.

Yet she sensed he was in there. Watching her.

Waiting for something.

Beth averted her gaze – afraid to stare too intently – and let Danny (Dennis?) guide her along the path around the field.

But as they rounded the second turn, Beth found herself looking back towards the street again.

At that dust-covered car.

She recognized the make. It was a lot like the one her parents used to drive so long ago.

What was it called again?

She had to strain to remember. It was there on the periphery of her mind, but not quite fully formed.

Then, finally, the effort paid off and it came. Another small victory for the lady with the bullet in her brain.

Whoever was out there, watching her, was driving a Town Car.

A Lincoln Town Car.

VARGAS

57

He drove for eleven hours straight, taking Highway 40 from Albuquerque, which, somewhere along the line, had turned into the 15. He stopped only to pee and for coffee, the only thing keeping him awake.

Around 1 a.m. he hit Los Angeles – or the outskirts of Burbank, to be more precise – where he lived in a tiny studio apartment that could best be described as shabby. One room, one bath. A bed, a desk, and a sliding glass door that led to a minuscule balcony overlooking a pockmarked street.

Despite this, it felt good to be home. After taking a shower to wash off the day, and shampooing his hair for the first time since he'd been attacked, he checked his wounds and saw that they were healing nicely.

He knew he should sleep, but there was something he wanted to do before hitting the sack. Taking the SD card from his wallet, he went to transfer the data and crime scene photos to his desktop PC, only to discover that it was turned off.

Not unusual in most households, he supposed, but Vargas always kept his computer *on*, even when he was away from home. A techie at the *Tribune* had once told him that the circuits lasted longer that way.

So why was it off?

He glanced at the clock next to his bed and saw that it was still keeping time, no flashing digits that would indicate a power loss. It was possible that the PC could have died, but as he looked around the room, he started to get a funny feeling in his gut.

Something not quite right, here.

Not that he could see it. Everything was in its usual place.

But somehow it just didn't feel right. As if his space had been invaded by a foreign presence.

The building manager, maybe?

No.

The guy was useless. Wouldn't even change the light bulbs in the stairwell unless the day ended with something other than a 'y'.

So it wasn't the manager.

And no one else had the key.

Vargas stared at his computer a moment, trying to fight the sudden chill in his bones, then leaned down and turned it on. A couple of beeps later, it came to life, booting up Windows, and he was starting to second guess himself, wondering if maybe he *had* turned it off, that maybe this feeling was just a touch of paranoia rearing its ugly—

His landline rang.

Vargas snatched the receiver from his desk, checked the screen and saw an 'unknown caller' message.

But he didn't need Caller ID to tell him who it was.

And while he'd made his decision to move forward with this story – damn the consequences – that didn't keep a wave of dread from washing through him.

He clicked the receiver button. 'Yes?'

'Imagine my surprise,' Mr Blister said, 'when I drove so far to see you and you were not at home.'

The dread deepened. Did they know what he'd been up to? Confronting Rojas had been a risk, yes, but since he was still alive, he figured he'd got away with it.

'I stopped off in Vegas to see an old friend,' he said. 'Wanted to try my luck at blackjack.'

'There is no luck, Mr Vargas. Only destiny. And at the moment, yours does not look promising.'

'Wait, now. I did what you asked and got the hell out of Texas. I didn't think it would matter if I took a detour.'

'Then you were mistaken. Were we mistaken as well?'

Vargas said nothing.

There was silence on the line and he tucked the phone under his chin, quickly grabbed his clothes from the floor and started pulling them on, just in case he had to move fast.

'As difficult as it may be for someone on the out-side to understand,' Mr Blister said, 'it is counter to our beliefs to do harm to those who do not deserve it. As I told you, Mr Vargas, we have no desire to punish the innocent. But perhaps we misjudged you. Perhaps you are not quite so innocent after all.'

'I've never claimed to be.'

'I do hope you realize that you are benefiting from our strong sense of benevolence.'

'So you keep telling me.'

'But we are not fools, either. So consider this call a reminder. Stay out of our business and we will stay out of yours.'

'You've made that pretty clear, too.'

'I do hope so. Because if you hear from us again, Mr Vargas, it will not be over the telephone. Understood?'

An image skittered through Vargas's mind. Mr Blister shooting Junior point-blank, then peering suspiciously into the darkness of the warehouse.

Staring straight at him.

'Understood,' Vargas said.

58

The moment the line clicked, Vargas moved.

He didn't give a damn what he'd been promised, he wasn't about to hang around hoping they'd leave him alone.

No matter how you sliced it, these were *not* benevolent people. He'd seen that at first hand. And despite his instinct to ask Mr Blister about La Santa Muerte, he had resisted. If you don't want a hornet to sting you, don't start poking at its nest.

But then that was exactly what he'd been doing, wasn't it?

And Mr Blister hadn't come all this way to sit in Vargas's hot tub.

Throwing on the rest of his clothes, Vargas grabbed his keys, the SD card, and the backpack in his closet that held his spare laptop, then doused the light, and went to his door.

Stopping short of opening it, he waited a moment, listening. The hallway outside had a cement floor and tended to echo, so he strained to hear any sound of movement.

Nothing.

Maybe a little too quiet.

Sucking in a breath, he opened the door a crack and peeked out, saw that the hallway was clear.

But just as he pulled the door wide and stepped past the threshold, a voice said:

'Mr Vargas?'

Turning with a start, he saw an LAPD patrol officer reaching the top of the stairwell and heading in his direction. A powerfully built Hispanic guy with the requisite cop haircut.

'I'm looking for Ignacio Vargas. Is that you?'

Vargas's heart was pounding. 'What's this about?'

'We had word of a disturbance. Is everything okay here?'

Disturbance? Vargas thought. What kind of disturbance? Had one of his neighbours heard Mr Blister breaking into his apartment and called the cops?

A nice theory, but most of the people living in this building – which leaned towards off-duty prostitutes and low-rent hucksters – had no interest in contacting the cops for any reason whatsoever. It seemed that the only time the LAPD ever showed up around here was to harass or arrest someone.

Besides, he doubted that Mr Blister would be so careless.

He was about to respond, when his gaze dropped to the officer's right hand, which was moving towards the weapon holstered on his hip. In a quick, fluid motion, the cop unsnapped the holster strap and pulled his gun free.

It was at that moment that Vargas decided that

either the La Santa Muerte cult had connections that reached far beyond a rogue border patrol agent, or this guy was not LAPD at all.

Whatever the case, one thing was obvious: Mr Blister had help. And as the gun came up, Vargas ducked.

The shot cracked, splintering wood somewhere above him as he rolled into his apartment, then suddenly realized that he'd just made a huge mistake.

There was nowhere to hide in here.

Jumping to his feet, he slung the backpack over his shoulder, bolted for the sliding glass door and flung it open.

Another shot cracked and the door shattered, glass flying everywhere as Vargas vaulted the balcony rail and jumped to the roof of a Grand Caravan parked at the kerb below. He hit it hard, denting the roof, and the alarm started squealing as he lost his footing and tumbled to the sidewalk, landing on his hands and knees.

The impact sent a jolt of pain through him. But, feeling eyes on him from the balcony above, he pushed past the pain, scrambled to his feet and ran.

There was a shout behind him, but no more gunshots. Then an engine revved and tyres squealed and headlights washed across his back.

Chancing a glance over his shoulder, he saw what looked like an LAPD patrol car heading towards him, but again, he couldn't be sure it was the real thing. The light bar mounted across the top was dark, and the glare of the car's headlights made it difficult to see.

Not that it mattered at this point. These were subjects for later debate – assuming there *was* a later.

He picked up speed, but he knew there was no way he'd ever outrun a car, so his only choice was to cut into a neighbouring apartment building. This was good in theory, but difficult in practice, because the building he was in front of right now was a bit more upscale than his place. The only way in was through one of the security gates that guarded the underground parking garage and the lobby entrance.

He didn't figure anyone would be buzzing in a half-crazed has-been newspaper reporter with a gun-toting assassin at his heels, so he cut across the street instead, heading towards the all-night gas station on the corner. There was a lot of light there, and surely they wouldn't try to shoot him in so public a place.

Assuming, of course, he was able to reach it.

The car roared behind him, and as he cleared the kerb and stepped onto the sidewalk, his breathing ragged, his body shouting at him to slow the fuck down, the car pulled up alongside him and—

—all he could think about was his brother Manny. Manny getting ambushed by a van full of punks, pulling up alongside him and firing that bullet that changed his life forever.

And at that moment, Vargas knew his brother's terror.

Then a shot cracked, quickly followed by another. And while the first one seemed to have gone wild, the second one made an impact and Vargas felt himself go down, pain blossoming somewhere in the region of his shoulder and the right side of his neck.

And as he hit the ground – knocking what little wind he had left completely out of him – he heard the squeal of tyres and the beefy roar of the car's engine as it tore away, disappearing around the corner.

Then, for the third time in as many days, everything went black.

59

The Mexican wrestlers were back.

He caught only fleeting glimpses of them as they grabbed hold of him and tossed him around as if he were nothing more than an over-sized suitcase. One of them said something to him, but in a language he didn't understand, and all he could do was groan in response. It must have been enough, however, because the crowd watching them cheered.

Then he was picked up again and tossed around and the next thing he knew there were blinding lights in his eyes and the wrestlers were gone, replaced now by angels in pastel greens and blues.

One of them was rubbing his aching shoulder, and suddenly the pain went away and he was gone again, only to awaken in a hospital bed, surrounded by curtains and the sound of voices and beeping machinery, his shirt and shoes gone, a patch of gauze taped to the space between his neck and his right shoulder, an IV attached to a tube in the back of his hand.

Only then did he remember what had happened and was surprised to discover that he was still alive.

He felt a presence nearby, someone moving around

next to him, playing with tubes or wires or buttons or whatever. Then one of the angels appeared in front of him, leaning forward, her pastel-blue-covered breasts brushing against his arm as she checked something above him.

He looked up at her and saw an attractive, short-haired Asian woman who smelled faintly of lilac.

'Welcome back,' she said.

'Did I go somewhere?'

'You drifted off a few times, but that was mostly because of the medication. The effects should wear off pretty soon.'

'How long have I been here?'

'Not long. The doctor will come by in a moment to fill in the details.'

'Somebody shot me.'

'That's the general consensus,' she said. 'But you got lucky. The bullet went straight through and didn't manage to do much damage. You lost some blood, but nothing substantial.'

'I can't feel a thing.'

A soft laugh. She patted his arm.

'You will when the local wears off. But then you probably already know that.' She gestured towards his stitches. 'Looks like you've had extensive experience in that area.'

She fussed with some of the machinery again, checked the tube in his hand, then turned and reached for the curtain.

'I'll let the police know you're awake. They'll want to see you as soon as the doctor is finished.'

Vargas's stomach dropped. 'Police?'

'They've been waiting to talk to you. We have to report all gunshot wounds.'

'What do they look like?'

She frowned at him. A question she hadn't anticipated. 'Look like?'

'Black, white, Hispanic?'

'They look like a couple of bored cops in uniform. What difference does it make?'

Vargas shook his head. 'Never mind,' he said. 'Thanks for your help.'

She studied him a moment, uncertainty in her eyes, then said, 'I'll get the doctor,' as she disappeared behind the curtain.

When she was gone, Vargas sat up, looking around the cubicle for his shirt and shoes. He didn't know if the cops out there were the same ones who had shot at him, but he sure as hell wasn't going to wait around to find out. Besides, even if they weren't, how could he know who to trust any more? La Santa Muerte might very well have tentacles that reached far and wide.

He felt a stab of pain as he yanked the IV free, then stood up, surveying the small space again, looking for his clothes and backpack. He found them under the gurney, his shirt neatly folded inside a plastic bag, but torn and covered with blood, his shoes and backpack lying next to it.

The shirt would make him a target, but so be it. It was all he had. He pulled it from the bag and slipped it on, felt the damp stickiness of the blood on his shoulder as he buttoned it up.

Then he slipped into his shoes, checked to make sure he still had his wallet and keys and cell phone, then slung his backpack over his good shoulder and moved to the curtain, peeking out into what looked like every other emergency room he'd ever seen:

A cluster of computers at the centre, people in scrubs moving about in a deliberate but hurried pace, shouting codewords to one another, a row of curtained cubicles on either side.

A clock on the wall read 4 a.m.

Vargas looked to his left and saw a short hallway that led to a set of double doors. Above them was a standard issue green exit sign.

His immediate destination.

Checking to make sure his nurse was nowhere around, he quickly slipped out of his cubicle and bee-lined it for the doors.

If anyone noticed him, they didn't say anything. Didn't try to stop him. And the next thing he knew he was through the doors and moving down a longer corridor past a row of vending machines.

He found another set of doors marked 'Exit', and pushed through them into the ambulance bay, which was pretty quiet at this time of morning.

There were a couple of LAPD patrol cars parked among the ambulances, but no cops visible, so Vargas kept moving, heading straight for the driveway and on into the street.

There was a thrift store on Magnolia that opened at 6 a.m. He'd grown up wearing thrift-store clothes, and he knew it would be a good place to buy a shirt for little cash.

So his first priority was to find an ATM, then call a cab.

BETH

60

She had another bad night.

One of the nurses found her wandering the halls, claiming she'd just been mugged by a man in a Meat Without Feet T-shirt.

She'd thought the nurse was a Mexican police officer, but then slowly came to her senses – doing it on her own this time, remembering where she was without having to be slapped back into reality.

Which, she supposed, was a good sign.

But the realization that Jen had been gone for nearly a year hurt just as much as ever. She didn't have the benefit of time to dampen her grief, because time would remain at a standstill until her brain healed and her memory returned.

Assuming it ever would.

She hadn't been able to sleep the rest of the night. She lay in bed, her head pounding, not wanting to close her eyes for fear that she'd wake up in Mexico again. Not that sleep had anything to do with the problem. It just seemed safer somehow to stay awake.

She watched the sun rise in her window. Then, at breakfast time, she climbed out of bed, shuffled to the dining room and sat alone, a plate of fruit and a soft-boiled egg in front of her.

But she didn't eat. Didn't have much of an appetite. Spent the next half-hour pushing the food around the plate, listening to the murmur of voices in the room – other patients, eating and talking, new bonds formed out of shared pain.

But Beth kept to herself. Was even less interested in making friends than she was in eating. She'd always been something of a loner anyway.

Her physical therapist came around shortly after breakfast and took her for a walk. As they moved around the field, she looked again at the street, wondering if the dusty Lincoln Town Car was still out there.

But she saw no sign of it.

She spent most of the morning in the day room, leafing through magazines, reading about troubled celebrities and thinking what a bunch of whiny, spoiled brats they were.

Try living my life for a few days and see how you like it.

But maybe *she* was a whiny, spoiled brat herself.

The good news was that she stayed lucid for the entire morning. No sudden trips to the past. No conversations with Jen or Rafael or Marta.

So maybe she *was* getting better.

Dr Stanley would be pleased.

As the clock rolled closer to noon, visiting hour came and the day room began to fill with friends and family. Not Beth's friends and family, of course. She had none. But she enjoyed watching the other patients' faces light up when a mother or father or husband or child came into the room. Hugs and kisses. Warm smiles.

Some of those patients had no idea who they were hugging and kissing, but it didn't much matter. It felt good to be loved. To know, even if only for that brief moment, that someone in this world cared about you.

Beth watched them all from behind a magazine. Every once in a while, a visitor would glance in her direction and she'd avert her gaze. Didn't want to be caught invading their special moment.

At one point, she felt herself being stared at and saw a small boy sitting quietly in a chair, a ragged stuffed animal in his lap. He looked at her, unsmiling, a bit bewildered by his surroundings. He couldn't have been much more than a year old. And for some reason Beth didn't look away this time. She had no idea whom he belonged to, but the sight of him made her heart break. He had somehow summoned up one of her buried memories, one that was too deep to grab hold of, but was painful nevertheless, and before she knew it, tears were rolling down her cheeks.

Embarrassed, she got up and went to the restroom and grabbed a tissue, staring at herself in the mirror as she wiped her eyes, not exactly pleased by what she saw.

Too thin. Too frightened. Too sad.

Was the old Beth in there somewhere?

Did it really matter any more?

At least her hair was growing back. She could still see the scar, but it was mostly covered by fresh new growth, and before long it would be completely hidden.

Maybe she'd have her memory back by then.

She almost laughed at that one.

'Elizabeth?'

Beth turned and saw one of the nurses standing in the doorway. A slender redhead with a face full of professional concern. Her name was Mary.

Marion?

'Are you okay?' she asked.

Beth frowned, not happy with the interruption. She was beginning to feel like a prisoner in this place.

'Can't I even go to the bathroom in peace?'

The words came out harsher than she'd meant them to be, but Mary/Marion didn't seem to notice.

'Better make yourself presentable. You have a visitor.'

Beth stared at her, surprised. 'Who?'

'One of the best-looking men I've seen around here in a long, long time.'

Peter?

Why would Peter be coming to see her? He could barely handle her on the phone.

Mary/Marion gestured for her to hurry up.

'Come on, girl. Trust me, you don't want to keep this one waiting.'

Curious now, Beth followed her out the door.

61

It wasn't Peter.

Mary/Marion led her back into the day room and pointed through the glass doors towards the courtyard, where an athletic looking man with dark hair stood with his back towards them, a backpack slung over his shoulder.

'He says he's an old friend from USC.'

Beth had been a USC undergrad, courtesy of her college trust fund, but hadn't really kept in touch with any of her classmates.

'He just heard about what happened to you and wanted to come by and see how you're doing. Isn't that sweet?'

Beth stared at him, and for a brief, panic-filled moment, thought he was Rafael Santiago.

But then he turned, looking through the glass at the other patients and their families, and, while he might have given Rafael a run for his money in the looks department, she didn't recall the face.

'My, my, my,' Mary/Marion said.

Beth wondered if she should order the woman a drool cup.

'Did he give you a name?'

'You don't recognize him?'

'You may not realize this,' Beth said, 'but my brain is a bit scrambled.'

Again, the words came out harsher than she'd meant them to be. But, honestly, if you work in a TBI rehabilitation clinic, shouldn't you know the territory?

Mary/Marion was as oblivious as ever.

'He says his name is Nick. Nick Vargas. Does that ring any bells?'

Beth ran the name through her head, straining to come up with a memory, but found nothing. Which was a bit odd, since the only memories she seemed to have problems with were post-Jen. Her college years had never been an issue.

She stared at the man, wondering for a moment if he drove a dusty Lincoln Town Car.

Then, at Mary/Marion's urging, she went out to the courtyard to greet him.

Closing the doors behind her, she said, 'Mr Vargas?'

He assessed her without apology, his eyes clear and direct – and mildly surprised. But in a good way. As if he liked what he saw.

'That's right,' he said. 'Ms Crawford?'

'Beth,' she told him. 'Please call me Beth. Nobody else seems to want to.'

'All right, Beth it is. And I'm Nick.'

He offered a hand to shake, and she must have looked unsteady on her feet, because when she hesitated, the hand went directly to her elbow and guided her to a nearby chair. Then he set his backpack down and pulled up a chair next to hers.

He winced slightly as he sat down, as if he were in some kind of pain. 'Now that we're on a first-name basis, I have to be honest with you. I lied to the nurse. We've never met before.'

'I didn't think so.'

'My brother had an injury similar to yours, and I know how difficult dealing with TBI can be. I don't want to confuse you.'

'I appreciate that,' Beth said. 'So why *are* you here?'

'I'm a reporter. Or at least I used to be. Now I'm writing a book.'

She frowned. She'd dealt with enough reporters in her time to know when to be wary. The majority of them were bottom feeders.

'What kind of book?'

'True crime.'

'And what does it have to do with me? Is this about one of my old cases?'

'It could be,' he said. 'But I'm not sure.'

'What does that mean?'

'It means I'm pretty much running blind at this point. And I'm hoping you can clear some things up.'

'Clearing things up is not exactly my strong suit these days. What about?'

'About what happened in Albuquerque.'

Beth stared at him. She couldn't fathom why anyone would be even remotely interested in what had happened to her. There was nothing exciting, or sexy or book-worthy about it, and she wondered if this was some kind of reporter's trick. Was he trying to play her?

But to what end?

Feeling anger start to burn inside her chest, she said, 'Why are you doing this? Why did you come here?'

'I just told you—'

'Can't you see that I'm in recovery? Was it really necessary to invade my privacy for whatever it is you're looking for?'

'I'm sorry. I have a story to write. I'm just trying to get to the truth.'

'Then you're out of luck, because I have no interest in talking to you.'

She started to rise, but he reached a hand out and touched her forearm.

'I didn't mean to upset you.'

She pulled away. 'Oh, I'm sure you didn't.' This time she intended the words to sound harsh. Hoped the sarcasm was clear. 'It was bad enough dealing with people like you before I got shot. I don't see any compelling reason to deal with you now. So if you're thinking the lady with the brain damage is gonna spill some confidential tidbit about one of her old cases, you're shit out of luck.'

She started for the glass doors, and he stood, wincing again as he moved after her.

'At least let me explain.'

'Why? What difference would it make?'

'I just got back from Mexico,' he said.

'How nice for you.'

'And I know how you wound up in that Taco Bell parking lot.'

This stopped her. She turned.

'What?'

His dark eyes didn't waver. 'I know the man who shot you.'

62

Beth wasn't quite sure she'd heard him right.

'How could you possibly know who shot me? The police can't even figure it out.'

'Until yesterday, the police didn't know what I know. So why don't we sit back down and I'll lay it all out for you.'

Beth had half a mind to suggest he go fuck himself, but what if this wasn't a ruse? What if he was telling the truth?

There was a time when she could spot a lying witness with very little effort. But when she looked into his eyes, she saw nothing there that gave him away one way or the other. Moving back to her chair, she sat and crossed her arms in front of her, feeling much as she did when she took a seat at the prosecution table, challenging a defence attorney to a courtroom duel.

'All right,' she said. 'Make your case.'

Vargas returned to his chair and sank into it, keeping his right shoulder still as he moved. The source of his pain.

He was quiet for a moment. Seemed to be searching for a place to start.

'A couple of months ago,' he said, 'I was watching the news on Channel Z. You know it?'

Beth nodded. They covered events relating to the local Hispanic community, but also broadcast news from Mexico and other Latin American countries.

'There was a report that never got much traction up here,' Vargas continued. 'About an abandoned old house near Juarez, where several women were found shot. A couple of them had slit throats. They called it the House of Death.'

He waited, as if expecting a reaction, so she gave him one. 'Sounds like a run for the border gone wrong.'

'That's exactly what the local *policía* thought. And as much as I hate to admit it, it's the kind of story I usually forget about five minutes after I've seen it. But for some reason this one resonated. Maybe I was feeling sentimental that day. My parents were illegals when they first came here.'

'This is fascinating,' Beth said, 'but what does it have to do with Albuquerque?'

He looked at her. 'None of this sounds even vaguely familiar to you?'

She looked right back. 'Two months ago I was in a coma. So, no, it doesn't sound familiar. Should it?'

'You really *don't* remember, do you.'

Okay, she thought. She'd given him enough slack. It was time for him to get to the point or get the hell out of here.

'What I know is that I've got a gap in my brain about the size of the Grand Canyon that seems to have swallowed up everything that happened to me for ten months. So if you know something that might help me fill that gap, I wish to Christ you'd get to it, because I've got some important magazine reading to do.'

He assessed her with those unapologetic eyes again, then found his backpack and unzipped it, pulling out a small netbook computer.

'My brother was pretty much a mess after his injury, and one of his biggest problems was his long-term memory. He had gaps, just like you.'

He lifted the lid of the netbook, pressed a key, and the computer began to hum, its small screen coming to life.

'I know every brain injury is different,' he said, 'so this may not work in your case. But we discovered that we could sometimes help my brother with visual cues. A photograph of the family at Christmas might be enough to bring on at least part of the memory, like putting a piece of a jigsaw puzzle in place.'

Beth gestured to the laptop. 'So I assume that's what you've got there. A piece of the puzzle?'

'Right,' Vargas said. 'But what I'm about to show you is pretty shocking.'

'I'm sure I can handle it.'

'These aren't family photos. I doubt your doctor would approve.'

Beth sighed. 'I've prosecuted rapists, paedophiles and murderers, so there isn't much I haven't seen. Now, are you going to keep me in suspense forever or are we gonna get on with this?'

Apparently satisfied with her response, Vargas ran

his finger along the touchpad, put the pointer over an icon and clicked.

A photograph filled the screen. A black and white shot of two dead women on a mattress soaked with blood.

Beth had seen enough crime scene photos in her time to know exactly what she was looking at. But what she'd never seen was *herself* in a crime scene photo, and one of the women lying on that mattress was surely her, USC sweatshirt and all.

The sight of her inert, bloodied body rendered her momentarily speechless.

Vargas tapped the touchpad again, showing her a new photo, shot from a different angle. Then a third, more distant shot that included most of the room, and three more dead bodies.

'These were taken right before they realized you were still breathing,' he said.

Beth struggled to find her voice. 'Before *who* realized? I don't see a head wound, and this sure as hell isn't a Taco Bell parking lot. What's going on here? Is this where I think it is?'

'The House of Death,' Vargas said. 'You were one of the victims.'

'That's impossible, how could I . . .'

But it *wasn't* impossible, was it? The evidence didn't lie. She was no expert in Photoshop manipulation, but she was pretty sure these were genuine.

But how had she gotten there? And why?

Beth reached across and tapped the touchpad, going back to the first photo. She stared at it, trying with everything she had to summon up the memory. But no matter how hard she concentrated, nothing came. It was a dark shape in an even darker room, and she'd need a much brighter light than a few photographs could provide.

'Please,' she said to Vargas, 'tell me everything you know.'

'It's not all that much. Most of it happened after these were taken, not before. With a lot of rumour thrown in for good measure.'

'I don't care,' Beth said, feeling a sudden urgent need wash over her. A need to know. 'Tell me what happened to me. Tell me how I got here.'

VARGAS

63

So Vargas told her, laying it out just as he had twenty-four hours ago for Detective Pasternak. He told her what was fact and what was rumour, about the nuns and Rojas and the Ainsworths, and about Pasternak's promise to take the investigation into her shooting down to Juarez.

But none of it broke through.

None of it was able to penetrate the wall her injured brain had erected around that part of her past.

When she had first appeared in the courtyard and introduced herself, Vargas had been surprised that she was walking on her own and seemed so clear headed. The way Pasternak had described her, he'd thought this visit might be premature. But it had quickly become obvious that in a few short weeks she had made more progress than Manny had made in fifteen long years.

Vargas had also been surprised to discover that she wasn't the woman from the passport photo. There were vague similarities, yes, but it was obvious to him now that the discrepancies between the passport and crime scene photos had nothing to do with age or gunshot wounds. It was much simpler than that.

The passport photo was merely a keepsake.

Crawford was the older sister.

And to Vargas's further surprise, he found himself attracted to her. She may not have been as drop-dead gorgeous as her sibling, but she was beautiful in her own way. And smart and vulnerable and not afraid to speak her mind.

And he liked that.

He liked it a lot.

'Is any of this helping?' he asked.

She stared at the image on the computer screen for a long moment, then lowered her head, looking down at her hands in her lap.

They were trembling.

He shifted his gaze to the scar on her scalp, the tufts of hair growing around it, and had the sudden urge to reach out and place his palm against it, wishing he could somehow heal her wounded psyche with his touch. Make her whole again. In his imaginary movie, her face would light up and all of the pieces of the puzzle that were missing would come to her in quick, dramatic flashes, and he would pull her into his arms and kiss her, celebrating the miraculous breakthrough.

But, once again, reality intruded. The conveniences of Hollywood wouldn't play here.

She looked up at him now, and there were tears in her eyes.

'Thank you,' she said softly. She wiped her tears with her sleeve. 'At least now I know *how* it happened. How I got this way. And that's something, isn't it?'

He nodded. 'But maybe you're better off not remembering.'

'I wouldn't go that far. I'd be happy to suffer a little emotional distress if it meant a fully functioning brain.'

'Point taken,' Vargas said. 'So let's try one last thing.'

She looked at him quizzically as he reached into his pocket and pulled out the string that held the hooded skull ring. La Santisima.

'The boy I told you about. Junior? He took this from you when they found you in the house.'

He placed it in her hands.

Beth stared at it, her brow furrowing.

Then suddenly she was crying again, a flood of uncontrolled tears rolling down her cheeks.

'Oh my God,' she said. 'Oh my God.'

64

Vargas felt helpless, wanting to console her, but not quite sure how to go about it.

'What is it? Do you remember something?'

'Yes . . .' she said. 'I—I mean, no, not in the way you think. This is the ring my sister Jen picked out for me in Playa Azul. She had one just like it. We bought them from a street vendor, right before she disappeared.'

She clutched the ring tightly in her hand and closed her eyes, getting lost in the moment. Then she looked at him, wiped her tears again.

'Sorry about that.'

'Nothing to be sorry about,' he said, then nodded to the ring. 'Do you know what that symbolizes?'

She looked at it, shrugged. 'I figure it's some kind of spooky, Goth thing. I'm sure the kids love them.'

'It's no Goth thing,' Vargas said. 'I'm pretty much convinced that what happened to you in that house may be related to a religious cult.'

'What?'

'That hooded skull is the symbol of La Santisima; Holy Death.'

She said nothing, but her face suddenly went pale, and Vargas knew he'd struck a nerve.

'What is it?'

'La Santisima. I've heard that before.'

'Where?'

'From Rafael.'

Vargas was at a loss. 'Rafael?'

'Rafael Santiago. We met him and his sister Marta on the cruise the night before Jen went missing. They took her back to their cabin. And I'm pretty sure they had something to do with her disappearance.'

'Are these the two the police checked into?'

She nodded. 'But they don't believe me. No one believes me. My own doctor thinks the Santiagos are a figment of my imagination.'

Vargas, who had his own share of credibility problems, could sympathize.

'What was it this Rafael guy said about La Santisima?'

'I ran into him on the street in Playa Azul. Although I'm not sure it was an accident. And he started talking about spirituality and some other b.s. to try to justify the fact that he was boffing his own sister.'

'What?'

'It's too disgusting to even get into. But he told me that they were blessed by La Santisima. That we all are.'

The words sounded chillingly familiar to Vargas. Unfortunately, it didn't really mean all that much.

'Let's not get too excited,' he said. 'Worship of La Santisima is pretty common in Mexico. This might just be a coincidence. Did he mention anything about La Santa Muerte or a guy called El Santo?'

She thought about it, then shook her head.

'But Jen said that Marta Santiago was a *bruja* and claimed that she could speak to the dead.'

'I'm afraid that's pretty common, too,' Vargas said. 'My own aunt liked to tell us she was a *bruja*. Scared the hell out of me. But the only dead person she ever spoke to was her husband, and usually to curse him.'

He could see the disappointment in Beth's eyes. He felt it, too.

Her shoulders slumped and she said, 'So what happens now?'

'What do you mean?'

'Now that I'm a big fat bust, your story's at a dead end – no pun intended. Where do you go from here?'

Vargas thought about this. There was really only one place left to go.

'Back to Mexico,' he told her. 'Down to Ciudad de Almas.'

'Why there?'

'That's where the nuns were from. A small church down there – the Church of the Sacred Heart. The priest was interviewed by the Chihuahua state police, but he wasn't much help. Maybe I'll have more luck with . . .' He paused. The look in Beth's eyes had changed. 'What is it?'

'Ciudad de Almas. That's where Rafael said he was from.'

'Probably just another coincidence,' Vargas said.

She shook her head. 'No. That's too many now.

I've worked a lot of cases, and when the coincidences start piling up, it means they aren't coincidences at all.' She paused, weighing a thought, then looked directly at him. 'Take me with you.'

'What?'

'To Mexico. This is all connected somehow. I know it is. I can feel it my gut.'

'I'm not sure that's a good idea.'

'Maybe all I need to jog the memories is to get out of this godforsaken place. Feel like I'm *doing* something, rather than sitting here like a warmed-over piece of meat.'

'You're not well,' Vargas said. 'The clinic would never release you.'

'I'm here of my own free will. I can leave whenever I want to.'

Vargas hesitated. 'You don't even know me. A few minutes ago you were ready to throw me out.'

She took hold of his hands, squeezed them.

'Please, Nick. Take me with you. We'll start in Playa Azul and work our way to Ciudad de Almas.'

'There are people trying to hurt me,' he told her. 'I can't get you mixed up in that.'

'Bullshit. I'm *already* mixed up in it. Why else would you be here?' She paused. 'You have to help me, Nick. Help me fill in this gap and find out what happened to Jen. I'm begging you.'

Vargas stared at her, at the desperation in her eyes. Despite her progress she still looked fragile and not particularly roadworthy.

But she needed to know the truth even more than

he did. And when he thought about it, her quest could well be the central theme of his book. He could build the story around her. *Through* her. Her presence would give it the emotion it needed.

Besides, there was something about this woman that compelled him to want to help her – that instant, undeniable attraction he'd felt the moment she walked into the courtyard. A feeling he'd never experienced before now.

'There's no guarantee we'll find what you're looking for,' he said.

'Maybe not. But I sure as hell won't find it here.'

PATIENT'S JOURNAL

Day 61?
2.00 p.m.

My last entry.

I'm not even sure why I'm writing this, because in a few minutes I'll be headed back to Playa Azul and everything I've said here will remain behind to gather dust and be forgotten.

I have no intention of telling the nurses or Dr Stanley that I'm leaving. They would only try to stop me. Would tell me that I'm not yet ready for the outside world.

Maybe that's true.

I have no idea how long I'll be able to maintain this clarity, but I can't stay in this place any more, wondering about those missing months. Not knowing what really happened.

I'm not sure if Nick knows about my 'episodes'. I couldn't tell him myself, for fear he'd have a change of heart and leave me stranded here. It was hard enough convincing him to take me with him in the first place.

So we'll deal with the problem if it arises.

When it arises.

As Jen always says, it's better to ask pardon than permission. Which, I guess, has always been the fundamental difference between us. I've spent too much of my life following the rules. Seeking approval.

But that's about to change.

As I sit here, waiting for the right moment to slip away, that small boy has caught my eye again – one arm cradling the stuffed dog, while the other is wrapped around his mother's leg.

I don't know why he stirs something inside me. Not sure why I feel like crying when I see him. But those dark, shapeless, almost-memories are back, struggling to break through the layers of tissue that separate me from my past.

Visiting hour is almost over. In a moment I'll go back to my room and quietly change into some street clothes. I'll wait for the crowd of family and loved ones to start migrating towards the exit, then slip away through the south doors and climb into Nick's waiting car.

For the first time in all the days I've spent here, I feel hope.

Real hope.

Dr Stanley once told me about a patient of his who spent her days in a fantasy world, getting up every morning to go to work, then sitting at the edge of her bed as if she were typing at an office desk.

When her relatives came to visit, she greeted them as fellow employees and took coffee breaks with them in the day room.

Then one morning she awoke and her fantasy world was gone. She knew exactly where she was and why she was there, and spoke with a lucidity she'd never before demonstrated. It was as if a simple switch had been flipped, and all was back to normal.

So maybe it *will* come back to me. All of it. A flick of a switch and I'll finally be whole again.

That's not too much to ask for, is it?

To be whole again?

THREE

DIA DE LOS MUERTOS

MR BLISTER

65

He spent his first night in Los Angeles at a believer's home near Silverlake.

As a gesture of respect, the father shared his oldest daughter with him, a slender nineteen-year-old who had been blessed by La Santisima with flawless beauty. She pretended not to notice his ruined face as she took him to her bed.

And he pretended not to care.

But when she straddled him and closed her eyes, quietly praising God as she worked her hips, grinding her body against his, he wondered if she was thinking of someone else.

Someone handsome.

Like *he* used to be.

Afterwards, they got dressed and had dinner with the family, followed by an hour of prayer.

The youngest daughter sang a song about Jesus, and he smiled politely and applauded, thinking that she was even more beautiful than her sister – and only a year or so away from her initiation into woman-hood.

Maybe he could convince her father to save her for him.

As a gesture of respect.

He had thought about driving by the rehabilitation clinic that night. But he was worn out by the sex and the long drive from El Paso, and the meal they'd served was weighing him down.

So he decided to go straight to bed.

In the middle of the night, he felt the mattress shift and opened his eyes to find the mother climbing in next to him, naked. She took his hand and placed it between her thighs, letting him feel her heat. Her wetness.

'It would be an honour,' she murmured, 'to serve the son of El Santo. To let my body be the vessel for his release.'

He was tired, but it would be an insult to the family to refuse her. And, unlike her daughter, she did not close her eyes. Instead, she stared at him with the gaze of the truly devoted as she received him in the name of God and La Santisima.

On his second night in Los Angeles, he went by the reporter's apartment. El Santo had ordered him to leave the man alone, and, while he understood the reasoning, he'd felt uneasy about the command ever since it had been given.

El Santo was getting old. And careless. And may have misinterpreted the signs.

His uneasiness grew when the believers he'd assigned to keep an eye on the reporter's apartment called and told him that Vargas had not yet returned.

So, after much prayer, he drove out to the Burbank apartment building and let himself in, checking the reporter's computer, his notes, for any indication that he might know more than they'd been led to believe.

He found nothing, but that didn't settle his uneasiness. And he knew that this wasn't over.

Sooner or later, something would have to be done.

That same night, he parked the Town Car near a street corner several yards from the rehabilitation clinic.

He had no right to be here.

Another of El Santo's commands.

'We made a promise,' the old man had told him. 'We leave her alone.'

'And if she remembers?'

'Then we will pray for guidance and act accordingly. Until that day, however, we must honour our pledge.'

But no matter how he tried, he could not bring himself to let it rest. To forget about her.

She was, after all, the woman who had changed his life forever. She was the reason he could not look into a mirror without feeling revulsion and anger consume him, aching to be released.

She was the woman he loved.

So he sat in his car, watching the building that housed her, wondering if she was asleep. All he would have to do was slip inside, put a pillow over her face, and that would be the end of it.

Clean. Quiet. Simple.

But then it wouldn't really be so simple, would it? Soon El Santo would find out, would know what he'd done, and he would face the threat of banishment, all his years of devotion marked by shame and humiliation.

'Leave her to La Santisima, my son. She has already been punished enough.'

But he couldn't leave her. He continued to watch the building until he could no longer keep his eyes open.

Then, the next morning, he came awake, surprised to find himself stretched across the seat.

And as he sat up, he received a message from God. What else could it be?

He saw her, walking along the edge of the field behind the clinic, a man in white guiding her, ready to catch her should she fall.

As they rounded a corner, she glanced back in his direction, and his heart momentarily stopped, but he didn't think she could see him from this distance.

She did, however, look much better than they'd been led to believe.

Thinner, perhaps. But healthy. Beautiful.

And he knew at that moment, that whatever the consequences, he could not wait for El Santo's permission to do what he knew must be done.

For his own sanity, if nothing else.

Soon he would return, find her in her room, and make his offering to La Santisima.

66

That night, it was the mother he chose to be with. While it was true that she was older and imperfect, she was still a handsome woman with skills her daughter had not yet perfected.

As she pleasured him with her golden tongue, the door opened behind her and her husband entered the room, naked, and took her from behind.

She groaned with pleasure, handling her task with even greater enthusiasm now.

He didn't object to this intrusion.

It was, after all, only natural for the husband to want to share in her joy before God.

They were sleeping when his cell phone rang.

He checked the screen and saw that it was one of the believers he'd assigned to watch Vargas.

'He has returned,' the caller said. 'What would you like us to do?'

'Keep your distance. I want to speak to him first.'

He clicked off, but didn't call the reporter imme-diately. It was past 1 a.m. and he wanted to give Vargas time to crawl into bed and fall asleep, then catch him at a moment of vulnerability, only half-awake and more likely to tell the truth.

So instead of calling, he made himself hard again, then rolled the mother over and thrust into her from behind, feeling her come awake with a soft moan, her muscles expanding, then contracting around him.

When they were done, he made the call, surprised to find Vargas still alert. And while he knew the man was lying – could sense it – it did not matter. He had already made up his mind that El Santo was wrong about this. That Vargas needed to go.

So he called the believers outside the reporter's apartment building and told them to get it done.

Late that morning he got word that Vargas had survived and was nowhere to be found.

Not only that, the Corolla was also missing from the apartment building parking lot, which meant that Vargas had been brave enough to return for it.

He couldn't help but admire the man for his willingness to take such a risk. But he knew now that he had underestimated Vargas and should not have left the task to someone else as he wasted time pleasuring his hostess. And all of this was further proof that the entire matter had been handled badly and that he should have killed Vargas back in Texas.

Perhaps El Santo wasn't merely old, but had taken leave of his senses. Perhaps La Santisima had abandoned him. And when the old man spoke to her, he was no longer in touch with her divine spirit, but merely speaking to voices inside his own addled brain.

Cursing himself for thinking such vile thoughts, he sent up a prayer, asking for forgiveness. And because he knew El Santo would soon learn of his disobedience, he called the old man and confessed.

But El Santo was in a merciful mood.

'What's done is done,' he said. 'You must come home, my son. The celebrations are about to begin. We will pray together and ask La Santisima to guide us.'

'Yes, father. I will leave today.'

But he didn't leave. Not immediately.

A few hours, he decided, would not make a difference, and if El Santo complained, he would explain that he had taken time to steal another car.

And this was true. He *did* steal a new car.

But that night, shortly past eight, he thanked the family for their hospitality, blessing them in the name of his father, then drove over to the rehabilitation clinic, parked across from the entrance and waited.

Then, when he saw the lone security guard step outside for a cigarette, he drove around to the back, vaulted the chain-link fence and entered the building through the courtyard, marvelling at how little attention they paid to securing the place.

This was, after all, a dangerous city.

The clinic was quiet. The patients all seemed to go to bed early, with only the guard and a single nurse on duty. Their charts hung on hooks outside their doors, so it took him no time whatsoever to find her room.

Which was dark inside.

Unlike a traditional hospital, there weren't bright lights all around, making it impossible to sleep. So he took a penlight from his pocket, flicked it on, then crossed to the bed, anxious to complete his task and leave.

But the bed was empty.

Surprised, he swept the beam around the room, but she wasn't here.

So where had she gone?

All but the night nurse and the security guard were fast asleep, so it made no sense that she wasn't in bed.

Crossing the room, he checked the small closet and found her robe hanging on a hook inside, along with several changes of clothing. He moved to a chest of drawers and found fresh pyjamas, underwear, T-shirts, jeans. There was a pile of *People* magazines on top.

So where was she?

Turning, he swept the beam around the room again, coming to a stop on the nightstand, where he saw a small, double hinged picture frame. Both photographs had been removed, and next to it lay a pen and a spiral-bound notebook.

Curious, he crossed to the nightstand, picked up the notebook and quickly leafed through it: a journal she'd been keeping of her time here. Flipping to the last page of writing, he stared down at her words, and his bewilderment suddenly turned to anger. A hot, white living thing that grew inside his chest with each new beat of his heart.

She wasn't just missing from her room. She had left the hospital entirely, abandoning what little she owned. Gone for good.

According to the journal entry she was headed for Playa Azul.

With someone called Nick.

The reporter.

Ignacio Vargas.

BETH

67

Before leaving Los Angeles that afternoon, they stopped at a thrift store to buy more clothes and a small suitcase to hold them. Then it was on to a supermarket for food and toiletries. They had no idea how long they'd be in Mexico, but it didn't hurt to prepare.

On the way to San Diego they encountered a traffic jam. A truck had jack-knifed on the freeway, and according to the traffic report, several cars were damaged and three people had been killed.

This was not, Beth thought, a good omen.

After she had told Nick the story of Jen's disappearance – with as many details as she figured he could stand – they spoke very little as they drove, each consumed by thoughts of their own. But what Beth found surprising was that there didn't seem to be any of the usual awkwardness between them. That feeling of discomfort when you spend a large amount of time with someone you've just met.

Despite their silence, Beth found herself at ease sitting next to him.

Was this because of the man himself? Or the fact that they shared a common goal?

Probably both, she thought.

But she couldn't be sure.

As they crawled past the accident, Beth saw a young family standing on the side of the road near their mangled car. All seemed to have escaped in one piece, but they looked shaken and slightly shell-shocked: a man and his young wife, who cradled their baby in her arms.

The baby was crying.

The sight of the child once again stirred something in Beth's mind: those shadowed memories that were trying hard to break through. And for one fleeting moment, she caught a glimpse of a face in the darkness.

But before it could fully register, it was gone – a barely remembered whisper – and she had no idea what to make of it.

'There's something I've been wanting to ask you,' Nick said. 'But you may not know the answer.'

'Which is?'

'Who's Angie?'

She looked at him. 'The police told you about that, did they?'

'Not the police,' Nick said. 'The boy. Junior. He told me you said it when they found you. He thought it was *your* name.'

'I've wondered about it ever since the police questioned me. But I don't remember an Angie or an Angela or anything close to that.'

Nick nodded and said nothing more, returning his concentration to the road. The traffic had started to clear and before long they were rolling into San Diego, where they took a bathroom break and picked up a couple of coffees. Beth noticed Nick quickly survey the area as if he were looking for someone. He continued to move stiffly, favouring his right shoulder, and she wondered if whoever had done that to him was out there somewhere, waiting to do it again.

Or worse.

When they got back in the car, Beth said, 'Are you ever going to tell me about your shoulder?'

Nick took a long sip of his coffee, then set it in the cup holder between the seats.

'I warned you, there are people who are after me.'

'Because of me.'

'No,' he said. 'Because we're dealing with some very secretive assholes who are into some very dangerous shit. I happened to stick my nose in where it doesn't belong and after a couple of fuck-ups on their part, they're pretty anxious to cut it off.'

'La Santa Muerte.'

'That's my guess, yeah.'

'I've been thinking about what you said. About Juarez.'

'What about it?'

'All those kidnappings Rojas was under pressure to solve. What if they have something to do with La Santa Muerte, too?'

Nick looked at her. 'You think they may have been recruiting women by snatching them off the street?'

'I spent enough years prosecuting special crimes to know never to underestimate the darkness of the human soul. And there's no reason these people wouldn't be just as active in Mexico City or Playa Azul or even onboard a cruise ship. Where all the tourists are.'

'Like you and your sister.'

'I think Jen was targeted on that cruise,' Beth said. 'By Rafael and Marta Santiago.'

'It's a theory. But it still doesn't explain what happened to *you*.'

Beth had been thinking about this, too. 'I guess I poked my nose in where it didn't belong,' she said, 'and got it cut off.'

68

By the time they reached Playa Azul, she could feel a headache coming on.

Nothing to be alarmed about just yet, but her episodes usually began and ended with a migraine, and there was no point in taking chances.

'I'm gonna need to lie down soon,' she said.

'You okay?'

'Just a headache. I'll be fine when I'm horizontal.'

This may or may not have been true. She had no way to predict what might happen in the next hour – or minutes, for that matter – but she saw no reason to alarm Nick.

'I know a hotel that has decent rooms,' he said, 'and even better rates.'

'Thanks.'

As they pulled into the city, caught up in another traffic jam, Beth looked out of her window and couldn't help feeling as if she'd never left this place – and in a way, she hadn't.

A cruise liner sat in the harbour, possibly the very same ship she and Jen had taken down from Long Beach almost a year ago.

Playa Azul's streets were bustling as usual, but there seemed to be an extra current of excitement in the air. Everywhere you looked there were flowers and multi-coloured banners, store fronts filled with candles and full-sized skeletons, wrapped in garlands and gold satin.

It occurred to Beth that today was Halloween in the States, but this didn't look like any Halloween she'd ever seen and she wasn't quite sure that that was what was going on here. All she could think about was Nick's talk of religious cults and the world of *brujas* and La Santisima.

Then, as they turned a corner, they drove past a storefront that featured a grinning skull on top of an ornate, flower-laden altar, bright red roses poking out of each eye socket.

Nick glanced at the display. 'All this time I've been spending in Mexico and I forgot all about the festival.'

'Festival?'

'Dia de los Muertos. The Day of the Dead.'

'How appropriate. I don't suppose this has any-thing to do with El Santo and company?'

'Hardly. Dia de los Muertos is a celebration that dates all the way back to the Aztecs. It's about families coming together to honour their lost loved ones.'

Nick turned the wheel and rounded another corner, pulling up in front of a small, boxy-looking hotel that couldn't have held more than ten rooms.

The sign out front read CORONA POSADA.

Climbing out of the car, they grabbed their things and went inside to the front desk, only to be told that because of the festival, there were no vacancies. But when Nick explained that they were only here for the night – slipping the desk clerk a fifty in the process – two adjoining rooms miraculously became available.

Ten minutes later Nick opened the door to Beth's room and ushered her inside, dropping her suitcase near the closet. The place was tiny, but clean and well maintained, with a view overlooking a beautifully manicured garden.

Beth was impressed. But then anything looked better than a hospital room.

'What did I tell you?' Nick said.

'Very nice. But I don't expect you to pay for this.'

'Don't worry about it.'

'I may have been out of commission for the last couple months, but I've still got money in the bank and I'm good for it.'

'Just get some rest, okay? We'll talk about this later.'

Beth smiled. Was he really this good a guy?

Yes, she thought. Maybe he was.

Nick crossed to the door, looking back at her, and she was surprised to find herself suddenly understanding Mary/Marion's unbridled enthusiasm this morning.

'I've gotta run an errand,' he said. 'But I should be back in about an hour or so. I'll be next door if you need me.'

'Would you mind leaving your computer? I'd like to look at those photos again.'

He nodded, then reached into his backpack, pulled out the netbook and set it on the table by the door.

'If you're up to it after I get back, we can start retracing your steps in town, see if it jars anything loose.'

Then he was gone.

Beth stared down at the garden for a moment, then retrieved the netbook and took it over to the bed. But her head was really pounding now, so she set the computer aside and lay back, trying to get her bearings, thinking how strange it felt not to be staring up at the ceiling of her hospital room.

Sleep. That's what she needed.

She hadn't had any since her episode last night.

So she closed her eyes, hoping the headache would go away without incident.

But when she opened them again, she was back on the deck of the cruise liner, looking out at the rolling ocean.

VARGAS

69

He found the house without difficulty, using Google Maps on his cell phone to guide him to a neighbourhood crowded with parked cars, some of which looked as if they hadn't moved in a couple of decades.

The Corolla fitted right in.

The roads in this part of the city were graded but unpaved, and the houses all had rings of dirt around them, looking worn and lived-in.

Back in LA, as Vargas had waited for Beth to pick out clothes at the thrift store, he'd made a call to his cousin Tito in Tijuana, who had hooked him up with a contact here in Playa Azul.

The contact, a guy named Ortiz, was said to be well connected in the area. But if Ortiz was making any money through those connections, it sure as hell didn't show in his choice of houses.

Vargas parked his car out front and emerged to find a couple of teenagers squatting in the front yard, smoking cigarettes. One of them eyed him suspiciously, then jumped to his feet and ran around the side of the house.

As Vargas worked his way up the drive, the kid

returned, accompanied by a hulk in a wife-beater T-shirt.

'You Ortiz?' Vargas said in Spanish.

The hulk replied by stopping him in his tracks, then spun him around and patted him down.

Satisfied that Vargas was unarmed, the hulk gestured for him to follow and they walked around the side of the house to the back yard, where a cluster of men were seated at a beaten-up picnic table passing a joint and drinking bottled beer.

The hulk made eye contact with one of them – a small, muscular guy – who looked up at Vargas and smiled.

'Hey, *pocho*, you finally made it.'

Pocho was not a term of endearment. It was a slur against Mexican Americans – which was ironic, considering Ortiz was a transplant, born and raised in San Diego. But Vargas let it pass.

As if he had a choice.

'Traffic,' he said. 'I assume you're Ortiz?'

'That's me,' the guy told him, then got to his feet and shouted towards the back of the house. 'Hey, Yolanda, open the shed.'

A moment later an attractive girl with a neck tattoo and a permanent scowl on her face emerged carrying a key dangling from a leather strap. They followed her across the yard to a walk-in shed, and Vargas couldn't help but notice that her jeans had been airbrushed on.

'Don't be staring at my cousin's ass, *pocho*. She's likely to take a razor to your *albondigas*.'

He smiled as he said it (Ortiz seemed to be one of

those guys who was always smiling) but the threat was clearly sincere, and Yolanda looked like just the girl to carry it out.

Averting his gaze, Vargas waited as she unlocked the shed, threw the door open, then turned on her heels and headed back to the house without a backward glance.

Ortiz stepped inside and flicked a light switch, revealing what looked like a typical tool shed with a variety of gardening and mechanic's tools lining its walls.

There were a couple of large, flattened cardboard boxes on the floor, and Ortiz shoved one of them aside, then reached down, flipped up a small metal handle and pulled, grunting as he opened a hatch.

A short set of steps led downwards, and Vargas realized that this was a bunker, not a shed, a nice, convenient hidey hole for Ortiz's wares.

They went down the steps, moving into a room that wasn't much larger than a walk-in closet. There were tools on the walls in here, too, but you wouldn't be repairing a car or raking the yard with any of them.

There were enough knives and guns here to start a revolution. And win.

'Make your choice, *pocho*. We have a discount today on small calibre weapons.'

Gun laws in Mexico were strict. Licences to carry were not only mandatory, but difficult to get, and weapons could only be purchased at a specific, government-run store in Mexico City. Not that this kept the locals from buying and trading at will.

For tourists, however, carrying a gun was next to impossible. The fines and prison sentences were hefty for anyone caught bringing a firearm or even ammunition into the country without prior consent, and Vargas hadn't been willing to cross the border with one in his possession.

But last night Mr Blister's men had tried to kill him, and now that he was potentially travelling in La Santa Muerte's playground, he wasn't about to continue this journey without some kind of protection.

He needed something small and easily concealed, and found it hanging from a hook directly in front of him.

A Beretta Tomcat.

'How much?' he asked, indicating his preference.

'Is that how you start a negotiation, *pocho*? How much? Why don't you make me an offer, instead.'

Vargas did and Ortiz laughed. 'Now I understand why you asked how much.'

He made a counter-offer and Vargas thought it was a bit steep, but didn't feeling like quibbling over it.

'Sold,' he said, and Ortiz laughed again.

'You're too easy. And you don't even try before you buy.'

'All I care is that it puts a hole in somebody when I need it to,' Vargas said.

Another laugh.

'It'll do that, amigo. That much I guarantee.'

70

When they were done making the exchange, Vargas tucked the Tomcat into his waistband, then covered it with his shirt and said, 'Tito tells me you're pretty well connected down here.'

'I know a few people.'

'I'm doing a favour for a friend. Looking for someone who disappeared here a little less than a year ago.'

'A year?' Ortiz said. 'Might as well be a century.'

'Yeah. I'm sure this is a long shot, but maybe you know something about her.'

He took the photo of Beth's sister from his back pocket and handed it to Ortiz. He'd bought some tape at the supermarket in LA and had taped the two pieces together.

'She was a cruise ship passenger. The sister says she disappeared after going into a leather goods shop downtown.'

Ortiz studied the photo. 'Nice piece of ass, but she doesn't look familiar. You've seen one tourista you've seen them all.'

'How many of them disappear without a trace?'

'Do I look like a statistician? This place is just like any other. Shit happens.'

Oh well, Vargas thought.

It was worth a try.

Ortiz started to hand back the photo but Vargas didn't take it.

'Do me a favour and keep that for now. Pass it around, see what you can find out. I'll make it worth your while.'

Ortiz shook his head. 'I ain't your errand boy, *pocho*.'

'As a favour to Tito.'

Ortiz snorted. 'You speaking for Tito now? That's a pretty bold move, amigo. He may be your cousin and all, but I'm not sure he'd appreciate you using his name like that. I know Yolanda wouldn't. Man racks up a debt, he should at least know about it, don't you think?'

'You're right,' Vargas said, then nodded to the photograph. 'I'm just trying to find out what happened to her.'

'You sure she wants you to? Maybe she'd rather not be found.'

'That's a possibility, but I doubt it. She and her sister were pretty tight.'

Ortiz looked at the photo again.

'Like I said, a year is ancient history. But maybe Little Fina knows something about her.'

'Little Fina?'

'She runs the local skin trade. And if this one got involved in anything kinky – voluntary or not – she'd have to go through Fina.'

'So where do I find her?'

Ortiz laughed. 'You don't. But I can make some calls, see if I can set up an introduction. You got a way for me to reach you?'

Vargas gave him his cell phone number. 'Thanks. I appreciate it.'

'Don't thank me too soon,' Ortiz said. 'Little Fina makes Yolanda look like a blushing schoolgirl. And that ain't easy to do.'

71

He stopped at a nearby *taqueria* before heading back to the hotel. All they'd had to eat and drink on the drive down were chips and sodas and coffee, and he hoped that some real food might help put a little colour back in Beth's face. She had looked pretty pale when he left, and he wondered if bringing her down here had not just been a bad idea, but a colossally stupid one.

Detective Pasternak had told him that she'd had trouble staying in the here and now, and while she'd seemed fine at the rehabilitation clinic and during the drive, that headache she'd complained about worried him.

Was he being irresponsible?

Should he have ignored her request and gone straight to Ciudad de Almas as he'd originally intended?

Had he let his desire for a story – or worse, his attraction to her – cloud his judgement?

It was too late, he supposed, to be asking such questions. He had always been a man who relied on his instincts, and sometimes he got it wrong.

Best to just leave it at that.

But if she did become a problem, what would he do? What *should* he do? Take her back?

Pulling into the hotel parking lot, he grabbed the sack of taquitos and burros from the passenger seat and headed up the steps to their rooms on the first floor. Letting himself into his own room, he went to the adjoining door and gently rapped on it, not wanting to startle her.

There was no answer.

He tried again. Waited.

Still nothing.

He knew he should let her sleep, but he was concerned about her. He'd been gone almost two hours.

'Beth?'

Again, no answer.

Slipping his key into the slot, he opened the door a crack and peeked inside.

The bed was empty. His netbook lying on it.

'Beth?'

He pushed the door wide, saw no sign of her. The bathroom was open, but he checked in there anyway and found it empty.

Moving to the nightstand, he picked up the phone and dialled the front desk.

When the clerk answered, Vargas said, 'Have you had any calls from this room?'

'Señor?'

'This is my friend's room. She's not here and I'm worried about her and I'm wondering if she may have called you, had some kind of problem.'

'No, señor, I've been here all afternoon and no calls. Would you like me to send security?'

'No,' Vargas said. 'I've got it.'

Thanking the man, he hung up, then left the bag of taquitos and burros on the nightstand and headed out of the door.

Five minutes later he was on Avenida Lopez Mateos, the heart of downtown Playa Azul.

72

The Day of the Dead festival didn't officially begin until tomorrow, but that didn't keep the tourists from starting early.

The streets and bars were packed shoulder to shoulder with people dressed in black, some of them wearing skull masks, others sporting hoods, almost all of them half-drunk and getting drunker. By nightfall, a good portion of them would be back in their hotel rooms or onboard their ship, decorating the carpet with the contents of their stomachs.

Pushing his way through the crowd, Vargas saw no sign of Beth, but hadn't really expected to. Instead, he narrowed his focus on finding the restaurant she'd told him about. Where she'd last seen her sister.

Problem was, he knew there were at least half a dozen outdoor cafes along the main drag and finding the right one, especially in this crowd, could prove to be difficult. And even if he *did* find it, there was no guarantee Beth would be in the vicinity.

Maybe he was concerned for no reason. Maybe she had simply got bored and decided to go for a walk, hoping to jog some of the memories that evaded her.

For all he knew, she could be back at the hotel by now, climbing the steps to her room.

But Vargas didn't think so. He'd spent enough time with Manny over the years to know that something was up and that Beth's headache could well have been a sign of worse things to come.

Cursing himself for leaving her alone, he continued moving, pushing through the crowd until he came upon his first outdoor cafe and knew immediately that this wasn't the one.

No leather goods shop in sight.

Moving on, he went a block and a half and found another one with umbrellaed tables taking up most of the sidewalk, tourists lined up nearby, waiting to be seated.

They were young and loud and Vargas marvelled at how Americans seemed to lose all sense of decorum when they were drunk and on vacation, coming into a foreign country as if they owned it and had the right to be served, screw anyone who got in their way.

Vargas himself tried to blend in whenever possible, no matter what country he might visit. And he was sure there were many Americans just like him. But the loud ones always got the attention and helped generate the anti-American sentiment that pervaded so many countries.

Stalled on the sidewalk, waiting for a crowd of oncoming tourists to pass, Vargas felt a tap on his shoulder and turned, hoping it was Beth.

Instead, he found a couple of glassy-eyed twenty-year-olds staring up at him, both wearing tight black dresses, their faces painted white, with smudges of black around the eye sockets.

'Aren't you that guy?' one of them said.

Vargas was at a loss. 'Guy?'

'The one from that *Desperado* movie.'

'Antonio Banderas,' the other one said, running a finger suggestively along the line of her cleavage. 'You're him, aren't you. Is it true Selma Hayek is only like five feet tall?'

'*No habla inglés,*' Vargas told her, then turned and continued up the street.

Two blocks later, he saw it. A leather goods shop directly across from an enclosed, oblong structure jutting out from the kerb, crowded with diners.

Vargas searched their faces, saw no sign of Beth, then crossed to the leather goods shop and went inside.

The place was jammed with tourists looking at handmade jackets and belts and handbags and luggage. Vargas worked his way to the cash register, told the woman behind the counter who he was looking for and did his best to describe Beth. The woman eyed him as if he were a crazy man and gestured to the half-dozen Beth lookalikes who crowded her store.

Nodding, Vargas went back outside.

Next stop: Armando's.

73

Armando's Cantina was an institution in Playa Azul. Opened in the late nineteenth century, it had seen the town grow up around it, turning into a thriving seaport. But the moment Vargas stepped inside, he knew he had wasted the trip. Not only was Beth not here, but the place was so crowded, the music and conversation and laughs so loud and obnoxious that if she *had* bothered to come by, he was pretty sure she would have fled immediately.

Stepping back out onto the sidewalk and closing the door behind him, a thought occurred to him:

Seaport.

The cruise liner.

He'd seen it docked in the harbour when they drove into town.

If Beth was in a bad way, if she were – as Pasternak had told him – reliving the same two days over and over, wasn't it possible that she would have gone to the ship, thinking that she was still a passenger?

Cutting across the street, he headed in the direction of the harbour. But as the ship came into view, his cell phone rang. He answered it without looking at the screen. 'Vargas.'

'Hey, *pocho*, you're on for midnight.'

'Little Fina?'

'She didn't want to talk to you, but I told her you were writing a book and might make her famous.'

Vargas hesitated. 'How did you know I was writing a book?'

'Come on, genius. Your cousin Tito, remember? You think I'm gonna sell merchandise to a guy, I don't know something about him? He told me your whole sad story.'

'I'll have to remember to thank him for that.'

'You can thank me, too, while you're at it. Where you staying? I'll pick you up around 11.45.'

'You don't need to do that. Just tell me how to get there.'

Ortiz snorted. 'It don't work that way, *pocho*. I drive or it don't happen.'

'Okay, fine,' Vargas said, then told him the name of his hotel. 'What kind of car do you drive?'

'Look for a blue-and-white taxi.'

'You're a cab driver?'

'Hey, man, you think I can make a living selling pop guns to cheap bastards like you? Tourism, baby. That's where the real money is.'

They hung up and Vargas continued west, waiting at the light to cross Avenida Reforma towards the Playa Azul port terminal.

Up ahead was a road leading directly to the ship.

The road was gated, with a security guard standing watch.

And there was Beth, yelling at him.

Vargas couldn't hear what she was saying. But the moment the light turned green, he darted across the street and approached them, and Beth's voice came into range:

'What do you mean, you can't let me in? I just got off the ship this morning.'

'No Seafarer card,' the man said in broken English. 'No Seafarer card, no enter.'

'I told you, I lost it. Now, if you can't—'

'Beth.'

She turned, saw Vargas approaching. Squinted at him. 'Yes?'

'It's me. Nick.'

She just stared at him. 'Nick? Nick who? How do you know my name?'

He gestured to the guard, said in Spanish, 'It's okay, she's with me.'

The guard nodded and turned away, going back to his booth.

'What did you just tell him?' Beth snapped. 'Who the hell *are* you?'

Vargas moved in close, took hold of her shoulders, but she jerked away. 'Let go of me!'

He reached for her again. 'Beth, it's me. Nick.'

'What the hell are you doing? Let me—'

'Stop. *Listen* to me.' He grabbed her shoulders and held firm. 'You didn't just get off that ship. You haven't been on it in months.'

'Get the hell away from me, you fucking perv—'

'*Listen to me*, Beth. You're not well. Your head was injured and you haven't been thinking straight. We came to Playa Azul to try to help you remember.'

'What are you talking about? Remember what?'

'*Concentrate*,' Vargas told her. 'Look at me and concentrate. I'm Nick Vargas. I'm writing a book about you and your sister, Jen.'

At the sound of her sister's name, Beth's eyes came into sharp focus and she stared at him. He could almost see her mind trying to put it all together.

Then there was a sudden shift in her gaze, a look of recognition, then realization, and she stopped resisting.

She was back. 'Oh my God . . .' she said. 'Oh my God . . .'

'It's okay.'

Her eyes filled with tears. 'I can't believe . . . I . . .'

'It's okay,' he said again, then pulled her into his arms, letting her cry against his chest. 'Don't worry about it. I'm here. You're gonna be fine. We're gonna be okay.'

And as she continued to cry, he wondered if that would ever be true.

74

'I've never been so embarrassed in all my life,' Beth said.

They were back in her hotel room now, and she didn't seem to be able to look him in the eye. She stood by the window, staring out at the courtyard, silhouetted against a darkening sky.

She looked waif like, vulnerable. But now that her headache had cleared and she'd regained her mental faculties, she sounded exactly like the hardened prosecutor she once was.

'I'm lucky that poor guard didn't have me arrested.'

'It's not like you jumped up on a table and did a striptease,' Vargas said. 'There's nothing to be embarrassed about.'

'That's easy for you to say. You weren't the one wandering the streets like a crazy woman.'

Vargas sighed. She had a point.

On the walk back, he'd been trying to figure out the best thing to do – what was best for *her* – and he'd come to only one conclusion.

'Listen, Beth. Maybe I should take you back to the clinic.'

She turned, looking at him now. 'Forget it.'

'You're not well,' he said. 'And as much as I hate to say it, you need supervision. God knows what would've happened if I hadn't found you.'

'I won't go back. You can leave me here if you want to, but I won't go back.'

'You aren't safe here. Besides, I'm not leaving you alone. Not again.'

'I'm alone in that clinic, aren't I? My parents are dead, my sister's gone, my cheating bastard of an ex-husband cringes every time I call him . . . I've got no one, Nick. Do you know what it's like to have no one?'

'As a matter of fact, I do.'

'Then don't make me go back there,' she said. 'I'm getting better. I can feel it. And if a headache starts to come on, you can lock me in the goddamn bathroom. I don't care.'

He moved to her.

'Look,' he said, 'you barely know me. I'm not good at being responsible for people. I'm not even good at taking care of myself.'

'You found me, didn't you? You kept me out of trouble.'

'I got lucky. We both did. But how can I pursue this thing if I always have to keep an eye on you?'

She paused. 'So I'm a burden, is that it?'

He didn't want to tell her yes. He didn't even want to be thinking it, but the answer must have been plain on his face, because her eyes grew hot and she pushed past him.

'Fine,' she said. 'Screw you.'

He grabbed her arm as she passed. 'Beth, wait . . .'

But she pulled away from him and spun round, her eyes burning now.

'For what? I don't need you, I don't need anyone. I'm sick and tired of everyone coddling me. I just want . . .' She paused again, trying to control her anger. 'I just want to remember. Why can't I fucking remember?'

Then the tears came again and Vargas moved in close, once again pulling her into his arms. He'd only just met this woman, yet he felt as if he understood her better than anyone he'd ever known.

He felt sorry for her, but it wasn't pity that drove him. He wasn't sure *what* it was. And before he could catch himself, he placed his hand on her head, against her scar, wanting more than anything to draw the pain out of her.

Then he bent down and kissed her cheek.

'I'm a fool,' he said. 'I shouldn't even have suggested taking you back. We're in this together now. And I'll help you remember. I promise.'

She brought her arms up around him then and turned her face towards his, pulling him into an embrace, kissing him. And as he felt the heat of her breath, Vargas thought: this is it, this is that magical movie moment I've been waiting for all my life.

Only it was real.

And the next thing he knew, they were pulling their clothes off and climbing onto her bed, and Vargas felt exhilarated and guilty at the same time, thinking he shouldn't be taking advantage of her vulnerability, her illness, but not wanting to stop.

She didn't seem to want to either. Pulling him towards her, she gently touched the bandage on his shoulder, then kissed him again, using her tongue this time.

And there was an urgency in the kiss – a need – that neither of them could, or wanted to fight.

BETH AND VARGAS

75

She couldn't explain it, wasn't sure why *now* and never with Peter, but the moment Nick pushed himself inside of her, his strong hands cupping her thighs, she felt something she'd never felt before.

It was as if his every kiss, every caress, every flick of the tongue had prepared her for just this moment – yet she wasn't prepared, and the rush of pleasure that consumed her was unexpectedly exquisite. All the muscles in her body seemed to tighten and she had this sudden, intense urge to pee. And when she let it loose – couldn't *stop* herself from letting it loose – a wave of electricity rolled through her, triggering tiny implosions inside her head, followed by a bigger, all-consuming burst of pure ecstasy.

And as she came, a long, guttural moan rose from inside her, and all at once she understood what Jen had been talking about so incessantly for so many years, had constantly been in search of.

Why it had eluded Beth for so long was anyone's guess, but this new sensation surely had a lot to do with the man who was inside her right now.

Not just her body, but inside her mind.

It had a lot to do with how she felt about him. But how exactly *did* she feel?

He was right, she barely knew him. But a connection had been made and why should she try to analyse it?

As he worked his way towards his own burst of ecstasy, she helped him along, moving her hips and her muscles, squeezing him until he finally came, throbbing inside her, releasing himself then collapsing against her as the last of his energy drained away.

Neither of them spoke for a long moment, listening instead to the soft syncopation of their beating hearts, their ragged breaths.

And all at once Beth felt as if she wasn't alone, that she'd never been alone. That this man had somehow been a part of her for as long as she had lived.

A part of her heart. Her mind.

Her body. Her soul.

Vargas lay still, not wanting to spoil the moment, wanting to stay inside her as long as he possibly could. But after a while, he had no choice, so he pulled away and lay beside her, reaching a hand out to stroke her, brushing his fingers across the scars on her chest.

She didn't flinch. Didn't protest.

The wounds were completely healed, yet they looked so painful. So raw. And he suddenly remembered the pain in his own shoulder, which had miraculously disappeared as they made love.

Beth turned to face him then, a drowsy smile on

her lips, and as he looked into her eyes, he wondered how anyone could be so achingly beautiful.

So perfectly fragile.

This is all happening too fast, he thought.

But it felt right somehow. Like it was meant to be.

There is no luck, Mr Blister had told him. *Only destiny*.

Maybe he was right about that.

After a while, Beth said, 'That was unexpected. So what happens now?'

'I think we got something wrong. We may have to try again.'

She laughed. 'That was about as right as I've ever gotten it. But practice makes perfect.'

'So they say. But I have a feeling that isn't what you were asking.' He paused. 'I meant what I said about not taking you back.'

'I know. Thank you.'

'Unfortunately, that creates a dilemma.'

'What do you mean?'

He told her about his upcoming meeting with Little Fina, and Ortiz's promise to pick him up at 11.45.

'No dilemma,' she said. 'I'll just go with you.'

'Probably not a good idea. These aren't friendly people and they won't be expecting you.'

'You keep forgetting what I used to do for a living. I was surrounded by people who weren't very friendly.'

'But always in a controlled environment,' Vargas said. 'This isn't the same.'

'Then I guess we do have a dilemma.'

He could sense that she was starting to get angry again, so he kissed her.

She kissed him back, holding it for a while, then said, 'Nice try, but it's not gonna work this time.'

'Then what do you want me to do? If you were to get hurt, I'd never forgive myself. And as much as I hate leaving you alone, I think you're safer here. The only other alternative is to cancel the meeting.'

She shook her head.

'If there's a chance this Little Fina woman has any information on Jen, I want to know about it.'

'Then, please, Beth, stay here. You can go over my notes, look at the photos again. And if you start to feel another headache coming on, just call me and I'll come right away.'

Beth sighed. 'All right. Fine. I don't want to fight about it. I'm exhausted anyway.'

Vargas smiled. 'Too exhausted for a little more practice?'

He was expecting a quick rejection, but she didn't even have to think about it.

'Nothing wrong with the pursuit of perfection,' she said. 'I think I'm about to make my sister proud.'

76

Ortiz pulled up in front of the hotel on schedule, driving a souped-up blue-and-white Volkswagen Beetle, the words BAJA TAXI painted on the side.

'No comments, *pocho*. I gotta make a living.'

Stifling a smile, Vargas climbed in.

'The way Tito described you, I thought you were some badass gangster.'

'Who says I'm not? These are tough times, amigo. Man's gotta feed his family. You'll never see Yolanda lift a finger to help, so somebody's gotta do it.'

He put the car in gear and pulled out, then turned to Vargas, a quizzical look on his face.

'Something different about you.'

'How so?'

'I don't know. You're smiling a lot more. If I had to guess, I'd say you just got laid.'

Vargas had no idea how he'd managed to figure that one out and didn't really want to know.

'Don't worry,' he said. 'It wasn't Yolanda.'

Ortiz laughed. 'You better hope not. She's done with a guy, she cuts off his privates and hangs 'em on her trophy wall.'

'It's nice to meet a man who has such love and affection for his family.'

Ortiz laughed again. 'You're a funny man, *pocho*.'

'I do my best,' Vargas said.

Ten minutes later, they pulled up to the kerb on a dimly lit side street. There was no sign of any whorehouses or bars in the vicinity, just a row of dilapidated buildings – nondescript businesses that were either closed or no longer operating.

'Where are we?' Vargas asked.

'Little Fina's place is just down the street. I wanted to come a little early so I can make sure you understand the rules.'

'Rules?'

'I told you. Fina makes my cousin look like a prom queen. You gotta be careful how you act around her or she'll have you gutted in about two seconds flat.'

'That's comforting,' Vargas said.

'Just remember, I'm the one bringing you to her, so what you say and do reflects on me. Understand?'

Vargas nodded. 'So what are these rules?'

Ortiz held up three fingers and started counting them off.

'Rule number one,' he said, 'you don't disrespect Little Fina. Rule number two: you don't disrespect Little Fina. Rule number three—'

'I'm sensing a pattern here.'

'I mean no offence when I say this, *pocho*, but you

strike me as a bit of a smartass. That's something you want to avoid in front of Fina.'

'Duly noted,' Vargas said. 'So when do I get to meet her?'

'You see that red door up the street?'

Ortiz pointed and Vargas looked towards the buildings and found the door he was referring to. The paint job was splotchy, but there was no missing it.

'Yeah, I see it.'

'When that door opens and a *cholo* in a white suit steps outside to smoke a cigarette, that's our signal.'

'Why the cloak and dagger?'

'Because that's the way Fina likes it. And don't be asking dumb questions like that in front of her.'

'I'm starting to get the feeling,' Vargas said, 'that your friend is into a lot more than the skin trade.'

'That's not something you want to be talking about either. Just stick to the business at hand.'

'You're really afraid of this woman, aren't you.'

'I'd be lying if I said I wasn't.'

'So then why are you helping me?'

Ortiz shrugged. 'You're a paying customer, *pocho*. And I believe good customer service is the cornerstone of a successful business.'

77

Beth lay in bed for a long time after Vargas left. For a moment she was worried that a fresh new headache might be coming on, but it was a false alarm.

Truth was, her entire body was throbbing. They'd made love three times before Vargas had gone downstairs to meet his contact, and each new orgasm had been stronger than the last.

Which was saying a lot.

Beth almost laughed at the thought. Less than a year ago, she would have said you were crazy if you'd told her she'd ever experience anything like this. And while she'd like to give the credit to Vargas, she had to wonder if the bullet fragments in her brain were somehow affecting her libido. All of which made her think of Jen again, and Albuquerque and the House of Death Vargas had told her about.

Climbing out of bed, she padded naked across the room and sat at the small desk where Vargas had left his netbook and cell phone. The cell phone was programmed to dial his contact Ortiz at the punch of a button.

Lifting the lid of the netbook, she pressed a key to

take it out of sleep mode, then spent the next several minutes going through his notes, which seemed to be more of a random jumble of thoughts than anything else. Certainly not the organized case files she was used to. Even her own journal had made more sense than this.

How he ever managed to assemble a cohesive narrative out of this stuff was beyond her. But she'd never been inside a writer's mind, and if this was any indication of how they worked, she'd just as soon stay out.

Flipping to the file index, she found the crime scene photos he'd shown her at the clinic.

She hesitated before opening them.

Did she really need to see them again?

Yes, she decided. While she knew she had to be patient and wait for her brain to heal, she didn't think it would hurt to give it another little nudge. One last try before she labelled herself a basket case and called it a day.

The first one she opened was the wide shot. The entire room, blood on the walls, on the floor, the mattress. The bodies frozen in motion, leaking fluids.

Her body. Sprawled across the mattress, eyes wide, staring at the ceiling.

No wonder they'd thought she was dead.

The next shot was closer, a high angle, shooting in a diagonal line towards the mattress. Nothing new here.

But in the third one – this one shot from directly above – something had changed. It was a subtle change, but she saw it as plain as can be.

Her mouth had been closed before, but now it

was slightly open. And her eyes didn't seem quite so vacant.

She could imagine the Mexican crime scene photographer staring down at her, noticing the slight movement, maybe even hearing a soft moan, then shouting to his fellow investigators.

'She's alive. This one's alive.'

Then that bastard Rojas – a name she'd never forget – taking her all the way up to Albuquerque and shooting her point-blank, all because he was afraid her presence at his crime scene might ruin a good thing.

She hoped to God that Detective Pasternak and the FBI would be able to get something on the guy. Because she'd love to be sitting in the courtroom when he went down.

But enough of this. She was only getting worked up again, and she'd so much rather bask in the afterglow of her time with Nick. Enjoy it while it lasted.

But then she noticed something else in the photograph. Her right hand, which hung at her side, was clutching something.

Unable to make out what it was, she clicked on the zoom tool and enlarged the image several times until the hand filled the screen.

The image was pixelated, but the original had been taken at a fairly high resolution and she had no trouble seeing what the object in her hand was.

A small wooden toy.

A baby's rattle.

And suddenly she was reminded of the child in the day room who had brought her to tears, and the baby along the highway, secure in his mother's arms. And in that instant, one of the dark, unformed memories they had stirred broke through in the form of letters – four of them, tumbling through her mind like baby blocks, like the pieces of one of her cognitive regeneration exercises:

Y

  D

    A

      N

But what did they mean?

Using every bit of concentration she could muster, Beth arranged those letters in a row, YDAN, but that wasn't even a word.

Pulling open the desk drawer, she found a pad and pen, and quickly wrote the letters down, again and again, working them like an anagram.

D-N-A-Y

Y-N-A-D

N-A-D-Y

A-D-N-Y

And then it hit her, like a sledgehammer directly to the brain:

A-N-D-Y

Andy.

And suddenly she knew. Wasn't sure it was a fully fledged memory, but she *knew* that that was the name she'd muttered over and over through blood-spattered lips as she lay there dying.

Not Angie – but *Andy*.

And for the first time since they'd scraped her off

that parking lot asphalt, she remembered something beyond Playa Azul. A face broke through the membrane – a child's face, a *baby's* face – staring up at her as she cradled him in her arms.

But not just any baby. *Jen's* baby.

Her little nephew.

Andy.

78

At five minutes past midnight, a man in a white suit emerged from the red door and lit up a cigarette.

'This is it,' Ortiz said.

He and Vargas climbed out of the taxi and moved up the street, Vargas once again feeling as if his imaginary movie had somehow overtaken the real world and come to life.

The man in white gestured as they approached. 'Hands.'

Vargas and Ortiz put their hands out, showing them empty, and the man stuck the cigarette between his lips and quickly patted them down, taking the Tomcat from Vargas and a Glock from Ortiz.

'You'll get these back when you leave,' he said, then held up Ortiz's cell phone. 'And this stays off as long as you're inside.'

Ortiz and Vargas said nothing as the man in white pocketed the weapons, then shut off the cell phone and handed it back to Ortiz. Ditching his cigarette, he opened the red door and ushered them inside.

They moved down a long, narrow corridor to another door, this one made of metal.

The man rapped on it and a moment later a slide opened, revealing a pair of female eyes. A pounding bass beat filtered out from behind her.

She eyeballed Vargas and Ortiz, then a latch clicked and the door swung open to reveal an attractive young girl wearing only a red leather thong and matching nipple clamps, as a blast of music hit them full force.

Inside was a large dark room, full of flashing lights and writhing, half-naked bodies, most of them women – a private, very exclusive dance club-slash-whorehouse-slash-S&M parlour with all the requisite accessories.

Too bad the Ainsworths weren't alive to see this place.

Ortiz seemed mesmerized, staring at Ms Red Leather's bobbling breasts with all the subtlety of a cat eyeing a ball of yarn.

The man in white pushed him past her and they skirted the crowd, moving to an enclosed set of stairs that wound upwards towards the first floor. They moved up the steps, the sound of the music growing muffled as they came to another door.

The man in white knocked, waved at the surveillance camera mounted above it, and a moment later the door was opened by a big guy wearing a gun in a shoulder holster.

Another Bullitt clone.

He gestured them inside and they all stepped into a room overlooking the dance floor, reminding Vargas of a box seat at a football stadium.

There were several men and women here, some

seated, some standing, drinks in hand, free hands roaming. Another woman in a red leather thong, *sans* the nipple clamps, was snorting a line of coke off a tabletop.

'Over here,' a voice said. 'Come over here.'

Vargas turned and several of the people stepped to one side, as a woman in a black leather bustier and fishnet nylons waved them away.

Little Fina, Vargas assumed.

Only there was something wrong with this picture.

Not only was Little Fina not little, she wasn't really a woman at all. She was most definitely a man dressed in drag, complete with a five o'clock shadow shading her jaw.

Vargas glanced at Ortiz, but either Ortiz didn't notice or he was too petrified to acknowledge the look.

Little Fina smiled, cutting straight to the chase.

'Ortiz here tells me you have a photograph you want me to look at. May I see it?'

Vargas took the mended passport photo out and handed it to her.

Little Fina studied it. 'Lovely creature. Is she a friend of yours?'

'I've never met her,' Vargas said. 'She's the sister of a friend.'

'And you've been tasked to find her, is that it?'

'More or less.'

Little Fina frowned. 'You know, I've never understood that phrase. Is it more or is it less? Seems to me there's quite a bit of difference between the two.'

'The answer is yes,' Vargas said. 'I've been tasked to find her.'

'And what does this have to do with the book you're writing? The one that Ortiz tells me will make me famous.'

'I think Ortiz may have overstated that a bit.'

'What a surprise,' Little Fina said. 'But he has a habit of doing that. He thinks he's a gangster, but he's really a frightened little boy who's all too eager to please. Isn't that right, Ortiz?'

Ortiz shifted uncomfortably next to Vargas, looking like he'd swallowed something sour. 'Yes, ma'am.'

Little Fina assessed him for a moment, then shifted her gaze to Vargas and handed the photo back.

'I'm sorry to disappoint you, Mr Vargas, but she's not one of mine. Never has been.'

'And you've never seen her before.'

Little Fina smiled. 'There are over five hundred thousand people in this city, Mr Vargas, and millions of tourists flow through here every week. I do my best, but it's hard to keep track of them all.'

'Then I guess we're done,' Vargas said.

He pocketed the photo and started to turn towards the door, when the temperature of Fina's voice dropped about forty degrees.

'We're done when I say we're done.'

Remembering Ortiz's warning, Vargas stopped himself and returned his gaze to her. 'I meant no disrespect.'

'Of course you didn't.' The warmth had returned as abruptly as it left. 'But I'm curious to know about this book of yours. What's it about?'

'Murder,' Vargas told her. 'The Casa de la Muerte murders.'

'Ahhh,' she said. 'The nuns up in Juarez. Poor dears.' She paused. 'Do you have any suspects?'

Vargas saw no harm in telling her.

'There's someone I've been looking at, yeah. And I guess I must have struck a chord, because they're after me now.' He pulled the collar of his shirt back to show her his bandage.

'Ohhh,' she said. 'That looks painful. Do *they* have a name?'

'A religious cult called La Santa Muerte.'

The moment the words left his mouth, the room suddenly went silent. Even the almost-naked woman snorting coke in the corner jerked her head up, white powder ringing her nose. Vargas would have laughed if it hadn't all been so deadly serious.

For a brief moment, Little Fina looked as if she'd been impaled. But she recovered quickly.

And fiercely.

'Ortiz, what were you thinking? The man is being hunted by La Santa Muerte, and you bring him here?'

Ortiz threw his hands up in protest. 'I didn't know. I swear I didn't.'

'What's wrong?' Vargas said to Fina. 'What do you know about them?'

'More than I want to.'

'Meaning what?'

'They're ghosts. Phantoms. They can be every-where and nowhere at the same time. And if they find out that you were in my club, I'll be as dead as you are.'

'Last I looked, I was still standing.'

'Then you're a lucky man,' she said. 'But your luck won't last long, so take your weapons and go. Trust me, you'll need them.'

'Where can I find these people? Do you know?'

Little Fina scowled at him. 'Haven't you been listening to me? Get out. Now. Before I kill you myself.'

She made a quick hand gesture and the man in the white suit grabbed both Vargas and Ortiz by the collar and shoved them towards the stairs.

And as they headed into the abyss below, Little Fina shouted, 'Come back here again, Ortiz, and I'll have your fucking head!'

79

She tried calling the number twice, and got Ortiz's voicemail both times.

Damn it, Nick.

So much for Plan B.

She knew she was only supposed to call if the headaches started again, but she was so bowled over by her sudden revelation that she needed to talk to him, as soon as possible.

On her third try, she left a message.

'Nick, get back here as soon as you can. I have news.'

But what *was* the news?

Sure, she'd remembered the name, and little Andy's face staring up at her, and she knew that he was Jen's child – Jen's *baby*, for godsakes – but how did she know this? And what exactly did it mean?

Was Jen was alive? And if so, where was she? And where was the baby?

It had been nearly a year since their trip to Playa Azul, but the face Beth saw staring up at her in her mind's eye was at least three months old, which meant that Jen had to have been pregnant during the cruise.

But why hadn't she told her?

And how on earth had she hidden it so well?

Beth had seen her naked, standing in their cramped stateroom, and maybe Jen had looked a little thicker than usual, but Beth had attributed that to the breast implants.

But she knew that many women don't start to show until the middle of their second trimester, so Jen could easily have been four months pregnant when she disappeared.

Beth thought back to their lunch together on that last day. She had relived the conversation so many times that she knew the words by heart:

There's something else I've been wanting to tell you. Something . . .

Jen had paused, unable to say the words. And Beth had been too stupid and self-absorbed to pick up on it.

But then this begged a whole new question, didn't it?

If Jen had disappeared before giving birth, how on earth could Beth have held little Andy in her arms?

Either she was confabulating big time – which would undoubtedly make Dr Stanley's day – or that day in Playa Azul was not the last time she'd seen Jen.

Far from it.

Sitting on the edge of her chair, Beth closed her eyes, straining to remember, working the image of little Andy's face through her mind, trying to connect it to a place or an event . . .

But nothing came.

Nothing.

Come on, come on, she thought, squeezing her eyelids tight and concentrating with everything she had.

Break through, goddamn it, break through.

But no matter how she tried, she could not dig deep enough to summon up the memory. The face and name were all she had – and it just wasn't enough.

Consumed by frustration, she jumped to her feet, began pacing the room. More than ever before, she felt trapped. Trapped by a brain that wouldn't cooperate. She moved to the nightstand and stared at herself in the mirror, at the scar on her head, and all she wanted to do was strike out at herself, pummel her brain into submission.

Remember, goddamn it.

Please, *just fucking remember* . . .

And then she began to cry again and hated herself for turning into a weepy little hag, but the tears were all she had, the only way she could purge the frustration. So she let them flow without hindrance, rolling down her cheeks and onto her bare chest. Then she suddenly swung her arms up, banging her fists against her reflection, cracking the glass.

Remember, remember, remember, remember, remember, remember, remember, remember, remember . . .

But it wouldn't come.

It would never come.

She knew that now.

Stumbling to the bed, she fell across the mattress and continued to cry into a pillow, wishing – not for the first time – that she had never made it out of that Taco Bell parking lot.

Because even death would be better than this.

Death was relief.

Release.

Freedom.

Peace.

And she continued to cry, crying until no more tears would come, until her eyes were so swollen she couldn't keep them open, and just as she was about to drift off into sleep, a familiar voice said, 'Hello, Elizabeth.'

Startled, she whipped around, yanking the bedsheets up to cover her naked body as she squinted towards the door and saw a dark figure standing there.

'Who the hell are you? What do you want?'

'It took me a while to find that little car, but I knew I would. And I knew if I found the reporter, I'd find you.'

Beth was frozen. Couldn't move.

Then the figure stepped into the light, and she sucked in a breath, not quite believing what she saw.

It was Rafael Santiago.

But not the perfect specimen she remembered.

This Rafael was different.

This one only had half a face.

80

'You should make me walk back to the hotel,' Vargas said. 'Sorry I screwed things up for you in there.'

Ortiz unlocked his car door and shook his head. 'Did you hear what that fucking *puta* called me?'

'I tend to ignore things that don't make any sense.'

'Damn right it don't make sense,' Ortiz said. 'Frightened little boy . . . She's lucky that *cholo* had my piece. I would've popped one in her hairy little ass right then and there.'

'So we're good?'

Ortiz opened his door and climbed in. 'Get in the car, *pocho*.'

Vargas climbed in next to him and Ortiz said, 'One thing you might've mentioned before we went in there . . .'

'What's that?'

'La Santa Muerte? You don't fuck around.'

'You know about them?'

'I know enough to keep my distance. And Little Fina's right. You got those locos on your ass, you're lucky to be alive.'

'So why aren't you afraid to be seen with me?'

Ortiz took his cell phone out of his pocket and turned it on. 'If I had to worry about all the people I hang out with, I wouldn't have any friends. Besides, they start coming after me, I'll just sic Yolanda on 'em.'

Vargas smiled, and Ortiz started the engine, checking his phone as he put the car in gear.

'What's this?' he said, looking surprised. 'I've got three calls. From *you*.'

Vargas turned. 'Those are from Beth. Let me see that.'

'What – I'm your answering machine now?'

'Just give me the phone.'

Ortiz gave it to him. 'Careful, *pocho*. You're stretching this whole customer service thing a little thin.'

Vargas checked the screen, saw one of the calls was a voicemail. He was about to ask Ortiz for his access code, when the phone rang.

'If that's Yolanda, tell her I'm busy.'

Vargas checked the screen, saw his name flashing, and clicked it on.

'Beth, what's wrong? Are you—'

'—He made me call you, Nick. I didn't want to call you.'

'What are you talking about? Are you getting another headache?'

'No,' Beth said. There was panic in her voice. 'This is real. It's Rafael. He's—'

There was a sudden loud rustling noise, a yelp of pain, then another voice came on the line:

'You've made this very personal, Mr Vargas.'

Vargas felt something thud in his stomach, then spread upward into his chest, paralysing him.

Mr Blister.

'You motherfucker. If you touch her . . .'

'Oh, it is much too late for that, I'm afraid. I've touched her in ways you have only begun to understand. Many times, for many months.'

'What do you want from me?'

'I think you know,' Mr Blister said. 'And this is not a negotiation.'

The line clicked and Vargas snapped his head towards Ortiz. 'Drive.'

'What's going on, *pocho*? Is something—'

'*Drive* . . .' Vargas shouted.

Without another word, Ortiz jammed his foot against the pedal and took off, retracing their route at twice the speed they'd come here, reaching the hotel in half the time.

Before they came to a complete stop in the hotel parking lot, Vargas had his door open and was out of the car, bounding the outside steps two at a time to the first floor.

But as he reached Beth's room, he slowed down, tried to catch his breath.

Her door was hanging open.

And he knew that Mr Blister was in there.

Waiting for him.

81

Pulling the Tomcat out, Vargas approached the room cautiously, pushed his way inside.

It was dim, lit only by a single light bulb, and Beth was on the bed, naked, staring up at him with terrified eyes. Her hands were tied behind her, her mouth covered with duct tape.

Mr Blister sat in a chair in the corner, his ruined face hidden by shadows, his gun pointed at her head.

'Your taxi driver deserves a generous tip, Mr Vargas. He got you here much sooner than I expected.'

Vargas levelled the Tomcat. 'Get away from her.'

Mr Blister smiled. 'Please, Nick, put the weapon down. The math is simple. You shoot me, I shoot her. You wouldn't want to have her blood on your hands, would you?'

'You still die in that equation.'

'Too true. But then so does she. And I have a very strong feeling you do not want that. So, please, put the weapon down.'

Vargas hesitated. If he followed Mr Blister's request, he'd be dead as soon as the Tomcat touched the floor.

But if he didn't do as he was told, he had no doubt that Beth would take the bullet instead.

And that wasn't acceptable.

Mr Blister waited patiently. Seemed to be working through some thoughts of his own.

'Tell me something,' he said.

'What?'

'It was you, wasn't it? In the warehouse.'

Vargas said nothing, but his eyes must have given him away.

Mr Blister smiled.

'Yes, I thought so. It is a shame I had to kill the younger one, but it couldn't be helped. And it seems I am to blame for this situation as well. If I had merely trusted my instincts that night, you would not be here right now.'

'Since we're sharing our deep dark secrets,' Vargas said, 'tell me about La Santa Muerte.'

'Ahhh. You know about us, do you? I am not surprised. But I'm afraid your stalling tactics will not change anything. So for the third and last time, please, carefully put your weapon on the floor.'

Again Vargas hesitated. Beth's eyes were burning him now, and she moaned against the duct tape, shaking her head, telling him not to do it. Then her gaze shifted almost imperceptibly, looking past Vargas's shoulder.

She'd seen something in the doorway behind him, out of Mr Blister's line of sight.

Ortiz?

Please let it be Ortiz.

'Shall I count to three?' Mr Blister asked.

'No,' Vargas told him. 'I'm putting it down. Just don't hurt her.'

'That's entirely up to you.'

'I get it, I get it,' Vargas said. 'You made your point.'

Then he lowered the Tomcat and started moving into a crouch to place it on the floor.

Mr Blister smiled again, then swung his weapon around, pointing it at Vargas as—

—Ortiz shouted from the doorway, 'Down, *pocho*!'

Vargas dived, the sound of gunfire erupting around him. As he turned, he saw Ortiz fall back, bullets splintering the doorframe.

And Mr Blister was on his feet now, leaking blood from his wrist, his gun on the carpet.

Grabbing Beth by the forearm, Mr Blister yanked her off the bed, pulling her close, locking his arm around her neck.

Vargas brought the Tomcat up, but before he could fire, Mr Blister kicked it out of his hand and produced a small, nasty-looking knife, holding it against Beth's abdomen.

'Keep moving,' he said, 'and I spill her intestines all over this beautiful carpet.'

Vargas froze.

'Very good, Nick. It's nice to see a man who values human life. Especially one so precious.'

Then suddenly Ortiz was in the doorway again, holding his Glock with both hands, pointed directly at Mr Blister's head.

'I've got a clear shot, *puta*. So let the lady go.'

But Mr Blister ignored him, looking at Vargas instead. 'Tell your friend to stand down. She will be dead before he pulls the trigger.'

Vargas knew it was true. 'Do what he says, Ortiz. Put the gun down.'

'What are you, loco? He's bluffing.'

'I've seen him work before. He's not bluffing. Do what he says.'

Mr Blister pressed the point of the blade into Beth's flesh, drawing blood, and she cried out, the sound muffled against the duct tape.

This was enough to change Ortiz's mind.

Nodding, he dropped the Glock at his feet, then kicked it aside and stepped away.

Vargas's heart was thumping.

'What now?' he asked.

Mr Blister smiled again, backing towards the adjoining doorway. 'She is my prize, Nick. My trophy. Just as she was before. I considered putting a pillow over her face for betraying me, but now that I see her like this, how beautiful she is, how could I do such a thing?'

The blood from his wrist was rolling down her chest now, snaking a trail between her breasts, working its way towards the dark patch between her legs.

'You're not taking her with you,' Vargas said.

'Oh? And what will you do to stop me?'

With this, he dragged her backwards through the adjoining doorway, moving quickly, Beth struggling against him as they disappeared into the darkness of Vargas's room.

The moment he heard the door slam, Vargas dived for the Tomcat and scooped it up.

By the time he reached the hallway, he heard another door slam – a fire exit at the end of the corridor.

Vargas ran, Ortiz emerging from the room behind him.

'This *puta madre* gonna die tonight.'

'Get your car,' Vargas said. 'Bring it round to the front. We can't let them get away.'

Ortiz turned on his heels and sprinted, as Vargas crashed through the fire exit, just in time to see Mr Blister and Beth on the landing below, pushing through the ground-floor doorway.

Vargas vaulted the steps, nearly losing his balance as he landed, using the walls to hold himself upright as he threw open the door and stumbled into the street. But Mr Blister was already on the opposite side, shoving Beth onto the backseat of a Jaguar XJ. Shutting her inside, he moved around to the driver's door and swung it open as—

—Vargas raised the Tomcat.

But he knew he was out of range and, if he fired, the chances of hitting anything significant were slim to none.

Then he heard the squeal of tyres and looked up to see Ortiz's taxi tearing around the corner, just as—

—Mr Blister reached inside the Jaguar and brought out a semi-automatic handgun.

He fired at the oncoming cab, decimating a side

mirror, puncturing the left front tyre. Ortiz swerved, struggling to control the wheel, heading straight for Vargas as—

—Mr Blister slid into the Jaguar, fired up the engine and tore away, leaving a long patch of rubber on the road.

Jumping clear of the cab, Vargas ran, chasing after the Jaguar with everything he had, bringing the Tomcat up again, ready to fire—

But it wasn't enough.

And as Ortiz came to a screeching halt behind him, the Jaguar careened around a corner and disappeared from sight.

Gone.

With Beth tied up in the back seat.

Vargas stopped in the middle of the street, his chest heaving, his shoulder aching, his head throbbing . . .

And a cold, dark tide washed through him.

82

'You must have many questions,' Rafael said.

They were driving along the coast road, several miles out of the city. Beth lay in the back with her head against the armrest, staring out at a black ocean lit only by the moon. She had no idea where he was taking her, but she had managed to quell her panic for the moment. She just wished he'd had the decency to cover her with a blanket. The last thing she should be worried about was being naked in front of him, but she felt embarrassed and humiliated.

And the thought of his blood drying on her body made her sick to her stomach.

'Do not worry, my love. I meant what I said back there. I will not harm you.' He paused. 'And if you promise to be good, I will remove the tape from your mouth. You would like that, *si*?'

Beth nodded, but wasn't sure if he saw her.

'Come closer,' he said.

Beth hesitated, then readjusted her body, doing as she was told, and he reached back, ripping the tape away. She let out a long breath then immediately backed away from him, returning her head to the armrest.

'What about my wrists?'

She was lying on top of them and her hands were starting to go numb.

'Not yet,' he said. 'But soon.'

'Can't you at least cover me?'

'I wasn't expecting you to be like this, so I am afraid I have no way of granting such a request. You can thank La Santisima for the heat.'

'Don't you have a blanket in the trunk or something?'

'No,' he said. 'But there is no reason to be ashamed of your body, Beth. As I've said many times, you are a beautiful woman.'

'You disgust me.'

'There is little I can do about that at the moment. But it will change. I promise.'

They drove in silence for a while, Beth quietly working on the rope around her wrists, trying desperately to loosen them. But he'd tied them too tight, and she wasn't having much success.

'Where are you taking me?' she asked.

'Back home, of course. Where you belong.'

'What do you mean? I've been there before?'

'Ahhh, yes. We have many memories together.' He paused. Shrugged. 'Well . . . *I* have many memories. What happened to you is unfortunate. But those who sin against La Santisima rarely go unpunished.'

'What do I have to do with La Santisima?'

'Much more than you know. You are a child of the Holy Mother.'

'Oh? And what about Jen? Is she a child of the Holy Mother, too?'

'We all are,' Rafael said.

'Where is she? What did you do to her?'

He paused again. 'We'll save that question for another time.'

He was silent for a moment, and Beth stared at his face in the rear-view mirror. The entire right side was a mess of mottled, blistery flesh.

He caught her looking at him.

'You must be wondering how this happened. The last you remember of me is our encounter in Playa Azul.'

'How do you know that? How could you possibly know what I remember?'

He smiled. 'There is someone in your life, Beth, who is not who he seems to be. He has been apprising us of your progress – although not quite as faithfully as I had hoped.'

'Who? Dr Stanley?'

He laughed softly. 'Your doctor knows nothing about us. No one at the hospital does.'

'Then who?'

Rafael said nothing, letting her turn the question in her mind.

Then it hit her. There was only one other person she'd had contact with since the shooting, besides the police.

'Oh my God,' she said. 'Peter?'

'He has been working with us for quite some time now. Long before you and I met. He has managed to facilitate many of our business transactions, while diverting attention away from us. At a price, of course. He is a valuable asset.'

'I don't believe you,' Beth said. 'Peter may be a lot of things, but he'd never get involved with people like you.'

'You think you know him, do you?'

'I was married to him for nearly four years.'

'Then you must know that he was sleeping with your sister.'

83

It took Beth several moments and a considerable amount of effort to recover from Rafael's bombshell.

She allowed herself to slip into a state of complete denial.

'Bullshit,' she said. 'Jen would never do that to me.'

'Jen is a creature of impulse, Beth. You know that better than anyone.'

He was right, but Beth refused to believe that her sister would betray her like that. It was true that she didn't seem to care much about who she slept with, as long as she got the rewards, but there's no way she would have taken on Peter. He was off-limits.

But then the concept of off-limits wasn't one that Jen truly understood, was it? She'd proven that more than once, like the night she'd flirted shamelessly with the newlywed, right in front of his wife.

Could Rafael be telling the truth?

Was she the woman Peter had been cheating with? The reason for their divorce?

As if he were reading her mind, Rafael said, 'It's a sad, unfortunate tale, Beth. But it goes well beyond an unfaithful husband and a sister's betrayal.'

'I don't understand.'

'How do you think Marta and I met you? Do you think it was an accident?'

'No,' Beth said. 'I think you and your little fuck buddy were on board that ship trolling for victims. You saw us in the restaurant and liked what you saw.'

'Yes,' Rafael told her. 'We did like what we saw. But we met Jennifer long before that cruise.'

That didn't make any sense.

'What the hell are you talking about?'

'I told you, Beth. Your ex-husband and La Santa Muerte have long had a business relationship. A little over a year go, Marta and I were visiting Los Angeles and we held a private party for our friends. A way to say thank you for their service to La Santisima.'

'What does this have to do with Jen?'

'Your sister was Peter's guest at the party, and quite a popular one at that – with both the men *and* the women.'

'Shut up, you disgusting pig.'

'I know this is painful for you, but I think it is important that you know the truth.'

Yes, Beth thought. The truth. Not these horrible lies.

She tried again to work the rope free, but still couldn't get it to budge.

'Marta took quite a liking to your sister that night. But Jennifer was so high on alcohol and drugs, I doubt if she remembered either of us. Marta, however, did not forget. And when Peter later found himself in a bit of . . . difficulty . . . Marta offered him a tempting solution.'

'What kind of difficulty?'

'He fathered your sister's child.'

Beth felt her skin go cold, her mind suddenly crowded by the image of the baby smiling up at her.

Jen's baby.

Peter's baby?

'Andy,' she said, almost involuntarily.

'Yes.' Rafael said, sounding surprised. 'You remember him?'

'Only a face. A face and the name.'

'Unfortunately for Jennifer, Peter had no interest in being a father. Especially out of wedlock. Especially when he was trying to win back his ex-wife.'

Beth remembered all the phone calls from Peter in the wake of the divorce, begging for her to take him back. The excuses to see her at the office. But she had rebuffed his advances every time. She'd been hurt enough, and she wasn't interested in giving him a chance to hurt her again.

'I still don't understand,' she said. 'What does any of this have to do with us meeting you and Marta on that cruise?'

'The whole thing was pre-arranged. Peter booked passage for Jennifer and her guest as a gift to her. A chance for her to get away and think about the pregnancy. But what she didn't know was that *she* was the gift. To *us.*'

'He was setting us up?'

'Not you,' Rafael said. 'He was not expecting you to be her guest.'

That's right, Beth thought. She'd been a last-minute substitute when Jen's best friend Debbie flaked out.

'Yet there you were, sitting in that restaurant, then later, standing at the ship's rail. And I knew I had to have you.'

Beth felt a ball of bile lodge in her throat. The thought that she'd let this guy even come close to her made her want to projectile vomit.

'But Marta wouldn't hear of it,' Rafael continued. 'You were not part of the deal.'

'That's what you two were arguing about in the bar.'

Rafael nodded. 'When Peter found out you would be there, he made a personal appeal to El Santo that you be left alone.'

'But you didn't listen.'

'I tried, my darling. And despite your rudeness towards me when I saw you sitting in that cafe in Playa Azul, it was very difficult to walk away.'

'How flattering. And Jen?'

'We had already taken her by then. But before the day was done, my prayer to La Santisima was answered. And we took you as well. Just as you were leaving the police station.'

'But why? Weren't you disobeying a direct order from your precious El Santo?'

'Yes,' Rafael said. 'And that is why I have *this*.' He gestured to his ravaged face. 'An offering of flesh as penance for my sins.'

'You've got to be fucking kidding me.'

'Oh no, my darling. We call it a cleansing. It is

373

quite painful – but without pain there is no glory before God. You will see.'

Beth stared at his face in the rear-view mirror again and renewed her effort to loosen the rope, a deep, dark well of dread bubbling in her intestines.

She had to get the hell out of this car.

84

Vargas could barely contain himself. 'Come on, Ortiz, we're wasting time. We have to get moving.'

He was standing in Ortiz's tool shed, looking down the steps into the hidey hole. Ortiz was moving around down there and taking forever.

'If we're going to kill a man, *pocho*, we'll need the right tools to do it. And not that pop gun you bought from me.'

'All right, fine, just hurry it up.'

A moment later Ortiz climbed up the steps, carrying an armload of weapons, then dumped them onto a work bench.

'A couple of these should do the trick.'

Vargas looked down at them, a variety of handguns, the makes and models of which he couldn't even name.

'Pick your poison, *pocho*. But I got dibs on the SIG.'

It was a classic case of overkill. They already had the Tomcat and the gun Mr Blister had left on the hotel room floor and Vargas just wanted to get on the road.

He grabbed a handgun and stuffed it in his belt. 'All right, you happy now? Let's go.'

'Wait a minute, wait a minute,' Ortiz said. 'Don't you think we'd better talk about where we're going, first?'

'I told you, Ciudad de Almas.'

Ortiz picked up the SIG. 'That's an all-night drive and then some, amigo. How do you know that's where he's taking her?'

'I don't. But it's all I've got.'

'This is where you say the dead nuns came from, right? From the church there?'

'Right,' Vargas said. 'Iglesia del Corazón Sagrado. But we can talk about all this on the road. We're wasting time.'

'That's another problem, Amigo.'

'What?'

He nodded towards the taxi, which was parked in the drive. The side mirror was history, but the car itself was still in pretty good shape.

'That spare tyre we put on is one of those temporary things. It won't last all the way to Ciudad de Almas.'

They'd thrown the spare on as quickly as possible, wanting to get away from the hotel before the police showed up. No way they'd be able to pass off the gunshots as pre-festival fireworks, and involving the Mexican cops in this thing was a recipe for disaster.

When Vargas had tried to retrieve his Corolla from the parking lot, he'd discovered the tyres had been slashed. Courtesy of Mr Blister, no doubt.

'Christ,' Vargas said. 'What about one of your friends, don't they have cars?'

'My friends find out we're fucking around with La Santa Muerte, they'll shoot us just to be merciful. So I wouldn't count on them.'

'Then what the hell are we supposed to do?'

Ortiz thought about it a moment, then an idea struck and his eyes lit up.

'We're about to go where no man has dared to tread, amigo.'

'What do you mean?'

Ortiz gestured. 'Come over here, let me show you something.'

They crossed the yard to a small garage at the end of the driveway. Glancing around, Ortiz grabbed hold of the door handle and yanked on it, rolling the door open.

Inside was a sight to behold: a pristine black 1970 Plymouth Barracuda with a monster hemi-head engine.

'Jesus Christ, Ortiz, how long have you been hiding this thing?'

'I haven't been, *pocho*. This is Yolanda's ride.'

85

Despite all of Rafael's talk, and all of his revelations about Peter and Jen and Marta and their sordid little orgy in the name of God and La Santisima, Beth still had a giant blank spot where those ten months should have been.

Still working at the rope, she asked, 'What happened after Playa Azul? Where did you take us?'

'I already told you. Home.'

'Ciudad de Almas?'

Rafael nodded.

'That's *your* home, not mine.'

'*Si*, but you came to accept it. You were quite a handful in the beginning, but like a wild mare, with time and patience you were tamed. You learned to laugh with us, pray with us . . . and share your flesh with us.'

The ball of bile in Beth's throat grew hotter, acidy. She really *was* going to throw up.

She didn't buy this for a minute. No way she'd ever let these sickos get control of her like that. She was a fighter. Always had been. But she also knew about the techniques religious cults used on their victims. She'd once prosecuted a sweet, elderly 'Christian' couple for imprisoning several teenage runaways and subjecting them to starvation and sleep deprivation and sexual depravity, all the while praying for their salvation.

The kids had resisted at first, but had finally broken. And the abuse might have gone on forever, if a suspicious neighbour hadn't called the police.

Beth was no teenager, but could she have been broken too?

'What about Jen?' she asked. 'You still haven't told me what happened to her.'

'Jennifer was quite another story,' Rafael said. 'She all but ran into our arms. But there were some complications in the beginning. She needed a bit of chemical persuasion. To show her the light, so to speak. But she came around quickly. And she and Marta have grown quite close.'

Beth felt a spark of relief. 'She's alive?'

'Alive and well and thriving in our community.'

Thank God, Beth thought. Thank God. 'And what about the baby? What about Andy?'

'A beautiful, healthy boy. Probably in his mother's arms as we speak.' He glanced back at her. 'You should be proud of your sister, Beth. She was instrumental in getting you to accept your destiny.'

Beth frowned. 'Which destiny is that?'

'The only one you have. She convinced you that the way to true glory was to offer yourself to La Santisima unconditionally, and to accept *me* as your master.'

'My *what*?'

Rafael paused again. In a way he reminded her of

Dr Stanley – eternally patient as he explained the facts of life to the girl with the battered brain pan.

'We have simple beliefs, Beth. The women in our family always serve at the pleasure of their men and their god.'

'Whether they like it or not.'

She kept working at the rope and felt it loosen slightly. Not enough, but it was a start.

'If my visit to Los Angeles these last few days is any indication, they like it quite a bit.'

'Oh? And what about Marta?'

'What about her?'

'She didn't strike me as particularly subservient. From what I could tell onboard that ship, she seemed to be running the show.'

'Marta is an exception. She is a *bruja*, and the direct descendant of El Santo.'

'How nice for her. But you're not fooling me, you know.'

'Fooling you?'

'There's no way Jen would voluntarily be part of this psycho-spiritual bullshit.'

'Perhaps you know your sister as well as you know your ex-husband.'

'Fuck you,' Beth said.

'Your anger is understandable. But before tomorrow night is over, you will see just how dedicated to La Santisima your sister is.'

Beth didn't like the sound of that. 'What are you saying?'

'As I told you, we have simple beliefs. And we practise those beliefs through certain rituals. Tomorrow we begin celebrating Dia de los Muertos. And at the mark of midnight, Jennifer will offer herself and her child in sacrifice to Holy Death.'

Beth hadn't heard him right. She couldn't have. 'What the hell did you just say?'

'You should be thanking me, Beth. Instead of putting a pillow over your face, I am bringing you to bear witness to one of the most glorious sights you will ever see.'

He turned, smiling at her.

'And with El Santo's approval,' he said. 'I think you should light the torch.'

86

Beth shook her head back and forth, trying to clear her mind.

Was this really happening?

Was it a nightmare?

Did Rafael really mean what she thought he meant?

'Tell me this is just a ritual,' she said. 'It's all make-believe, just going through the motions, like drinking wine and eating crackers in church.'

He gestured to his face. 'Does this look like make-believe to you?'

All at once Beth felt as if her mind had just been separated from her body, threatening to float away. Then an all-consuming anger enveloped her, bringing her back to earth. She moved her wrists behind her, straining the rope that bound them, and finally pulled one of her hands free.

'You will see, Beth. You will see just how beautiful it is. A moment we will share together in God's embrace, celebrating the cleansing of Jennifer's soul. It's a moment you will *never* for—'

Without warning, Beth sprang forwards, bringing her hands out in front of her, snapping the rope taut between them. Before Rafael could react, she slipped it over his head and around his neck and pulled, pushing her knee into the back of his seat for leverage.

Rafael's head snapped against the headrest. He made a gurgling sound and let go of the wheel, grabbing at his neck with both hands, trying desperately to pry the rope loose.

But Beth pulled harder, rage consuming her, and felt the springs of the seat digging into her kneecap. But she didn't care, all she wanted was to silence this fucking monster, to take from him what he had taken from so many others.

Glancing in the rear-view mirror, she saw the blisters on his face turn crimson, his eyes bulging hideously. And she looked away, not wanting to see the effects of her handiwork for fear she'd have pity on him and loosen her hold. Instead she concentrated on the face of little Andy.

And of Jen.

Suddenly the car started to swerve, and Rafael's right hand left his neck. But instead of grabbing for the wheel, he reached to the passenger seat, fingers scrabbling, trying to get hold of the gun that lay there.

And all Beth could think was, why won't you die already? Just fucking die.

She couldn't keep this up much longer.

Then, as the car started to veer off the road, Rafael got hold of the gun. But rather than grip the trigger, he used it as bludgeon, bringing his arm back and slamming the weapon against her head.

Pain radiated through Beth's skull and she was

suddenly back in that Playa Azul alleyway, that Hispanic thug using his fist as a club, knocking her to the alley floor.

The gun came up again, hitting her a second time, and Beth fell back, letting go of the rope.

Coughing and spitting and gasping for air, Rafael quickly grabbed hold of the wheel and hit the brakes, trying to get control of the car.

But it was too late. The tyres hit gravel and the car spun, barrelling backwards over the side of the road and into a ditch, coming to an abrupt stop against an outcrop of rocks, windows shattering, metal bending and twisting around them.

The impact knocked them both around the interior of the Jaguar, Beth hitting her head against something solid—

— another devastating blow and one too many . . .

And a moment later she was gone.

87

The Barracuda tore down the coast road, Ortiz looking much more at home behind its wheel than he had when he was driving the taxi.

'Tell me the truth,' Vargas said. 'This isn't the first time you've taken Yolanda's car for a late-night drive.'

'Don't know what you're talking about, *pocho.*'

'Don't worry, I'm not gonna say anything. I'll probably never see her again.'

'Then you're a lucky man. Because when she gets up in the morning and opens that garage, she gonna be pissed.'

'That's what I don't get,' Vargas said.

'What's that?'

'Why you're willing to risk her wrath to help me. And why you're risking your life to take me to Ciudad de Almas. After that reaction from Little Fina's crowd, I figure you'd be running for cover just like everyone else. And don't give me any bullshit about customer service.'

Ortiz shrugged. 'Maybe I got my own axe to grind with these circus freaks.'

'Like what?'

'That *pendejo* shot at me. I don't like people who shoot at me.'

'And?'

Ortiz hesitated, then shook his head. 'There is no and.'

'Come on, Ortiz. What do you know about these people that you aren't telling me?'

'You hear stories, but you never know what's truth and what's fiction. People use La Santa Muerte and El Santo like the bogeyman. Scare their kids into doing their chores.'

'Only the bogeymen are real in this case.'

'I know they do some business in Playa Azul, and all along the Baja coast, and they make enough money off the drug and sex trade to make them extremely dangerous people. But Little Fina was right. They're ghosts. They're very private and want to stay that way. You don't get in their face, they won't get in yours.'

'So what's your beef with them?'

'What difference does it make?'

'Come on, Ortiz.'

Ortiz sighed. 'There was this girl I met up in Tijuana a few years back. Gracilia. She worked in a factory making seat belts and airbags for American cars.'

He looked out at the ocean as he drove. And for once he didn't have a smile on his face.

'One day she and a couple of her co-workers just up and disappeared. Police couldn't figure it out. But the rumours started that El Santo was behind it. And not the eat-your-vegetables version, either.'

'And you believe it?'

'No reason I should,' Ortiz said. 'But yeah. People say El Santo steals these women and uses them either as sex slaves, or as human sacrifices to appease his god. Tells his people that the sacrifices bring them blessings and good fortune.'

'Jesus. And nobody's been able to confirm this?'

'Like I said, *pocho*. Ghosts.'

'And this girl in Tijuana. She must've been pretty special.'

Ortiz shrugged again. 'I didn't really know Gracilia all that well. But I could have, amigo. I could have.'

Vargas thought about Beth. Despite what they'd been through, he didn't really know *her* all that well, either. But he hoped to hell he wouldn't one day be saying he could have.

He knew he had every reason to blame himself for what had happened tonight. But he'd already been through the blame game with Manny, feeling like he should've been a better brother. Thinking if he'd done something different, Manny would still be alive.

No point in retreading that territory. He'd made choices tonight, and they'd had consequences. Besides, this wasn't over. And he had no intention of leaving Mexico without Beth.

They cruised in silence for a while, then Ortiz's cell phone rang.

Swearing under his breath, Ortiz pulled it out of his pocket and glanced at the screen.

'Holy shit, *pocho*. It's you again.'

Vargas turned sharply and snatched the phone from him, clicking it on. 'She'd better be alive, asshole.'

'. . . Nick?'

It was Beth.

'Jesus Christ, Beth, where are you? Are you okay?'

She started to cry, her voice trembling. 'I think I killed him, Nick. We wrecked the car and I found your phone in his pocket. I . . . I think he's dead.'

'Are you hurt?'

'No . . . I don't know. I shouldn't have killed him . . . he knows where she is . . . But I couldn't help myself, I . . .'

'Where *are* you?'

'By the ocean,' she said. 'I'm by the ocean, near a lighthouse. I need clothes. He wouldn't even give me a blanket . . . a fucking blanket . . .'

'Just hold on, Beth, we're coming.'

'We have to get to Ciudad de Almas . . . They've got Jen there . . . We have to get there before . . . before . . .'

There was a long silence.

'Beth?'

Then the phone went dead.

'Shit,' Vargas said, turning to Ortiz. 'Is there a lighthouse around here?'

'Down the road. About thirty minutes.'

Vargas dialled his number and listened to it ring. 'Make it twenty,' he said.

And Ortiz hit the gas.

They found her on the beach, using the ring of the cell phone to guide them. The lighthouse sat shining in the distance, on a rocky patch of land that jutted out towards the ocean.

She was lying face up in the sand, a pale, naked figure, out cold, still clutching Vargas's phone in her hand.

Vargas's first instinct was to panic, but then he felt for a pulse and got a strong one.

She was alive. A bit battered and bruised, but alive.

Ortiz brought a blanket from the trunk of the Barracuda and they wrapped it around her. And as Vargas pulled her into his arms, Beth stirred, looking up at him.

'Easy,' he said. 'Easy.'

When she realized who it was, she heaved a soft sigh and threw her arms around him.

'Nick . . .'

They kissed, and Vargas suddenly realized how worried he'd been. He'd kept his emotions crammed deep, but now that he'd found her and she was alive and in one piece, his relief was a tangible, living thing.

When he'd seen the condition of the Jaguar, and Mr Blister's broken body inside, he couldn't fathom how Beth had managed to escape.

Breaking from the kiss, Beth said, 'We have to go. We have get to Ciudad de Almas.'

'We're not going anywhere until you see a doctor.'

She pulled away from him. 'No, we have to go now. Rafael told me they have Jennifer and Andy.'

'Andy? Who's Andy?'

'I'll explain in the car. I tried checking his phone for numbers, but it was broken in the crash. We can't waste any time. We have to find them before midnight tomorrow.'

'I don't mean to rain on your parade,' Ortiz said. 'But that could be a problem unless you got a map with an X on it. Ciudad de Almas is almost as big as Playa Azul.'

Ignoring him, Vargas said to Beth, 'What happens at midnight?'

Despite the heat, she shivered, pulling the blanket close. 'That's when the cleansing begins. A cleansing by fire.'

88

Ortiz hadn't been lying about needing a map with an X on it.

Once a small fishing village off the Sea of Cortez, Ciudad de Almas had at least quadrupled in size over the decades, taking up a long stretch of coastline.

The city was a mix of old and new: retro adobe buildings nestled between modern business offices and tourist shops.

But what stood out were the cliffs that overlooked the place, like all-seeing, all-knowing gods.

The sun was up well before they arrived. The drive had been long – Ortiz refusing to relinquish the wheel – so Vargas and Beth had slept in the back seat, arms entwined.

When they pulled into town, the Dia de los Muertos festival had begun in earnest. Everywhere you turned, there was celebration: a street parade full of papier-mâché skulls, mariachi bands, dancing children with painted faces, tourists and locals wearing skull masks, all under the watchful eye of the local *policía*.

It was, for the most part, a harmless exercise in tradition, a joyous occasion for everyone involved. But somewhere in town, that X was marked, and the lives of a woman and her son depended on them finding it.

While Vargas bought Beth a pair of jeans and a Day of the Dead T-shirt and waited for her to dress under the blanket in the car, Ortiz tracked down a local map. None of them was hungry, but they knew they needed something to give them energy, so they found a small cafe, ordered espressos and Mexican pastries and unfolded the map in front of them.

'Here's the listing of landmarks,' Beth said, then ran her finger down the page.

There was a fierceness to her demeanour that Vargas hadn't seen before. A clarity of purpose. He couldn't be sure, of course – he was no expert – but he sensed that after last night's violence, she had turned some kind of corner, and had seen the last of her headaches.

Her refusal to visit a doctor hadn't surprised him. Despite the emotional seesaw she'd been riding, she was a strong, stubborn woman, as determined as she was beautiful.

'Here it is,' she said. 'Iglesia del Corazón Sagrado. Church of the Sacred Heart.'

'You realize,' Vargas told her, 'there's no guarantee this priest will know anything.'

Ortiz cut in before Beth could respond. 'Like you said last night. It's the only thing we've got.'

'He knows something,' Beth said. She had a faraway look in her eyes. Had gone inward for a moment.

'How can you be sure?'

She focused on Vargas now. 'There's something about this place that speaks to me, Nick. Rafael said it was my home for a while, and I definitely feel like I've been here before.'

'You're starting to remember?'

She shook her head. 'Not exactly. It's like what I told you about the whole Andy thing – I see these dark shapes, and I'm just waiting for them to surface.'

Vargas had been thrown by the Andy/Angie revelation. There had never been any indication that a child was involved in this, but each new day he spent with this story seemed to bring a fresh new surprise.

'And the priest is one of those shapes?'

'He'd have to be, wouldn't he? The nuns in that house didn't just happen to bump into me on the road. Whatever we were up to, we were in it together and the priest knows about it. I'm sure he does.'

'How far is the church?' Vargas asked.

Ortiz was measuring the distance with his fingers. 'Not far,' he said. 'We could drive, but with everything going on around here, we might be better off on foot.'

Vargas looked at Beth. 'You up to walking?'

She shot him a look. 'I just killed a man with two hands and a piece of rope, Nick. I think I can manage to walk a few blocks.'

'Easy, kiddo, I'm not the enemy.'

She softened. 'I'm sorry. I'm just worried about Jen and Andy.'

She stood up, a bundle of adrenalin. She hadn't touched her espresso or her pastry.

'I can't sit here any more. Let's do it.'

89

They had to dodge the parade and an outdoor food fair to get to the church.

With each new block, they drew closer to the cliffs, as the buildings and houses and roads grew more and more decrepit, reflecting an even older Mexico that hadn't kept up with the times.

There wasn't much celebrating going on in this part of town. Some of the houses had makeshift altars in their windows, with burning candles, offerings of fruit and photos of their dead loved ones. But most of them were silent and empty.

After a while, they came to a short dirt road with a battered sign that read: IGLESIA DEL CORAZÓN SAGRADO.

At the end of the road stood a large, rustic adobe structure with a leaning bell tower that looked as if it might topple at any moment.

Church of the Sacred Heart.

They stood at the mouth of the road, gaping at it.

'You sure this is the right one?' Vargas asked.

Ortiz checked his map. 'This is it, *pocho.*'

'Maybe there's more than one Church of the Sacred—'

'*La iglesia esta cerrada*,' a voice said.

They turned to find an old woman on a bicycle staring at them from across the street. A plastic sack full of *conchas* – Mexican sweet breads – hung from one of the handlebars.

'*La iglesia esta cerrada*,' she repeated. The church is closed.

Vargas asked her for how long.

'Many weeks,' she said in Spanish. 'After Father Gerard left.'

Ortiz's eyebrows went up. 'The priest is gone?'

'Yes,' the woman said. 'One day the police came to speak to him, the next day, no more Gerard.'

Ortiz and Vargas exchanged looks and Vargas turned to translate for Beth.

But Beth wasn't paying any attention to them, her gaze fixed on the church.

'Go home,' the old woman said. 'There is nothing to see here.'

Then she turned her bike around and rode away, the sack of *conchas* swinging from the handlebar.

Ortiz watched her. 'That was weird.'

Vargas nodded. 'She came all the way out here with those sweet breads. I wonder who they were for.'

Ortiz shrugged. 'Maybe she was selling them.'

Vargas turned to Beth again, but she was still staring at the church. Seemed transfixed.

'We need to come up with another game plan,' he told her. 'The old woman says the priest is gone.'

'I know this place,' Beth said, then started up the road towards it.

Beth approached the entrance to the church, a jumble of half-memories swirling through her mind, trying to break through.

She *did* know this place. She was sure she'd been here before.

Moving up to the double doors, she ran a hand across their warped wooden surface.

It felt familiar to her.

There was a chain and padlock on the door handles, but when Beth pulled on the lock, it sprang free in her hand. It hadn't been fastened properly.

Unwinding the chain, she dropped it aside and pushed the doors open, the old hinges groaning. Inside was a cavernous room with at least a dozen rows of pews, all facing an altar that featured a larger than life-sized figure of Jesus on the cross. Sunlight slanted in from a skylight above, and through stained-glass windows high along each side.

Beth had never been religious, but as she moved down the aisle, there was no denying the power here. The feeling that you were in the presence of something larger than you. Greater.

She stopped in front of the altar, stared up at the watchful eyes of Christ.

'Beth, what is it?'

She turned. Vargas and Ortiz were standing in the doorway.

'I'm not sure,' she said. 'There's something about this place. I . . .'

She heard a shuffling sound from above and stopped herself, shifting her gaze to the balcony over the doorway.

To her surprise, a boy stood near the rail, staring down at her. Wide-eyed.

He couldn't have been more than fourteen years old, a Mexican child wearing only a dark pair of pants. There were burn scars on the right side of his neck and down his arm.

He stared at Beth intently, then broke into a smile. 'Elizabeth?'

Startled by the sound of her name, Beth stepped backwards. The boy suddenly turned and ran, disappearing from sight, his footsteps clattering on the stairs.

And as Vargas and Ortiz stepped inside to see what the commotion was, the boy emerged at a full sprint and shot past them, coming straight towards Beth – the smile even wider now – a smile of joy as he threw his arms around her and hugged her.

'You came back for us,' he said. 'I tell the others you would, but they don't believe.'

He squeezed her tighter.

'You came back, Elizabeth. You came back.'

90

The boy's name was Cristo.

He seemed hurt when Beth couldn't remember it.

They were sitting in a pew now, and he was holding her hands, not wanting to let them go. Vargas and Ortiz sat several pews away, watching and listening, giving them room.

'Someone hurt me,' Beth told the boy, then bent forward and showed him the scar on her scalp. 'Some bad people did this to me and it makes me forget sometimes.'

She looked at the burn marks on his neck and arm and knew that he was no stranger to bad people himself. That feeling of anger she'd felt in the car with Rafael threatened to overcome her again.

'What do you forget?' he asked.

'All kinds of things. Names, places. Like this place. I think I've been here before, but I'm not sure.'

'*Si*,' he said. 'You come here many times. But how do you forget about me?'

Beth's heart was breaking.

'I'm sorry, Cristo.' She touched her chest. 'I can feel you here . . .' Then her head. 'But I can't find you in here.'

He looked confused. 'Is this why you don't come back for so long? Because you cannot find us?'

'Yes,' she said. 'So help me remember. Tell me how I know you and why I came here.'

The boy said nothing, staring down at their hands now, his smile gone.

'Please, Cristo. Please help me remember.'

When he looked up at her again, there were tears in his eyes. 'How do you forget me, Elizabeth? I bring you food when you are hungry. Like the old woman brings food for us.'

'The woman on the bicycle?'

'*Si*,' he said. 'She is a friend of Father Gerard. She take care of us when they kill him.'

Beth glanced at Vargas and Ortiz.

'Who killed him? La Santa Muerte?'

Cristo nodded. 'I watch from up there,' he said, pointing to the balcony. 'They cut his throat, and let him bleed in front of Jesus. They tell him he is a traitor to El Santo because of what he did.'

'Because he helped you?'

'*Si*. Just like you help us, when you were strong again. They keep you in the cage, give you poisons, try to make you one of them. But I bring you food. I make you strong. I take care of you.'

Beth squeezed his hands. 'Tell me everything, Cristo. Be my memory for me.'

He let go of her then and stood up.

'Better I show you,' he said, then squeezed past her and started down the aisle towards the altar.

Beth got to her feet, gesturing to Vargas and Ortiz. 'Can my friends come, too?'

Cristo stopped and turned. '*Si*,' he said, 'I show you all.'

They followed him as he moved past the choir stall and opened a door, gesturing them inside. He led them down a narrow hallway to a tiny, cluttered office, then moved to a wall that was dominated by a large, woven reredo, depicting the birth of Christ. Grabbing it by the corner, he pulled it back to reveal a hole in the wall where a door used to be.

Cristo took a small flashlight from his pocket, flicked it on, then led them down a set of wooden steps to a storeroom crowded with the shadowy remnants of the church's past: old lecterns, several floor candlesticks, a broken font, and at least two wooden kneelers.

He crossed to another door, produced a key from the same pocket, then unlocked it and threw it open. Behind it was a small cramped closet, with several cardboard boxes piled up inside. Cristo shoved the boxes aside to reveal another hole, this one low to the ground. Stepping through it, he waved for them to follow.

Beth, Vargas and Ortiz exchanged looks, then stooped down and climbed through the hole, finding themselves in a long, narrow tunnel, its mud walls braced by thick pieces of lumber.

'Come,' Cristo said, and, using the flashlight to guide them, he moved towards the far end of the tunnel, where it abruptly turned left.

As she walked, Beth began to get that feeling of déjà vu again, knowing that she'd been down here before.

'What is this place?' she asked.

'Father Gerard say the church use the tunnels to smuggle guns and hide freedom fighters during the Revolution.'

They reached a junction, the tunnel splitting off in several directions, and took another left. Beth was surprised to hear the faint echo of waves crashing.

And just beneath this, something else . . .

'Do you hear that?' she asked Vargas.

'Sounds like kids,' he said. 'Playing.'

Beth's heartbeat began to accelerate as they followed Cristo along a curve in the tunnel, the sounds growing louder with every step.

A moment later they were standing in a large cave, carved out of the cliff. And beyond it, the Sea of Cortez stretched out endlessly towards the horizon.

There were about a dozen children here, some playing, others eating fruit and rolls, while still others lay asleep on straw mats. It looked as if every single one of them had burn marks on their bodies: face, hands, legs – some worse than others.

A young girl, whose forehead was mottled with scars, saw them and shouted, 'Elizabeth!' and one by one they turned to look at Beth.

And the next thing she knew they were all crowding around her, hugging her, touching her, saying her name.

91

Five boys and seven girls.

Refugees. Victims of the La Santa Muerte cleansing rituals, and brought here one by one by Cristo.

Cristo had been the first to flee, shortly after his third cleansing, when his burns were still raw and festering, the pain nearly unbearable.

He had escaped late at night, through a labyrinth of underground tunnels and caves beneath the La Santa Muerte compound. This, he told them, was where the cleansings and fire ceremonies took place.

When Beth asked about these fire ceremonies, Cristo explained that many women who were brought into the compound were forced to work in private brothels throughout the country. Those who did not succumb to the will of El Santo were offered in sacrifice to La Santisima, strapped to the Holy Chair and burned alive.

Beth thought of Jen and Andy, and what Rafael had told her, and again a nearly uncontrollable anger rose in her chest. But she fought it off. She had to keep a rational mind.

Children were also brought to the compound,

Cristo said. Some from as far away as Monterrey and Piedras Negras. They were snatched from the slums – sometimes in broad daylight – then brought to the compound to be indoctrinated and trained to go out into the streets of the cities to deliver drugs for the local dealers. Some of them were sold into sexual slavery and auctioned off to the highest bidder.

Most of the children came from poverty and neglect and were happy to have food and shelter. But those who revolted or misbehaved were cleansed during the nightly prayer. And sometimes they, too, were sacrificed on Holy Friday.

When Vargas asked why no one went to the police about this, Cristo told him that the police and the politicians could not be trusted. Many of them were believers, followers of El Santo, and La Santa Muerte's network extended far and wide. Even non-believers protected and worked with them, lining their pockets with El Santo's gold.

And those who had managed to escape, like Cristo, and had the opportunity to expose the cult, were hunted down and killed. Cristo and his brothers and sisters here in the cave were the lucky ones, thanks to Father Gerard.

And Elizabeth.

When Elizabeth and her sister were brought to the compound they were separated, and the sister, Jennifer – who was with child – was kept in the High House with Marta and Rafael.

Elizabeth, however, was taken to the cages, where, at Rafael's command, she was chained to the floor like a mongrel and beaten and starved and fed drugs. Cristo, who was in charge of washing down the cages, felt sorry for her, and late at night he would sneak back and bring her food and try to talk to her. They did not speak the same words, but after a while, with Elizabeth's help, Cristo began to learn her language.

El Santo and Rafael thought they could break her, as they had so easily broken her sister. But Cristo knew better. Elizabeth was strong willed and would not bend. But she wasn't stupid. She pretended to go along with them, allowing Rafael and El Santo and whoever they chose to defile her.

Elizabeth soon became Rafael's trophy, Cristo told them, and was free to roam the compound – which was heavily guarded by men with guns. She was even given access to the High House, all the while plotting with Cristo to escape.

And to take Jennifer with them.

Then one night Cristo made a discovery: a part of the tunnels that was hidden from view, blocked by fallen rock. There was a hole in the wall, and through that hole he found more tunnels and more caves and soon he was standing in the church.

'The tunnels lead here?' Ortiz asked.

'*Si*,' Cristo said. 'They lead many places. They run like a maze beneath the city, and most who know about them stay away for fear of getting lost forever.'

In his exploration of the tunnels, it was not unusual for Cristo to come across old bones or a rotting corpse.

When he found the church, Cristo shared his discovery with Elizabeth and they knew that this would be their way out. But before they could execute a plan,

Jennifer gave birth and Elizabeth said they must wait until the baby was strong enough to travel.

Then Cristo was caught stealing an extra ration of food and was taken for a cleansing, and in his pain that night he fled, coming straight to the church before collapsing beneath the statue of Jesus. He was discovered the next morning by Father Gerard and the sisters, who took care of his wounds and nursed him to health.

And when he was healed, he told Father Gerard of La Santa Muerte and where he was from.

'Are there more children like you?' the father asked.

'*Si*,' Cristo said. 'Many more.'

Father Gerard, who was very, very old, had once lived in a far away place. And during a great war, he worked with many people to smuggle refugees out of their country. He asked Cristo if he was willing to go back into the tunnels and bring more children to the church.

Cristo agreed, and late at night he returned to the compound and found Elizabeth, who was overjoyed to see him. He told her of Father Gerard's request, and the two of them worked together to bring many of Cristo's friends to safety.

The sisters from the church then travelled with them by fishing boat across the bay to Mazatalan. They made many trips, ferrying two or three children at a time.

But with so many disappearing from the compound, the elders began searching the tunnels, suspicious that the children had found a way out. They never discovered the secret passage, but Elizabeth became nervous, afraid that it was only a matter of time before they did.

When El Santo announced that the next child caught trying to escape would be dealt with on Holy Friday, the children began to refuse to leave with Cristo, for fear they would be sacrificed. And Elizabeth knew that her time had come.

'What about the baby?' Beth asked.

'He was old enough by then,' Cristo said. 'But convincing the mother to go was not so easy.'

Jennifer had been brainwashed. Was so deep under Marta's spell that she would not leave. Elizabeth begged her to go, but Jennifer refused, and when she threatened to expose Elizabeth to El Santo, Elizabeth had no choice but to take the baby and run.

'The last time I saw you,' Cristo said, pointing towards the ocean, 'you were standing with the sisters on the fishing boat with Andilito in your arms. You did not want to leave us, but there was no room, and Father Gerard insisted that the baby must come first. That the sisters would travel with you through Mexico to Juarez and smuggle you across the border.'

Cristo stood then, remembering the moment.

'You said you would come back for us. That you knew many people in America and they would do everything they could to destroy El Santo's empire. But then many days went by and you did not return. No Elizabeth, no sisters, no fishing boats. And after many weeks passed, the elders came and killed Father Gerard. But they did not find us. So we stayed down here in the cave, waiting for you to return.'

Beth turned to Vargas and Ortiz. 'They must have tracked us. Found us hiding in that house in Chihuahua, then shot us all and took the baby.'

'That would be my guess,' Vargas said, then looked at Cristo. 'Would you be willing to go into the tunnels again? Take us to El Santo's compound?'

'*Si*,' Cristo said. 'But it is not safe to travel by day. There are too many elders with big guns in the tunnels. Better we wait until tonight, when everyone is in the Great Chamber for the celebration of Dia de los Muertos.'

Vargas turned to Beth and she nodded.

'Tonight it is, then,' he said, then turned to Ortiz. 'We're going to need some supplies.'

Ortiz responded to him, but Beth had stopped listening. Her thoughts were elsewhere at the moment, her mind struggling with those dark shapes again, kneading them, trying to push them into the light.

There was something about her story that seemed unfinished. The final piece of the puzzle that had not yet been put into place. Something about Juarez.

But it didn't matter.

It was all coming to an end in just a few hours, and Jennifer and Andy would soon be safe.

FOUR
LOS HOMBRES MUERTOS

MARTA

92

Marta was worried. It had been many hours since she'd last heard from Rafael, and it was unlike him not to keep in touch with her.

Here they were, so close to the great ceremony and her brother was still out there somewhere, defying the will of El Santo – as he so often did.

Any other man would have been killed by now. But Rafael, like Marta, had the benefit of being related to El Santo by blood, so the old man was merciful towards him. In fact, he often seemed amused by Rafael's transgressions, and El Santo was not easily amused.

Despite Marta's standing in the community, however – her status as a *bruja* – El Santo seemed to have little patience with her, and she was often envious of the affection Rafael received. But then Rafael was a second-born son and would always live with that mark upon him, so she knew that her envy was misplaced.

She also knew where her brother was. Ever since the night they'd met her precious Jennifer, he had been obsessed with the sister. Elizabeth. She was, he had once told Marta, an angel sent to him by La Santisima. The missing piece to an incomplete soul.

That she was a lying, conniving, sinful whore, meant nothing to Rafael.

He often pretended to hate her now, to want her dead, but Marta knew his true feelings. Many times, when she and her brother and Jennifer made love, Marta knew he was thinking of his prize, wishing she were back home with them where she belonged.

But Beth didn't belong here. She had got what she deserved and, despite Rafael's foolish yearning for her, she belonged in that hospital, where she could rot and die, for all Marta cared.

She had not liked Beth from the moment they met. Did not trust her. And Rafael's obsession with her was a constant source of frustration and annoyance.

So Marta knew he was still in Los Angeles, pining away for his lost love, thinking he could somehow change her. Mould her. Bring her back to him.

But Marta knew that Beth was not the type to be moulded. Her time here had proven that, had it not?

And if El Santo were to find out about Rafael's obsession, he might not be so merciful this time.

La Santa Muerte had made a deal with the ex-husband, the lawyer, to leave her alone, and El Santo did not go back on his pledges. And if Rafael again disobeyed El Santo's command to honour that deal, Marta feared she would soon lose her only living brother.

It was bad enough that she was losing her precious Jennifer tonight.

Jennifer.

Marta knew this was supposed to be a joyous occasion. She knew that the sacrifice Jennifer was about to make, on this holiest of nights, was a high honour that would deliver her into the waiting arms of La Santisima and God. But that did not keep her from dreading the moment. From wishing that someone else had been chosen.

Jennifer and the baby were down in the preparation room now – down near the Great Chamber – their bodies being rubbed with holy oils. But Marta had decided to stay up here in their room for a while. Had thought about missing the ceremony altogether.

She knew, however, that Jennifer would need her in her final moments, would want to hold her hand until El Santo lowered the torch.

So Marta would be there, dressed in her finest robe, looking on stoically as her one true love was given to God in a burst of flames.

93

Cristo drew them a map of the portion of the tunnels that lay directly beneath La Santa Muerte's compound. It was crude and done by memory, but Vargas was confident it would help them should they get lost. He didn't want to wind up like one of the corpses the boy had found down there.

'How far is this from here?' he asked.

'Four, maybe five miles.'

Close enough, Vargas thought, but such a trek might take as much as an hour and a half, so they'd have to leave soon if they wanted to get there before the ceremony began.

While Beth had stayed with the children, Vargas and Ortiz had gone back into town to pick up the Barracuda and a few supplies.

The Dia de los Muertos celebration was in full swing and many of the shops and services had been closed, but they'd managed to find what they needed: several small flashlights, a twelve-pack of mandarin Jarritos in glass bottles, two gallons of gasoline, two backpacks and a bundle of rags.

'Leave the Tomcat,' Ortiz said, 'and the *pendejo*'s

piece of shit. With all this weight, we'll want to keep the hardware to a minimum.' He gestured to the gun in Vargas's waistband. 'The Glock is all you'll need, anyway.'

Vargas nodded, then they climbed into the Barracuda and headed back to the church.

Time to get busy.

They gathered in the cave at 10 p.m., the supplies distributed under the light of the moon. Many of the children were asleep now and despite the churning ocean, there was a calmness here. No fear or trepidation – at least not for Vargas. When he looked into Beth's eyes, he knew this was the right thing to do.

Five minutes later Cristo said, 'We go' and they all flicked on their flashlights and followed him into the tunnel, leaving the sounds of the ocean behind them. When they reached the junction, Cristo took the second tunnel on the left, which then curved away to the right and branched off again in several different directions.

Vargas was already confused and decided that Cristo must have some unearthly sense of direction to be able to remember the correct path. The boy travelled effortlessly, without thought, as if he'd done this hundreds of times before. Which, Vargas knew, he had.

Then, a good hour into their trek, they came to a small cave, where Cristo stopped near a pile of large, fallen rocks. Gesturing for help, he began pulling the rocks away, and the others joined in until an opening in the cave wall was revealed.

The opening was large enough for Cristo to crawl through easily, but the others had to remove their backpacks and pass them to the boy before squeezing through themselves.

Once on the other side, they found another pile of rocks and stacked them up to hide the hole.

They were now inside another small cave, and Cristo pointed to a tunnel on the right.

'Through there,' he said. 'We go straight for a while, then make two lefts and a right and we are beneath La Santa Muerte's compound.'

'And where's the Great Chamber?' Beth asked.

'You will know as soon as we get there. Just follow the others.'

'How are we supposed to do that?' Ortiz said. 'Don't you think we'll stick out a little?'

'People from all over the country come here for the Holy Night. Besides, we will be wearing masks, and robes.'

'I didn't see those on the supply list.'

'They are provided for us. I will show you.'

'No, Cristo,' Beth said. 'I can't let you go any farther. I'd never forgive myself if you were hurt.'

Cristo gestured to the scars on his neck and arm. 'What could they do to me that is worse than this?'

He was right, Vargas thought. Any kid who could go through what this one had and come out of it still sane was not someone you needed to be worrying about.

'They could kill you,' Beth said. 'I can't let you do it.'

'And how will you find Jennifer and the baby?'

'I'll find them.'

'No, they keep them in a special room before the ceremony, where they prepare them for the fire. If I do not show you, it may be too late.'

'Tell me something,' Vargas said. 'Why the baby? Why would they sacrifice an innocent child?'

Cristo looked at him as if this was a silly question. 'It is tradition,' he said. 'He is the first-born male.'

And with this, Cristo crossed the cave and stepped into the tunnel on the right.

'Cristo, no,' Beth said.

But the boy ignored her, once again signalling for them to follow.

BETH

94

When they drew close to the compound, Cristo told them they would have to turn off their flashlights. The tunnels were lit by torches after the next turn.

Beth was surprised. With the kind of money El Santo had to be making through his drug and prostitution rings, you'd think he would have wired the place for electricity.

But since the cult seemed to be living in a kind of netherworld between the old and the new, basing their lives on traditions and rituals that were modelled on some ancient pagan society, maybe torches was the way to go. What would a good old-fashioned cleansing or ritual sacrifice be without the proper ambiance?

'Wait here,' Cristo said, and started to leave.

Beth grabbed his hand. 'Where are you going?'

'I come back soon,' he said, pulling away. Then he darted through the tunnel, stopped at a junction to peek around the corner, then continued on, disappearing from sight.

Beth had butterflies in her stomach. The plan, they had decided, was for Beth to find Jen and the baby and get them out of there as quickly as possible before the ceremony began.

Meanwhile, Ortiz and Vargas would go to the cages and release any women who might be held there, then round up as many of the children as they could find and take them all to safety.

It was an ambitious and maybe even a foolhardy plan, but they thought they might be able to pull it off while all attention was centred on the festivities in the Great Chamber.

Even the guards attended these festivities, Cristo had told them. So if everything worked out right, they'd have plenty of time to do what they needed to do and remain undetected.

Maybe.

Based on the story Cristo had told them earlier, it was painfully obvious that such plans don't always work.

After several nervous minutes, Cristo returned, carrying black hooded robes and gold skull masks and handed them out. As Beth put hers on, she suddenly remembered a Stanley Kubrick movie she'd seen a few years back, when Tom Cruise and Sidney Pollack dressed up in robes and watched people have anonymous sex in a New York mansion. The filthy rich caught up in a decadent fantasy.

It wouldn't surprise her, she thought, to discover that many of the people who attended this shindig were equally rich – and emotionally empty. People who rationalized their callous indifference to the suffering of others by wrapping it in pseudo-religious hokum.

It would almost be laughable if it all weren't so deadly serious.

Nevertheless, Beth felt ridiculous wearing this thing. But she had to admit it was a great way to enter the place undetected.

Their backpacks, which were filled with the Jarrito bottles, would have to be left behind. So Vargas and Ortiz stuffed their pockets with as many of the bottles as they could fit. Which wasn't many.

'Where's *your* robe?' Beth asked Cristo.

'The children do not wear robes,' he said. Then showed her his skull mask, which was white instead of gold. 'Come. The ceremony is about to begin. I show you where they keep Jennifer.'

Feeling the butterflies fluttering away, Beth followed him.

95

As they turned the first corner, the tunnel started to narrow slightly and, as promised, its walls were lined with torches, lighting their way. Beth heard the buzz of conversation ahead, and when they turned the next corner, they stepped into yet another cave, this one at least twice the size of any of the previous caves. It was filled with two or three hundred people, standing shoulder to shoulder, every one of them wearing a black robe and gold skull mask.

Beth, Vargas and Ortiz followed Cristo into the crowd, Beth suddenly feeling exposed, waiting for someone to point a finger and shout, 'Stop her! She's not one of us!'

But as they continued through, there were no shouts, no accusations, only the excited hum of spectators waiting for the show to begin.

All eyes were fixed on the front of the cave, which was dominated by several large stone statues of La Santa Muerte. A huge, circular slab of intricately carved stone lay at their feet, looking like something out of an Aztec nightmare. Flaming torches lined the circle, throwing light on the focus of everyone's attention: a large fire pit with a crude stone chair standing at its centre. And high above it was a man-made wind tunnel, carved into the roof of the cave, where smoke from the torches funnelled into the night sky.

Beth stared at the stone chair, knowing that if they didn't work fast, Jen and little Andy would soon be sitting in it, waiting to die.

Cristo cut abruptly to the right. Beth turned quickly to make sure that Vargas and Ortiz were behind her, then followed the boy out of the crowd towards yet another tunnel.

Stopping at the mouth of the tunnel, Cristo waited for Beth and the others to catch up, then pointed past the crowd towards a small stone archway on the far right side of the sacrificial altar.

'In there,' he said. 'She will be alone with the baby. Given a last moment of reflection before the final walk.'

Moving deeper into the tunnel, Cristo shoved a large rock aside and came away carrying another black robe and gold skull mask.

'She will be dressed in red,' he told Beth. 'You must change her into this and hide the baby under your robe.'

Nodding, Beth took them from him as Cristo turned to Vargas and Ortiz. 'I will go with Elizabeth. Do you have the map?'

Vargas reached under his robe and brought out the drawing. Cristo traced their route with an index finger.

'You must follow this tunnel to the cages,' he said. 'Then go here, where the children sleep. Many of them will not want to come, but you must tell them that Cristo says it is safe.'

Vargas nodded, then reached under his robe again and brought out the Glock, offering it to Beth. 'I don't want you going in there without protection.'

Beth stared at it a moment, then took it from him and tucked it into the top of her pants, beneath her robe.

Suddenly the loud, musical blast of a horn echoed through the cave and excited murmurs rose from the crowd. Then a tall female figure in a gold robe and red skull mask stepped out from behind one of the statues and the crowd erupted in applause and cheers.

The woman raised her arms, signalling for them to quiet down. Then she began to sing, her sweet, soulful voice filling the air.

At the sound of that voice, Beth felt a chill of recognition run through her. Images of her night aboard the cruise liner filled her head: sitting with Rafael in the jazz bar.

The singer was Marta Santiago.

'We must hurry,' Cristo whispered. 'Next El Santo will speak and then the sacrifice will begin.'

As Marta continued to sing, all eyes riveted to her, Beth nodded, then followed Cristo to the stone archway.

Gesturing her inside, Cristo stepped back into the shadows to wait.

96

When she entered the small chamber, Beth felt her heart skip a beat.

Jen was sitting on a wooden cot, wearing a red hooded robe, a black skull mask covering her face.

Little Andy was in her arms, sleeping quietly.

Outside, Marta finished singing her song and the crowd cheered and applauded, and Beth knew she had to work fast.

'Hello, Jen.'

The hooded head jerked up sharply. The baby stirred in her arms.

'Who's there? Who are you?'

'It's me, Jen, Beth. I've come to get you out of here.'

Her first instinct was to throw her arms around her sister and hug her. But there was time for that later. Instead, she reached up and lifted her mask.

Outside, the crowd began to chant: 'Santo, Santo, Santo, Santo . . .'

And Beth heard Cristo's voice behind her in the doorway:

'Hurry. We must hurry.'

Jen was looking at her, eyes wide behind the mask. 'Is this some kind of trick? Beth is dead.'

So they hadn't told her. Probably thought she'd be easier to handle this way.

'Look at me,' Beth said. 'Do I look dead to you?'

'You're not Beth. Beth was shot.'

Her speech was slow, lethargic. It occurred to Beth that Jen may have been drugged in preparation for the ceremony. She moved closer, crouching down in front of her, stroking little Andy's head.

He didn't stir. Had he been drugged, too?

'It's me,' she said to Jen. 'I'm here. They may have stopped me, but they couldn't kill me.'

Jen pulled the baby away from Beth and hugged him to her breast. She began muttering rapidly in Spanish. Words Beth didn't understand. A prayer of some kind.

What the hell had they done to her?

But then she knew, didn't she? Cristo had told her what El Santo did to his women, and the irony of all this suddenly came home to her. A man who worships an all-powerful female entity, yet treats the women in his life like dogs.

Then again, judging by the burns on Rafael and Cristo, maybe this was equal-opportunity degradation.

'We have to hurry,' she said to Jen. 'You need to change into this mask and robe.'

Beth reached to remove Jen's mask, but Jen brought a hand up, stopping her.

'No,' she said, her voice rising. 'You're not Beth.'

'We don't have time to argue about this,' Beth

told her, then reached for the mask again, grabbing it firmly.

But as she pulled it off, Jen said, 'Beth is dead. I know she is. I know because I shot her.'

And then the mask came off and her hood fell away revealing a sight so shocking that Beth felt her heart freeze in her chest, and she stood up, stumbling backwards.

Jen's hair was gone, her bald scalp shining in the candlelight. But that was nothing. That wasn't the worst of it. That was something that could be remedied with time.

But what couldn't be remedied was Jen's face.

Every inch of it was covered with burn scars, as if she'd been dipped in acid and left to dry. She had no nose, no lips, no eyebrows, no ears, her skin a blotchy, waxy, melted mass of flesh.

And suddenly Beth felt it. The switch being flipped. And all the dark shapes that had been struggling to get through, finally came to the surface, and she saw herself huddled in that desolate house in the desert, little Andy in her arms, sisters Imelda and Christina and Miranda and Lasarte standing around her as the door flew open and two men entered the room, followed by Marta and the hideous creature who had once been Jen. Then the guns started blazing and the sisters were screaming as Jen snatched the baby from Beth's arms, then pushed her towards the mattress, raised a pistol and shot her twice in the chest.

And Beth fell in slow motion, landing next to Sister Christina – who was surely as dead as Beth would soon be – blood spreading out beneath her, her energy draining away as Jen looked down at her, only the eyes recognizable, a fierce, untamed hatred in them as she spat on Beth and said, 'He's mine, you fucking whore.'

And then she was gone.

Beth looked at her sister now, sitting there in the candlelight, clutching the baby, and the weight of those final moments came crashing down on her, disbelief spreading through her as the crowd continued to chant, 'Santo, Santo, Santo, Santo,' and Beth heard Cristo shout behind her:

'Elizabeth! Look out!'

And as she turned, she saw Marta coming straight for her, swinging something heavy at her head, and before she could duck, it connected, knocking her sideways.

The gun in her waistband clattered to the floor and she went down.

Hard.

'What are you doing?'

The drug they had given Jennifer seemed to have worn off a bit.

But that didn't matter now.

'What does it look like,' Marta said. 'I'm taking her robe off.'

'But why?'

Marta looked up at Jennifer. She was no longer the beautiful young woman she'd met at that party in Los Angeles so long ago. Would never again be the object of desire that she was that night – using her hands and body and mouth and tongue to spread the joy of God – but Marta still loved her with her heart and soul and did not want to see her die.

Even if it was meant to be, even if El Santo commanded it, Marta could not bear the thought of a life without her Jennifer.

And this was her chance to change that.

Elizabeth's presence here was a surprise, but coupled with Rafael's sudden failure to call, it meant only one thing to Marta. That Rafael was gone, and this bitch surely had something to do with it. So it seemed only fitting that Elizabeth take Jennifer's place. El Santo would be angry when he found out, but when Marta explained that this was vengeance for their beloved Rafael, he would understand. And he would forgive.

'You're not going to die tonight,' she told Jennifer. 'Take your robe off and help me put it on her.'

'What?'

'It's simple,' Marta said patiently. 'We will dress her in the ceremonial robe, put the baby in her arms, and be done with her.'

Jennifer shook her head. 'No . . . I have offered myself and the life of my child to La Santisima. I won't let you or her take that from me.'

Marta went to her, kissed her. 'And I will not let La Santisima take *you* from me. Not now.'

But Jennifer pulled away. 'Why?' she cried. 'Why would you do this after all the promises that this day would come? Look at me. Look at what I've done to myself. Look at what I did to my own sister. Do you think I take my commitment lightly? I want to prove my love to La Santisima. To offer her my soul, and the soul of my—'

Marta slapped her across the face. 'I am the daughter of El Santo,' she said. 'You do not dictate what will and will not be done.'

Tears sprang into Jennifer's eyes. 'You lied to me. First you say my sister is dead, then you promise me a chance to see my mother and father in the loving arms of La Santisima. But it was all lies, wasn't it?'

Marta stared at her. No matter how she felt about

this woman, Jennifer had no right to speak to her this way.

Reaching to the floor, she picked up the gun that lay near Beth and pointed it at Jennifer. She had no intention of using it, but Jennifer didn't know that.

'The decision is made,' she said. 'And you will obey me.'

Then a horn sounded and the crowd roared, and Marta snapped her fingers.

'The robe. Give me the robe.'

98

It had taken Vargas and Ortiz longer than they expected to find the cages. Vargas had misinterpreted Cristo's map and had taken a left when he should have gone right. So they had doubled back, finally finding two small caves fronted by iron bars and locked with chains and padlocks.

At first he thought no one was inside them. But as they drew closer, he saw them: several women in each, huddled in the shadows at the back of the cells. They were dressed in frayed and dirty street clothes – probably the very clothes they'd been wearing when they were snatched off the street – some of them drugged, others mumbling incoherently, and still others crying softly, bewildered looks on their faces.

As Vargas and Ortiz approached the bars, several of them recoiled, retreating to the very back of their caves.

There was the distinct smell of faeces and urine in the air, and in a corner of each cave a small bucket overflowed with waste. The two men looked at each other in surprise and disgust. And though he had listened to

Cristo's story, Vargas couldn't have imagined anything like this.

He knew that human beings were often the cruellest creatures on earth. History had proved this time and again. But to see it first hand, the stark reality of it, was as painful as a dagger to the chest.

Turning again, he noticed that Ortiz was staring intently into the two cages, looking at all the faces, studying them – and he knew exactly who Ortiz was looking for.

'You won't find her here,' he said. 'It's been too long. She's either been shipped off to one of the brothels or she's dead.'

Ortiz nodded and his face hardened. 'We don't have all night, *pocho*. Let's get these fucking things open.'

Then he pulled the SIG from his belt, pointed it at the first lock and fired, blowing it off the chain. The shot echoed loudly in the tunnel, several of the women flinching and yelping in surprise, but Vargas was pretty sure the roar of the crowd upstairs had kept the sound from escaping the immediate area.

Ortiz aimed again, blowing open the second lock, then they threw open the cage doors, expecting the women to jump to their feet.

But no one moved. Just stared at them with wide, frightened expressions on their faces.

Then Vargas removed his mask and looked in at them, smiling. 'Come,' he said. 'Come with us. You're free.'

And as his words sank in, several of the women

rose to their feet, tentative but hopeful looks on their faces.

'You're free,' Vargas repeated, gesturing for them to step out of the cages. 'Come. We'll take you out of this place.'

Then the smiles came, the looks of relief, as they began helping one another to their feet, the drugged or injured women carried along by the healthier ones as they stumbled out, moving faster with each step.

'Stay together,' Vargas said.

Vargas and Ortiz led them through the tunnel, moving as quickly as they could—

—but as they rounded a corner, Vargas saw Cristo running in his direction, a frantic look on his face.

'Señor Vargas! Señor Vargas!'

'What is it? What's wrong?'

Cristo was out of breath, could barely get the words out. '. . . Elizabeth,' he said. 'They have Elizabeth.'

'Who does? El Santo?'

'Marta and Jennifer. They put her in the sacrificial robes.'

'What?'

'Come quick! They take her to the altar!'

99

Beth felt woozy. Knew that her head was bleeding.

Marta had stuffed something in her mouth – a balled-up rag, she thought, pushed deep to prevent her from crying out. Marta was yelling at Jen now, but Beth couldn't quite make out the words as they drifted in and out like a bad radio signal. And all she could think about was that house in Juarez and Jennifer's waxy face as she pointed a gun at Beth.

He's mine, you fucking whore.

What had they done to her? How could they have warped her this way? Bled her of all humanity and turned her into some brain-dead true believer?

It wasn't unusual for people like this to go after the emotionally vulnerable, but while Jen may have been constantly searching for some kind of meaning in her life, she had also been strong willed and stubborn – traits the sisters had always shared.

Beth remembered now the nights in the cage, the drugs, the beatings – some of them administered by Rafael himself – but if *she* had managed to resist, why hadn't Jennifer? Was Jen's dissatisfaction with her life

434

enough to force her to relinquish all power to these maniacs?

Apparently so.

Beth felt herself being lifted now, but the blow to her head had rendered her too weak to resist as her arms were shoved into the sleeves of a robe and a mask was placed over her face. She smelled the faint odour of what she thought might be kerosene and realized that the robe and mask had been treated with a flammable liquid.

Then Marta moved to a nearby curtain and pushed it aside, uttering a sharp command to someone behind it.

She pushed little Andy into Beth's arms as two men entered the room and grabbed Beth by the elbows, pulling her towards a dark doorway.

Despite her wooziness, she knew what was beyond that door. Could see the flicker of the altar torches at the far end of another tunnel.

Someone was standing out there now, a tall, powerfully built, barrel-chested old man in a white robe, his arms raised, standing in front of a sea of masked faces.

She recognized him. Had seen him many times, had forced herself to share his bed – as she had with Rafael and Marta – participating in their pagan rituals as a way of survival, a necessary sacrifice to facilitate the escape of the children and little Andy.

It was El Santo. The Holy One. The direct descendant of God and La Santisima. A man whose evil seemed to know no limits. A man whose followers would do anything to promote his cause.

They were cheering for him now.

Their Messiah.

And as he lowered his arms, a silence fell over the cavern, and he spoke to them in Spanish. Beth had heard the words many times in the months she'd spent here, words that Cristo had translated for her:

'Oh, Holy Death, our great treasure, we offer you these gifts as a symbol of our love, and ask only that you smile down upon us. That you protect your children and give us food and shelter. That you provide us with an abundance of riches and hide us from those who mean us harm.

'Oh, Queen of Darkness, please hear our prayer and take these souls as your own.'

And as he finished his prayer, El Santo waved his arms and the two men holding Beth moved forward, walking, half-dragging her and Andy out onto the semicircle, towards the stone chair.

Beth started to struggle now, but was still feeling weak, and there wasn't much she could do with little Andy in her arms. The men carrying her tightened their grip. They were used to this, a last-minute change of heart that always came too late. The crowd began cheering as they brought her and Andy out onto the altar and sat her down, draping the bottom of her robe over the large stack of twigs at the foot of the chair.

Andy began crying now, the roar of the crowd frightening him, and the two men stood on either side of Beth, each with a firm hand on one of her shoulders, holding her down.

Then El Santo moved in front of her, placing his

palm first on her head, then on Andy's, and said, 'Go with God, my children.'

Reaching down to an urn by her feet, he picked it up and held it high in the air and the crowd's cheers grew louder, wilder, the chants beginning again: 'Santo! Santo! Santo! Santo!'

El Santo brought the urn down and began pouring liquid over the twigs, the smell of kerosene rising into Beth's nostrils – and Andy's too.

And as they both coughed and choked, Beth desperately looking for a way out of this, El Santo reached for one of the torches—

—and smiled at them.

100

By the time Vargas reached the cavern, they had already put Beth and the baby in the chair.

He pushed frantically through the crowd towards her, watching as the man in the white robe – El Santo, he presumed – placed his hands on Beth's and the baby's head, then stepped over to one of the torches and picked it up.

El Santo turned, smiling at them, holding the torch high, and the crowd roared around Vargas, hungry for blood. He continued forwards, shoving people aside, hoping he could reach the altar before that torch touched those twigs.

But he knew he wouldn't make it, there wasn't enough time.

If only he hadn't given his gun to Beth.

Reaching under his robe as he moved, he grabbed one of the Jarrito bottles and he knew he was taking a chance, knew he might miss, but he had no choice. So he wound back and hurled the bottle – which he and Ortiz had filled with gasoline – straight at El Santo's head.

El Santo didn't see it coming – no one did – and

a moment later, Vargas saw that his aim had been good, as the bottle slammed against El Santo's skull and shattered, flooding his face and robe with gasoline—

—and the torch in his hand exploded in flames, engulfing him quickly as the two men holding Beth stumbled back in surprise, and—

—Vargas reached the front of the crowd and leaped onto the altar, grabbing hold of Beth and the baby and pulling them away from El Santo, ripping Beth's robe off, as the old man screamed in agony and fell to the floor, his flesh bubbling hideously as the fire consumed him.

And suddenly the room was filled with screams and cries of horror, people rushing to the altar to help El Santo as others turned and fled, and still others swarmed around Vargas and Beth.

Then, from out of nowhere, came another Jarrito bottle, this one with a flaming rag stuffed in it – a Molotov cocktail. It hit the back of one of their attackers and shattered against the cavern floor, bursting into flames. The attacker's robe caught fire and he screamed, tearing it off, as—

—Vargas saw Ortiz across the cavern, lobbing another Jarrito bottle, creating a distraction as Cristo led the women towards the tunnel they'd started from. There were kids with them now, running alongside as—

—another bottle hit the ground, exploding in flames—

—And now Ortiz was firing his handgun into the air, the echo of gunshots scattering people in every direction, as Vargas ripped his robe and mask off, shouting, 'Let's get the fuck out of here!'

Beth seemed dazed, but she didn't hesitate, she didn't falter as she pulled a wad of cloth from her mouth, then clutched the baby to her chest and ran, the three of them tearing down the tunnel.

As they rounded the bend, Vargas slowed down, reaching for his flashlight, when Beth suddenly shoved the baby at him.

'What's this?' he asked.

'Jen. She's still back there. We came to get her out of here. I can't just leave her.'

'All right, I'll go with you.'

But Beth wasn't having any. 'No,' she said. 'You need to take care of Andy.'

Then she turned abruptly and ran back towards the Great Chamber, leaving Vargas with the squirming baby in his arms.

101

When she got back to the Great Chamber, much of the crowd was gone, but several people were huddled over El Santo, who lay still near the altar, looking like something fresh off a Labor Day barbecue spit.

Beth battled a savage stab of nausea as she pushed past them, looking around the cavern, seeing no sign of Jen or Marta.

Which meant they couldn't have been around when this all happened. They must have left shortly after Marta had hijacked Beth. Otherwise, Marta would be at the centre of that huddle, sobbing her eyes out.

And Beth knew there was only one place they could have gone.

The High House.

The house was a large, multi-roomed mansion that stood near the edge of a cliff overlooking the Sea of Cortez. It was the centre of the La Santa Muerte compound – the centre of La Santa Muerte itself – where El Santo had sat like a king, overlooking his criminal enterprise.

The clarity with which Beth remembered all this was shocking to her, and she wondered if one of the bullet fragments in her brain had shifted somehow, taking pressure off the section that had been causing her memory loss.

She knew that the room behind the altar held another curtained doorway, this one with a set of steps that led up to the High House.

Slipping into the room, she found the stairs, then took her flashlight from her pocket, flicked it on, and started up them.

As she reached the top, Beth hung back, hearing the sound of running footsteps, car engines starting. The party had been ruined and El Santo's so-called followers were fleeing the scene, skittering back to the holes they'd come from.

The house was usually heavily guarded, but as she peeked past the doorway at the top of the stairs, Beth saw no sign of any guards now, figuring they had either fled, too, or were still down in the tunnels, looking for Vargas and Ortiz.

And her.

Beth stepped through the doorway and quickly made her way down a corridor to another set of steps – a wide stairway that led to the first floor. Marta and Rafael's suite was up there, and Beth had no doubt that this was where Marta had taken Jen.

She heard sobbing when she got to the first-floor corridor. A sound muffled by walls and doors, but she knew exactly where it was coming from. She had been in that room more times than she could count, acting out her charade as she had dreamed of escaping this terrible place. Of taking Jen and Andy far away from here.

Back in Playa Azul, when Beth had complained of always being forced to play the mother, Jen had told her that it was a role she had chosen for herself. And Beth now knew that she was right. She was Beth the Dutiful, and it had been her nature to do whatever it took to protect her cub.

But she had failed. Despite her own narrow escape, the Santiagos had won, simply by virtue of the fact that they had managed to steal Jen's soul.

But maybe the deaths of Rafael and El Santo would change all that.

Marta's private room was at the end of the corridor. Beth quietly approached the door, listening to Jen's sobs, and felt her heart break. What they'd done to her, what Jen had done to herself, was unspeakable. Unforgivable.

Beth reached a hand out, slowly turned the knob, and pushed into the room.

Jen was on the bed, face down, sobbing into a pillow, Marta sitting next to her, her back to the doorway, rubbing Jen's shoulders.

Beth spotted Vargas's pistol lying on a nearby chair. It was almost, she thought, as if God had been expecting her.

Destiny, you might say.

Marta continued to rub Jen's back. 'It's all right, *cielito*. You'll see.'

'You lied to me,' Jen said. 'You all lied to me.'

'No, my darling. We told you only truth. But I could not bear to let you go. You can understand that, *si*?'

'How true can it all be, if you can bend the word of God to suit you? If I was meant to give myself today, why am I still alive?'

'The fact that you are alive must mean that it is God's will, no? And in the end, El Santo will surely bless you.'

'El Santo won't be blessing anyone,' Beth said.

Both Jen and Marta looked up sharply, staring at Beth, who now held Vargas's gun in her hand.

Marta's eyes narrowed. 'How could you still be alive?'

Beth nodded towards the bedroom window. 'Look outside. The rats are abandoning ship.'

Marta frowned and climbed off the bed, moving to the window. She parted the curtain, staring at all the activity below, then turned and looked at Beth again.

'What happened? Where is El Santo?'

'He's got a bit of sunburn,' Beth said. 'I don't think he's gonna make it.'

Marta's face went through several different expressions, most of them involving some form of disbelief.

'No,' she said, moving back to Jen. 'You lie. It is not true.'

'I'm afraid so, sweetie. Your lecherous, murderous, drug-smuggling, daughter-fucking asshole of a father is dead and headed straight to hell, exactly where he belongs.'

She raised the gun.

'Now do me a favour and get away from my sister so I can send you there, too.'

And as the truth sank in, Marta's look of disbelief slowly turned to sorrow, then anger, then rage. And with a blood-curdling scream, she launched herself at Beth like something straight out of a vampire movie, her teeth bared, a crazed, feral look in her eyes as she went for Beth's throat—

—and Beth squeezed the trigger, putting a bullet in her brain, dropping her right there on the bedroom floor.

Jen screamed then and scrambled off the bed, moving to Marta, who now lay wide-eyed, blood leaking all over her carpet. Jen stood over the dead woman, tears filling her eyes.

Beth was trembling. Lowered the pistol. Not quite believing she'd just what she'd done.

But she'd had no choice, right?

'Come on, Jen. We need to get you out of here.'

Then Jen looked up at her, the tears now streaming down that hideous face. There was a clarity in her eyes that hadn't been there before. The drugs had worn off.

'What about Andy? Is he . . . ?'

'He's fine,' Beth said. 'He's with my friends.'

'Thank God, thank God. I can't believe I almost killed him tonight.'

'It's not your fault, Jen. They warped your mind. Drugged you. Manipulated you. Took advantage of your vulnerability. It's what they do.' She paused, gestured. 'Now, come on. Let's go.'

'No,' Jen said. 'My whole life I've been a burden to you. I can't be that any more.'

'You've never been anything but my little sister. And no matter what you've done, I've always loved you and I always will.'

'Then let me go.'

Beth frowned. 'What are you saying?'

'Look at me. Look at my face. Look at what I did to myself. And to you. I could spend a hundred years trying to heal, trying to forgive myself, but I'll never be whole again. I'll never be what I was before.' She paused. 'I was willing to give my life to God tonight. And that hasn't changed.'

'What do you mean?'

Jen stared her, intently. Beth could barely stand to look at her face, so she concentrated on the eyes instead, remembering the laughing girl onboard that ship who just wanted to get laid.

'Send me to God,' Jen said. 'Help me do what I should have done when I climbed that clock tower at school all those years ago.'

'Stop, Jen, you're talking nonsense.'

'Am I? Think about it, Beth. Would you want to look like this for the rest of your life? Could you live with yourself, knowing that you had almost sent your son to his death? If you have any mercy at all, if you love me, you'll do what I ask.'

Beth shook her head, not wanting to listen to this, but some small part of her knew that Jen was right. If she were in the same position, she wouldn't want to live either.

'What about Andy? He needs his mother.'

'You'll be a better mother to him than I could ever be.'

'That's crazy talk.'

'Please, Beth. If you truly do love me, if you have any mercy in your heart for the girl who tried to kill you . . .'

Beth continued to stare at her, thinking about all their years together, all the laughter and pain and grieving and frustration – and this is what it had come down to. A damaged soul, asking to be set free.

'Please, Beth. Please . . .'

And as Jen stared up at her, Beth the Dutiful raised the pistol again and pulled the trigger.

PATIENT'S JOURNAL

Day 92?
11.00 a.m.

They say that time heals, but I'm not quite sure that's really true.

Time may lessen the sting, may allow you to relegate the pain to another part of your mind, to box it up and store it away, only to be brought out on special occasions – those melancholy moments that remind us of who we are . . .

But we can never be truly healed.

That's the thing about memories. There is so much we wish we could forget. We go through our lives wanting to erase the data banks, to start anew, but even if we could, what would we lose in the process?

I cherish the memories I have. Both the good and the bad. I remember them clearly and in great detail and do not regret that.

I've done things. Horrible things. But I know deep down that they were justified. That they needed to be done.

And I know that at this very moment, Jen is in the

loving arms of our parents. Which, in truth, is the only place she ever wanted to be.

After I said my goodbyes to her that night, I found Nick and Cristo waiting for me in the tunnels, ready to guide me back to the church. But I didn't need a guide. After so many months of travelling through them, I knew those passages as if they'd been etched into my brain.

In the days that followed, Nick's detective friends, both here and in Mexico, were able to rally together and put a stop to what was left of La Santa Muerte. The brothels were closed, the smuggling operation shut down, and before we knew it, the so-called believers were turning on one another, exposing a network of criminals and corrupt law-enforcement agents that spread not just through Mexico, but all the way into the United States and even parts of Canada.

There was a brief investigation into the shooting deaths of Marta and Jen, but, with no witnesses and little evidence, the Mexican police hit a dead end.

The man who shot me in Albuquerque – Rojas – was stripped of his job and thrown in jail.

Peter has been arrested and charged with criminal conspiracy. He's scheduled to be arraigned in a few days, and I've been asked to testify.

Cristo and his young friends were reunited with their families. And after we bid Ortiz goodbye and returned to the United States, I decided to check myself back into the clinic, to be kept under observation until Dr Stanley tells me I'm ready to go.

That should be any day now.

Little Andy has been taken into temporary foster care here in Los Angeles. I've filed for custody, and my attorney thinks that, given my steady progress, the judge will grant it. The foster parents regularly email photos of him, and I can't help seeing Jen in his eyes.

He is her legacy. Her gift to me.

Nick comes to see me every morning, and brings me new pages of his book. I may be biased – no doubt about it, in fact – but I think he's got something there. A real stab at reversing some of the damage he did to his career.

My own career is still waiting for me. After the scandal of Peter's arrest, the district attorney decided it would be good publicity to allow me to return to my old job, with a substantial bump in pay.

But I haven't decided whether I'll return. I'm not sure I want to go back to a world so full of darkness. I would be content to live my days alone with Nick and Andy, listening to him read his words to me.

This isn't a realistic prospect, of course. Merely a dream. I know that when I walk out of here, I'll have to find something to do with myself. Something to help me push away the pain. To help me move forward.

There is, however, in the back of my mind, one small concern. It's probably nothing, but I've lived with it every day – a mild but constant bit of paranoia that just doesn't seem to want to leave me alone. And what it stems from is this:

When the Mexican police found the crumpled Jaguar on the side of the road, Rafael was not inside. All that was left was a bit of blood on the seat.

And sometimes, late at night, I wake up in the darkness of my room and feel as if someone has been watching me.

Watching and waiting.

So a few days ago, I asked Nick to bring me one of the pistols Ortiz gave him.

And I keep it under my pillow.

Just in case.

Acknowledgements

I want to again thank all the usual suspects – you know who you are.

Thanks also to Emmanuel Ruiz, for his invaluable assistance with the Spanish translations; agents extraordinaire, Scott Miller and Claire Roberts, of Trident Media Group.

And thank you to my new editor at Pan Macmillan, Trisha Jackson, whose insight has made this a better book. She has a tough job and she does it brilliantly.

extracts reading groups

competitions books new

discounts extracts

competitions

books

new events books extracts reading groups

events books reading groups

new titles reading groups

interviews

books events extracts extracts new books

discounts events

new books events interviews new books extracts

events new

discounts extracts discounts

www.panmacmillan.com

extracts events reading groups

competitions books extracts new